SHADOWS IN THE RAIN

Anna Barrie was born in 1946 and lives with her husband in a village near Bath. She trained as a painter and taught Art for a while, but now devotes all her time to writing. Her first novel, under the pseudonym Patricia Barrie, was published in 1986. *Shadows in the Rain* is her first novel under the name Anna Barrie.

ANNA BARRIE

SHADOWS
— *in the* —
RAIN

PAN BOOKS
LONDON, SYDNEY AND AUCKLAND

First published 1993 by Judy Piatkus (Publishers) Ltd

This edition published 1994 by Pan Books Limited
a division of Pan Macmillan Publishers Limited
Cavaye Place London SW10 9PG
and Basingstoke

Associated companies throughout the world

ISBN 0 330 33127 2

Some of the events in this book were inspired by the West Country floods of July 1968; however, all the characters are fictitious and to the best of the author's knowledge bear no resemblance to any living person.

1 3 5 7 9 8 6 4 2

A CIP catalogue record for this book is available from the British Library

Phototypeset by CentraCet Limited, Cambridge
Printed and bound in Great Britain by
Cox & Wyman Ltd, Reading, Berkshire

For Keith and Shelagh, with loving memories of their mother, Mary Barber

With grateful thanks to Beth Reeves and Marianne Edwards and to the farmers and market gardeners whose advice I sought during the writing of this book

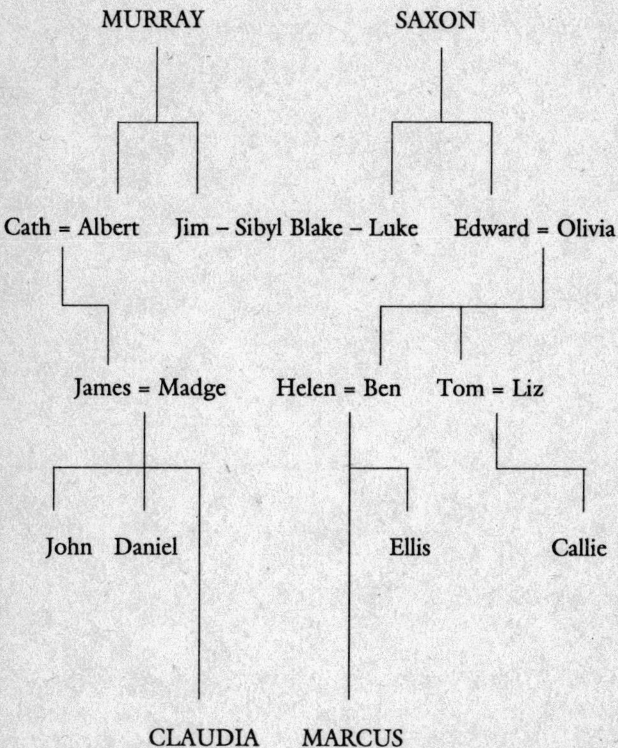
MURRAY
SAXON
Cath = Albert
Jim – Sibyl Blake – Luke
Edward = Olivia
James = Madge
Helen = Ben
Tom = Liz
John
Daniel
Ellis
Callie
CLAUDIA
MARCUS

Chapter One

Larcombe village hall. Old Georgie Flicker and his accordion were propped against a bale of straw, both of them wheezing slightly after a strenuous hour of music making. The old man was red in the face and steaming, as were most of the people who'd thrown themselves to rest after a last frantic gallop through 'The Dashing White Sergeant'.

Mrs Chislett's bosom was heaving with exertion. She scarcely had breath enough to speak but attempted it anyway, taking three gasps and a chuckle between each word.

'Ooh – oh – Gaw – blimey! I reckon – I'm – gettin' a bit – old for this – sorta caper!'

'Old?' Georgie Flicker scoffed generously. 'Get on with you! You'm only sempty!' He thumped his chest after the manner of a gorilla in its prime. 'Look at I! Sempty-eight come Whitsuntide and still as strong – ' He broke down in a fit of coughing. 'Strong as a flamin' – ' He covered his mouth with a politely clenched fist and coughed until his forehead turned purple. 'Straw dust,' he said sheepishly at last. 'Sticks in me throat.'

'Ah, I expect it do,' Mrs Chislett said cynically. 'That bronchitis you 'ad's stickin' there, too. You be careful, Georgie. Don't go so hard at it.'

'Careful? The day I gets careful I'll be laid out in me box!'

'Huh.' Mrs Chislett rolled her eyes towards the small orange record-player which the youngsters had set up in a corner of the village hall. 'You'll be wishing you was in a minute!'

Her voice was drowned by a sudden blast of rock music, and she shrieked, 'Oh, save us!' and covered her ears with her hands.

Claudia Murray eyed the old woman with wary hostility, wishing – if only vaguely – that someone would shoot her. Mrs Chislett was reputed to have a heart of gold, but Claudia had never seen so much as a glint of it. True, she did a lot of things for charity (this village social was one of them), and she visited people when they were ill and went to church twice on Sundays; but since Mrs Chislett *liked* being bossy, interfering and sanctimonious, Claudia didn't think these things were greatly to her credit.

Anyway, she had very small eyes, several large chins, and a tongue like a razor, which could cut you in half the minute you set a foot out of place. She also had a moustache: sparse, white and wiry, like the thread-like albino spiders which lurked in the darkest corners of the Murrays' old air-raid shelter. Claudia shrieked with revulsion every time she saw one of those spiders. She felt much the same about Mrs Chislett's moustache.

'What you gawping at I like that fer, Claudia Murray?'

Claudia jumped and blinked, her dark grey eyes widening at the challenge. She could hardly say she'd been wondering if Mrs Chislett's moustache would suddenly scuttle off to hide behind her ears . . .

She smiled nervously. Mrs Chislett was almost twice her size and nearly six times her age; which meant (or so Claudia's mother said) that she was entitled to respect, even if she didn't always deserve it. Claudia had never seen the justice in that, and for her own part she showed Mrs Chislett the proper respect only because there'd be hell to pay if she didn't.

'I was thinking you looked – er – thirsty,' she said. 'Would you like some orangeade?'

'Huh!' Mrs Chislett scoffed. 'I s'pose that means *you* wants some! Ain't you brought no money with you?'

Claudia's cheeks reddened with annoyance. She should be accustomed by now to Mrs Chislett's suspicious mind, but it never failed to catch her off her guard.

'Yes, thank you,' she said frigidly. 'I have plenty of money.'

'Ooh, Rockerfeller,' the old woman said.

Claudia narrowed her eyes and flounced off to the refreshments table in the corner, where she forked out a precious threepence for a small, scratched glass of brightly coloured orangeade.

Mrs Chislett did not hide her astonishment when the gift was duly proffered. 'Oh, now, my love,' she said anxiously. 'Oh, now, no. I didn't mean for you to . . .'

Claudia smiled stiffly and flounced off again; honour satisfied – for the moment.

All she had to do now was to catch the bigger of her two big brothers (the one who could dance), and she could go home happy. But time was running out. She had to be home at nine o'clock, and John had promised to teach her to jive. Brothers' promises didn't count for much, of course, especially the ones they made under duress while running to catch the school bus; but that was by-the-by. A promise was a promise, and as soon as John finished dancing with Rita Tapscott, Claudia would grab him.

John was a wonderful dancer, the best in the village, which meant that Claudia wasn't the only girl stalking him with narrowed eyes – eyes which widened with admiration as Rita Tapscott dived between his legs feet first, to emerge on the other side in a flurry of white frills and stocking-tops.

'Ooh!' Mrs Chislett gasped. 'She'm showin' her drawers! Well, of all the – !'

Mrs Chislett hated rock and roll. So did Claudia's father who, when he heard the twang of a guitar issuing from the wireless, invariably snapped, 'Switch that heathen noise off! It's time for the weather forecast!'

He'd also said that Claudia was too young to learn to dance; a pronouncement so patently ridiculous that she hadn't even bothered to argue with it. How on earth could anyone be too young to *dance*? But she'd been careful not to mention that there'd be rock and roll at the social tonight. If he'd known, he'd never have let her come. As it was, the permission had had to be wrung out of him, and a promise wrung out of John 'to keep an eye on her, just in case'.

The 'case' in question hadn't been mentioned. It never was although they all knew its name and hated it. But no one of that name had arrived tonight, and now – it was a quarter to nine already! – no one would. They were probably too stuck up to attend a humble village social, anyway.

As the final bars of 'Peggy Sue' thundered through the hall, John Murray swung Rita Tapscott into the air, bounced her off his hip and threw her away again, catching her hand at the last moment to give her a final twirl. The music stopped. Claudia cried, 'John!' and went up on her toes with excited anticipation.

'Yer, Claudia!'

Claudia heard Mrs Chislett's voice and valiantly ignored it, but was foiled as a fat, work-reddened hand clamped her wrist, forcing her to a standstill.

Mrs Chislett was smiling broadly, her little brood of white spiders tickling her nostrils. 'Now, you look 'ere, my love,' she said kindly. 'Rockerfeller you may be, but I'm not – '

'Oh, Mrs Chislett!' Claudia wailed as Eddie Tinknell hurried to change the record.

'No, no, my love, I won't 'ear of it. It was very good of you, but – '

Claudia twisted her head to look frantically over her shoulder. 'John! Wait!'

'But I'm not having you spending your money on me, and that's me last word. So yer's your threepence back, my love. Buy yourself an ice-cream. Oh, blimmin' heck, they'm off again!'

This last exclamation was to herald the wild, heady chant of 'One-two-three o'clock, four o'clock, rock!' which now thumped tinnily across the floor. But John hadn't released Rita Tapscott's hand, and as the beat caught his feet he snatched her briefly to his chest and hurled her away, making her spin.

'John!' Clutching her threepence, Claudia dashed across the floor to grab his arm. 'Ohhh, *John*! It's five to nine!'

'Better go home, then. Dad'll kill you if you're late.'

'But you *promised*!'

'Let go of me!' He shook her off and gave Rita a confiding wink before whirling her away to the far end of the hall.

For a moment Claudia could only stare, her dark grey eyes brimming with pained disappointment. Then she grabbed her school blazer from a nearby bale of straw and marched angrily toward the exit. She noticed, vaguely, that the doorway was full of people, but when Claudia Murray was in a rage she expected everyone to respect the fact and get out of the way.

She was small for her age and rather thin with a cloud of fine, wheat-coloured hair which only emphasised the impression that a puff of wind might blow her away. But with her chin up, and twitching slightly, she saw herself as something powerful, invincible; a relentless force, like earthquakes and thunderstorms.

Most of the Murray family, and at least some of the villagers, knew this; but the man who hovered in the doorway evidently didn't, for he stood his ground long enough for Claudia to step on his foot and stub her nose on his waistcoat. He smelled of Palmolive soap, fruit-cake and saddle leather. A pleasant enough combination, but not pleasant enough to change Claudia's mood.

'Hey, hey,' the man laughed as she again tried to force her way past. 'What's this?'

His voice was both hard and soft: an educated voice, with round plummy vowels and crisp consonants. It was a voice Claudia had heard only rarely, and never so close.

She went rigid with shock, but her mind was racing. What should she do? Spit in his eye, kick him in the shin, or simply demand (in the nastiest voice she could muster) that he get out of her way? She decided that this last course would be more dignified (and a good deal safer) and, as the man set her away from him, gently holding her arms, she jerked her head back to glare up into his eyes. But his eyes weren't where she'd thought they'd be – they were several inches higher: a bright, clean, hyacinth blue which glinted with suppressed laughter – and the sheer size of him stopped her words in her throat.

The man released her as soon as he saw her face; his smile fading, his blue eyes cooling with contempt. 'Manners,' he said softly. 'Too much to hope, I suppose.'

Claudia fled down the flight of rickety wooden steps and stood at the bottom for a moment, gasping for breath.

Manners. It was the sort of thing everyone said; but not everyone said it like that: so cold, so contemptuous, so –

hateful! Claudia was trembling with reaction, almost in tears. God, what a rotten night! She'd only gone to Mrs Chislett's stupid social because John had promised to dance with her! And then to bump into Mr Saxon at the last minute . . . And have him brush her off as if she were nothing!

She shuddered and bit back a sob before turning to glare at the dimly lit windows of the hall. 'Stinking Saxons,' she muttered.

The church clock struck nine, and Claudia, kicking a stone into what was left of the river, squared her shoulders to face yet more trouble. Where his daughter's curfew was concerned, James Murray was a fanatic and it would be ten minutes at least before Claudia could get home. By daylight, after a year of unremitting drought, she would have run down the river bank and jumped the feeble stream which trickled down the middle, but by night it was too risky. Rats and foxes, made desperate by thirst, could be down there, drinking in the dark.

She hated that river. Everyone in Larcombe hated it, for it was of no use at all unless you happened to be a duck. It didn't even have any worthwhile fish in it. In dry weather it stank; in wet weather (Claudia could scarcely remember wet weather) it flooded; and, worst of all, it cut the village in half, with only an ancient single-track bridge to connect the two sides.

All the important things – the bus-stop, the church, the village hall and the shops – were on the wrong side of the bridge, and the fifteenth-century idiot who had built it had built it at the wrong end. If he'd built it at the right end Claudia could have been home in two minutes and saved herself a telling-off. Worse, perhaps, for she'd been late on Tuesday, too.

It was all John's fault. John's, old Ma Chislett's, stinking Mr Saxon's. And she couldn't use any of them as an excuse.

John was safe because Claudia was 'too young' to dance, Mrs Chislett because she was *entitled* to respect, and *him* because if she even mentioned *him* her father would go crazy with rage. She'd just have to brazen it out. Keep her mouth shut and look humble.

The village loomed over her like a cliff: squared faces of grey stone tunnelled through with dim lights. Even eleven years after the war's end, few people had forgotten the blackout, and except for three small yellow pools where the street-lamps shone, the river valley was as dark as a well. Claudia had persuaded herself some time ago that she was not afraid of the dark; but still she ran past the end of the Bristol road, where the mouth of the night yawned widest.

The bridge, a narrow hump of masonry with cottages clustering at either end, was the worst part of her walk, for one of the street lights shone behind it, strangely emphasising its squat, hunchbacked shape so that it looked like a crouched animal: vast, scaly and malevolent, sleeping with one eye open. It wasn't safe to step on it. It wasn't wise to wake it . . .

Even in daylight Claudia never felt comfortable on that bridge; she always wanted to get over it as quickly as possible, before something dreadful could happen to her. It wasn't because she feared it would collapse (after five hundred years, collapse seemed unlikely), but because . . . She didn't quite know why. She knew it couldn't get up on its hind legs and carry her away, but somehow she always feared it might. It seemed *alive*.

Flickering reflections played under the arches and little splashes, drips and scuffles echoed up from the shadows. But the worst thing of all was the passing place: a chill, dark alcove set into the stone parapet where pedestrians could step clear of the traffic. Claudia never approached that spot without feeling she'd be overcome by dread. It was impossible not to utter a little gasp of relief when she reached the opposite bank still in one piece.

From the far side of the river, the village looked little better than the hole Claudia's mother often called it; a deep hole, and dark, and cold. The sun set here an hour earlier than it did elsewhere, and frost fell like a stone, crushing the flowers. It seemed the worst place on earth for a market garden, but in fact the alley fanned out at the far end, and Murray & Son could claim thirty acres of wide, sunlit land between the river and the hill.

Luckily for Claudia, if not for her mother's flowers which shivered and shrivelled in the frost-bitten April nights, the Murray house had been built at the narrow end of the fan, nearest the village. Only the width of the road divided it from the river. Behind it, to the north, rose the steep, protective slope of Saxons' wood; but like all things Saxon this was more a curse than a blessing, for the hillside funnelled the east wind into the gap, making Murray's one of the coldest houses in the village.

It was also one of the most brightly lit, and the lamp over the kitchen door had comforted Claudia through many a gloomy walk in the days when she *had* been afraid of the dark. She wasn't afraid now. Her heart was thudding just because she was late; and she was running past the shady skirts of the woods for the same reason. She wasn't scared. She would be twelve next week, and she wasn't scared – except of her father.

Yet she was unaccountably glad to see James Murray's stocky, bow-legged silhouette as he marched down the road to meet her.

'There you are, you little blighter! Have you any idea what time it is?'

He had come out without a jacket, but Claudia knew that he was trembling, not shivering. He always trembled when he was angry. Claudia suffered the same handicap, and if anyone had the bad manners to mention it, was liable to stop being angry and go into all-out hysterics. Her father was the same; and having seen him in hysterics once or twice, it was not an experience she wanted to repeat.

'Sorry, Dad. I lost track of the time.'

He caught her roughly by the elbow and hustled her through the gate. 'I'll give you lost track, young lady! You've no call to lose track! What's that on your wrist? What's that on your wrist?'

'A watch,' Claudia muttered. 'Sorry.'

'Yes, a watch!' her father snapped bitterly as he prodded her through the kitchen door. 'Proud of that watch, aren't you? Well, madam, unless you learn what it's for, you won't have your precious watch much longer! I'll throw the damn thing in the river, that's what I'll do! Perhaps then you'll have an *excuse* for losing track of time! Selfish, impudent . . . ! You *know* how your mother worries!'

James glanced frantically at his wife who was sitting at the kitchen table, calmly pondering the crossword in the *Bristol Evening Post*. She blinked and made an attempt to look worried, but the effort failed. She was a placid, gentle woman, strong of soul. She could achieve more with a few calm, well-chosen words than James or Claudia could do with all their explosions of temper.

Madge loathed tantrums, and when Claudia had them she was inclined to shut her in the broom cupboard and let her get on with it. But she couldn't shut James in the broom cupboard, and even if it had been possible, she wouldn't have done it. 'My husband, right or wrong' was her motto, and had he resolved to throw all three of their children, complete with their wrist watches, into the Chew, she wouldn't have raised a hand to stop him. Diversion was more in her line. A subtle change of direction. A pin gently applied to the bubble of his rage.

She yawned and stretched her arms above her head.

'Well,' she said mildly, 'if Claudia's too thoughtless to worry about us – '

'Thoughtless! This isn't *thoughtlessness*, Madge! Twice in one week is sheer insolence! She doesn't care, that's her trouble! And it'll have to stop! I won't have it! I won't have it, I tell you!'

'Oh, well. If Claudia doesn't care about us, we won't care about Claudia. A taste of her own medicine will do her the world of good. We'll see how much she cares when her birthday comes round.'

Something kicked on the inside of Claudia's chest. Her chin went up, her eyes blazed; but she knew better than to scream at her mother. She had been quivering slightly ever since John had ditched her for Rita Tapscott. Now she was quaking all over, and the difficulty of saying something reasonable, when she wanted to throw crockery instead, had beaten her many times before this. 'I do care,' she said through her teeth. 'I *said* I was sorry. Twice!'

'I'm sorry, too, Claudia. Your father's sorry. We are sorry ten times over. Does it change anything? Does it put the clock back? It doesn't. Go to bed.'

She watched, resting her chin in the palm of her hand, as her enraged daughter steamed towards the door. 'Slam it . . .' she warned quietly, and Claudia, taking a deep breath, did not slam it. But her feet pounded the stairs like thunder and, after a brief suspense-filled silence, her bedroom door swung to with an almighty crash.

The back door flew open. James, swinging into the kitchen on one leg, yelled, 'Rain!'

Madge slid the bacon from the stove and looked sideways at her stunned, silent family. Daniel and John seemed to have turned to stone, with loaded spoons of Puffed Wheat held half-way to their mouths.

'All hands on deck,' Madge prompted grimly. 'Come on, move! John, give your nan a shout. Claudia, put something on your feet and help set the buckets. God, make it a downpour!'

Within seconds the kitchen was empty and Claudia was racing across the yard to fetch the buckets. Except for the occasional light drizzle and short-lived shower, no rain had fallen since the autumn; and the summer before that had been one of the hottest and driest on record. In some localities the piped water supply was now cut off for eighteen hours a day, and if housewives ran out between times they were forced to queue at standpipes in the street. A water tanker made daily deliveries to the farms and market gardens, but it could never bring enough. All over the south-west people were crying for rain, praying for rain, setting buckets to catch each drop. For every drop, now, was as precious as an ounce of gold.

James, in a last-ditch attempt to save his thousands of spring seedlings, had set some of them on wheeled trolleys, and when the least smattering of rain touched his face, he dragged the precious plants out of the glasshouses to catch what moisture they could. He rarely got them all out in time. Though the clouds gathered, darkening and lowering, filling his heart with hope, they usually withered away again, their promises all broken.

If the drought didn't end soon, he, and hundreds like him, would face ruin. He had not told anyone how scared he was. Not even Madge. But everyone knew. Even his mother, convinced that her 'three-score years and ten' would soon be the death of her, could gallop like a two-year-old the minute he shouted: 'Rain!'

Rain! And this lot was heavier than they'd had in months! 'Keep it coming, you blighter!' he roared up to heaven. 'Keep it coming!' He hitched himself to the first of the trolleys and leaned forward, heaving it over the ramp.

From the corner of his eye, he saw John racing towards another glasshouse. Daniel was already going back for his second load, and Claudia and Madge were tearing down the track, clanking six buckets apiece.

The thin curtain of rain sagged and whispered, drawing back from its clear blue window of sky.

'Come on! Come on! Oh, come *on*, will you?' James stood in his tracks, shaking his fists at the clouds. 'Give me a chance! *Please*!' His screams fell into silence. The others had all stopped work and stood watching him, their eyes bleak with pity. The rain had ceased.

'Oh, leave it!' he roared. 'Damn it! Damn it! Go home!' Madge, stuffing her hands into the pockets of her cardigan, made a move to approach him. 'All of you!' he added frantically, for he couldn't bear to let a woman see him cry, even if she was his wife. She had seen him cry many times before this but he still couldn't bear it. She didn't understand. She didn't believe that he was doomed, that every move he made was a futility, born out of desperation. He was like a butterfly on a pin, fluttering because he had to, not because he saw any point to it.

'Pin . . . Point . . . Pun,' he muttered, and his rage, like the rain, sagged and whispered, leaving him dry.

By the time everyone had finished breakfast, the sun was shining again, and the boys were arguing about the best way to spend their Saturday.

'I don't suppose anyone's going to Bristol?' Daniel asked hopefully, darting a sly glance at his father.

'Ask your mother,' James growled. '*I* don't know.'

'Well . . .' Madge said, watching him.

'Might as well,' he said. 'Look at it.' He gazed mournfully from the window. 'Not a cloud in sight. Well, who's coming and who's staying?'

Claudia blushed and looked at her hands, hoping she would be included in the outing. She usually was; but after last night's little difficulty, it couldn't be guaranteed. Her father hadn't yet spoken to her, and her mother had said very little, very coolly. She didn't dare ask. Not in front of the boys. If the answer was no, they'd laugh; and she couldn't bear that. Not today. If John laughed at her, she'd kill him.

'I could do with some shoes,' Nan said brightly, and everyone stared at her as if she'd volunteered for a trip to the moon. The last time Catherine Murray had ventured into Bristol was on the day King George had died, and she'd felt guilty about it ever since.

'Have you checked on Her Majesty's health?' James teased dourly. 'Sure you want to risk it?'

Registering the change in his mood, everyone began to talk at once and, in the cross-fire, Daniel secured his own seat in the car while John was persuaded to stay at home with Claudia.

'Can I wallop her if she's naughty?' he enquired thoughtfully. 'It's about time someone did.'

'I think Claudia is beginning to realise that,' Madge replied. 'We can but hope.' She smiled at her daughter, encouragingly and without rancour, but it was the worst thing Claudia could remember her saying. It meant something big, something serious. It meant that her mother had had enough; and when Madge Murray had had enough, it was final.

For some time past, Claudia had begun to suspect that things were changing, that the old days had gone and that she was moving into unknown territory. All her life until now she had been the pet of the family, loved and protected, comforted, spoiled. She could remember a time when John and Daniel had let her tag along when they went fishing for minnows, allowed her to climb trees with them and to join in their football games. They had taught her to fight, to skate, to ride her first little fairy-cycle. Now they ignored her, shook her off, told her to find some friends of her own age.

Claudia didn't have any really close friends. With her brothers for company she'd never needed them; and the old circle of village girls had broken up after the eleven-plus exams. Claudia didn't like girls very much. She had never yet met a girl who was like her mother; never yet met a girl who was like her brothers. And if her mother and her brothers no longer liked her, it seemed she would be lonely for the rest of her life.

When the family had gone, and John had retreated to his room to keep out of Claudia's way, she wandered miserably through the silent house, picking things up, putting them down, looking for something to do. The house, built just before the First World War, had originally been an uncomplicated cube, with four rooms upstairs and three rooms down; but it had spread a little since then, and now boasted two extensions, one at each side. Nan now occupied the two front rooms of the original house. She hadn't used the stairs for years, and claimed to be unable to manage them, although she could sprint up the Post Office steps on pension day. But Nan's sprinting was like Dad's trembling: no one was mean enough to mention it.

Nan's living room was the nicest place in the house; warm and dark and thickly layered, like a bird's nest. It was full of old things, some of them precious, most of them worthless and prized only for their memories.

Claudia's favourite things were the photograph albums. There were fourteen of them, beginning on Nan's wedding day (Grandad had looked a bit crabby, even then) and ending – just for the time being – with Claudia's first Grammar School portrait, her arms demurely folded, her school tie askew. The later albums, in fact, were mostly embarrassing. They were full of things she remembered and didn't much like. Dad building the new extension, for instance. He was smiling in the photograph, but Claudia remembered the building work only for his bad temper. The day he'd fitted the plate-glass window – and broken it – would remain in her memory until the day she died.

The best albums were the early ones. Pictures of the village when it was just a single street, with lots of trees and no lamp-posts. Old-fashioned clothes, old-fashioned hair styles. Sibyl Blake, standing shyly at the bridge in an ugly, low-waisted frock, with a silly, snail-shell hat pulled down over her eyes.

Nan always said that Sibyl Blake had been beautiful. She narrowed her eyes when she said it, and her sharp, no-nonsense voice became hushed and sad. 'Oh, she was a *beautiful* girl!'

They'd had different ideas of beauty in the olden days, of course. They must have done, for if they'd known how awful those hats were, they couldn't have looked so pleased with themselves.

'And here's your Great-Uncle Jim. Now he was a *lovely* man, before . . .'

Before he had died in prison, of grief and tuberculosis, Great Uncle Jim had loved Sibyl Blake, and the album was full of snaps of them: laughing, solemn, fooling on the river bank, having tea on the lawn. One photograph, which Claudia had never seen, had been taken at a picnic in Saxons' orchard, with Saxons, Blakes and Murrays all lined up together in a single laughing group. Where that picture had been was now an empty space. And it wasn't the only space. When Grandad had torn the Saxons from his album he had refused to fill the gaps with something else. Each space was like a two-minute silence, a stained grey square full of ghosts.

Claudia slammed the album closed and threw it down.

Without Nan to explain who everyone was (or wasn't), the photographs were no fun at all.

Oh, this was a hopeless way to spend a Saturday! Claudia was bored. She was lonely. She'd have to make it up with John.

'I'm making coffee!' she called up the stairs. 'D'you want some or don't you?'

John did not reply and Claudia swallowed a throatful of tears.

'Blow you, then!' she snapped. 'See if I care!'

Twitching her chin, she marched into the kitchen and slammed the door, half hoping that sheer annoyance would bring John down. She filled the kettle and stroked a tear from the corner of her eye. The silence lengthened. He wasn't coming down. Damn it, she'd been sent to Coventry, just for being ten minutes late!

While she waited for the kettle to boil, Claudia wandered to the window, her eyes glazing over with the utter blankness of utter boredom; and through the unfocused mists she saw a shadow passing over the flagstoned yard, as if a cloud had crossed the sun. She blinked, refocused her eyes and leapt for the door.

'Rain!' she yelled.

The rain shadow had overtaken her before she reached the first of the glasshouses, each chill drop penetrating her grey Shetland jumper like a bullet. But the newly formed clouds had more to offer. How much more didn't matter, just as long as she could get some of the trolleys out to catch it.

She had hauled out three loads before John overtook her, and after that she didn't count the trolleys. Her head had gone fuzzy with the strain, and her legs wouldn't hold her up unless she was bracing them against a ton-weight of wood, compost, and bean seedlings. She fell over more times than she could count, her ears roaring like the river in flood. Then, from the end of the track, the last of the glasshouses, John yelled, 'Done it! We've done it!'

Claudia was lying on the ground, and time seemed to have passed, for the person leaning over her wasn't John. It was James, his best grey trilby dripping with rain.

'Hey, Dad,' Claudia murmured drunkenly. 'We done it . . .'

Chapter Two

Even had she not known her father-in-law, Madge would have guessed he was a recluse from the design of his house, which turned a blank wall to the south, snubbing the village. The house faced west, affording clear views of the road, so that if Albert saw anyone coming, he could quickly nip out at the back door, muttering, 'If it's for me, I'm out.'

He was dead now, killed by a hunting pair of Jehovah's Witnesses. When he'd seen them approaching the front gate, Albert had nipped out the back in his slippers and stepped on a newly pruned rose bush. Having twisted his ankle, he'd been in too much of a state to notice the thorn which had penetrated his toe, and afterwards, when it poisoned his foot, he'd been too shy to go to the doctor.

'That'll wear off,' he'd said grimly, and so it had, in a way.

Three months later, Albert had come home from the hospital minus the bottom half of his leg, stumbling so clumsily on the artificial one that even the back steps had proved too much for him. No longer able to escape, subjected to the attentions of the curate, the district nurse and every other well-meaning soul in the community, he had simply shrivelled up, like a minnow on the river bank, and died within the year. He'd been muttering something when he died, and although Madge hadn't been able to make it out, her mother-in-law swore he'd said, 'I never did have much luck with bloody roses.'

True or not, it made a good story to tell at the funeral. Madge had been surprised – in fact, rather shocked – to find that virtually the whole village had turned out 'to see Albert off'. She'd silently called them hypocrites, which had been stupid of her, for she'd known all along that Albert's troubles, like James's, were mostly of his own making. He'd lacked courage, he'd lacked hope; and worst of all, he'd lacked forgiveness.

'But *we* never turned from 'un,' old Georgie Flicker had said a trifle heatedly when the ham sandwiches and the whisky were passed round afterwards. 'It were just damn difficult, that were all, to look 'un in the eye right after. Wait for it to blow over, that was all we could do, like. But it never did blow over. He shut hisself away, Mrs Murray, and 'ouldn't let us nigh 'im. But we knowed it weren't his fault. We knowed he were a good 'un.'

'Jim, too,' said old Mrs Chislett stoutly. 'Aye, Jim too. Jim were a lovely lad, and there's not nobody, save for Saxons and the Judge, who've ever said no different. I'll 'ave a drop of that whisky, James Murray, if you'm having trouble getting rid of it. My, this is a lovely room you built! Just right for a funeral. Mind, my heart ached for you in the buildin' of it. Reckon you never had no rest at all, this past year, my lad.'

No one had had any rest that year, with Albert fading away in the front room, and the mess of the building work spreading through the house like a plague. Not to mention the plague of James's temper. Looking back, Madge was surprised to find that any of them had survived the experience.

Still, it was all over now. The new kitchen was beautiful,

large and labour-saving. The new living room faced south, soaking up the sun as no room in this house had ever done, and the big, sunny window had given Madge the thing she had longed for all her married life: a clear view of the village.

Not that she had much time to look at it. With three children, an emotional husband and a malingering mother-in-law, a woman could work twenty hours a day and never find a minute for window gazing. But twenty-hour days were against Madge's religion. At two o'clock each afternoon she threw down her dish-cloth, locked herself in the bathroom and emerged half an hour later in a fresh skirt and blouse, her dark, greying hair carefully groomed and a gracious smile lipsticked firmly into place. Then she'd sit by the window for an hour, sipping Earl Grey tea and thinking of higher things.

Madge usually had a few dozen higher things to think of, but just lately they had all come under one heading: Claudia. When the boys had been Claudia's age, Madge had thought of Art, Literature and Philosophy while she sipped her afternoon tea (at least, she'd tried to); but the boys had been such straightforward characters. Neither of them had inherited James's temperament, and she thanked God for that. But Claudia . . .

There was the difficulty, of course, of not knowing how much was heredity, how much upbringing (they *had* spoiled her a bit) and how much the onset of adolescence.

Claudia was not yet, officially, an adolescent, although her chest was beginning to fill out, and the time could not be far off. Madge had already told her what to expect, and it hadn't been easy, for Claudia hadn't believed a word of it at first. Then, after listening to her mother's firm repetition of the facts, she'd said,

'Oh . . . Well, thank you for telling me, Mum, but I don't think I'll bother with all that. It sounds disgusting.'

When Madge had told her she didn't have the choice of opting out, she'd thought she was being victimised. 'You say the boys won't have periods?'

'No. Only women have periods.'

'Why? Oh, Mum, it's not fair! Why does everything have to happen to *me*?'

She'd pinched that line from her father, who had lived most of his life in the firm conviction that the world had it in for him. The drought, for instance. He knew that everyone in the south-west was gasping for water, but he still thought the rain was being withheld especially to spite him.

It had its funny side but when you came down to it, it was sheer selfishness, a twisted version of egomania. Who did he think he was that even the weather should change for him – or against him? Why couldn't he acknowledge that other people suffered, and that the slings and arrows which stung him so hard, stung other people too, sometimes a darn sight harder? He saw other people's blessings, not their griefs; saw his own griefs, not his blessings. Or, rather, he saw his blessings all too clearly, and lived in terror of losing them.

On Saturday, when the rain had come, they'd been in the new Broadmead shopping centre, looking for a parking place; and Madge, knowing what was likely to happen next, had bundled everyone out into the street before James could whisk them home again. 'We'll catch the bus home,' she'd said, but he'd been on his way before she'd finished speaking, and at least half of Broadmead's shoppers were taking note of his car number as they'd leapt out of his path.

The Lord only knew how many lives he had risked as he'd driven the ten miles home. He'd confessed later that during the entire drive he'd been working out how much rain he could have saved if he'd fitted the Rover up with drainpipes and a water tank. It hadn't occurred to him to thank God for all the gallons of rain which were soaking into his land, nourishing his broad beans and spring cabbages. It certainly hadn't occurred to him to think that Claudia and John would haul his precious seedlings out of the glasshouses before he could get home.

Poor old Clo. She hadn't been able to move the next day, and even this morning she'd gone off to school with her teeth gritted, wincing at every sudden movement. For Claudia, who was barely five feet tall and as thin as a reed, hauling those trolleys had been a superhuman effort, and James, the fool, had known it. But two hours later, as he watched the rain still falling, he'd said, 'All that effort wasted, love. If you'd waited for me, I could still have got everything out in time.'

He still couldn't understand why Claudia had spent the rest of the day in tears. He'd thought it was because her back was hurting.

It was useless to explain anything to him, and Madge rarely wasted time in pursuit of useless projects. But when James said something negative, she tried to say something positive, hoping that Claudia and the boys would find this more interesting – and influential. Influence mattered just as much as heredity, and if any of her children had inherited James's thumbs-down attitude to life, Madge felt pretty confident of laughing it out of their systems. Pretty confident, but not entirely so. Claudia was proving to be harder work than the boys had been, and no amount of smiles and encouragement had cheered her up on Saturday. She'd even declined Madge's offer of a birthday party.

Madge finished her tea, washed her cup and saucer, set the table for the children's tea and wandered through to her mother-in-law.

'Feel like a walk? I thought I'd go and meet Claudia.'

'Well, I'd like to, Madge . . .' Cath rubbed her left leg

and winced discreetly. 'But I'm just beginning to decrease for the sleeves, and you know how muddled I get if I leave off when I'm counting. Getting old, I'm afraid.'

And lazy, and sly, and selfish, Madge remarked inwardly. She had made a big mistake with Catherine Murray. Cosseted her too much after Albert's death, done too much for her. Cath had learned to like it, and now no one could tell which of her aches and pains was genuine and which laid on for effect.

Still, Madge was happier to walk on her own, and even the habitual longing for rain couldn't detract from her pleasure in the crisp, sunny afternoon. The village looked almost pretty in the sunshine, almost lovable, although Madge had to strain a few emotional muscles even to think of loving Larcombe. She'd been born higher up, on the edge of the Mendips. Coming to live in Larcombe had been like falling down a well. On dark days, even twenty years later, she still itched to climb out of it.

The brakes of the ancient school bus were already groaning on the steep Bristol road as Madge crossed the bridge. The bus was almost empty, for Larcombe was one of its last ports of call, and Madge could clearly distinguish Claudia as she staggered down the central aisle, loaded down with satchel and gym-bag. She came down the steps very gingerly, biting her lip.

'Hello, soldier. Still aching?'

'Mum! Where've you been? We had Games last lesson. It was awful! I thought I was going to pass out.'

'But you didn't.'

'No, we were on the gravel courts so I fought it off. I wouldn't have bothered if we'd been on grass. Where did you say you were going?'

Madge laughed. 'Nowhere. Give me your satchel.'

'So where've you been? You look really nice in that coat.

I'd like a camel-hair coat, Mum. Where did you say you'd been?'

'I've been,' Madge said solemnly, 'to meet a friend. To discuss a matter of great importance.'

'Oh,' Claudia said tetchily. 'What? W.I. again?'

She was as white as a ghost and there were purple shadows around her eyes, adding to the ghostly look. But without her heavy school satchel she seemed to be walking quite normally and, as usual, was trailing her finger along the low wall which edged the river bank. She looked so young when she did that; and her school uniform didn't help, for Madge had bought it with growth in mind, and Claudia hadn't grown as much as she should. She was probably going to be small, like her grandmother, and if she'd done herself an injury with those trolleys, she might well end up stunted for life.

'So where does it hurt now?' Madge asked cautiously.

'Nowhere, really. All over, but not very much. What matter of great importance?'

'Your birthday. I take it you didn't mean what you said about a party, so if you want one – '

'I don't. I hate parties.'

'Oh. Do you, darling?'

'Yes. When you're fourteen you can invite boys, and when you're ten you can have musical chairs as usual, but when you're twelve . . .' She sighed heavily. 'Oh, I don't know, Mum. Do you know what I'd really like to do? I'd like to do what you do on your birthday – invite a friend to lunch, in the dining room, with no one else allowed in!'

'That's what I do on my birthday?' Madge frowned.

'Yes! It's what you did last year, anyway. Remember? You invited Aunty Val.' Claudia scowled petulantly. 'And *we* all had to eat in the kitchen and not interrupt!'

Madge laughed rather hollowly. 'Oh, that was my birthday, was it?' She nodded grimly, having laid on that special lunch to comfort a friend whose husband had recently died. Val had wept through the entire meal. Such fun.

'Well, darling,' she said. 'Each to his own. Are you sure that's what you want?'

'Yes, but absolutely *private*. Just the two of us. Please, Mum? Please?'

Madge smiled. 'Hmmm,' she said cautiously. 'Well, if you'll do me one small favour, I'll mention it to your father and see what we can arrange.'

The ghostly look left Claudia's face. She turned pink and her mouth dropped open with delight. 'Oh! Really, Mum? You mean it?'

'I mean . . . what I say. If you'll do me that little favour I mentioned.'

'What?'

'Go to bed early. You look awful.'

Madge glanced up from her book. She'd been doing Greek Civilisation at an evening class in Keynsham, and was now reading a translation of Plato's *The Republic*. Jolly interesting it was, too; although Madge had had a great many of Plato's ideas before she'd even heard of him.

'Nearly finished, Clo?'

'Mm.' Claudia went on writing in the miraculously neat script which was Larcombe Junior School's only claim to fame.

Madge deemed herself fortunate to have had three children who were naturally bright, but they had all found their first year at Grammar School a struggle. Claudia, on occasion, was inclined to give up the struggle and go under. This was why Madge had joined her evening class. It was an excuse to say, 'Come on, Clo, let's do our homework.'

They usually did it at the kitchen table, within cosy reach of the Rayburn.

'Ten minutes, dear. It's your turn for a bath, remember?'

'Bath,' Claudia muttered. 'Paddle, you mean! Mum?' She wrote a few more words and slammed a full stop into place. 'There! Finished! I hate Geography. Mum, how long would it have to rain before they'd turn the water back on properly?'

'I don't know, dear. A few weeks, I should think.'

'A few weeks! Oh, God . . . I hate it, Mum. Everything's so smelly. I hate having to flush the toilet with a bucket. I hate – '

'We all hate it, Claudia.' Madge fixed her daughter with a cool, forbidding stare.

'Can't I just *say*?'

'Yes, but it's always a good idea to think before you say. You hate having to flush the toilet with a bucket. So do I. I also hate having to fill the blasted bucket from the tank and carry it upstairs ten times a day. You catch my drift?'

Claudia was silent, but her eyes widened and her mouth pinched into a small, pained rosebud; half repentance, half resentment.

'Well,' she said, after a few moments' thought, 'I hate Miss Johnson anyway.'

Madge made another attempt at a cool, forbidding stare, but her lips twitched, and when Claudia responded with a grin of her own, there was nothing to do but laugh. 'All right, why do you hate Miss Johnson?' she enquired comfortingly.

Claudia cheered up, leaning across the table with a bright, confidential smile. She looked not unlike old Mrs Chislett when she'd found a 'fallen woman' to gossip about. Madge half expected her daughter to hiss, 'Three months gone, and no talk of a wedding!'

'Well!' Claudia glanced warily into every corner of the kitchen, checking for eavesdroppers. 'Well, Miss Johnson said we had to write an essay, called "The Quarrel". She said it had to be something we knew about, something that might happen in a family. So I – ' She lowered her voice to a whisper ' – I did mine about Uncle Jim and Luke Saxon!'

'Oh, Claudia,' Madge groaned. 'You shouldn't. What if your father should see it? You know how he – '

'He won't see it,' Claudia said scornfully. 'Anyway, that's not the point, Mum! The point is – ' Again her voice fell to a tortured hiss. 'I wrote it exactly the way Nan told me, Mum. The truth, the whole truth and nothing but the truth. And guess what the old bag wrote on the bottom? You'll never believe it!'

She scrabbled in her satchel for her English exercise book and slapped it open with an angry flourish. 'There!'

Miss Johnson, in her youth, could not have attended Larcombe Junior School, for her handwriting, scrawled in red ink at the bottom of Claudia's essay, was barely decipherable, with only a few letters of each word properly defined.

'Very nicely written, Claudia,' Madge read out slowly. 'But rather far-fetched. Try to be more realistic.'

'You'll have to write her a note,' Claudia said huffily. 'Tell her it's true! Crumbs, Mum, she only gave me six out of ten!'

'Hmm,' Madge murmured. 'Just a minute, dear. I'll just . . .'

She scanned through the essay, pressing her fingers to her lips to quell a rising bubble of laughter. Claudia had certainly told the truth – as far as she knew it. But there was something *very* far-fetched in a story which ran: 'Then Luke Saxon kissed Sibil Blake, and she did not like it, so she cumitted sewerside on her aunty's gas stove in Totterdown, because they did not have any gas stoves in Larcombe, and they still haven't.'

'That's true,' Madge murmured.

'See?' Claudia said. 'Will you write her a note, Mum?'

Madge swallowed. 'Er . . .' she said. 'I don't think she's marked you down for the – er – content, darling. It's your spelling. And . . . and your – er . . .'

'My what?'

'Comprehension, dear.' Madge stared intently at the floor which was covered with pale green lino. Very modern. It showed every mark.

'Comprehension?' Claudia said irritably. 'It's not supposed to be Comprehension, Mum. It's an essay!'

'I meant "understanding", darling. You see, Luke didn't just kiss Sibyl Blake. He . . . Well, you remember what I told you about periods, Clo?'

'Oh, Mum,' Claudia groaned. 'I know all that! But I couldn't very well write it in an *essay*, could I?'

Madge turned a little cold. 'You know?' she asked faintly. 'Who told you?'

'Diane Bridges. I was really disgusted, Mum. Well, I can tell you this: what with periods and *that*, I'm never going to get married!'

Madge turned even colder. She took Claudia's hand and patted it gently. 'I think you'd better tell me what Diane said, dear. She's only a few months older than you. She might have got it wrong, you know.'

'No, she didn't. She saw Tony Tinknell doing it to Maureen Paisley, before they got married.'

'Diane . . . saw . . . ?'

Again Claudia lowered her voice to a whisper. 'He stuck his *tongue* into Maureen Paisley's *mouth*! And she's expecting a baby now, so that proves it!'

Chapter Three

Mary Fisher was not Claudia's best friend. She was Claudia's only friend; and the condition was mutual. They'd met at the Grammar School only six months earlier, and had, in all the confusion of their first day, somehow been thrown together. They didn't like each other; but although 'breaking friends' was easy, making new ones was more difficult, and they always came together again, muttering haughtily, 'I'll make friends with you if you like.'

One of Claudia's many reasons for not liking Mary was that she was a two-faced creep. At lunch, consisting of all of Claudia's favourite foods, Mary had complained that she didn't like lamb chops, mint sauce and banana trifle. Now she was in the kitchen with her hands held demurely behind her back, simpering. 'Thank you for my lovely dinner, Mrs Murray, and thank you *very* much for inviting me.'

'Come on, Mary,' Claudia groaned. 'We're supposed to be going for a walk.'

'Oh!' Mary carolled sweetly. 'Shouldn't we help with the dishes? Would you like us to help, Mrs Murray?'

Claudia sucked in her cheeks and stared at the ceiling.

Her mother said dryly, 'No, thank you, dear. You go off and enjoy yourselves. That's what birthdays are for.'

The girls trailed out to the garden, each of them wearing a new summer frock to match the bright April weather. Claudia's frock – a pink candy striped shirt-waister – was the most grown-up garment she had ever possessed and she couldn't help feeling glad that Mary's frock, although equally new, was a dull green gingham with hardly any gathers in the skirt.

Claudia eyed this inferior garment from the corner of her eye. 'Did your mother make your frock?' she asked.

'No, my Aunty Eileen did.'

'My mother made mine. But then, *she's* very good at sewing.'

'I love your mother,' Mary said wistfully as they set off down the path. 'You're ever so lucky, Clo. You don't know how lucky you are.'

This was true. Claudia had no idea how lucky she was. All she knew was that she had the best mother, the best brothers and the best grandmother in the world; and that she, somehow, had organised it that way. Fathers were different, of course. Fathers just fell on you from above, like pigeon droppings.

'Where are we going?' Mary asked nervously. 'I hope we aren't going very far. I don't want to get my new sandals muddy.'

'How can they get muddy?' Claudia scoffed. 'It hasn't rained for years!'

'Liar! It rained last Saturday!'

'Well? *So*? It's dried up by now!'

They glared at each other, their eyes sparking with hostility, but Mary backed down first. 'So where *are* we going? Let's go through the woods. I like woods. We might find some primroses.'

'The woods?' Claudia gasped. 'Are you crazy?' They're Saxons' woods!'

'So?'

'So! We hate the Saxons!'

Claudia clawed her fingers dangerously close to Mary's face. 'You'll break out in boils if you go in there,' she cackled wickedly. 'They've put an evil spell on it!'

Mary shrieked and ran away, and by the time Claudia caught her they were both laughing helplessly, leaning on one another and clutching their stomachs. Neither of them had the least idea what was so funny, and they stopped laughing almost as suddenly as they had begun. But the tension between them had broken.

'Why do you hate them, then?' Mary asked cheerfully.

'Because they stink,' Claudia said.

'No, really.'

'It's a secret.' Claudia looped her arm through Mary's and hissed into her ear, 'A dirty secret!'

'It isn't!'

'It is. You know what I told you about making babies? Well, it's not true. It's worse than that, but it's illegal until you're sixteen, so I don't know what it is yet. I'm not sure, but I think it's got something to do with periods.'

Mary stared at her, appalled. 'You mean . . . in the same place?'

Equally appalled, Claudia stared back, her lip curling with distaste. 'No,' she said uncertainly. 'It can't be, can it?'

And yet, incredible as it seemed, she had a nasty suspicion that it *was* in the same place, for if not, why should her mother be so secretive about it? There weren't any other secret places. Except busts. Relief made her smile. It also made her forget her grandmother's endlessly repeated warning: 'And we don't talk about your Uncle Jim outside this room, Claudia! Never. Not to your father, not to your brothers, not to anyone!'

'It's probably something to do with busts,' she said. 'But I'm not sure what. Whatever it is, that's what Luke Saxon did to Sibyl Blake. And they weren't even *married*!'

'Who's Sibyl Blake?' Mary gasped. 'Do I know her?'

'No! She's dead. She gassed herself. Years and years ago, this was. Even *I* didn't know her.'

'My God! Why'd she gas herself, for heaven's sake?'

'Because she was having a baby, you fool!'

Mary's face crumpled with bewilderment. 'But what's that got to do with you? If you didn't know her . . .'

'She was engaged to my Great-Uncle Jim,' Claudia explained importantly. 'My grandad's brother. Luke Saxon was Uncle Jim's best friend, and they both fell in love with Sibyl Blake, but she only fell in love with Uncle Jim, so Luke Saxon got jealous, and then, when Sibyl wouldn't go out with him, he . . . did it to her.'

'Did what?'

'It! You know! Gave her a baby! My nan told me he just kissed her, but it wasn't just that. It was the other. Whatever it is.'

'I wonder how it works,' Mary mused thoughtfully. 'I wonder what they *do* to you. Do you know what Gaynor Richards said they do?'

'No! What?'

'Come here,' Mary muttered through her teeth. 'I'll have to whisper.'

She whispered, cupping her hand to Claudia's ear to ensure that no word of her message escaped its target. Then, at precisely the same moment, they both exploded with laughter and fell, shrieking, into each other's arms.

'No,' Claudia said knowledgeably when they'd subsided again. 'They're just for weeing with. I should know. I've got two brothers.'

'Ah-ha!' Mary held up a finger. 'But if they're just for weeing with, why haven't girls got them?'

'Oh, I know that! My mum told me. It's because of men going to war, so they don't have to keep pulling their trousers down in the face of the enemy. Think of all those knights in armour in the olden days. What if they'd had to take it all off when they wanted a wee?'

'Oh!' Mary said wonderingly. 'I never thought of that. Just wait until I tell Gaynor Richards. She thinks she knows everything. Just because her father's a dentist. What's so good about dentists? I *hate* dentists.'

'I hate Gaynor Richards,' Claudia said amiably. 'Her bottom wobbles when she runs.'

After a short silence, during which she'd evidently been casting around for someone else to hate, Mary said, 'So is that *it*? You mean you hate the Saxons just because Sylvia gassed herself?'

'Sibyl!' Claudia corrected excitedly. 'No, I didn't finish telling you. When my Uncle Jim found out what had happened, he went up to Saxons', had a fight with Luke – ' She paused for dramatic effect, grabbing Mary's elbow to ensure her complete attention. 'And chopped his arm off!' she crowed.

'He didn't!'

'He did. They were in the barn, and Uncle Jim took a scythe off the wall, and . . . whoosh! Luke nearly bled to death!'

'He chopped it right *off*?'

'No, but it was just dangling by a bit of gristle, so he lost it anyway. And he very nearly died. But they saved him, hard luck,' she added bitterly.

'And your uncle got *away* with it?'

'No, that's the whole *point*. He had to go to prison, but it wasn't fair because it was all Luke's fault. And he was horrible, and Uncle Jim was nice. But he had to go to prison for ten years, and he got TB and died in there.' Her eyes blazing, she added furiously, 'And Luke got *all* the sympathy! No one blamed him for what he'd done to Sibyl. No one said he'd killed her, and he had really, because it was even worse, in those days, to have a baby if you weren't married.'

They had reached a gateway at the side of the road, and now, quivering with outrage, Claudia flung out an arm and pointed across the fields to a group of tall cedars, outbuildings and the roof of a large thatched house. 'That's them,' she announced viciously. 'That's where they live, the rotten devils!'

The girls laid their arms and chins on the top bar of the gate and, for the best part of fifteen seconds, were silent, staring gloomily at the view. Several fields divided them from Saxons' farmstead, where the thatched house turned its back to them, its face to the sun.

'I like thatched cottages,' Mary mused dreamily.

'It's not a cottage. It's a house. Those trees are hiding half of it. It's got eight bedrooms. My mum went there once, in the olden days, before she got married, so she knows. Mind you, they need a big house. There are hundreds of them in there.' She counted on her fingers. 'Well, nine of them, anyway,' she amended flatly.

'Any kids?'

'Only Callie. She's thirteen, but there's something wrong with her. She used to go to Juniors when I was in the Infants, but she doesn't go to school now.' Sighing, she added glumly, 'I wish *I* didn't.'

'Is she – ?' Mary twirled a finger at her temple. 'You know.'

'No, I don't think so. She's different from the others, though. I feel sorry for her. I bet they're cruel to her. Marcus and Ellis – they're her cousins not her brothers – are horrible. Our John used to fight with Marcus when they were young.'

'Crikey!' Mary's eyes widened. 'Who won?'

Claudia pinched her mouth into a pained rosebud. 'Who d'you think?' she snapped angrily. 'John, of course!'

Mary laughed, a mocking gleam in her eyes. 'Did he chop his arm off?' she demanded derisively.

Claudia felt a nasty little pain under her heart. Fear? Or anger? She wasn't certain. She wasn't even certain what Mary was getting at . . . Unless she'd guessed the truth – that after his one and only fight with Marcus Saxon, John had come home with a bloody nose and a cauliflower ear, muttering, 'He's fast, Mum. I'll say that much for him.' (But he told James he'd acquired his battle scars on the rugby pitch.)

'Oh, shut up, Mary,' Claudia sneered. 'You're really stupid sometimes, aren't you?'

But that ominous little pain was still there, making her heart thump. She wished she hadn't told Mary about the Saxons. She wasn't sure why but a cold, creepy feeling had come over her when she'd said the bit about Uncle Jim going to prison. And then, when Mary had laughed . . . It had felt very bad. It had made Claudia think about her father.

James had been Claudia's age when Uncle Jim went to prison. Now he was forty-five, which was a long, long time to bear a grudge which wasn't even *his* grudge. She had once overheard Madge talking to him about it. 'It's over! It's gone!' she'd said. 'For the love of God, James, forget it!'

But he couldn't. The very mention of the name 'Saxon' terrified him, enraged him, turned his face to a mask of fury. It made him shake, just as Claudia, just a few moments ago, had shaken and raged and bared her teeth. She wished she hadn't. She felt a bit sick now, as if she'd eaten something mouldy.

'Does Luke still live down there?' Mary asked.

'No. He's dead, thank goodness.'

Again there was silence, broken only by birdsong and the groaning of brakes as a small, square-topped lorry crept down the hill towards the village. It was this sound which made Claudia realise suddenly where their walk had led them. 'Oh, blow,' she said. 'We've come the wrong way. Now we've got to turn round and go back again. I hate that, don't you? I like walking in a circle, so you don't see the same things twice over.'

'We haven't come very far,' Mary observed thankfully. 'I thought we'd walked miles, but I can still see the village down there.' She climbed a few bars of the gate and leaned over, peering downhill, beyond the crown of Saxons' woods. 'I can even see your house.'

'The road curves around the hill,' Claudia explained. 'It's two miles long. If it went straight down, it would probably be half that.'

Mary laughed. 'So?' she said. 'Let's go straight down!'

'We can't! It's Saxons' land!'

'Scaredy cat!' Mary scoffed. 'They can't hurt you. It's against the law.' And then, to Claudia's horror, she slid down the far side of the gate, ran a few yards downhill and turned, grinning defiantly. 'Come on!'

Claudia took a step backwards, her face draining of colour. She had never in her life set foot on Saxon land. She'd convinced herself that Saxon land, and all that grew on it, was poisonous. Even if you only stood on it, your feet would drop off.

'Oooh, she's scared!' Mary taunted merrily.

'I am not!'

'Okay then, come on, I dare you!' Mary laughed, her voice changing to a mocking, high-pitched sing-song: 'Cowardy, cowardy custard, your face is made of mustard!'

Under normal circumstances this would have been enough to bring Claudia flying over the gate, but not this time. She seemed rooted to the spot, her face stone-white, her eyes blazing with a mixture of fear and frustrated rage.

'Oh, come on,' Mary coaxed. 'It'll be much quicker this way, and my feet are killing me.' Her voice softened to a sly, persuasive purr. 'Look, tell you what, if you come, I promise I won't tell anyone that your uncle was a dirty jail-bird!'

They had covered the width of the field and almost reached the middle of the next before Claudia caught up with Mary, but by that time they were too out of breath to fight.

Claudia made a grab for Mary's arm, but only managed to pull her cardigan out of shape. 'I'll kill you,' she gasped. 'I'll scratch your eyes out for that, Mary Fisher!'

'I didn't mean it!' Mary fell to the ground, dragging Claudia with her, where, red in the face and steaming with exertion, they struggled to catch their breath.

Claudia felt sick again. She knew it was partly because she'd eaten Mary's share of the banana trifle; but it was mostly because of Uncle Jim. She shouldn't have told! Nan had warned her not to tell anyone, and now she knew why. For the first time in her life she understood how her father felt, understood what it was he was so frightened of – and it wasn't just the Saxons!

Claudia had been protected from it until now. She'd been shown the photographs of Uncle Jim when he was happy and smiling; had been told, over and over again, that he was wonderful: a kind, gentle man with a *lovely* sense of humour. 'Not like your grandad,' Nan had said wistfully. 'Jim could laugh about anything, and make you laugh, too. Even on a rainy Monday . . .'

It was how Claudia had always thought of him: kind and gentle, happy and laughing; a good man, a brave man, a hero. But he wasn't. He was a *jail-bird*!

'Hey, this is fun!' Mary remarked at last. 'Much better than going on the road. And no one'll know. See?' She looked around, waving her arms to indicate their solitude. 'Not a Saxon in sight!'

There was not a Saxon in sight. Instead, just rounding the brow of the hill and advancing at a tentative trot, came a small group of Hereford cattle, shouldering each other aside to get the best view of the unexpected company.

Mary leapt as if she'd sat on a thistle. 'Bulls!' she shrieked. 'Oh, my God, oh, my God! They'll kill us!'

Mary had lived all her life in Bristol and could hardly be expected to know the difference between bulls and steers. Claudia knew the difference. Bulls had a droopy pink bag dangling between their back legs and steers didn't. Daniel had told her so, and Daniel wouldn't tell lies about things like that. Not that she'd ever put his veracity to the test. Until now, Claudia had avoided cattle of every persuasion, just in case she made a mistake. But you couldn't be wrong about steers . . . She hoped.

'They're not bulls,' she said lazily. 'They're steers. Steers can't hurt you.'

'Says you!' Mary yelled. 'I'm going!' Scrambling to her feet, she ran a few yards in the direction they had come, only to halt with a frightening yelp as yet more cattle appeared on the horizon. 'Oh, God,' she whispered. 'We can't get back!'

Claudia observed Mary's terror with profound satisfaction. The steers had halted some distance away, strung out in a long, curving line, their pretty red and white faces alert with curiosity. But Mary was in too much of a panic to notice their faces. She was much more interested in their horns. And she was trembling.

Claudia smiled. 'Scaredy cat,' she murmured softly. 'Cowardy, cowardy custard.'

'I want to go home!' Mary wailed. 'Oh, Clo, we're stuck! What are we going to do?'

Claudia shrugged. 'Dunno,' she said idly. 'It wasn't my idea to come here in the first place, was it? I wouldn't have come if you hadn't called my uncle a dirty jail-bird.' She turned away, making a bee-line for the woods. 'Oh, well,' she said airily. 'Ta-ta. I'm going home.'

'No!' Mary leapt towards her, clutching her arm. 'I'm sorry! I'm sorry about what I said. I didn't mean it, honest! I was only joking!'

'And you won't tell anyone?'

'No! Cross my heart! I swear! On my life!'

Claudia thought about it. She knew that when Mary crossed her heart and swore on her life, it didn't mean very much; but there was nothing she could do about that.

'Come on, then,' she said. 'See that gap in the hedge? If we just walk quietly towards it the steers won't take any notice. God, you're such a nit, Mary! Steers can't hurt you!'

Still clutching Claudia's arm, Mary began to walk, but after only a few steps she glanced warily over her shoulder. 'Crikey!' she howled. 'They're coming!'

They were coming. First at a gentle trot and then, as Mary took to her heels, at a frisky, thundering gallop.

'Oh, my God!' Claudia roared. 'Bulls!'

The gap in the hedge was tightly strung with barbed wire. Claudia leapt over it, Mary dived under; and they landed in a ditch, on a bed of young nettles. Sobbing and gasping, they crawled away to examine their wounds, which, apart from nettle rash and a few scratches, were confined mostly to their clothing. Claudia's new dress was ripped at the hem. A frayed strip of Mary's green gingham had been left on the wire, where it hung like a surrender flag, feebly fluttering.

They sat in silence, staring at each other, too appalled to speak; while on the far side of the fence, the cattle lost interest and began quietly to browse.

'They're not bulls, they're steers!' Mary sneered venomously. '*Steers* can't hurt you!'

Claudia closed her eyes. She was remembering that this was her birthday. She was wishing she was dead.

'This is a brand new dress,' Mary added shakily.

Claudia looked away, and then swiftly back again, her eyes staring with horror. 'Mary!' she whispered. 'Oh, God . . . Over there! It's Marcus Saxon, and he's got a gun!'

'A *gun*?'

'Sssh! He hasn't noticed us! Quick, get back in the ditch!'

Claudia had been lying in the ditch with her eyes shut for the best part of a minute before she realised she was on her own.

'Oh, hello,' she heard Mary call brightly. 'I wonder if you could possibly show me the way out of here? I'm afraid I'm lost.'

Then Claudia heard Marcus, and her blood ran cold with loathing. He had a curious voice, hard and soft at the same time, like his father's. They never seemed to shout, and there was always a faint hum of laughter in their voices, even when they were being nasty; but each word seemed to emerge on its own, as clear and cold as an icicle.

'Lost?' Marcus said. 'All by yourself, or is your friend lost too?'

'My friend?' Mary gasped innocently. 'What friend?'

'The one lying in the ditch,' he said sweetly. 'This one.'

Claudia groaned and opened her eyes – and saw the toe of Marcus's brown leather boot just inches above her nose. He was standing against the sun, almost completely silhouetted and looking twice as tall as she remembered him; but he'd broken his gun and now held it loosely over his arm, which at least meant that he wasn't going to shoot anyone . . . Yet.

'Why, it's little Miss Murray,' he mocked. 'What a surprise!'

Claudia closed her eyes again. There seemed nothing else she could do. The necessity for speed had plunged her back into the nettles, and she was burning all over, although the heat wasn't all nettle rash. Some of it was humiliation.

'She's scared!' Mary announced with scorn. 'I told her you wouldn't hurt us, but she wouldn't believe me.'

Marcus ignored her. He crouched at the rim of the ditch, observing Claudia's plight with a satisfied smile. 'Are you quite comfortable down there?'

Claudia's face flamed. 'Yes, thank you,' she lied frigidly.

He laughed and reached down a hand to pull her up.

'Don't you touch me!' she wailed. 'You leave me alone! I hate you!'

Again he laughed. 'But you're lying in a bed of nettles, you fool!' His hand flashed out to grab her wrist and Claudia, trying to twist clear, turned her face into the nettles and gasped with pain. But Marcus had her, and he wasn't letting go. 'Get up. Come on.' He pulled her to her feet, his eyes widening at the rash of pink weals on her legs, hands and face. 'Good God,' he muttered. 'You'll still be smarting a month from now.'

Claudia could scarcely dispute it. It was agony: worse on her face than anywhere else, and one of her eyelids was swelling up. She wanted to cry but couldn't, not in front of him. And he was still holding her wrist! Twisting her arm, she struggled to free herself, but Marcus's fingers tightened, tugging her to an ungainly standstill.

'Wait a minute,' he said sharply. 'Let's have a look at you.'

She'd thought she would survive until he said that. She'd thought that if she could just put a few yards between them, her courage would come back. But he was looking her over the way Madge did after breakfast each morning, apparently checking that she'd washed her face and brushed her hair properly. And, oh, she was such a mess! She could have fought him off if she'd been tidy!

'How did you do this?' He had found a gash on the back of her leg which, with all the nettle stings she'd suffered, had entirely escaped her notice.

'I expect she caught it on the wire,' Mary offered helpfully. 'She jumped over it when the bulls were chasing us.'

'Bulls?' He glanced sideways, grinning knowledgeably. 'Oh, *those* bulls.'

'I thought they were steers,' Claudia whispered.

'Didn't you check?'

'Yes, but . . . They chased us!'

His grin widened. 'Just curiosity, I imagine. They've never seen a Murray this close up before.'

Claudia gulped, realising that she had never seen Marcus Saxon this close up before. Not that she could really see him. Her eyes had fogged over, reducing his features to an indistinct blur. But there was no mistaking him for Ellis or his father. Most people said the Saxon men were like peas from one pod, for they were all slim, dark and blue-eyed, but Claudia could tell which was which from a mile off. Ben was rather more thick-set than his sons, and, walking at speed across a distant meadow, would thrust his shoulders forward, as if hoping by this means to get there sooner. Ellis's movements were distinctive only because they were without distinction: save for his colouring, he could be anyone. But Marcus was straight. Whatever he was doing – running, walking, riding a horse or driving a tractor – his back was as straight as a die. He gave the impression that, whatever happened, he wouldn't give an inch.

He was only eighteen: just a few months older than John and, like him, still at school; but it was impossible to think of Marcus in the same terms. John was a boy, with at least some of his childish weaknesses still evident – and still exploitable – but Marcus was a man. He was dangerous, he was the enemy – and he wouldn't let go of her arm!

But now he said the words she'd been longing for, praying for. 'You'd better go home. Get your mother to wash that leg and put something on it. And tell her it was barbed wire, or you'll end up with blood poisoning.'

'Thank you.' She tugged free at last, and staggered backwards, half-turning towards the woods. Again Marcus caught her, held her.

'Where are you going?'

'Home! You said . . .'

'Oh, you can't go that way.' Her jerked his head towards the gap in the hedge, where the bulls still grazed and Mary's forlorn strip of gingham still clung to the wire. 'Thataway.'

Claudia could only stare at him, her blushes slowly fading as comprehension dawned. She'd known he would do something terrible, but not this terrible! He couldn't make them go back through a field of bulls! They were almost home! But Marcus was smiling, his eyes widening as he judged her reaction. Claudia could hear Mary jabbering about the bulls, could see her fingers, plucking urgently at Marcus's sleeve; but he took no notice, and even Claudia saw them only dimly. She wouldn't break down, she wouldn't! He wanted her to cry, just as Mary was crying; to beg, to plead, to clutch at his sleeve; but she wouldn't!

Her eyes narrowing, she peered into the field, noticing thankfully that most of the cattle were facing downhill, their under-bellies in clear view, innocent of any large, pink appendages. And what had Marcus said?

'Bulls?' he'd said. 'Just curiosity,' he'd said. Not that anything he said could be trusted; but if all she had was a choice between trusting him and pleading with him, she had no choice at all.

'All right,' she said flatly. 'Let's go, Mary.'

She turned away, feeling very weak, warm and strangely weightless. Marcus had taken the bones from her body and stuffed her legs with cotton wool. Her ears, too, for although she could still hear Mary (she was threatening to set the police on him now!), her voice seemed very faint, as if she was screaming her rage from a hole in the ground.

Claudia climbed shakily through the fence, standing with her back to Marcus, her face to the steers. 'Come on, Mary,' she encouraged bravely.

At first the steers didn't notice them, but then, as Claudia quickened her pace, they looked up; and, as if they'd all been tugged by the same string, they turned in their tracks and began to follow. Her heart hammering, Claudia halted. The steers halted. She took a deep, calming breath.

'It's all right, Mary,' she said tremulously. 'They're just curious. It's all right. It's all right . . .'

She had an awful feeling that Mary had been struck dumb with terror, but except to keep up her soft chant of encouragement, Claudia could do nothing to help. Mary had lowered herself. She had cried. She had begged for mercy. Claudia would not be seen to do the same thing. She knew in her bones that Marcus was still watching them, but he could watch for ever before Claudia would make it worth his while. She wouldn't even look back, and if Mary fell down . . . Well, that was Mary's hard luck.

She walked. The steers followed, their hooves rumbling ominously on the dry, hard-baked ground. She stopped. The cattle stopped. She took a few more steps forward and the steers followed; at every step coming closer until she heard the rasp of their breath and felt – if only in her imagination – the points of their horns nudging her back.

She was getting weaker and more shaky with every step, and her heart was beating so violently she began to think she'd die anyway, even if the steers didn't kill her, but it was against Claudia's nature to give in without a fight. Suddenly she turned, waving her arms like a windmill. 'Yah!' she yelled. 'Get away from me!'

To her astonishment, the steers came to a sudden halt and staggered backwards, bumping into one another, tripping over their feet. They were scared!

'They're scared!' she laughed. 'Oh, Mary, look! They're scared!' She glanced around. She turned on her heel, raking the field with her eyes.

'Mary?' she gasped faintly.

But Mary wasn't there.

Chapter Four

Madge sighed and viewed the tea-table with a critical eye. Claudia had insisted that, for this birthday tea, she didn't want anything childish. No jelly and blancmange, balloons or party hats. She wanted sausage rolls, chocolate eclairs, and very thin sandwiches with the crusts cut off.

Narrowing her eyes, Madge surveyed the table again. Something was missing . . . 'Oops!' she giggled. 'The birthday cake!'

She scuttled out to the kitchen to fetch it, almost bumping into her mother-in-law, who had been out for her pension and was scuttling in the opposite direction, with her hat all askew.

'Where's Claudia?' she gasped. 'It's that dreadful Jack Horner! He's back!'

Nothing could brighten Cath's eyes so well as a spot of smutty gossip, and the news of Jack Horner had made them gleam with excited malice. 'The men'll lynch him if they catch him!' she gasped.

'Nonsense,' Madge said mildly. But she was thinking, the women might . . .

No one knew Jack Horner's real name. A tramp, he'd been coming through the village for years, usually camping in Saxons' wood for a few days before wandering off to bother someone else. Winter and summer alike, he wore an Army greatcoat which, over the years, had absorbed so much dirt that it gleamed like bronze. Jack had never bothered anyone except to ask humbly, 'Spare us a pinch o' tea, missus?' And few women ever refused him. They gave him food, old clothes and boots: whatever he asked for, within reason.

Then, after a polite, 'Thank 'ee kindly,' he'd shuffle away, muttering, 'Liddle Jack Orner, zad'n uz corner, ead'n uz Chrizmuz poy . . . 'E pud in uz thumb an' pulled out a plum . . .'

Last year, however, he'd recited his rhyme to one of the village girls – a very young village girl who had listened and watched with innocent fascination – but the plum he'd pulled out on *that* occasion . . . ! He wasn't made so welcome here now.

Madge thought about it. 'Oh, Clo'll be all right,' she decided at last. 'And Mary's with her. If they're not back soon, I'll send the boys out to find them.'

'Where are the boys?'

Madge smiled wryly. 'How should I know? But they'll be back. Have you ever known them miss a birthday tea?'

'Huh! Some tea!' Cath scoffed indignantly. 'No jelly? I never heard such a thing. I reckon Mariah Chislett might be right about Claudia, you know. Too many fancy ideas by half. Cut the crusts off, indeed. She'll be wanting us to hire a butler next.'

Laughing, Madge fetched the birthday cake from its tin. It was iced in white, with lacy pipings at the edges and Claudia's name picked out in silver dragees. There was nothing in the least childish about it – always assuming you didn't notice that there were twelve candles, rather than the sixteen Claudia would have preferred . . .

Oh, Clo, Madge thought wistfully. If only you knew how much better it is to be twelve.

But the years sped by so fast, and it would be no time at all before Claudia *would* be sixteen. Wearing a brassiere and lipstick. Going courting! Oh God . . .

Her eyes misting, Madge carried the cake through to the dining room, silently rehearsing the facts which, too soon, she would have to face. I have three grown-up children. They've all left home. And I'm stuck with their father for the rest of my days.

They were words she had never said and would never say to a living soul; words she was ashamed even to think. But, just lately, that shame had come upon her with sickening regularity, coupled with a crazy yearning to have yet more children while she still could. She couldn't bear the thought of living without them, without their needs putting a buffer between her and –

'Oh, shut up,' she said out loud and jerked her gaze to the French windows by way of distraction.

Immediately she looked up she saw something pale, something moving, deep in the woods. Jack Horner? No . . .

Frowning, she stood watching for a moment. Pale . . . green. With two skinny legs and, beside them . . . a khaki-clad leg, gleaming like bronze! Even before she'd thrown open the windows and stepped outside, the pale green frock and the skinny legs had identified themselves as Mary Fisher but the rest was just a dark shape moving swiftly among the trees, a man, who *must* be – ! Oh, dear God! But where was Claudia?

The words 'Leave that child alone!' had already curled her tongue into place; but before she could utter a sound the man stepped clear of the trees, and her mouth snapped shut with astonishment. Ben Saxon! No, not Ben . . .

Marcus! She stared at him for what seemed like hours before the shock wore off. And it *was* a shock: a drowning sort of shock, where your entire life – past, present and future – passes through your mind like a steam train, roaring and shrieking, leaving you with nothing, save a dry, sucked-out feeling of unbearable loss.

She hadn't seen Marcus for years – not this close, anyway – and he'd grown. He'd changed. But the likeness was astonishing. Save for his eyes, he could so easily have been Ben. Even the expression on his face was the same: bland and cool, with everything which meant anything hidden – and not quite hidden – just beneath the surface. Ben had hated to 'have his mind read', especially by women; and he seemed to have passed this aversion to his son, for Marcus's spine was as uncompromisingly straight, his eyes as bright with disguising laughter as Ben's had always been. Yet Marcus's eyes were not Ben's eyes. They were his own: so pale and clear a blue that they seemed almost freakish against his dark skin and thickly fringed black lashes. So like Ben . . . Yet not the same.

Mary, who had been only a few steps behind him, now struggled wearily to his side, her dress torn, her face filthy and streaked with tears. Her mouth opened as if to bawl for help, and then collapsed in a silent, sulky line as Marcus said coldly, 'Be quiet.'

Madge felt as if she'd touched a hot wire. Her entire body leapt – and didn't move. *Where was Claudia*?

'Marcus?' she breathed.

'Claudia's all right,' he said. 'She's coming home by the road. On her own, thanks to this one.'

Her eyes closing, Madge inhaled deeply. Mingled with her relief was a gratitude which verged upon passion. Marcus could have said anything – or nothing at all – but he'd said the only words she wanted to hear, and he'd said them first! 'Claudia's all right.' So everything was all right, and Madge was herself again.

She produced a patient, long-suffering smile. 'Well,' she said, 'what have they been up to?'

Again Mary's mouth opened, and again snapped shut as Marcus's finger slid warningly past the end of her nose. Madge almost giggled, but she swallowed the urge, remembering James.

Marcus, too, was remembering James. He leaned forward, glancing warily from left to right before patting the broken breech of his shotgun to draw it to Madge's notice.

'Nothing, really,' he said quietly. 'But Jack Horner's back, and they're talking of chasing him out. Dad thought it would be kinder to get to him first.'

'A shotgun's kinder?'

Marcus's mouth quirked to one side. 'At least he knows what it means. If I told him to make a run for it he wouldn't understand, but if I point a gun at him . . .' He paused, as if waiting for Madge's approval. 'Come on, Mrs Murray,' he chided softly. 'Old Ma Chislett and her cronies? Could you really wish that on him?'

Having so recently thought something very similar, Madge could scarcely deny it now; and having a shotgun aimed at his person was probably all in a day's work for Jack.

'Well,' she smiled ruefully. 'You could be right. But where – ? Did Jack – ? Where were the girls? In the woods?'

'No. I was just going down to look for Jack when I saw this one.' He jerked his head contemptuously in Mary's direction. 'They'd been through a field of steers.'

'Bulls!' Mary wailed, but very softly, as if hoping Marcus wouldn't notice.

'Claudia was lying in a ditch – hiding from me, I think.' He laughed suddenly. 'The ditch was full of nettles, so she was in a bit of a mess, but I couldn't let them come home this way in case they met Jack. Not that he'd hurt them.' He looked down at his boots, disguising a grin. 'But they'd need blindfolds, wouldn't they?'

Madge bit her lip on a smile and said nothing.

'So they had to go back through the steers. I meant to go with them, or at least to see them through safely, but this one ran off and, on balance, I decided she needed an escort more than Claudia did.'

'Well,' Madge gasped feebly. 'Thank you, Marcus, you've been very – er – kind.' She flapped her hands at the sagging hurdle fence which lay between them. 'Would you lift Mary over?'

He did it with one arm, carelessly hoisting the child and dropping her on to the lawn as if she were a bale of hay, all the better for a good shaking. She burst into tears almost before she hit the ground, wailing miserably, 'I want to go home!'

'You shall, poppet.' Madge slid an arm around her shoulder, an automatic gesture born out of years of practice. 'Don't cry, there's a dear. It's all over now.'

Marcus grinned again. 'Is it?' he asked, and before Madge could ask what he meant, his gaze slid away to the cinder track near the glasshouse, where James, his shoulders squared aggressively, was marching swiftly towards them.

'Well,' Marcus said, his voice smooth with contempt, 'I think I'll say goodbye.'

Save for the violent click of Madge's knitting needles, the house was silent. Save for the click of her needles and the thud of her heart, Madge was silent. Had she ever been so angry? Probably, but she'd been younger then. She was certain it hadn't hurt so much, and there was nothing she could do to stop it . . . except *kill* someone. James, for preference.

She stared at him for a moment, hating him even more because the sight moved her to pity. He didn't deserve pity! And yet, what else was there to do with him? Even when he knew he was wrong he claimed rightness. He seemed to think that being wrong was the same as having 'flu. It *entitled* him to feel sorry for himself, *entitled* him to sympathy! And the awful thing was, it worked; for even while Madge wanted to tear him limb from limb, she was *still* sorry for the bugger!

It all went back to the sainted Uncle Jim, of course. The Murray martyr, the Murray mug. He'd marked James for life, ruined and maimed him just as effectively as he'd maimed Luke Saxon. How could a man, whatever the provocation, slice off another man's arm and still be *right*? Only in the Murray household. But then, they were mad. They were stark staring mad, and Madge was stuck with them!

She saw their point of view, of course. She saw, too, that Uncle Jim wasn't half so much to blame as was Albert, his brother. Madge could understand Uncle Jim, for he – when you came down to it – had had a number of good reasons for attacking Luke. But none of the Murrays was clever in a fight. Even when John had been small he couldn't get the better of Marcus. They'd been the same size, the same weight; but John had rendered himself helpless with temper, allowing Marcus, quite coolly, to beat merry hell out of him.

She didn't know, but she could guess, that Luke had done something similar with Uncle Jim; and when you've set out to punish a man for the rape and the death of your fiancée and instead been beaten to a pulp . . . Yes, Madge could understand Uncle Jim. In his position she, too, might have grabbed the scythe and swung it, for some things are not to be borne.

Madge knew for a fact that the Saxons, at the time, had had more sympathy for Jim than for Luke who, in their opinion, had been given his just deserts. But such attitudes had been beyond Albert's comprehension. All he could see was that a Saxon had been the cause of Jim's imprisonment, and that Jim's imprisonment was the Murrays' shame. It was the shame – Albert's not Uncle Jim's! – which had marked James and turned him into . . . Madge wasn't sure what he'd turned into, but whatever it was, it was warped. It was painful. It was . . . incurable.

How could you not pity him? He hadn't moved for hours. Hadn't spoken. And his pain was almost tangible, almost audible. But what, and who, had caused it? Had he been Madge – had he been anyone remotely normal – the source of his pain would have been obvious, for he had lost his temper and struck his little daughter (in fact he'd almost choked her), and now he was sorry. Now he was ashamed.

But no, that wasn't it. No, he wasn't blaming himself. He was blaming John! For John, in defending his sister, had 'come out on the Saxons' side'!

'My own son,' James had whispered incredulously. 'My own son . . . He struck me!' And Madge, surveying the small, purple contusion on his cheek-bone, had been hard put not to add grimly, 'Pity he didn't make a better job of it.'

As birthdays went, this one had been . . . well, memorable if nothing else. Madge had spent the best part of an hour cleaning Mary up, shutting Mary up, trying to keep her out of James's way; but the beastly child had still managed to spill more beans than had ever been in the sack. Little cat! Lying, sly, sneaky little toad! She'd turned James into a walking time-bomb, unable to say anything except,

'Just wait until she gets home! Just wait until I get my hands on her!'

Not that this was unusual. When any of the kids was in trouble he said the same thing, but Madge had usually managed to calm him down before he could catch them.

Well, she hadn't managed it this time. Thanks to sweet little Mary, who had wanted to go home, she hadn't managed it. But she'd tried. When, almost an hour after Mary's return there was still no sign of Claudia, Madge had sent the boys out to find her.

'But don't bring her back!' she'd said. 'Give me an hour to take Mary home and get your father smoothed down, and then . . .'

Daniel had found Claudia in the churchyard. She'd been sick, poor little kid, and had sobbed herself dry, and all she could say was, 'I think Mary's dead. I think Mary's dead . . .'

Mary had been trampled to death by Saxons' steers, or so Claudia had imagined. 'But I couldn't go back and look for her, Daniel! I was scared! She called Uncle Jim a dirty jail-bird and I wanted to kill her. And now I *have*! Oh, Daniel, what am I going to *do*?'

'Try again,' he'd said glumly. 'She survived.'

Madge frequently found herself thanking God for Daniel – and praying that he wouldn't change. The prickly Murray temperament seemed to have missed him entirely; and although both boys vaguely resembled Madge's father, Daniel was his spitting image. He had the same gentle mannerisms, the same sleepy, indulgent smile. Daniel seemed to get sleepier in proportion to the urgency of the crisis he was facing – he'd suffered most of James's outbursts, over the years, with his eyes half closed. But that was deceptive, for he was at his most alert when he seemed on the verge of passing out.

Daniel had used up much of his allotted hour persuading

Claudia that Mary was alive and that everything (barring James) was all right.

'But Mum's sorting Dad out,' he'd said confidently; which was a shame, because Madge had still been sorting out Mary's tight-lipped harridan of a mother, while James . . . James was still being James.

Madge stared at her husband again, shaking her head despairingly.

He'd caught Claudia by the hair before she'd even crossed the threshold, and proceeded to shake her to her knees before attempting to slap her. Daniel, having dived between them, had taken the first blow; and in the resulting chaos James had held his daughter by the throat, pinned her against the wall and slammed into her poor little flank as if he'd been trying to put a fire out.

That was when John had hit him; and that, too, was when Madge had come home. It had been like paying a visit to the violent ward of the Barrow asylum. James was stretched out on the stairs, clutching his eye. Daniel was in a heap on the floor, clutching his nose. Claudia was crouching on her haunches, screaming, 'Wah, wah, wah!' like a tiny baby tormented by colic.

And then there was Cath, feebly slapping at John's raised fist as if it were a large blue-bottle she'd found in the pantry.

'Don't you dare strike your father again!' she'd sobbed. 'Oh, how dare you, how dare you! You ought to have more *respect*!'

Madge hadn't known where to turn. Her mind had gone a complete blank. And then, into the blankness, had come a memory . . . She'd remembered the advice her Aunt Vick had given her on the night of the Mendip Farmers' Hunt Ball – the first grown-up ball Madge had ever attended.

'Now, remember,' Aunt Vick had said sternly. 'If your drawers fall down while you're dancing, just step out of them, keep dancing . . . *and make out they belong to someone else!*'

Madge had knitted the best part of a sleeve before her rage subsided. In its wake came despair; and now – perhaps for the first time in her life – she recognised it. It wasn't new. It had been with her a long time, but she'd refused to give it a name, refused to admit it was there.

She put her knitting down, jammed her thumbnail between her teeth and looked despair in the face. She was surprised to discover that it bore no resemblance to James. Despair wore Ben Saxon's face. No, no, not Ben's: Marcus's; but they were the same thing – save for the eyes. Strange eyes. Freakish. Pale. Quite different from Ben's.

She'd seen Ben just a few weeks ago when she was in Keynsham paying the electricity bill, and his eyes had been as brightly blue as ever. But Madge hadn't felt a thing. Perhaps it was because, where Ben was concerned, she was still eighteen, and eighteen-year-olds don't – generally – feel very much for men in their forties whose dark, springy hair is going grey at the temples and receding, ever so slightly, at the crown. But Marcus *was* eighteen. Marcus was Ben as she remembered him, Ben as she'd wanted him, Ben – who'd been too hot to handle.

No, she was getting muddled. *She'd* been eighteen, not Ben. Ben had been twenty-four, and oh, so beautiful . . . Sometimes, when James was asleep, her thoughts drifted to Ben as if pulled by a magnet. She couldn't help it, even though she deemed it little better than adultery. 'Thou shalt not covet thy neighbour's skin, nor his hands, nor his legs, nor his eyes, nor anything that is his.' Yet she could have had him. She might have married him. And she'd turned him down.

'Why?' she whispered.

The answer had been fairly obvious at the time, but now it just seemed silly. More than silly. He'd been too strong for her. The only authority Ben had ever recognised was God's. With everyone else (and everything else which did not count as God's prime responsibility), Ben was master. And Madge hadn't wanted a master, except . . . Well, they hadn't reached that stage. She'd fought it off. God only knew how, for she'd been jelly from the neck down since their first dance at the Mendip Hunt Ball. She'd taken a firm grip on her drawers then, and never let go . . .

She'd always regretted it. But at the same time she'd always known she'd been right, and that if she'd married Ben she'd never have had a chance to be right again. No, that wasn't fair, but you had to be up very early in the morning to beat a Saxon at his own game. There were very few men, let alone women, who had ever got the better of them. Even Luke . . . Even without his arm . . . Yes, even he'd got the better of poor Uncle Jim.

As for Marcus . . . He'd told Mouthy Mary to be quiet, and the kid had almost bitten her tongue off in her haste to obey. It had scared Madge rigid. She'd already been scared, wondering what had happened to Claudia, but that was different, separate. It was Marcus's power which had scared her. It had brought her whole life crashing around her ears like an avalanche. She'd thought, If I'd married you, I'd have been safe.

Safe? From what? From feeling that she was the last, Godforsaken outpost in a crumbling civilisation. The only one with any strength, the only one with any sense, the only one . . .

Madge closed her eyes, and when she opened them again she saw James. He was no different, in his way, from Claudia, whom she had bathed, kissed, fed and comforted and tucked up in bed with her teddy bear. 'But,' she'd said firmly, 'you were very naughty, Claudia. You shouldn't have told Mary about the Saxons. You made the choice and you've paid the price. And that, young lady, is as fair as life ever gets, so you needn't tell *me* how unfair it is.'

Yes, that was how it was. You made a choice, and you paid the price. Despair or no despair, regrets or no regrets – James, God help her, was still her husband.

'I don't understand it,' he said bleakly. 'I've been a good father to him, a good father to them all . . .'

'Yes. But had it been another man hurting Claudia, wouldn't you have been glad that John defended her? You were choking her, James.'

'I didn't mean to! I didn't!'

It was the nearest Madge would ever bring him to an apology. I didn't mean it! My hand slipped! It was an accident. And anyway, it was all Saxons' fault!

Chapter Five

The drought broke in earnest on Easter Monday, but instead of lying down in a puddle and thanking God for it, James shook his fist at heaven and yelled, 'That's right, that's right, ruin my Bank Holiday!'

Poor James. He scarcely ever noticed Bank Holidays – they were his busiest time – but on Easter Monday he'd planned to take the family to Weston. Largely, Madge suspected, because the family hadn't yet forgiven him for Claudia's birthday. Admit it he would not, but in his heart he knew he'd gone too far. He was sensitive enough to want to make amends; not sensitive enough to know that a trip to Weston was the last thing the children wanted.

There was only one thing James's children wanted from him. They wanted him to change. Yet, at the same time, they'd accepted that it could never happen. James had no power to change himself.

His power to change others, however, was remarkable: once you'd seen James Murray in a temper you were never the same again.

Even Madge hadn't bounced back as she usually did, and the lack of bounce worried her slightly, made her wonder if she'd ever manage to pick up all the pieces. It was almost as if 'Madge-the-optimist' had been a porcelain figure which James had knocked to the ground once too often. Until now, only its head or its arm had snapped off, and she'd stuck them back on again, cheerfully exclaiming, 'There! Good as new!' But this time . . . This time, she'd lost a few bits. She'd run out of glue. She couldn't be bothered.

It was in this quiet and depressed state of mind that she discussed the situation with John, and discovered that he, too, had changed. He'd grown up.

'I'm not going to apologise this time, Mum.'

'No, dear. I wouldn't ask you to.'

'Mum?' he'd said after a long pause. 'Dad's not really well, is he? I mean . . . mentally.'

What could she say? Disloyalty to James was beyond her; and yet, for the first time in his life, John was thinking about his father instead of just reacting against him, and his concern deserved respect – and honesty, as far as honesty ever went.

'I wouldn't go that far,' she said. 'Your father's lost his sense of humour, that's all. He's not ill, he's not mad. He just can't see the funny side of anything – especially the funny side of himself.'

Madge had spoken very softly, looking at her hands, and when John didn't respond she glanced up and realised that her words had gone far deeper than she'd intended.

'Hey,' she smiled. 'It's not that bad!'

'No. But it's worse than you said, Mum. I think he does see the funny side of himself. That's why he goes so . . . berserk. Because he can't bear the thought of people laughing at him.'

Yes, her son had grown up. He understood. Too well.

Daniel, too, spoke about his father. Not in the same terms, but with a similar concern. Unlike John, he pretended to be doing something else while he talked, and his worries emerged through a spray of dry Weetabix and promises to sweep up the crumbs.

'Hey, Mum. You ever noticed I'm the youngest? Not counting Clo, of course. John got the first bag, really, didn't he?'

'The first bag at what, dear?'

'Well, a career.' He disappeared into the pantry. 'Where's the thingummy? The dustpan.'

'Not in the pantry, dear.'

'And there's Murray's to think of, isn't there?' His eyelids drooped. 'Murray and *Son*, I mean, so if it's not in the pantry it must be . . . in the broom cupboard.'

'Gosh,' Madge remarked dryly. 'You ought to be a detective.'

'Hey, I've thought of that! Or a vet. But if John gets away first . . . See what I'm getting at? I wouldn't want Dad to think . . . But he does. He keeps telling me how to prick things out, Mum. He keeps telling me about *compost*. And I'm not – ah, here it is! – not all that interested, really. But I haven't quite got round to mentioning it. I don't want to hurt him.'

Even though his voice had broken some time ago, Daniel still spoke in a series of soft yelps, growls and gulps which gave the impression he was riding on a switch-back. His vocal problems were emotional rather than physical, however, and Madge knew from experience that the things nearest his heart were the ones which barely passed his lips.

'A vet? Is that just a notion, or a burning ambition?'

'Well . . .' Daniel had got as far as kneeling on the floor with the dustpan and brush; but now he closed his eyes and collapsed sideways against the table leg. 'Well, I've been thinking about it ever since we found that hedgehog. Remember that hedgehog? It was all squashed at the back end and oozing with – '

'I remember the hedgehog,' Madge said hurriedly. 'And your father wouldn't dream of standing in your way, Daniel, whatever you decide to do. I feel exactly the same, so if you decide to sweep up those crumbs, dear . . . Just go ahead and *do* it.'

'But he's always . . . saying things. I'm sure he expects . . . Or wants, anyway. And who could blame him? What'll he do when he retires, for instance? It'd kill him to sell up, wouldn't it?'

'He's only forty-five, Daniel. Anything can happen in twenty years. It's not worth worrying about, darling.'

Not worth worrying about . . . Oh, God. In twenty years, Claudia would be thirty-two, John going on forty! Madge would be a *granny*!

The rest of the Easter holidays were completely rained out, and although after his first outburst James revelled in the rain, Madge found herself resenting it more each day.

The worst thing of all was the overcrowding. Everywhere she turned she tripped over someone: someone bored, boorish and bewildered who said hopelessly, 'When will it ever stop?' or, 'God, just as the cricket season got started,' or (and this always when she'd just got the floor dry), 'Hand us a towel, Mum! I'm dripping wet!'

She said levelly, 'This is a large house. We have three living rooms. Why do you all have to be in the kitchen?'

She said through gritted teeth, 'Will you all – please – go elsewhere? I'm trying – to cook – lunch.'

Finally she yelled, 'Get out! Get out from under my feet *at once*, now this *minute*, before I kill one of you!'

Mortified, Madge collapsed into a chair, hid her face in her hands and sobbed; hating herself so violently that the tears dried at their source, leaving her staring into space like a zombie. The silence was awful.

[illegible] typical?' she murmured weakly. 'Just when you [illegible] shoulder to cry on, they all go off and leave you.'

She hadn't cried for years. On the day of Claudia's birth she'd told the midwife, 'If I have another boy, I'll cry until he grows up and leaves home.' But she'd had a girl, and had then proceeded to sob her way happily through James's entire supply of clean hankies.

That was the last time she'd really let herself go; and she'd sworn never to do it again, if only because the headache she'd had afterwards had lasted the best part of a week. She had a headache now, although the tears could hardly be blamed for that. The bloody rain was to blame for that. Of all the times for a drought to break – in the middle of the school holidays!

Oh, God, now she was quoting James; and with all of Shakespeare to choose from, where was her excuse?

What was happening to her? Why had everything become so difficult all of a sudden? Her talks with the boys should have cheered her up, not plunged her into the depths. She'd lived all their lives in the terror that James would mark them, as Albert had marked him; and he hadn't. They hadn't come through unscathed, but the experience had at least given them wisdom.

The kitchen door opened – one inch at a time – and Claudia's shocked little face insinuated itself into the gap.

'Want a cup of tea, Mum?' she whispered. 'It's all right, I've shut the boys in the living room.'

Madge produced a tired little laugh. 'How did you manage that? I've been trying to do that all week!'

'I think they're scared.'

Claudia was scared too, and Madge could hardly blame her. It just wasn't done for Mum to blow a gasket. That was exclusively James's department. But Madge had feelings too, and the effort of bottling them up, day after day, year after year . . .

But perhaps that was where the trouble lay? Perhaps she'd filled herself up with feelings, like a kilner-jar with bottling-plums, and begun to overflow. Or perhaps it was just the dreaded Change creeping up on her. Next thing she knew, she'd be screaming at the grocer, sobbing in the street, having all the village know-alls whispering behind her back. 'She's on the change, poor dear. Must be dreadful, mustn't it, losing control of yourself like that?'

Not to mention the facial hair . . . God, to end up with a moustache like Mrs Chislett's!

'Yes, let's have a cup of tea,' she said hurriedly. 'Thank you, Clo. You're a pal.'

It was all Claudia needed. She turned pink and slid her arms lovingly around Madge's neck. 'And you forgive me for my birthday?'

'Your birthday?' Madge smiled wearily. That day had had so many strange repercussions, she'd almost forgotten that Claudia had been the cause of them all. 'Good Lord, yes,' she murmured. 'Water off a duck's back, dear.'

She woke soon after four with a strange roaring in her ears and an even stranger headache. The ache wasn't in her temples or behind her eyes, as usual. More on the top of her head, as if someone had thwacked her with a mallet. But what the hell was that funny noise? Rain?

She crept out of bed, pressing the top of her head as if to keep the ache in. She twitched back the curtain and peered out. Only a thin, peaceful drizzle was falling now, although it must have come down like stair-rods during the night, for the river – a mere brook the last time she'd noticed it – had swollen to its outer limits and was not far short of overbrimming the banks.

'Good God,' she murmured. 'Talk about the sublime and the oh-gorblimey!'

'Uhh?' James groaned. 'What's goin' on?'

Madge didn't feel like explaining. She felt rather sick, even mildly frightened by the extraordinary forces of nature. It had only been raining a week, and for the first three days, at least, it had made little difference to the river.

She'd always hated that river; but, as the drought had grown worse and the river-bed drier, she'd forgotten all about it. In previous years it had often broken its banks, washing the bulbs out of her garden and the profits out of James's. The house had been built on a small rise in the land so they'd never actually been flooded, but Madge had often feared a flood, with all the filth, discomfort and expense that would entail.

Poor Miss Derby had been flooded more times than she could count, and, as a consequence, had given up many years ago her ambition to have a carpet in the parlour. She could shovel the filth from bare stone floors and chuck it out the door. But, oh, what a way to live! And the whiff of sewage, drowned sheep and mildew lived in the walls for ever afterwards.

'Ugh!'

Shuddering, Madge dived back into bed, giving James a shove to push him out on the other side. 'It's time,' she muttered, hoping that before James was dressed for his trip to market she'd be fast asleep; but her headache wanted attention, and by half-past five she was up again, knowing that this time it was permanent.

Madge's morning routine was quick and efficient and – after years of practice – mostly performed unconsciously; but this morning every move she made seemed fraught with difficulty. Her toothbrush slipped just as she made a lateral attack on her molars, almost forcing the brush out through her cheek. And then she jabbed a cream-laden finger in her eye, and was still seeing things through a film of grease two hours later.

Still, 'teachers' rest, mothers' ruin', otherw nown as the school holiday, was over at last; which was as well, because there was a W.I. meeting tonight . . .

'It's W.I. tonight,' she said off-handedly as James t the house after breakfast.

'Oh.' His tone spoke volumes, even without the v look he threw at her as he marched off to his glasshouses.

Madge sighed. He'd discovered a few months ago that Liz and Helen Saxon were members of the Institute, and that they'd been attending meetings for the best part of three years. James had been all for Madge resigning on the spot, and she still didn't know how they'd got through the resulting argument without coming to blows. But he hadn't forgiven her. He probably never would.

'You actually *speak* to them?' he'd howled incredulously. 'You're actually *civil* to them?'

'I'm a civilised person, James. I was civilised enough to have warned you, many years ago, that I would not be drawn into your quarrel with the Saxons. And you accepted it – like the gentleman you *were* in those days.'

Cruel, perhaps. But effective. And true. James had been a very gentlemanly man at one time. He'd had a lovely smile . . . He'd been calmer, softer, more reasonable; and had stayed that way – give or take the odd lapse – until . . . Well, looking back, Madge couldn't find the join. The odd lapses had simply become more frequent as the strain of the years took their toll. Money worries, family problems, war. The bloody weather.

But James the gentleman hadn't been a myth. He hadn't been a deception. He'd just been a porcelain figure, made of finer, more fragile clay than that of his wife, the optimist.

'You've been depressed before,' she whispered helplessly. 'You have, Madge. You have. Remember the alterations? Remember visiting Albert in hospital?'

But tha[illegible] different. With the alterations, with Albert, she'd kn[illegible] it would end, sooner or later. But this, whatever it [illegible] . . . it felt like a sickness that would go on and on.

H[illegible] eyes widened. 'Fool!' she gasped. 'That's it! You've h[illegible] a headache for days! You're sickening for something!'

She felt better immediately. The common cold, bless its black little heart, had come to the rescue. It would probably go right through the house, and she'd be boiling up handkerchiefs for weeks to come. But it would end!

Madge took another Beecham's and forgot all about it.

The monthly meeting of the Women's Institute, especially for its President, offered an excuse for dressing up, and dressing up was one of Madge's favourite occupations. Even at forty-three her figure was still good, her complexion still clear, and her fine, dark brown hair was turning grey in the nicest of ways: in well-defined streaks rather than the accursed 'pepper-and-salt' which drove so many desperate women to the dye bottle.

She had hoped to wear a new summer frock for tonight's meeting, but the rain had put paid to that. A costume was called for; and since Madge – like most worthy women of her class – had bought a new one for Easter, the choice was simple enough. And deeply satisfying, for she'd seen a costume very like it in a copy of *Vogue* at the hairdresser's. And she looked so sleek in a pencil-skirt, with the jacket hugging her waist and just a peep of white lace at the throat to brighten her complexion. Not that her complexion depended entirely upon white lace. There was rouge, too; a light coating of powder; a double application of lipstick, carefully blotted.

'Oh, Mum, I'll be so glad when I'm old enough to wear lipstick! You look lovely.'

'So do you, darling,' Madge smiled. 'Even without lipstick.'

She was lying. Claudia had come home from school in desperate need of lipstick, for her mouth was as white as her face, her eyes haunted and bruised-looking. Madge guessed that things had been bad at school, with Mary Fisher getting her first chance to spread the scandal about Uncle Jim. Not to mention Marcus Saxon and the steers!

Poor little Clo. But there was nothing Madge could do. The cruelties a child suffered at school were just as much a training for life as were lessons in Maths and Geography; and if this little lot hadn't taught Claudia to keep her mouth shut, nothing would.

It seemed that James, too, had learned to keep his mouth shut – on the subject of the W.I. at least – for as Madge swept through the living room, collecting her bag, her keys, her papers, he remained hidden behind the pages of the *Evening Post* and said nothing at all.

'There's a Dundee cake in the tin, James, if you feel peckish later on. All right? I'll be off, then. See you later, dear.'

James said not a word but his disapproval was almost tangible, seeming to make the air quiver like an August heat haze.

For a moment Madge glared at him, wanting to tear the paper down the middle and shout 'Yah, sucks!' through the gap. Instead, she tip-toed to the door and said – to an entirely deserted hallway – 'Sssh . . . Your father's nodded off, bless him.'

She was still grinning as she crossed the bridge ten minutes later. That was the way to handle him – kill the blighter with kindness! Good old Shakespeare. Shakespeare had an answer for everything. She might look him up later. See if he had a cure for facial hair . . .

'What you smirkin' at?' Mrs Chislett demanded suspiciously as they met on the far side of the bridge. 'Won on Ernie, have ya?'

'No.' Madge shook her head. 'Missed it by a whisker.'

Mariah Chislett sat in the front row, giving only half her mind to the speaker, who was talking about the education system in Canada and not making a very good job of it. Even when the talk was a good one Mariah didn't always listen. The Women's Institute was at its most interesting when you studied its members, noticing their little foibles, mannerisms, enmities and friendships. Liz Saxon and Madge Murray were an interesting pair. They didn't chat very much, but the glances they exchanged told a story or two.

Different as chalk and cheese to look at, of course. Liz was a small girl, with softly rounded edges, while Madge was tall, sometimes a mite gaunt-looking, but always exuding a motherly kind of elegance which somehow caught at the heart. She was the sort of woman everyone turned to in a crisis; not because she could fix the burst pipes or cure the sick child, but because, whatever went wrong, she made you feel able to bear it.

Liz wasn't the same; but, within her lights, she was just as strong, just as warm and kind. They should have been chums, those two, and they knew it. They understood each other. Yet they'd never been seen to put their heads together and talk. Exchange recipes for fairy-cakes, yes. But talk, never. And that was a bitter shame. It was James Murray's shame. Silly devil.

Still, Mariah had said it once and she'd say it again (if she could get anyone to listen); a woman was only as good as the trouble she'd borne; and both Liz and Madge had borne plenty, one way and another. Liz should have married

Ben, really. If she'd married Ben and Helen had married his brother Tom, they'd all have been happier. But then, life wasn't meant to be happy. People who had no trouble never amounted to much.

Mariah had realised this many years ago; and the funny thing was, she'd been happy ever since. Not the sort of happiness which made you laugh, not even the sort of happiness which kept you from crying when things went wrong. It was a deep-down kind of thing, a solid base which nothing could shift; so that when a tree fell through the roof, or the river flooded the parlour and drowned the cat, you could scream your head off and still know (somehow or other) that you were happy underneath.

Mariah suspected that Madge hadn't yet discovered this, for there was always something a bit sad about her. Something wistful, as if she still had dreams. And dreams were ruin, if only because the dratted things never came true. Liz Saxon didn't have dreams. She'd looked reality in the face long since, and accepted it for what it was. A cruel reality, too, for when you have but the one child, and that child slowly dying . . .

Helen wasn't up to much. Mariah liked her well enough, for there was nothing much to dislike; but the sweetness of her smile and the softness of her voice reminded Mariah of an egg custard. It offered no resistance to the spoon and gave your teeth nothing to grind against. It was nice, and there were no gritty bits to stick under your plate. But that was all you could say about it.

The speaker concluded with a little joke about kids being the same the world over, and Mariah led the applause, beaming widely as she swivelled in her seat to say loudly, 'Now, that *was* interesting!'

Miss Derby had nodded off, Mariah shook her wrist. 'All about *Canada*!'

'I always think Canada's interesting,' Miss Derby murmured sadly, and then, her eyes brightening, 'Oh! Is it time for tea?'

Tea time wasn't just about cakes and tea. It was about gossip; and everyone made the best of it because it only lasted fifteen minutes.

Mariah grabbed a butterfly cake and a cup of tea and made a beeline for Mrs Hall, whose daughter had been seen in a clinch, in the woods, with a dark-haired man in a nice tweed jacket. Marcus Saxon, some said it was, and Caroline was only fifteen, so there'd be an awful shindig if it was true. Lord, that boy had more arms than an octopus!

'Mrs Hall? Oh, Mrs Hall!' Mariah pushed through the crowds, waving her butterfly cake in the air, seeing everything, hearing everything, summing it all up. She noticed that Madge Murray was sitting on her own, staring into space, which was most unlike her. Something must be wrong; but there wasn't time to go back and ask, now, drat it.

'Oh, Mrs Hall!' Mariah beamed. 'I just bin thinking how I haven't seen your Caroline just lately. She must be getting quite grown up now – sixteen, seventeen? Courting, is she?'

There wasn't time to get back to Madge. There should have been, because the tea break went on for an unprecedented twenty minutes, and even then the President didn't clap her hands to bring it to an end. She just stood on the stage and waited for silence.

But Madge didn't speak. A few people nudged each other and giggled, but Mariah Chislett sat forward suddenly, her heart leaping with fright.

Madge's face was rigid, her eyes dull and cold, and her skin was the sickly, brick-dust colour of baker's yeast.

'Quick!' Mariah struggled to her feet. 'She's feeling bad! Give her a chair!'

But it was too late. Before anyone could move to help her, Madge fell to the boards like a stone.

Chapter Six

Marcus had arranged to leave school while everyone else was at lunch. He'd been through all the farewell ceremonies, the nostalgia, the exchanges of mementoes, addresses and invitations, and been thoroughly unbalanced by it all. Goodbyes, on top of all that, would probably have made him cry. He'd lived the past ten years in the firm conviction that he hated Clifton and all it stood for; and the irony of discovering – at the very last gasp – that he loved every inch of it, was too much to take.

He was glad his mother hadn't come to fetch him. For one thing, she wouldn't have driven the Alvis. She didn't understand the essentially masculine things about cars: the assurance – or, in this case, reassurance – the right car could give a man; and the Alvis was exactly the right car: sleek, powerful, expensive and elegantly discreet.

And Helen would have asked questions. She was as sensitive to hidden emotions as blackbirds are to underground worms. She would even put her head on one side to listen for them, her eyes bright and knowing as she murmured, 'What's up, Marcus?'

There were times when he wanted to tell her, but he hadn't reached that stage yet. He just felt hurt and sad and bewildered, almost as bad as he'd felt ten years ago, when he'd first set eyes on the bloody place.

He'd felt as if he'd spent those ten years climbing a ladder which was actually *leaning* against something, actually *leading* somewhere. A place where everything was right, and you could look down on all the idiots still wallowing at the bottom and feel you'd achieved something. Yesterday, he'd reached the top rung of that ladder. He'd stood at the brink of glory, shouting, 'I've done it!' Today, he'd discovered that the ladder was free-standing. When you stepped off the top you crashed straight to the bottom again.

'Is that everything?' As his father threw the last of the bags into the car, he grinned as if he knew precisely how Marcus felt; but his eyes skimmed away, refusing to get involved. It was just as Marcus wanted it, but he felt hurt just the same.

'Yes, that's the lot.' He smiled, but they'd travelled the best part of three miles before he wanted to speak again. He wanted to speak of the future, to get it into some sort of perspective, to re-establish himself in the world; but he could think of nothing to say. Eventually he asked, 'Did you get all the hay in?'

'Mm-hm.'

Marcus could never talk to his father. They shared a mutual respect which at times felt dangerously like hatred. Even more dangerously, it sometimes felt like love: a strong, yearning, helpless kind of love which never came to anything. It was as if someone had erected an electric fence between them. They couldn't touch each other without first touching it; so they didn't try any more. But sometimes the yearning to touch became more painful than the fear of touching, and the urge to break down the barriers was too strong to resist.

Marcus chuckled, very softly, as if to himself. 'Bit of a

letdown, really,' he said. 'All that talk about fresh fields and pastures new. I suppose it would be different if I was planning to be a surgeon.'

'There's nothing to stop you being a surgeon. *Be* a surgeon if you want to.'

'Thanks,' Marcus said bitterly. 'I don't want to.'

'So what are you complaining about?'

'I'm not complaining.' Marcus spoke through his teeth. 'I was making an ironic observation about the terminology – "fresh fields and pastures new". We've been farming the same fields and pastures for nearly three hundred years.'

'Hmph. You're teaching your grandmother to suck eggs. Why do you suppose I sent you away to school? Why do you suppose I want you to take a degree? Because – '

'All right. I know.'

He knew more than his father guessed he knew. The justification – that he was too intelligent to grow up knowing nothing except farming and no one except farmers – had a ring of truth about it which Marcus was too intelligent to dispute. But that wasn't the real reason. The real reason was that Ben would have killed him if he'd stayed at home; and this was a thing which, for all his intelligence, Marcus had *never* understood. Even now, his father seemed all too anxious to get rid of him. 'Be a surgeon.' Get lost.

'So what would you do if I *did* decide to do medicine?' he demanded. 'Ellis won't take the place on. He'd rather die.'

'He's young yet,' Ben muttered defensively.

'He's twenty, for God's sake! If he doesn't want it now, he'll never want it!'

'You hope!'

They had reached too far. They always did. And the pain was so bad, Marcus wondered how he could have been fool enough to risk it again.

Yes, he hoped Ellis would never want the farm, because, as the elder son, Ellis was entitled to it, as Ben had been – and Tom had not. Not that it had mattered so much in their case. Ben had been the better farmer, the stronger man. But if Ellis took over . . . The very thought of it turned Marcus's stomach. It was the only reason he'd agreed to go to university: to give himself an escape route if the worst happened. But it wouldn't happen. Marcus would sooner kill his brother than let it happen. Or kill himself.

And that was another thing he didn't understand. Why should a stupid parcel of land mean so much? He'd never met anyone whose roots and soul were so inextricably joined. Most of his age group (including Ellis) could scarcely wait to break free of their roots, to hurl their souls skyward and see where they would fall. Oxford, Cambridge, London – as far from home as they could get. But Marcus was going to Bristol, staying close, keeping a hold on the things that were *his*.

The route home took them past a Victorian girls' school, where the older girls sat on the walls with their skirts hitched up, browning their legs in the sun. Ben slowed down, turning his head to admire the view; and Marcus followed his lead, knowing that it would break the tension between them. 'The blonde on the end?' he ventured thoughtfully.

'Mm. Nice legs, but top-heavy. You don't go for these eye-poker-outers, do you?'

'In a perfect world, no. But if she's willing . . .'

'Not too willing, Marcus. If they're too willing, you miss all the thrill of the chase.'

'Fond of a good chase, are you, Dad?'

Ben laughed. 'Just as long as I don't catch something at the end of it!' He frowned now, glancing anxiously in Marcus's direction. 'You are careful about that sort of thing, aren't you?'

'Yes, yes . . .' Marcus raised a despairing eyebrow. He'd learned the mechanics of sex in the farmyard, probably before he'd learned the alphabet; and Ben had given him a lecture on venereal diseases on his sixteenth birthday. This had been followed by a gentlemanly discussion on the subject of rape, which began, 'Never, Marcus! Never, never! Once in this family was enough!'

Since then, a few misunderstandings had arisen between them on the subject of sex. Ben seemed to imagine that because Marcus knew all about it, he did it every night and twice on Sundays – which wasn't true at all. He had a reputation for randiness in the village, too. Not wholly undeserved: he'd certainly cultivated it with a view to making it true some day, but it wasn't as easy as it looked. He quite understood that the girl had to be willing, but so few of them were; and even if they were panting for it they backed off at the last minute, gasping, 'No, no, what if I get pregnant?' Perhaps he'd have more luck at university . . .

The silence which fell now was easier than before; but a mile further on Ben slowed down again. 'That's funny,' he said.

'What?'

'It's not end of term for the other schools, is it?'

'No, they've got another three weeks or so. Why?'

'Oh . . . I saw the little Murray girl earlier, a couple of miles outside the village. She wasn't in school uniform, though.'

Marcus wasn't interested, but it was something else to talk about. 'Any news of Mrs Murray?'

Ben sighed heavily and shook his head. 'Hanging on, the last I heard.'

Marcus wasn't surprised to hear the edge of grief in his father's voice. Mrs Murray had always been different from the rest of her family. She was a kind, gentle, humorous woman. Even when she said no more than hello, she made you feel loved.

'I hope she pulls through,' he said.

'I don't,' Ben growled. 'I wish to God she'd die. What kind of life will she have if she survives? She can't walk, can't talk, can't feed herself. I've seen strokes before, Marcus. It's a living death. And Madge, of all women . . .'

'Yes . . .' But Marcus was too familiar with the idea of living death to want to talk about it. 'I like Daniel, too,' he said hurriedly.

'Daniel? Which one's he?'

'The younger boy. He doesn't really look like him, but he always reminds me of Harpo Marx. He's got that sort of astonished look, as if he's just been woken up by a loud noise.'

'Ha!' Ben laughed. 'Probably scared of you!'

'No, oddly enough, he's the only one who isn't. He talks to me sometimes. He's quite clever, too. Wants to be a vet.'

'Now that,' Ben said excitedly, 'is something *you* could do! Be a vet!'

'Christ.' Marcus turned away and stared determinedly out of the side window, watching the hedges flash past. Be a vet. Be a surgeon. Join the bloody Navy and be a bloody Admiral. In short, be anything you like, as long as it takes for ever and keeps you away from home.

'Oh-oh . . .' Ben's sorrowful murmur had nothing to do with Marcus. It was the sort of expletive which went with a puncture or an empty petrol tank, and it meant, 'Disaster is upon us, but let's not panic, chaps.'

'What's up?'

Even as he spoke Marcus saw the disaster approaching and understood it. Claudia Murray was now at least six miles from home. She was sunburnt and limping, but the blank, emotionless expression on her face reminded Marcus of a film he'd seen of refugees, walking in shock, not feeling a thing. She certainly hadn't seen them drive past, for Marcus swivelled in his seat to watch her. She didn't look back.

They drove on in silence for a few minutes. 'Dad?' Marcus said.

'Hmm?'

'She's only twelve.'

'Mm. I was just wondering what we'd do with her. If she puts up a fight we could get arrested.'

But he turned at the next gateway and drove back the way they had come. 'You'd better speak to her.' He sounded nervous. 'She thinks I'm a monster.'

'Oh . . . Aren't you?'

Ben's hand strayed from the gear stick, patting the air as if he'd intended to pat Marcus's knee and thought better of it. 'I know you don't believe it, but I'm only thinking of you, you know. Farming produces more shit than satisfaction, and . . . And we don't get on. We're too alike. We're too . . . Dear God, just look at the kid! She's walking barefoot!'

Claudia had taken her socks and sandals off since they'd first seen her, and now was wearing them around her neck, like a scarf. Her heels were bleeding, but at least she wasn't limping any more.

They both stared at Claudia's bleeding heels as they passed; but Marcus wasn't especially concerned. He wanted to go on talking, to reach some kind of understanding with his father.

'Being alike,' he said, 'means we should understand one another, not fly at each other's throats at every other word.'

'But it doesn't. It's *because* we understand each other that we . . . Oh, damn it, Marcus! This isn't the time for this sort of thing! Get out. See what she's up to.'

Marcus bit back a sigh. Just as they were getting somewhere. Trust little Miss Murray to ruin it.

But as soon as he saw Claudia's face, his resentment died.

He hadn't seen her since the Easter holidays, and although she'd been a mess then, she'd been a healthy, flourishing mess. She wasn't flourishing now. She was thin and grubby, and the tired shadows around her eyes had little to do with this walk of hers. When Madge had first been taken ill, Marcus had wondered how Claudia would manage without her. Now he knew.

They were barely ten yards apart, and she was looking straight at him, but she'd come almost within touching distance before a glimmer of recognition dawned. She was dead on her feet.

'Hello,' Marcus said quietly. 'This is a long walk for a hot day, isn't it?'

She blinked. Then, after barely a second's pause, she was off again, plodding blindly into the road to get around the car. Marcus caught her elbow. 'Claudia? Where are you going?'

She blinked again, and this time the exercise seemed to wake her up, for she gave him a stare which was strongly reminiscent of her usual, venomous, self. 'Let me go!' she yelled hoarsely. 'I'm going to see my mother, and you can't stop me!'

'But the hospital's miles away! You can't – '

He bit his tongue as Claudia lashed out suddenly, catching his jaw with the back of her hand. 'I can, I can!' She hit him again, a feeble punch to the shoulder. 'And don't tell me she's dead, you bastard! She's *not* dead! She's *not* dead! She's not!'

With every repetition she hit him, her voice rising to a scream; but, as he always did in a physical conflict, Marcus detached himself from the words and dealt with the blows. It was more difficult with girls. You couldn't hit back; could only dodge, restrain, put their arms out of action; and with Claudia in the state she was in, he was almost afraid to do that.

Marcus had never been so glad to see Ben coming to the rescue. He caught Claudia from behind, taking her in a bear hug which, Marcus knew from experience, was inescapable. In Marcus's case, his father had then proceeded to squeeze all the air out of his lungs and, when he was near to fainting, flip him over and beat almighty hell out of him. Claudia was luckier. Ben just squeezed until she stopped screaming, then turned her around in his arms and let her sob. It didn't take long. She'd been exhausted to start with. Now, the strength went from her legs and, as they sagged, Ben picked her up and put her in the back seat of the car.

'Get in the other side, Marcus. Give her your handkerchief.'

But Claudia, although desperately in need of it, hadn't the strength to use a handkerchief, and Marcus ended up doing the honours, although he knew she'd start again as soon as she was fit to talk.

'Who told you she was dead?' Ben asked softly at last.

'N-no one! But D-Dad . . . My father . . .' Her face twisted into an agonised mask. 'I heard my nan!' she wailed. 'She . . . she rang the undertaker! And she's *not* dead, I know she's not! Sometimes she just *looks* dead, and if they bury her – !'

Ben produced his own handkerchief. He took her in his arms and rocked her, murmuring, 'There, there. Don't cry any more.' When she'd quietened a little he added softly, 'Are your brothers at home?'

'No! Their bus goes earlier than mine. I – I was upstairs when the phone rang, and Dad . . . Dad . . .' Again her voice rose to an agonised wail. 'He *screamed*!' She struggled free of Ben's embrace, adding breathlessly, 'So I hid, and then I . . . She's *not* dead! She's not! Oh, please, *please*! I want to *see* her!'

'Right. We'll – er – find a telephone. I'll ring the hospital and . . . And ask. And we'll take it from there. Will that help?'

As soon as Ben was back in the driving seat, Claudia calmed down and tried to pull herself together, huddling in the corner with her knees drawn up, shutting herself away. Marcus had never seen anyone more alone. Her mother was dead. He had no doubt of it. But how could the Murrays have left Claudia in so much doubt? *He screamed*! And he was probably still screaming, the bastard, leaving his poor little kid to sort things out for herself.

Ben went into the telephone box alone; but Marcus knew, the minute the operator put him through, that he hadn't phoned the hospital. Ben grimaced and held the receiver a yard clear of his ear, which meant that Mrs Chislett was at the other end. She'd only had the phone installed a few months ago – a birthday present from her son – but she didn't understand the mechanics of it. She thought it was the same as a loud hailer. It was ironic that she had a telephone at all, for even without one she'd always been able to tell what was happening ten miles away.

Claudia had uncurled from her corner and was sitting forward, trying to read Ben's lips. A faint, tinny echo of Mrs Chislett's voice escaped the call box and crept into the car, and Marcus spoke over it, drowning it out. 'Don't worry,' he said firmly. 'Dad's pretty good in a crisis. If he can help, he will.'

She didn't seem to hear him. Every nerve she possessed was straining towards Ben who, in one of his 'good father' phases, had told his younger son, 'Don't show your feelings through your spine, Marcus. It doesn't matter what words you say; if your spine says something different, that's what people will believe.' In his more frequent 'bad father' moods, he'd said, 'Don't do as I do, do as I say!' and the bad father was much in evidence now, for Ben's spine was saying more than Claudia could bear to hear.

'Hang on,' Marcus said gently.

Her breath escaping in a soft, shuddering sigh, Claudia turned towards him, her wide, dark eyes blanked out with despair. And somehow he knew that she knew the worst, had known all along and simply refused to believe it. It was odd that a pair of 'lousy Saxons' should be the ones to convince her . . .

Ben returned, kneeling backwards in the front passenger seat to hold Claudia's face in his hands. 'Listen,' he said softly, 'when someone dies, or seems to die, the doctors are very, very careful not to make a mistake. They make absolutely sure, Claudia. Dying isn't like being asleep, you see. And your mother . . . is not just asleep. She had another stroke early this morning and passed away very quietly, without any pain. I'm very, very sorry, my dear, but it *is* the truth.'

Ben's eyes were wide with sympathy. And desperation. Marcus could almost hear him praying: Dear God, don't let her have hysterics!

But Claudia was silent. Strangely silent, as if she, too, had died; and she didn't speak again until they delivered her to Mrs Chislett, twenty minutes later.

One of Marcus's most recent Common Room discussions had been about the things people would miss most if they went to live on the moon. Some of the boys had been remarkably honest. One had even gone so far as to say, 'My mother'. Marcus had said, 'Girls, cars and jugged hare,' and although they were true enough, these things came nowhere near the top of his list. The things at the top of his list were ridiculously sentimental. They were – in reverse order – Christmas carols, bluebells and coming home.

Coming home was the best of them because it was so complete an experience, satisfying every one of his needs except the most basic. The first sigh of satisfaction usually passed his lips as he reached the top of the Bristol road and saw, far below him, the lichened stone pinnacles of Larcombe church tower, poking through a green froth of elm trees and yews. He sometimes thought this view was so satisfying because he looked down on it, knowing that although these were the highest points of his life, he was above them, and could always rise above them if he chose. At other times, he thought it was because, at this moment, he was beginning the descent into his true self, letting it swallow him, envelop him, like a warm feather bed on a cold night. He preferred the first idea, but was afraid the second might be closer to the truth.

The village itself was like a portrait of himself, for he'd explored it all, as a small child, in more detail than he had ever, since, explored anything else. It had marked him out and moulded him, awakened his senses.

He'd scrumped apples from every orchard, crawled into every culvert and chased all the ducks, geese and hens that had ever been hatched. Virtually all of Larcombe's male residents at one time or another had boxed his ears; and only the sweetest of women had not screamed at his rapidly departing heels, 'I'll tell your dad on you, you wicked little perisher!'

The old women told him now that he'd been a remarkably wicked child; but Marcus found it rather puzzling that they should think it true. He hadn't felt very wicked. As a child, he'd felt very much as he felt now, as full of possessive pride in the place as if he'd built it with his own hands. He'd also felt hurt that people didn't understand this, especially when he'd tried to explain his point of view and been accused of 'ruddy cheek'.

The cattle-grid at the end of the farm drive produced the only sad moment of his homecoming. As the car went over it, there was a rumble like thunder and a sudden rattle of teeth and bones. This part of the drive cut through a corner of the woods, a shocking plunge into deep shade. It lasted only a moment or two, but it never failed to chill Marcus's heart. Sour memories, griefs and resentments; and then they were free, soaring upwards, with the house rising out of the hillside like the sun from dark clouds.

Marcus loved that house as he loved nothing else. It was old, very old, for the earliest part, now the kitchen, had been built almost a thousand years ago. Originally, as far as could be made out, it had consisted of two rooms – one for the livestock – with a sleeping loft in the thatch. Now there were eight bedrooms and two bathrooms in the thatch, for as the centuries went by the house had been extended several times, always in a straight line, until it was five times its original length. In the eighteenth century, having realised it would end up in London if it continued in linear fashion, someone had added a new wing at the rear, and now the house was roughly T-shaped, and big enough to house three generations of Saxons without feeling crowded.

'You can unload the car,' Ben growled as they pulled into the yard. 'After you've done your tour of inspection, I suppose.'

Ben had been unnerved by their meeting with Claudia. Now he was being bitter and sarcastic, apparently implying that Marcus might have handled things better if he'd tried. Marcus disagreed. He'd tried to imagine a similar disaster happening to him – Ellis taking over the farm, for instance – and had decided that, in such circumstances, he'd have killed anyone who tried to comfort him.

The house was deserted when he went inside. He strolled through it, noticing everything, checking that all was as it should be. The refectory table in the dining room was laid for the two o'clock lunch: eight places, which meant that Ellis wasn't home, thank God. Not that their paths crossed very much even when they were both in residence, but Marcus felt his brother's presence like a rash on his skin: he always wanted to be scratching it, and was never content until he'd drawn blood.

Hidden in a corner of the dining room, a steep flight of stone steps (one of three staircases the house contained) led straight up to Marcus's own rooms. Ellis had a similar apartment – a small study with a bedroom opening off it – at the other end of the house, which usually looked like the aftermath of a jumble sale. But Marcus was neat, knowing the precise location of his every possession, so that with one glance over his territory he could tell that all was well. His mother had put a jug of yellow roses on his desk, and he smiled and shook his head: somebody loved him.

He changed his clothes, and afterwards took the main staircase down to the drawing room, which was always deserted at this time of day and satisfyingly immaculate. It was an enormous room: low-ceilinged, with huge grey beams and a massive inglenook fireplace where, in summer, a black cauldron hung, filled with fresh flowers. Marcus held his breath, letting his gaze rove lovingly over every chair, table and sofa; the dark sheen of carved oak and rich, polished walnut. It was a masculine room, a place where the men came to rest at the end of the day, yet in no other room in the house was Marcus made so deeply aware of the women of the house and his need of them.

But now they were all outside, enjoying the sun. Marcus knelt on the window-seat and watched them for a few moments: his mother standing by the bird-bath, checking her reflection in the water; his grandmother knitting; Liz guiding Callie through the pea sticks with a basket on her arm.

Marcus always found Callie surprising – probably because she was always changing. She'd be fourteen next month, but she could easily be mistaken for an eighteen-year-old. She was tall and slim and incredibly graceful – incredibly, because she was almost completely blind now and as weak as a starved cat. But she did everything in slow motion. Even when she stumbled and fumbled, she did it slowly, stretching her fingers and stroking the air as if teasing soft chords from a harp.

And Callie was always smiling: the vague, half-formed smile of an overly polite visitor, afraid of giving offence. But even Callie's smile was a part of her illness; a strange ghost of the emotions she could no longer feel. Her brain worked too slowly now for emotions to register; yet, even more strangely, she could still maintain a simple conversation, still understand what was said to her.

Callie had been born in this house, and he'd held her in his arms when she was only a day old. He'd been four, and had been told in advance of the birth that his aunt was 'bringing him a baby'. Apparently he'd asked (typically), 'Will it be mine to *keep*? I won't have to share it with Ellis, will I?'

He knew he was too possessive. And he knew it was a fault, if only because he'd been punished for it so often. Sometimes he feared that he'd go on being punished until he was cured. Callie's illness would soon take her from him. If Ellis took the farm, too . . .

'Marcus? You home, then?'

Marcus turned his gaze into the violet shadows of the hallway, where his grandfather was shambling through from the rear of the house, leaning heavily on a walking stick. 'Oh, hello, Grandad,' he smiled. 'Yes, I'm home. How are you? Not out enjoying the sun?'

'No, no.' The old man's voice was slow, dour and gravelly, belying the sharp glint of humour in his eyes. 'Busman's holiday is sunbathing, my lad.' He shuffled closer to the window, his head on one side. 'Inspecting the flocks, are you? Like a bloody old sheepdog, you are. Find any missing?'

Marcus grinned. 'Only the black wether, Grandad.'

'Wether?' The old man feigned shock. 'Here, that's a bit hard, my boy. Ellis hasn't been castrated yet, s'far as I've heard, any road.'

'No,' Marcus murmured faintly. 'Not yet.'

'Ah, 'tis a shame about you two.' The old man shook his head, turning as if to walk away. 'You be careful, Marcus,' he added thoughtfully. 'Sometimes I think there's a lot of our Luke in you.'

Had Ben said the same thing, Marcus would have been deeply offended, for Ben held Luke's memory in contempt and would say nothing good of him. But Edward Saxon was Luke's brother, and he'd loved him. He'd loved him as God loves sinners, with more sadness than pleasure; forgiving, but not excusing him; understanding, but not condoning.

'What do you mean?' Marcus asked softly.

'You sets your heart too much on things, Marcus. Sets your sights on 'em and won't look to right nor left – nor right nor wrong – for fear of losing 'em. And that's not the way to go about it, my boy. Not when it brings you to hate your own brother.'

'I don't hate him, Grandad.'

This was true, as far as it went. Most of the things he hated *about* Ellis weren't Ellis's fault. He couldn't help being two years older. He couldn't help being his father's favourite – indeed, he struggled against the pressures it put on him, asking Marcus to cover his tracks. There were times, in fact, when Marcus was almost fond of his brother; fond of his weaknesses, his casual attitudes: the things which posed Marcus no threat. The day Ellis sobered up and came down to earth – Marcus's earth – would be soon enough to hate him. And then . . .

But it wouldn't happen.

Chapter Seven

Liz was never comfortable with Marcus's homecomings which, for a short while, seemed to throw the entire household out of kilter. The way he strolled about, inspecting his territory, made her think of a medieval lord, coming home from the Crusades after a long absence: an absence during which everyone had learned to do without him – and to like it.

Life was certainly a darn sight more comfortable when Marcus was elsewhere; but comfort and pleasure were not necessarily synonymous, and the pleasure Liz felt when she saw his face was the least comfortable state she could imagine. It was like walking with a shoe full of gravel: she hardly knew where to tread without doubling the agony. She wanted to cry out, 'It hurts!' and have Marcus carry her, or at least stick a plaster on the blisters.

She was probably going mad. They said you could go mad without even noticing, taking the strain bit by bit until you simply ran out of steam and went crackers.

And she *was* mad to depend so much on Marcus. He was only a kid: eighteen, just out of school, and in greater need of sticking plasters than Liz was. He was sensitive, vulnerable, and she had no *right* to lean on him. No *wish*. No *intention*. Yet somehow she couldn't help it. She needed him.

'Hello, Liz. How's things?'

'Fine. Welcome home.'

He laid his hand on her shoulder. She laid hers on his arm. He kissed her cheek, she his neck (it was as high as she could reach), and then quickly turned away, pretending her delight was all for Callie.

'Callie, Marcus is home!'

Callie turned her dimmed gaze in roughly the right direction, smiled politely and thought about it for a while; but her uncertainty didn't last long. Just the way he spoke to her inspired confidence, for he always made time to watch her before he approached, judging her, assessing the changes since he'd seen her last and taking them all in his stride.

'Come on, then, lazy bones. Let's finish picking these peas, or they won't give us any lunch.'

And that was it: absolute take-over; leaving Liz free for the first time in weeks to just walk away. Freedom! It was all she could do not to kick her heels and shout 'Yippee!' Or to burst into tears and kiss his feet . . .

It wasn't that the others didn't help; but she didn't trust the others. They took Callie for granted, not bothering to watch her, perhaps not wanting to notice the little changes which weakened her, day by day. But Marcus noticed everything, and cared enough to anticipate and make the proper allowances.

That was the difference, of course. The others cared, but not enough. Ellis had been home last weekend. He'd talked to Callie. He'd walked with her. He'd held her arm, keeping her close to his side. But he'd forgotten to tell her where the steps were. In the very act of leading a blind girl, he'd forgotten she was blind.

Marcus scarcely touched her. He guided her with words

and with his fingertips, giving her time to work things out for herself and to move at her own pace. Yet an arm was always ready to support her if she stumbled: a quick, strong arm, with its strength contained to gentleness. He never relaxed his guard; which meant, of course, that when Marcus was there, Liz could relax hers.

And she loved him for it. Just for that. *Only* that. Well, sometimes he was good to talk to. And sometimes he could make Liz laugh, make her forget for a few moments that . . . Oh, for a few moments he could make her forget everything: that she was fast pushing forty, that her marriage was a desert, that her daughter was dying . . .

Liz had pondered her feelings about Marcus many times and reached many different conclusions about them, few of which were at all comfortable to live with. He seemed so different from the rest of the family. He had different weaknesses, different strengths – different eyes. Given enough nerve, Liz could have gazed into his eyes for hours, just wondering how he'd got them. But even when he was a child she hadn't had the nerve – except to tease him with the song:

Jeepers, creepers, where'd you get those peepers?
Gosh, those weepers, how they hypnotise!

'Hypnotise' wasn't the right word, exactly. 'Terrify' was nearer the mark, especially when she chose the wrong moment to tease him about them!

He was as prickly as a thicket of blackthorn. When he was at home the entire household seemed to hum, like a short piece of elastic stretched to its limits. He made people wary. He made them polite. You could almost hear them muttering, 'For God's sake, Marcus, don't let go at your end!'

'The peas,' Callie said slowly, 'are for supper, I think, not for lunch.'

Marcus smiled, watching while she groped painstakingly among the pea-sticks for one more pod to add to the mere dozen she'd picked in the past half hour.

'Just as well,' he said dryly; and Liz, suppressing a giggle, turned on her heel and returned to the house without sparing her daughter a backward glance.

Helen had preceded Liz into the kitchen and now looked up, producing one of the gently gracious smiles which served her for every occasion. If it was a happy occasion, she smiled and murmured, 'Oh, this is splendid', and if it was a disaster she smiled and murmured, 'Oh, what a dreadful shame . . .'

Liz spent half her time envying her sister-in-law that all-purpose smile and the other half wanting to slap it off her face; but you couldn't have everything. Helen wasn't exciting company, but she was *easy*. Amenable. Well-trained. She hadn't always been so, but you needed a very strong constitution to live twenty-five years in this house without losing your taste for a fight. Fight all you liked, you usually ended up doing as you were told anyway.

'Potatoes done?' Liz asked briskly. 'Soup hot? Apple pies ready?'

'Yes, yes. All we need now is someone to eat it.'

Helen glanced at the clock. It was ten to two. She went to the window and peered out into the yard, looking for their respective husbands. She had once been very beautiful. Now she was just a woman who had once been very beautiful. All the elements of beauty were still there: the height, the grace, the big blue eyes, the impeccable taste in clothes. But some things had gone: her natural vitality, her mischief and giggles; and some other things had arrived: a few crows' feet around the eyes and two deep, unhappy lines each side of her mouth which, at their worst, resembled the hinges at the mouth of a ventriloquist's dummy.

It was hard to believe, now, that Helen had once been

Liz's idea of the perfect woman. That was in the old days, of course, the sweet days of youth, when appearances mattered more than anything else. In her youth, Liz would have paid thousands for Helen's figure, Helen's skin, Helen's hair; and she might still consider coughing up a fiver or two for a straight swap. It was no fun being short, plump and mousey. There was no dignity in having freckles.

Yes, Helen had been fortunate. She had two healthy sons and a husband who (in his way) adored her; but nevertheless Liz pitied her, for she'd never been given the most important thing of all: fire in the belly. Liz had plenty of that, even though, on occasion, it felt much the same as heartburn.

'Ah, they're coming.'

'Good-oh, Father! Call the troops. Lunch is ready!'

There was a huge pot of carrot soup; a glazed baked ham stuck with cloves; new potatoes from the garden; a salad of firm, sweet-hearted lettuce. Ben presided over the ham at the head of the table. The others sat where they landed – or seemed to; but Helen was next to Ben where she felt she belonged, Callie between Liz and Marcus, and her father as far from Callie as he could get without actually eating in the kitchen.

Given time, he would speak to her but he spoke to Marcus first, his tanned face alight with the cheerful, cold-eyed smile which was the Saxon men's secret weapon, their invisible shield. No one could get past it. Few people tried. And those who did needed a month to get over the shock.

'Finished school, Marcus?'

Marcus produced a similar cold-eyed smile. 'Mm-hm.'

'So you're happy at last?'

'Yes, thanks. For the moment.'

'Well, that's something.'

In mixed company, Tom was a man of few words; so few in fact that a list of them could quite easily be compiled on the back of matchbox. Yet put him in a room with a few other men and he'd talk all night, spilling out words by the thousand. 'Artificial insemination', 'diversification', 'contagious', 'amalgamated', even 'philosophical' (which wasn't all that easy after three whiskies). Yet three hours later, when Liz asked what he'd been talking about, he'd say, 'Oh, nothing.'

'*Nothing*? You've been talking all night!'

'Oh . . . Have I?'

But even Tom hadn't always been the same. He'd always been quiet, but he'd been more open, more generous with his words. Now he was afraid of words, the way some people were afraid of water. They could dip their toes in, perhaps even paddle in the shallows; but as soon as a wave splashed their knees they grew afraid of being sucked under, afraid of drowning. Tom had turned his back on the sea – on his daughter's illness – hoping it would go away. But the sea could stand any amount of neglect. You could bury your head in the sand all you liked; the tide still came in, eventually.

They were half way through the soup before Tom spoke again. 'How's Callie today?'

He always spoke to her in the third person, hoping, Liz guessed, that a third person would answer him. It was the equivalent of asking someone braver, 'What's it like in?' instead of testing the water for oneself.

'Callie,' Liz prompted briskly, 'Daddy's speaking to you, darling.'

Callie turned her head in the direction of his voice, smiling blindly into Marcus's shoulder. 'Oh, fine, thank you,' she said. 'I've been picking peas for supper.'

'Good,' Tom said. 'Good, good. Pass the bread, will you, Mother?'

'I hope you picked enough peas, Callie,' his mother said

sternly. 'Now that Marcus is home there'll be one more for supper. How many does that make?'

She meant well. The schoolmistress she had once been had never quite died in her; and, cancer notwithstanding, she thought all minds could grow if they were made to work hard enough.

'Mother?' Ben's interruption was discreetly timed. 'Did Marcus tell you what happened on the way home?'

'On the way home? No. What happened on the way home?'

'We met the little Murray girl, just this side of Whitchurch.'

'*Met* her? What on earth do you mean, *met* her?'

'She was walking to the hospital. She'd had some bad news and taken it very hard, poor child.'

All eyes turned to him, and he nodded. 'Another stroke, early this morning. Funeral's on Tuesday, Mrs Chislett says.'

Liz shut her eyes to stem an unexpected rush of tears. She'd known it would happen, of course; had almost hoped it would, for there'd been little hope of a worthwhile recovery. But she'd loved Madge, needed her. She'd prayed for her in the long, lonely reaches of the night. No, prayed for herself; for with Madge gone and Callie fast retreating into the dark, impenetrable corners where none could reach, it seemed that there was no one left, as if the whole world was empty and she was quite alone.

Titch Flicker led the cows down to Long Meadow and Marcus followed, smacking rumps and shouting encouragement in the strangely pitched voice – half-yodel, half-growl – which cows were supposed to understand best. 'Yarrgh! Get a move on, Sal! A-yah! Hoy-up!'

In April, when the cows first took a sniff at the fresh, young grass, you couldn't stop them. They cantered out to pasture, kicking their heels; but that didn't last. Within a week they were back to normal: slow, lazy and stubborn, munching the hedges, admiring the view. Marcus admired it, too, but with a possessive and critical eye, noticing the state of the hedges and ditches, the condition of the grass.

Titch was waiting by the gate, his shoulders slumped, his hands sunk deep into the pockets of his khaki dungarees, watching without interest as the cows lumbered past him.

'All right, Titch?'

'Ah.'

The Flicker men rarely communicated in English, reserving its complexities for times of national emergency or the early stages of courtship; but there were a hundred different ways of saying 'Ah'.

Titch had said it from the side of his mouth, abruptly, with a slight curl of his lip. It meant, 'No, I'm not all right', but Marcus knew the futility of making deeper enquiries. Give him a day or two and Titch would get over it. Either that, or he wouldn't.

The last of the cows stepped gingerly over the stony ground at the entrance to Long Meadow, and Marcus swung the gate closed and turned away, expecting Titch to fall into step beside him. But he hung back, thoughtfully inspecting his boots.

'Ah,' he said. 'Ah.'

'Hmm?'

'Only I bin after a job, see, Marcus. I sid'n in the paper and I thought . . . Well, it's a good bit more money, like, and with me and Janice . . . Ah.'

This last 'ah' was pronounced with a hopeless finality which meant, 'I've said enough. Work out the rest for yourself.'

It was easy enough to do. Titch had been courting Janice

Tapscott for five years and wanted to get married. He'd been offered a job with better pay and wanted to take it; but he was afraid of giving offence, afraid of letting Ben down, afraid of breaking with ancient tradition.

There had been at least one Georgie Flicker working at Saxons' since before anyone could remember. Even in Marcus's lifetime there'd been Old Georgie Flicker, Young Georgie Flicker, Little Georgie Flicker and Titch. Little Georgie was still hard at work on the farm and was likely to remain so until he retired. Noddy Bridges would stay too (he thought he owned the place, anyway); but even Noddy couldn't last for ever, and the two boys who made up the rest of the workforce would soon go the way of all boys these days: elsewhere.

Times were changing. People who, before the war, could scarcely afford to own a pushbike, were now buying their own motor cars, even their own houses. But Titch couldn't. He didn't earn enough. He couldn't even look forward to a tied cottage in the foreseeable future, for the Saxons owned only four, and they were all occupied – two of them by Titch's own family.

'I see,' Marcus said. 'And the job's definite, is it?'

'Ah. I can start next Monday week, if your dad'll let I go.'

'Let you go?' Marcus laughed uncomfortably. 'He doesn't own you, Titch!'

'Ah. Still. 'E won't like it, will 'un?'

No, Ben wouldn't like it, for his chances of replacing Titch were slight, and likely to get worse as the village became more prosperous. It was no longer a matter of earning enough to feed a family; that was taken for granted these days. Now they wanted cars and new carpets, washing machines, refrigerators, holidays at West Bay . . .

Marcus thought about it for the best part of a week before Ben brought the subject up. But, as he always did when he was worried, he laughed it off, joking. 'It's all Noddy's fault. If he'd had three sons, instead of those silly daughters of his, we'd be set up for life.'

'No,' Marcus countered softly. 'You're missing the point, Dad.'

Again Ben laughed, his eyes cold and hard, rejecting Marcus's opinion before he could voice it. 'Well, that's only to be expected,' he remarked cuttingly. 'Compared with you, I know nothing at all.'

Marcus's eyes had hardened too. He had lost more battles with his father than he had ever won, but the day he stopped fighting would be the day he lost the farm, and he would *never* do that.

'If Noddy had had sons,' he said pleasantly, 'they'd be doing what Titch is doing: finding a job elsewhere.'

'Rubbish. Noddy's family's been on the land since – '

'So has Titch Flicker's family. But times have changed, Dad. They've got more choice now, and if the factories offer more money, they'll take it. If we don't think this through – '

Ben grinned. 'Oh, it's "we" now! Taking over already, are you?'

Marcus closed his eyes and took a deep breath, trying to ease the sudden pounding of his heart. As a child, he had lived for the day when he'd be big enough to punch his father in the teeth; but life never worked out quite like that. He still wanted to punch his father in the teeth, but he needed something quite different. Friendship, partnership. Understanding. And you didn't get that sort of thing with your fists.

'All right,' he said levelly. 'If *you* don't think this through, *Ellis* might end up with a farm he can't work because he's got no labour. This place, as it stands, can't be run with fewer than six men, so perhaps you ought to be thinking in terms of greater efficiency rather than – '

'Oh! *Efficiency*! So we need to be more *efficient*, do we? How very interesting!' Ben stood up and walked to the window, shoving his hands into his pockets. He stared out for a moment before turning gracefully on his heel, his smile sweet enough to charm the birds from the trees. 'Well, thank you for your advice, Marcus. I'll give it some thought.'

He might have been speaking to an insurance salesman.

Marcus stood for a long time when his father had left the room, fighting the urge to run after him and shake him until his teeth rattled. But he knew he'd gone as far as he could – for the moment. And Ben *would* think about it. He wasn't stupid or ill-informed. He must know which way the wind was blowing. And perhaps that was why he'd been so annoyed; he thought Marcus was 'teaching his grandmother to suck eggs' again. Yet if Ellis had said the same thing Ben would have discussed it quite happily, not thrown it back in his face, spiked with contempt. What the hell was the difference?

The telephone rang and, glad of the diversion, Marcus went to answer it; but his mother got there first.

'Saxons',' she said dully, and then, with a little more animation, 'Oh, hello, darling.'

It was Ellis. Marcus leaned against the door-jamb, watching her; interpreting her smiling little murmurs with perfect accuracy.

'Oh, splendid. When?'

He was coming home.

'Well, yes, of course, dear. Salmon, I think.'

He was coming today. In time for lunch.

'Is she? How nice. Well, I'll look forward to meeting her, darling.'

He was bringing a girl friend.

'No, I'm afraid not, darling. She's thrown a shoe and the farrier can't get here before Saturday. Oh, you *are*? Well, that's splendid.'

And they were staying at least a week, and wanted to go riding.

Marcus shrugged dispiritedly and walked away.

Olivia Saxon sat in a hard, high-backed chair beside the drawing-room window, knitting the thirty-third square of one of her white honeycomb blankets. She'd knitted seventeen of them in forty-nine years of marriage: the first six as an economy measure, the next few out of habit, and the last just for something to do when her legs gave out.

Growing old was a wretched business which had always struck Olivia as cruelly unfair. You worked like a navvy for fifty years, deeming it worthwhile just for all the fun you could have when you'd finished; and then you were finished. Spine nobbled, knees hobbled; digestion, sight and hearing mere phantoms of their former selves.

But the worst thing of all was the cynicism: the feeling you had that you'd met everyone, heard everything, seen it all before; and couldn't, even if they paid you, be surprised. Or even shocked. Which was just as well, or she'd have died of shock a thousand times just looking in the mirror. She had once been tall and straight and lithe, with an apple blossom complexion. Now she was a good deal shorter, bent and stiff, with a hide like crazy paving.

So what was left? Love? No, not really. She'd spent too much time thinking about it, wondering what it was and where it sprang from, and she knew the answer now. Love was self-interest, and it sprang from nothing more sacred than the primitive urge to survive, to eat, to be sheltered, to have someone warm to curl up to on freezing winter nights and someone (or two, or seven) to take care of you when you were old. That was love.

Then there was religion, but even that had been devalued. She believed in God just as much when she was seventy-five as she had done at seventeen. Just as much, but quite differently; although she hadn't made the final adjustment until quite recently, at the end of the war, when the truth had come out about Hitler and the Jews.

It had been enough to rock the foundations of anyone's faith; but while Olivia's was still rocking she'd read an article in *The Geographic* about termites and that had finished her off. Clever little blighters, termites. A darn sight more clever than humans. They were organised, cooperative, hard-working and virtually self-sufficient. They left nothing to God, and if they acknowledged Him at all it was only to say, 'Thank you for creating termites. And now run along, we're busy.'

It made sense. It made perfect sense and it explained everything: all the cruelties, the injustices, the billions of unanswered prayers. Oh, all those pitiful billions of unanswered prayers . . .

No, God wasn't meant to answer your prayers. He'd made you, in precisely the way he'd made termites, building into the design all the help you'd ever need. After that, it was your duty just to say, 'Thank you for creating me: my hands, my legs, my senses, my mind. And now, run along. I'm busy.'

It was just a matter of humility, really. Man hadn't yet acquired the humility to understand all he'd been told. He believed only the fancy bits – that he'd been made in God's image – and had forgotten the simplicities – that the Lord cared for sparrows just as much. That was where the answer lay: not in God's image but in his creation. The sparrows, the lilies of the field, the clever little termites.

Olivia had missed supper for two reasons, neither of which was polite enough to mention. The first was wind, the result of the cucumber salad she'd eaten at lunch. The second was Ellis's new girlfriend, Annette, who (if first impressions counted for anything) was the most irritating creature to have survived its juvenile state since the invention of DDT.

There was something wrong with Ellis. He was intelligent enough underneath; but that's where he kept it: underneath. Still, as Ben so often said (making it sound like a prayer), 'He's young yet. There's plenty of time.'

And he was right. That was the most interesting thing about people. They could change, and very often did; even quite late in life when you'd think they'd lost their chances. But it was trouble which changed them, and Ellis had never had any. Wasn't likely to get any, either, with his father aiding and abetting him, favouring him, petting him . . .

Olivia shook her head, and was still shaking it when the door opened and Marcus came in, only to shut it again and lean against it with his eyes closed, breathing in patience, exhaling blue murder.

Olivia was deeply fond of Marcus; but a good deal fonder of him at a distance than when he was right under her nose. He'd battled his way through his childhood in an almost permanent rage, more often resembling a cornered animal than a close relative of Olivia's; and then suddenly had changed. He'd harnessed his temper and his intelligence, becoming more reasonable, more amenable, infinitely more civilised. But the rage was still there. You could see it in his eyes. White-hot, like the heart of a furnace.

It was one of Olivia's ambitions to put that fire out before it drove him mad, but she had no idea how to go about it. She couldn't kill Ben; and after forty-seven years of trying, she couldn't change him, either. But Ben was at the root of it. He'd never loved anyone he couldn't manipulate and trying to manipulate Marcus was like trying to spread cold butter.

'Don't tell me,' she said crisply. 'I know.'

Marcus took another long draught of air. 'Huh,' he scoffed. 'You know everything, don't you?'

'No. I still don't know how to make hay-seed, but I suppose it's only a matter of time. And patience, of course.'

'Patience!' Marcus stretched his mouth in the bitter approximation of a smile and threw himself into the blue brocade armchair opposite, clutching the arms until his knuckles whitened. 'I don't understand it,' he muttered angrily. 'If I brought a little – a girl like that into the house – I'd never live it down! Yet *he*!'

'Now, now . . .'

'She's *stupid*! Her manners are appalling. She was asking about Callie, asking what's wrong with her! I suppose Callie doesn't care, but Tom! I thought he was going to hit her!'

'Hmm. Well, that's Tom's problem, not yours.'

Olivia turned her knitting and began another row.

'It's a pity men don't knit any more,' she said calmly. 'It used to be very much a man's craft. When I was a girl you'd still see a few old men knitting at their doorsteps, and sailors have done it until quite recently. It soothes the heart and directs the mind. It's also a marvellous way of sticking needles into people who drive you past your limits.'

Marcus's eyes widened, revealing a stray glint of humour. 'So that's what you're doing. *Killing* people!'

'That's right. And you thought it such a harmless little hobby, didn't you?'

He laughed at last. 'And you're saved all the bother of making little wax effigies.'

'Quite. Embroidery's the same. Those linen pillowcases with the butterflies, the ones your mother's so fond of – Jim Murray's in those. Or, rather, his judge and jury. *Pitiless*.' She paused and gazed thoughtfully into a shadowy corner of the room. 'Ten years,' she mused sadly. 'As if he hadn't enough grief to bear, poor man. That's what he died of, of course. Grief, not TB.'

She looked up at the ceiling, frowning thoughtfully. 'What will people do with their grief now they've brought out penicillin, I wonder? Commit suicide nineteen to the dozen, I suppose . . .'

'Perhaps they'll just put up with it, Grandma.'

'Yes, perhaps so. Good thing, too. Dying leaves you with so little to look forward to, doesn't it?'

She knitted a few more rows, peeping furtively over her spectacles as her grandson, by slow degrees, relaxed and stared thoughtfully into the fire.

'Better?' she demanded sharply.

Marcus shrugged. 'No, not really. Every time it happens I tell myself to admit defeat and have done with it, but I don't seem to be able to. I suppose it's not Ellis's fault . . . It's *Dad*. He's so . . . He's so *inconsistent*!'

Wrong word, Olivia thought waspishly, knowing that Marcus had chosen it in preference to the right one. He didn't want to admit that unjust was the right word. Unwise. And unkind.

'Well, no one's perfect, Marcus. Present company excepted, of course.'

Again he glared at her. 'Did *I* say I was perfect?'

'No, I did.'

'But you were lying.'

'I thought your ego might need a boost.'

Marcus laughed again – at himself this time – and Olivia's heart warmed with gratitude. But she waited until his gaze left her face before she smiled her approval.

'He's been telling Ellis we have to be more efficient,' Marcus said quietly.

'Isn't that a good thing?'

'Yes. But that's what I was telling *him*, just this morning, and he rejected the idea out of hand. I don't understand it. Why is it all right to discuss it with Ellis and not with me? Ellis doesn't care.'

'And what was Ellis's view of it? This efficiency thing.'

'He agreed. He always does.'

'Then perhaps that's your answer. Have you ever discussed *anything* with your father without turning it into an argument?'

'I'm not sure that *I* turn it into an argument. I hate arguing with him. I sometimes think he deliberately misunderstands me or that he . . . No.'

Olivia maintained a discreet silence. Intelligence was a funny thing. It didn't seem to matter how much of it you had, you could still reject its reasonings and opt for the answer you liked best. *No*. Even when the truth was *yes*.

'I almost got through to him once,' Marcus reflected sadly. 'It was the day I left Clifton; the day Mrs Murray died. I was asking him why we always end up fighting. He said it was because we're so alike, and that – '

'He's wrong.'

'*Wrong*, Grandma?' (As if it was impossible!)

'Wrong,' Olivia repeated firmly.

'In what way?'

Olivia knitted, peering intently through the thick, pebble lenses of wire-framed spectacles, her mouth working as she silently recited each phrase: 'Knit one, make one, knit two together . . .'

'Breeding,' she said at last. 'Farmers know all about breeding, or think they do; but men and women don't come in pedigree strains like Ayrshires and Shorthorns. You can't put them together with any certainty of how they'll turn out.'

She paused, and Marcus scowled impatiently. 'Yes. And?'

'And I believe your difficulties with your father are mostly to do with Luke.'

Marcus had been watching her face. Now suddenly he turned, stiff-necked, to stare into the fire again. 'I see,' he murmured.

'See what? I haven't said anything yet!'

'But Dad hated Luke, and if I'm like him – ?'

'*You*? Like *Luke*? Nonsense! You aren't a bit like Luke, except in looks, and since that's true of every Saxon ever spawned, it hardly counts. No, no. Your father's like Luke. You're like me. And before you explode with insult, being like me isn't such a bad thing. We're clever, we're honest, we know how to think and how to work. We're *powerful*, Marcus.'

She'd been talking more quickly than usual, trying to hide her bombshell in the middle of a less than honest diversion, for she'd often wondered who Marcus was like!

But the diversion hadn't worked. Marcus was staring at her as if she'd sprouted horns.

'Dad's . . . like *Luke*?'

'In some ways, yes. And even that's not as bad as it sounds, you know. Luke wasn't the animal your father makes him out to be. There's one thing you don't know about Luke; and although it doesn't change what he did, it puts a different complexion on it. He loved that girl.'

'Loved her,' Marcus repeated scathingly. 'And *raped* her?'

'It's not that simple. Girls were more innocent in those days, Marcus. Ignorant. I doubt Sibyl even knew that sex existed, let alone guessed the effect it could have on a man when his emotions were caught up with his lusts. I don't excuse him. He was wrong. But he wasn't *all* wrong.' She jabbed her finger in the general direction of Marcus's nose. 'And,' she went on vengefully, 'your father isn't all *right*! He just *thinks* he is!'

'True,' Marcus remarked wryly. 'But I still don't see how it affects me. In what way is he like Luke?'

Olivia sighed. 'In many ways, but only one that really matters. He lacks humility, Marcus. He can't bear to be outdone. He can't bear to be challenged. That's where your problem lies. You challenge him. Ellis doesn't.'

Marcus was silent for several minutes. He stared into the fire. He tipped back his head and stared at the ceiling. He stared at the floor. 'So,' he said grimly at last, 'I've just got to keep my mouth shut, have I, and let everything go?'

Olivia pursed her mouth to hide another smile. 'Not *necessarily*,' she said.

Chapter Eight

The men made coffee and doorsteps of toast before their day's work began, but the family breakfast was at nine; and this, too, was what Ben called 'the board meeting', when the work was organised and everyone's plans discussed and synchronised for the day.

'Are you in or out today, Ellis?'

'Out. I thought I'd show Annette around Bristol . . . If no one wants me?'

'Marcus?'

'I have to go to Bath for a few hours. Otherwise I'm in.'

'Those ewe lambs need to be moved from Top Barrow to North Reach. Could you see to it before you go out? Noddy'll give you a hand. Now, how's everyone else? Mother?'

'I'm all right, thank you.'

Ben took a second helping of scrambled eggs. 'Helen?'

'Mmm,' she smiled. 'Well, it's not absolutely *vital* – '

'Yes, it is,' Liz said crisply. 'If we don't get it done now – '

'Get what done?'

Liz glowered at Helen. 'Well? Speak up! It was my turn to be unpopular last week!'

Ellis, Marcus noticed, was shrinking as far back in his chair as he could get without sliding under the table, for the women rarely asked for help with anything quick and painless. Cleaning all the upstairs windows was more their style, or trimming five hundred yards of yew hedge. It all took time, muscle and perspiration; and, unlike farming, 'family work' didn't pay.

'Well,' Helen finished hurriedly, 'if we don't get the autumn digging done before the boys go back to college . . .'

'Ah, I see!' Ben leaned back in his chair to direct a bright, challenging smile down the table. 'Any offers?'

Marcus turned away to butter some toast for Callie. He hated gardening. The vegetable plot was all right, but that wasn't what they meant. They meant flowers. Some to be burned, some to be dug up, split and replanted, and some in the 'touch my delphiniums and you're dead' category. Marcus couldn't tell which was which and didn't greatly care.

Silence reigned for several uncomfortable moments before Annette tactlessly broke it. 'Er – is this a quarrel?'

'No,' Liz confided kindly. 'They're terrified, that's all. Nothing to worry about.'

'I'm not terrified,' Ellis scoffed. 'I'd like to help but Annette's only got a few days, and it seems a bit mean to leave her while I – '

'Oh, please,' she offered anxiously. 'Don't mind me. I can see Bristol any time.'

Marcus heaved a sigh. Annette was a pain but she didn't deserve this. Ellis was a fool to have brought her – especially if he really liked her. Having tried it once or twice, Marcus had long ago given up bringing his girlfriends home, for they were invariably overwhelmed by the experience. Not only were there too many people, but too many hidden undercurrents between them: adorations and enmities, silent griefs and private jokes, tensions so powerful – and so volatile – that they could be triggered by the soft tip-toe of a stranger's footfall. And Annette, poor cow, was wearing iron-clad boots with bells on. It would probably be better for everyone if Ellis took her out.

'Well . . .' Ellis said painfully.

Marcus reached for the marmalade. It was against his principles to give in; and, having elected to be 'in' on the farm, he had right on his side: he couldn't be expected to do everything. On the other hand . . . He cast a narrow glance in his grandmother's direction and found her looking at him over the rim of her glasses.

Yes, it would be better if Ellis went out.

'All right,' he conceded at last. 'I'll do it.'

Ellis's eyes widened. 'Hey . . . Thanks, Marcus.'

Marcus ignored him.

Helen stood over him for a while, navigating him through the tall perennials, clematis and bush roses at the back of the border; but she wandered back to the house eventually, murmuring, 'Those antirrhinums can come out, but everything else . . .'

Marcus shook his head and rested both arms on the spade, gazing about him despairingly. He could identify fifty different species of grass and almost as many weeds, but antirrhinums had him beat.

'Mother!' he roared, looking up at the front door as if fully expecting her to shoot out on roller skates at his call. Instead, he saw Callie, feeling her way across the brass-clad door-step, her hands groping the air. It seemed she was alone; a fact which irritated Marcus even more than his mother's defection had done.

Callie could see nothing at all now, save the difference between light and dark; and, recently, she'd been moving towards the light, following it compulsively, like a moth drawn to a candle flame.

She never went far; she was too weak to cover more than a few yards at a time and generally made for the garden seat under the dining room window. This was all right as long as the path was clear, but today there was a garden rake and a heap of terracotta flower pots in the way; and Callie didn't grope with her feet, looking for things which might trip her up. She groped with her hands, for things which might bump her on the nose.

'Stand still!' Marcus roared. 'Callie! Wait for me!'

His boots, heavy with soft garden soil, slowed him as he ran up the long, sloping lawn. But Callie did as she was told, standing quite still, with her head up, sniffing the air.

During the past few months, Marcus had observed his cousin's deterioration with the cool detachment which, he'd decided long ago, was his only hope of enduring it; but for some reason, as he hurried towards her, it struck him with unusual force. She wasn't a person any more. She wasn't Callie. Muscle wastage had turned her arms and legs into soft, shapeless columns, like the limbs of a rag doll; and her eyes were like chips of broken glass, obscuring her soul.

And she'd had such a beautiful soul. She'd been so *good*; perhaps the only truly good person ever to be born a Saxon; the only one they had all loved without stint. But none of them was any good at losing. They'd refused to lose her, preferring – each in his own manner – to reject her, before death could take her from them. Even Tom, her own father, barely acknowledged her existence now.

Marcus caught her hand, holding it tightly; yet her face stayed blank for two or three seconds before she registered his touch and smiled. 'Argh!' he growled softly. 'You bad girl. You mustn't come out alone. You might fall.'

'Marcus?'

'Yes, it's me.'

'I'm not alone. Mummy's bringing you . . .' She frowned.

'Bringing me what?'

He guided her to the seat and sat beside her, stroking a stray loop of damson-dark hair from her face. She was still frowning, still puzzling her way through the conversation they'd had so far.

'Coffee,' she said at last. 'She's bringing you coffee. It's tea time, but you don't like tea, and you're a hero so you must have what you like.'

He smiled. 'Did Liz say that?'

The idea pleased him. He had a suspicion that it pleased him more than it should, and that he and Liz were sometimes in danger of flirting with each other. But what the hell? She was a lovely person: strong, brave and full of sweetness. He laughed and patted Callie's hand, suddenly realising that – in spite of the gardening – he was happy.

His talk with Olivia – something he'd fallen into more by accident than design, for she invariably upset him with her ruthless plain-speaking – had had a different effect on him from usual. For one thing, it had made him feel more fond of her, less . . . scared. Yes, regrettable though it was, 'scared' was the word; for although she could barely see a hand in front of her face without her glasses on, with or without them she could look straight through you, and it was an extremely unpleasant feeling.

But one thing she'd never been guilty of was empty boasting, and when she'd said she was powerful she'd been selling herself short. Had she left it at that, he'd have emerged from the discussion with his feathers badly ruffled, but she hadn't. She'd included him, drawn him into the circle of her power, told him he was the same.

'Did Mummy say what?' Callie asked anxiously.

'That I'm a – ah, here she is.' He raised his voice slightly. 'She's a disgrace: letting you out by yourself, leaving all this junk on the path. What kind of a mother is she, anyway?'

'Oh, don't nag,' Liz remarked pleasantly. 'And you can blame *your* kind of mother for the junk. I don't know how often I've told her to leave the path clear. But does she listen? Nope.'

The coffee came in a Coronation mug; strong and black, with the faintly nutty flavour of dark brown sugar.

'Ahh,' Marcus sighed after tasting it. 'Just the ticket. Hey, what colour's an antirrhinum, Liz?'

'An antirrhinum? I dunno. What colour's an antirrhinum?

'It's not a *joke*, you fool!'

'Oh, isn't it?' She burst out laughing and pulled her face straight again, her eyes brimming with mischief. 'Sorry, Marcus. Sorry. They're pink.'

'Thanks.'

'And yellow. And red. And white.'

'Oh.' He folded his arms. 'I don't know why I bother. Being a hero doesn't seem to pay, these days. All I get for it is abuse.'

Liz laughed again. 'Callie! You shouldn't have told him that! Now we'll never get his head down to size!'

She sat beside him, wriggling into the rather limited space he'd left for her. 'Shove up, Marcus.'

'Huh. Before you start worrying about the size of my head, perhaps you should give your bottom some thought.'

'Ooh! I've lost weight, you rotten lout!'

They were quiet for a while, smiling at the sun. 'I do like an Indian summer,' Liz remarked at last. 'It's like an extra hour in bed. You can almost feel it doing you good.'

'Mm.'

'It *was* heroic of you to volunteer for the garden. I know how much you hate it, but I thought Ellis . . . Well, I thought you'd hold out until he gave in gracefully. Why didn't you?'

Marcus laughed. 'I've changed my tactics.'

'How exciting! What does it mean?'

'Nothing, really. I had a chat with Grandma the other day. It made me think, that's all.'

And what an understatement that was, for he'd lain awake half the night thinking, readjusting his ideas and trying to sort them into some kind of order. Ben like *Luke*? The idea had shocked him rigid at first; he'd rejected it out of hand. But it was extraordinary how soon he'd accepted the truth of it and begun to find it comforting. His father wasn't perfect!

Not that he'd ever believed he was. No, never. Yet Ben's faults, as Marcus had perceived them, had seemed to have some hidden meaning: like the clues to a cryptic crossword which could be found to make sense if you puzzled over them for long enough. But they had no meaning. They just *were*: as his eyes were, and his hair was, and the shape of his hands . . .

Marcus stretched out his legs and curved his arm around Callie's shoulder. 'Liz? How would you describe humility?'

'Humility? Do you mean honesty?'

'No. They're completely different, aren't they?'

'I can't say I've ever heard of humility. Honesty's a purple flower with silvery seed-heads. Look, there's some over there, by the – *Oh*!' She threw back her head despairingly. 'One-track mind. Sorry, Marcus. What was the question again?'

'You're nuts.'

'I know. It's beginning to worry me. Umm. Humility. I'd say . . . I'd say it was being able to laugh at yourself. Not take yourself too seriously, I mean. No . . . I don't mean that.'

'Well,' Marcus teased. 'As long as you're sure. Been thinking it over for some time, have you?'

'Oh, *you*!' She thought about it again. 'No, you're wrong,' she said at last. 'Honesty and humility aren't so very different. If you have humility you have to be honest – and vice versa, of course. Why do you ask? Grandma again?'

'Yes. She was talking about Luke. She said he lacked humility.'

'Ha! He wasn't alone!'

'Grandma said that, too.'

'Hmm. She and I have a great deal in common. The only difference . . . Well, she enjoys pitting herself against the old slings and arrows, while I . . . I don't share her conviction – your conviction, too, I suspect – that the struggle's worthwhile.'

'Are you convinced that it's *not* worthwhile?'

'No. Only suicides are convinced of that. The rest of us are just a bit *suspicious*. Olivia thinks it'll work out all right in the end, you see: perhaps a few millennia after she's gone, but all right nevertheless. That's true humility. Making a lifetime of effort for a world you'll never know, and laughing all the while at the sheer insignificance of your contribution.'

'Does Grandma laugh at herself?'

'Constantly. And at the rest of us. She doesn't take anything seriously.' She affected a childish pout. 'Not even *me*! Can you *believe* that?'

Marcus tousled her hair. It made little difference to her general appearance except to brighten her eyes a little and bring a soft flush of pink to her cheeks.

'Yes, I can believe that,' he said, pretending scorn. 'What's the point of taking *you* seriously? You're a dope.'

'True.'

He laughed. 'You'd say humility's a good thing, then?'

'Oh, yes . . . In moderation, of course, like everything else. You've been brought up to be proud: to take pride in your work, pride in your intelligence, pride in your home and family; and all that's good stuff. In moderation. But none of it actually matters, you know. You can take pride until the cows come home, and still lose – everything you take pride in. Then what do you have?'

The mood had changed. The laughter was over. Liz was talking about Callie.

'I don't know, Liz,' Marcus said gently. 'Do you?'

'Yes, I think so . . . You have yourself. Just yourself. And without – all the other things – it doesn't amount to much. It's very small . . . And rather hard, like a clenched fist. But it's all you've got. Perhaps *that's* humility: knowing that you can lose everything, and be reduced to nothing bigger than . . .' She clenched her hand and stared at it bleakly, her eyes glittering with tears. '*This*.'

Marcus covered her fist with his hand. 'It's a phoenix,' he said quietly. 'It'll rise from the ashes, Liz.'

She swallowed. She said nothing. But she opened her fingers and slid them around his hand, holding it tightly for a moment before hurriedly letting go.

Marcus set off for his first day at college with his teeth defensively gritted, but he came home (as in his heart he'd known he would) smiling like a cherub.

His mother came out to the car to meet him. 'How was it, darling?'

'Fine.'

'What did you have to do?

'Nothing. It was like one of your drinks parties, with stacks of paper being passed round instead of gin.' He shrugged dismissively. 'I suppose we'll get properly started tomorrow. Any coffee?'

His mother's smile was smug and secretive: the sort which seems to say, 'All that fuss for nothing,' although he was certain he hadn't made a fuss. On the contrary, he'd spent the past few days in a state of monastic silence, getting through more work in one weekend than his father would have asked him to do in a month of Sundays. He'd even cleaned out the gun room, a job which had been awaiting attention for the best part of a year. When he'd finally finished, Ben had asked him why he hadn't whitewashed the coalhouse as well.

'What were the people like?' Helen asked as she made his coffee. 'Did you meet anyone nice?'

'They seemed okay. Many and various.'

'Any girls?'

'Lots, but only two doing Chemistry in my year. Both redheads.'

'Oooh!'

'With complexions like Harris tweed.'

'Oh, dear. But you aren't confined to the Chemistry department, I take it?'

Marcus grinned. 'By no means. The scope seems virtually limitless.'

She poured two cups of coffee and sat opposite him at the kitchen table. 'I'm glad,' she said. 'We've all been a bit nervous, just in case it met *your* expectations, rather than ours.'

'My expectations?'

'Well, you can't say you've been looking forward to it, darling.'

'No, I suppose not.'

'And now?'

'Hmm.' He grinned again. 'You aren't asking me to admit you were right, I hope?'

'Oh, no, heaven forbid. But we *were* right.' She threw him a sideways smile. 'Weren't we?'

'I'll think about it. Ask me again when I've taken my degree.'

But it didn't take that long. After barely a week of student life Marcus knew they'd been right and was grateful. He hadn't been ready to limit his life to the rigid disciplines and social isolation which farming involved. He'd simply thought it safer to do so: and not just because he was afraid that Ellis, the cuckoo in the nest, might push him out. No, his insecurities went deeper than that; and most of them arose from his relationship with his father.

He was no closer to understanding their relationship now than he had ever been, but Olivia's revelations had made it less important, if only by demoting Ben from god to man. And University had made it less important by promoting Marcus from *boy* to man: his father's equal in nomenclature if in nothing else.

It was a change which seemed to happen almost overnight, but Marcus had sense enough to realise that he hadn't suffered some strange, biological transformation while he slept. It had nothing much to do with him, and everything to do with other people's responses to him. The Ugly Duckling had to be *told* he was a swan, and even then it took some believing. Not that Marcus had ever thought himself a mere *duck*. He'd known he was a cygnet. But he hadn't expected to acquire the full complement of snowy plumage quite so soon, let alone so suddenly.

He'd never been so happy. Life had never been so easy. The only problem he had was to tear himself away from it each night. Home was still the best place in the world; but – for the first time in his life – Marcus began to feel that it could manage without him for a while.

Olivia had advised him to let go a little, to seem to surrender his claims so that Ben should feel less threatened; and although Marcus had known it was good advice he'd been too scared to accept it in its entirety. But now, for some reason, he wasn't scared any more. He felt calmer, more confident. After all, the farm wouldn't go away; and, as Olivia had said, 'If the hawk is yours, it'll always fly back to you.'

He found an unfurnished garret flat in one of the streets

just off Whiteladies. He bought a divan bed, a table, two chairs and a gas ring – and a large keg of beer for the house-warming.

Three of his guests failed to go home when the party was over. He rolled two of them (they were blotto) in a rug to keep them warm. The other (she was blonde) he rolled into bed to keep *him* warm.

'I hope you know what you're doing,' she giggled nervously.

'Oh, I do,' he said. 'I do.'

The only thing he didn't know was her name.

Marcus drove home for the Christmas holidays in a beatific state of mind, having decided that his life was as good as anyone had any right to expect. His pre-war Wolseley Hornet was cold and draughty, and there was a tiny hole in the cloth roof which let in the rain, but he barely noticed these discomforts.

A broad, happy grin lit his face as he rounded the crest of the last hill and saw Larcombe's church tower gleaming wetly among the trees. Home and Christmas carols! Liz and Callie! (And the others . . .) Oh, God, life was good!

At their worst his brakes didn't work, and even at their best they couldn't stop him. Marcus slapped his foot up and down, pumping brake fluid until he could safely change into third gear, and then into second for the sharp left-hand turn at the foot of the hill. But the school bus had preceded him and was just about to move off, blocking the bridge. Marcus pumped the brake pedal again, slammed on the hand-brake and veered to the right, stopping at last with half an inch to spare between his front wheels and the river.

He barely acknowledged this little difficulty. No harm was done, and as long as he hadn't killed anyone (and he hadn't yet) he reckoned he was doing pretty well. He thrust the gearstick into reverse, put his foot down and, as an afterthought, swivelled his head around to see where he was going. He was just in time to see Claudia Murray, also in reverse, narrowly escaping the edge of his rear bumper as she leapt hurriedly over Mrs Tapscott's garden wall. Marcus laughed and bit his lip. *Now* he was in trouble . . .

His face was as apologetic as he could make it as he got out of the car; but when he leaned cautiously over the wall to see where Claudia had landed (she had landed in a rose bush and was sitting in the middle of it as if in a large, comfortable armchair), he threw back his head and howled with laughter.

Claudia didn't move. Her school hat was askew, her bottle-green socks in concertina folds around her ankles and she was being thoroughly rained on by the chill December drizzle; but her face was impassive, bored, resigned. It was as if she did this sort of thing every day and had long grown accustomed to it.

Marcus clamped his teeth on another burst of hilarity, reminding himself that life wasn't as peachy for Claudia as it was for him. He couldn't ask her to see the funny side of it, especially when her underside was well peppered with rose thorns.

'I'm terribly sorry, Claudia,' he muttered. 'I'm afraid I didn't see you.'

She said nothing. She looked at her feet. Her face was the colour of raspberry sauce, an agony of embarrassment.

'Er – don't move.' Marcus climbed over the wall. 'If we get you out the way you came in, it'll probably be less painful. Forward and upward, okay?'

Claudia flung him a look of pained resentment, but said nothing at all.

Marcus was astonished to find her so light in his arms, for she'd grown a few inches since he'd seen her last and no longer resembled the undersized rabbit he'd scraped up from the side of the road not so long ago.

No, not long ago. Six months? But it seemed like a lifetime. He had a nasty feeling that it had seemed even longer for Claudia. They had both begun new lives since then. They had changed, and only one of them for the better.

He set Claudia down on the far side of the wall and passed over her satchel. 'Are you all right?'

She blinked and looked at the ground. 'I wish you'd killed me,' she murmured sullenly.

Marcus frowned, more with irritation than sorrow. 'Don't be silly,' he said crisply. 'I wasn't going fast enough to kill you. Anyway, if that's what you wanted, why did you jump over the wall?'

Claudia narrowed her eyes and darted him a look of pure venom from under the brim of her hat.

'Hey, come on,' he encouraged nervously. 'Cheer up. It's nearly Christmas. Season of goodwill? All that?'

Claudia shrugged and walked away, dragging her feet.

Marcus felt like slapping her. Instead, he gave Mrs Tapscott's wall a good, hard kick.

'And a Merry Christmas to you, too,' he said.

The advent of tractors and combine harvesters had been the death of the traditional Harvest Supper, but Saxons had kept the feast alive in their own way, moving it along to Midwinter Night when they gave a Christmas party. This had originally been a party for 'the men' and their families, but in recent years, as the number of men had dwindled, the guest list had been extended to include a few others.

Miss Derby came because she didn't have much fun (and even less to eat); and old Mrs Chislett because they didn't dare leave her out – she'd still be complaining come Midsummer. In spite of his departure from the farm, Titch was invited; and Janice and Mrs Tapscott, because Titch wouldn't come without Janice, and Janice wouldn't come without her mother. Then there was the Bridges family: Noddy, 'Mrs Nod' (no one ever called her Mrs Bridges), with their three little girls, Carol, Diane and Irene. And Fred and Mrs Haines, both in their nineties, who had worked for Saxons long, long before 'them ruddy gurt trattors come and buggered up the country'.

The last five were all Flickers, making a total of eighteen guests, but only twenty people sat down to eat the traditional Christmas dinner. Edward presided at the head of the table and Olivia at its foot. The rest of the family staffed the kitchen, waited at table and did the washing up: a combined operation so efficient that, by the time the guests were down to the last of the walnuts, everything (save a few aching feet) was back to normal again.

Even as he approached his nineteenth birthday, Marcus was almost as excited by Midwinter Night as he had been when he was nine, when the mere sight of his father washing dishes had been enough to send him into giggling raptures. But it was all like that: no one was the same as usual. It was as if they all – family and guests alike – cast off the cold shells of themselves and became, just for one night, as warm, as loving and as lovable as Marcus *always* was – beneath his shell.

Save for Mrs Chislett, the guests arrived in a state of shyness which verged upon paralysis. In their best clothes and well-polished shoes, they looked nothing like (and, evidently, felt nothing like) the comfortably familiar people whom Marcus had known all his life. Noddy and Little Georgie, who'd been cussing in the farmyard just a few hours before, now cleared their throats, shuffled their feet and murmured, 'Good of 'ee, Marcus, very good of 'ee,' when he offered to take their coats. The ladies smiled with painted mouths which, in spite of their efforts, refused to come unpursed. The Bridges girls suffered even worse agonies. As brazen as monkeys when they roamed the village, now they hung their heads to hide purple blushes, bumped into the furniture and tied themselves in knots with the sleeves of their cardigans.

Marcus found it all very touching. Not one of the guests, young, old or middling, answered to anyone's description of beauty. Or even charm. And none of them was educated – old Mr Haines, in fact, had never learned to read. Yet they had a special kind of beauty, not lent to them just for Midwinter Night but constant and enduring; something deeper than wrinkles, something sweeter than charm.

Even Ellis looked unusually sweet, although it had to be said that he owed a lot to his frilly apron and pink party hat.

They met at the kitchen door, Ellis laden with dirty crockery, Marcus with Christmas puddings.

Marcus blew his brother a kiss.

'Yer, gerroff,' Ellis simpered shyly. 'Our Ma've told I about blokes like 'ee.'

'Stop it, you two,' Liz giggled. 'Someone in there might get the wrong idea.'

When the meal was over, there was a strong arm to help each of the elderly folk into the drawing room, and drinks were passed to those who would indulge. Then – after a short, embarrassed silence – the talk began.

'Yer, Marcus. What was you doin' with poor Claudia Murray, t'other day? I sid 'ee chuckin' her over Mrs Tapscott's wall, but I couldn' for the life o' me – '

'Chuckin' Claudia Murray over my wall? Why ever – ? Yer, I bin wonderin' what come of that rose bush o'mine. Remember, I said to 'ee, Janice – whatever come of that rose bush, I said. 'Er wuz upright as a good Christian woman t'other day, I said, and now 'er's leanin over like a drunken flippen sailor! What you go and chuck Claudia in my rose bush fer, Marcus?'

'I didn't. I fished her out of it. No, that's not quite true . . .'

It took some explaining, but it raised a laugh, as well as a few insults about his driving.

Marcus hadn't mentioned the Claudia incident at home, for the simple reason that he'd forgotten it; but he noticed Ben's eyebrows go up with mute disapproval, and his mother's lower with anxiety.

Mrs Chislett shook her head. 'I don't s'pose she noticed,' she said flatly. 'Poor little kiddie. The life's went right out of her since Madge passed on. As for James Murray . . . There'd be ruin starin' that man in the face if tweren't for his mother – '

'Cath?' Olivia interrupted sharply. 'Why? What's *she* doing? She had one foot in the grave the last I heard!'

'Ah. Well, that's life, see, Mrs Saxon. We does what we'm called to do, and if no one don't call, we don't dang well answer. Madge never called much on Cath after Albert passed on but she'm been called now, right enough – and she'm *answerin'*! Complains a good bit, mind you.'

'Hmph!' Olivia said. 'She would.'

'But – be fair – it's a hard job, Mrs Saxon, and Cath ain't no chicken. Sempty-one, see, come next March. Just the thought of it makes me feel tired, I can tell 'ee. House, family, business: she'm tryin' to keep it all up together. And James . . . Oh, James. Say what you like about James – and even *I* say he were never no more'n a poorish specimen – he loved his wife, Mrs Saxon. Leant on her too much though, see, and can't hold up without her. Sobs himself to sleep he do, night after night, and the whole house achin' at the sound of un.'

There was a short, mournful silence.

'Ah. Well.' Old Georgie grinned. 'Ta very much, Mariah, m'dear. Cheered us up no end, that did!'

Mrs Chislett let forth a wild shriek of laughter and clapped her hands with glee. 'Oh, ah, life an' soul of the party, that's me!' she claimed merrily. 'Yer! Come on, Marcus! Give us a song! Youngest starts, oldest finishes!'

Marcus grinned and crept up on Irene Bridges, who, having realised that *she* was the youngest, was already turning purple again and trying to disappear through the floor.

'Oh, *I'm* not the youngest,' he teased. '*Irene's* the youngest. Come on, Irene. On your feet, my darling!'

He tugged her hair and tickled her ribs, but she covered her face with her hands and wailed. 'Yer, gerroff! Oy, our Dad! *Tell* 'im!'

So Marcus and Ellis, as they always did, began the carols.

> 'The boar's head in hand bear I,
> Bedecked with bays and rosemary;
> And I pray you my masters, be merry,
> *Quot estis in convivio* . . .'

Even at this early stage, the guests were mellow enough to have tears in their eyes when the boys had finished.

'Proper old song that 'un be. You don't quite catch the words, like, but the tune oils you up just nice.'

'That's not the tune! That's the whisky, Georgie!'

'No, it ain't! 'Tis the tune, I tell 'ee! Right then, who'll give us another? Make it one I knows, and I'll pick it out on me squeeze-box for 'ee.'

The men sang 'Good King Wenceslas', the women 'The Coventry Carol', and the Flickers stood up *en masse* for 'While Shepherds Watched'. Finally, they all launched into the 'Somerset Wassail' with old Mr Haines, which drew the night to a close.

'Yer! Just look at this time, Georgie Flicker! Time these

good people was in bed, after all the work they put in for us today, and *they* can't bide in bed tomorrer, not like *some* we could mention! Ooh, we've had a lovely night of it, Mrs Saxon – and Liz – and Helen. Aw, look at your Irene, Mrs Nod. Noddin' off, she be, bless 'er. Oooh! *Noddin' off*! Oh, ain't *I* a card?'

They were not the people they'd been when they arrived. These people laughed, teased, kissed and shook hands; and only little Irene, faced with the prospect of kissing Marcus and Ellis, still retained strength enough to hold on to her best party manners.

'Gerroff,' she muttered shyly; and, at a violent prod from her mother, 'And fanks very much for havin' I.'

Chapter Nine

Callie sat in an armchair, hour after hour, her blind eyes seeming to squint into the corners as if trying to identify something small and strange, beyond the bounds of her memory. She still smiled when she was spoken to, and still – after a while – produced an answer of sorts; but the strength and the meaning were going out of her and Marcus prayed that she would die.

In the middle of the afternoon, on a rainy Sunday in March, he walked through the twilit kitchen and found Liz leaning over the sink as if she'd just been sick. But she was crying.

'Liz?'

He touched her shoulder and she turned into his arms, her face running with tears. 'I know!' she sobbed. 'I know I'm a fool, but sometimes – !'

'You're no fool, Liz.'

'I feel so alone! I feel – I feel as if I'm the only one who loves her, Marcus, the only one who . . . needs her. Yet at the same time . . . Oh, *how* can I wish her dead when I'd give anything to keep her? But not like this, Marcus!' She twisted clear, throwing her head back to glare up at heaven.

'Callie's not a *termite*! You can't just *step* on her! She's my daughter!'

'Grandma and her famous termites,' Marcus murmured sadly. He pulled a chair clear of the table and guided Liz into it. 'Got a hanky?'

'Yes!'

But it was already sopping wet. Marcus gave her his and put the kettle on. He'd been on his way to help with the milking. Ellis hadn't been home since Christmas, Noddy had 'flu, the day's work wasn't nearly finished; and the first thing Marcus had learned about farming was that farming came first – even if the house was on fire. He'd learned it, but didn't necessarily accept it.

When Marcus's house was on fire, nothing could keep him from putting it out.

'You aren't the only one who loves her,' he said quietly. 'But you're her mother, it's bound to hurt you most.'

He had made two cups of Nescafé and now slid Liz's across the table.

Her mouth went down like a child's as she struggled against a fresh onset of tears. 'But you're all . . . You're all so bloody *tough*! I want someone to cry *with*, not at! As for my being Callie's mother, what about – ?'

She stopped suddenly, biting her lip, but Marcus knew what she'd been going to say. What about Callie's father?

'James Murray,' he said bitterly. 'Think of him, Liz, and ask yourself if you'd prefer Tom to express his grief *that* way. We may be bloody tough, as you put it, but for most of us – Tom included – it's just a shell. You can't ask him to cry with you, because if he once began he'd never stop.'

Marcus reached out to take Liz's hand, smothering it in both of his. 'I can see that Tom's way leaves you . . . lonely, but it also leaves you free to concentrate your efforts on Callie. He gives you no apparent support, no comfort. But he takes nothing, either. James Murray takes everything.

Christ, it makes me furious. Would you rather Tom was like that?'

'I don't know.' Liz bowed her head. 'I hate him sometimes,' she whispered. 'I think that's why . . . I think that's what brings me down like this; because when Callie's gone . . . there'll be nothing left. No child. No marriage. No *point*.'

Her eyes widened, and the look in them was one of pure horror. 'I know how James Murray feels!' she wailed softly. 'When you've lost everything, what's the point of being brave?'

'You never lose everything, Liz. James Murray certainly hasn't. He's got three children, for God's sake! Anyway, someone once told me that when you seem to have lost everything, you still have yourself. I can't remember who it was, but she was a wise old duck, and I think she was probably right.'

Liz blew her nose again. 'Less of the *old*,' she muttered. 'And I'm not wise. I just talk off the top of my head. I don't really believe it. Neither should you.'

'But I do. Drink your coffee.'

Liz laughed tearfully. 'And pull yourself together, woman. Look on the bright side . . . Count your blessings.'

'I didn't say that. I didn't mean it.'

'No . . . No, I know.'

'I like you when you're all weak and feeble,' he teased gently. 'It does wonders for your nose. Day-glo pink really suits you.'

'Flatterer.' She sighed heavily. 'No wonder you have all the girls eating out of your hand.'

'That's not quite what they do,' he said solemnly, and was rewarded with another smile. She was recovering.

Marcus watched her for a moment, making certain that the tears were over. He would have liked to talk more, to try to bolster her faith in herself before the long slide into darkness, but he knew it would do no good. Liz was like a goldfinch, her flight taking a swooping path in which the downs were as essential to her progress as the ups. Using the same analogy, he supposed Tom was a swift. He'd rather fly through the night than make a landing, just in case he couldn't take off again. Poor little birds . . .

He frowned and took Liz's hand again, squeezing it tightly. 'Listen,' he said. 'We all have to grieve in our own way, but some ways are better than others.'

'I know,' she said, and her face reddened with embarrassment. 'I won't do it again, I promise. Not in the kitchen, anyway.'

Marcus smiled. 'That's not what I meant. I meant . . . that your way is the best, and Tom's probably the worst. I used to think he'd taken it on the chin when Callie was in hospital last year; and that, since then, he'd just been absorbing it, like a bruise. But I'm not so sure now.'

'What do you mean?'

'I mean . . . Maybe he didn't take it on the chin. Perhaps he dodged. And if his pain is all still to come, Liz, he'll *need* you.'

Her face hardened and grew cold. 'Yes,' she said wearily. 'I know. And when he needs me, I suppose I'll be there – regardless of the fact that when I needed *him* – !'

With a struggle, she dispelled the bitterness from her eyes and patted Marcus's hand. 'Never mind. I've got you.'

'Yes.'

'But you're too young to be carrying my burdens, Marcus.'

'Ha! Tell that to Claudia Murray.'

Liz smiled. 'Ooh, you *are* furious, aren't you?'

'Well.' He drummed his fingers on the table. 'It does bother me a bit. I think it's guilt. When I saw her sitting in Mrs Tapscott's rose bush I laughed my head off. She looked so funny. But she said she wished I'd run her down, she wished I'd killed her.'

'Poor little kid.'

'Yes. I was annoyed at the time. It seemed so stupid, so melodramatic – not to say depressing! But then when Mrs Chislett . . . What she said about James . . .' He shook his head. 'Christ, she chooses her words well, doesn't she? I can't seem to forget it. I keep thinking of him sobbing his guts up night after night, and that poor little kid . . . Just *aching*.'

Liz was silent. She stirred her coffee and stared into the cup, a half-formed smile playing at the corners of her mouth.

'My,' she said dryly at last. 'You *are* a clever boy, aren't you?'

'Why?'

'Because . . . Oh, you just are.'

Marcus stood up, remembering the milking now that he'd put the fire out at home.

'Well, that's a comfort,' he said flatly. 'I don't know how I'd have got through the day without you, Liz.'

They laughed. Marcus attempted to tousle her hair, but she ducked away, blushing, to hide her face in her hands.

Liz lay in bed, flat on her back, running her hands thoughtfully over her ribs. She'd never been fat, but she'd always been the well-padded type; the type who really *needed* a roll-on when she wore slender skirts. She didn't need it any more. She could actually count her ribs, and her tummy went in instead of out, a state of affairs she'd been longing for all her life.

She chuckled cynically. 'When I'm really *thin*,' had been one of the dreams she'd often talked about when she was younger. 'When I'm really *thin*, I'll pinch Tom's wallet, drive up to London and go through Harrod's like a dose of salts . . .'

On quiet winter evenings, when everyone was gathered in the drawing room and Marcus was looking for mischief, he'd suddenly pipe up, 'What will you do when you're really *thin*, Liz?'

He'd been a maddening little brat. He'd learned logic at a very early age. He'd understood human nature and used it as a weapon. He'd read books which were far too old for him. He'd also read the *Farmer's Weekly*, reciting it at breakfast, teaching his father the best way to breed sheep. *Maddening*.

But Liz had loved him, even then. And she'd loved him because he'd loved Callie. No, not loved her – worshipped her. He could tear out of one room in a killing rage, and if he met Callie in the next room he'd skid to a halt, smile, say something gentle, civilised and contained, pat her on the head and tear off again, still raging. They had all (even Ben) observed this phenomenon with a wonderment which verged upon heartbreak, for his patience never snapped, his gentleness never failed, his concern for Callie never faltered; and it was impossible not to grieve that he could give her so much and them so little.

Yet even that wasn't true. The truth was that Callie had given *him* so much; for, unlike the family at large, Callie had *listened* to him. She'd respected him. She'd given his virtues room to expand; and that – more or less – was all he'd required from any of them. But Ben had no real respect for anyone, so it was too much to hope that he would respect a kid of eight, ten, thirteen. All that could be hoped was that he wouldn't strangle him before he grew to be a kid of sixteen and big enough to fight back.

But the alchemy of adolescence had saved them from bloody murder. Marcus had gone back to school one

Christmas (screaming as usual) and come home at Easter with a supercilious smile and a line in deadly sarcasm which could strip the skin off an ox at a range of fifty paces. Hmm. That had taught the buggers respect . . .

It had taught Liz respect, too. Until then, Marcus had been like her own son, a little boy she could tease, scold and – in his occasional soft moods – cuddle. But that had changed. Now, he made Liz feel like a young girl: shy, bewildered and insecure, ever turning to him for strength and comfort. He could be very comforting at times. Too comforting. Yet never comforting enough.

She turned over and sank her teeth in the pillow to avoid disturbing Tom. She had been able to contain her tears once, but no more, no more. She was too tired, now, for the strenuous business of self-control. She cried when she was feeding Callie, or changing her, or changing the bed. Or she locked herself in the bathroom and sobbed her heart out in blissful privacy, using Olivia's embroidered huckaback towels for handkerchiefs. And sometimes, when even the bathroom offered no relief, she marched over the fields to the top of Old Barrow, and just stood there, all by herself, howling into the wind, 'Oh, God, God, it's not *fair*!'

But at least she was thin . . .

And Marcus would be home today. He didn't do his Homecoming Crusader inspection any more. He dumped his bag in the kitchen, kissed his mother and came straight upstairs to Callie's room, bearing a bunch of jonquils in one hand and a glass of whisky in the other. The jonquils were to scent the room, which, in spite of the open window, always smelled of encroaching death. And the whisky was to fell Liz in her tracks, which it did with no trouble at all. She didn't sleep much usually. Even when she risked lying down for an hour or two, her ears were always pricked for a sound from Callie's room across the landing. A sound?

No. A cease, a peace, the perfect stillness which would say that the struggle was over. And Liz didn't want to miss that. She wanted to be there.

Not that it mattered to Callie, poor child. Callie had gone somewhere else, and wouldn't have noticed if she'd been left alone for a month of Sundays. But Liz (she was mad, of course) couldn't believe that some flicker of feeling didn't survive. An ability to recognise that the hands that touched her belonged to hearts that loved her. Her mother's hands. Her cousin's hands.

Yes, Liz could sleep while Marcus was there. He wrote up his lecture notes and lab reports at Callie's dressing table and at half-hourly intervals he turned Callie over. He could change her nightdress too. Change the sheets. Liz had actually watched him doing it, lifting Callie's helpless dead-weight from one side of the bed to the other as if she were no more substantial than a sack of feathers. And there was no nonsense about it, either. Not like the other men who, with just as much strength at their disposal, blushed and fumbled through the entire business, worrying about the *propriety* of the thing! Christ! As if it mattered!

Liz sat up and blew her nose, wondering what the hell time it was. Sleeplessness was a funny thing. You could lie there for hours: hour after hour after miserable hour; and then, when you gave up trying and staggered off to make a pot of tea, you discovered you'd only been in bed twenty minutes.

Liz got up, inch by inch, trying not to rock the bed or create a draught as she peeled off the blankets. It was cold. She stuck her nose through the gap in the curtains. There was a clear sky and a full moon and . . . yes, a frost.

'Everything all right, Liz?'

She arrested her movements in mid-sneak, raising her eyebrows despairingly. He'd been awake all along, damn him.

'Yes. fine. Can't sleep, that's all.'

'Same here.'

He sounded so sad. More than sad. Her eyes pricking with yet another rush of tears, Liz thought of James Murray, whose house ached to the sound of his misery. This house ached, too; not to the sound, but to the silence . . .

Yes, Marcus had been right: Tom's way was best. It was braver, kinder, less selfish. He'd known his own limitations and kept sternly within them; suffering, suffering, but suffering alone.

'It's all right,' she whispered brokenly. 'I understand.'

It was too dark to see his face, but she heard his throat working and knew that, but for the sobs, he was weeping.

'But you've been so brave! You've done so much, while I – !'

Liz sighed and sat at the foot of the bed, grasping Tom's foot, which was so much easier to reach than his hand.

'Hush,' she said gently. 'We both . . . love her, Tom, and we're both . . . losing her. Let's just take it for granted that it hurts us both just as much. You've nothing to blame yourself for. You're a man. If there'd been anything you could have done to save her you'd have done what men do: fought tooth and claw, risked life and limb. And I'd be lying where you are now, blaming myself. "You were so brave," I'd say. "And what did I do? Nothing."'

Tom shuffled down the bed to wrap his arms around Liz's waist, to bury his face in her lap. 'Yes, but that's not – '

'Hush. You've kept your peace this long, Tom. Keep it a little longer, will you? Because it helps, you see. It helps.'

She looked up at the ceiling, wearily thanking God for Marcus. He had helped her so much over the past few months, but she'd never believed what he'd said about Tom. She hadn't believed that he'd been as brave as he could, done the best he could. But he had. In his way. For Tom's grief and Tom's guilt, on top of everything else, would have been too great a burden for her to carry.

She stroked his hair. They'd scarcely touched each other for months. Not for years. Well, more than a year, anyway. And his arms were warm and strong, absorbing some of her pain, taking it away. This was the comfort she craved from Marcus; this close, hard, seemingly unbreakable contact of skin and muscle and bone which hurt, yet took the pain away. Well, she couldn't have Marcus; and Tom was all she had.

'Just do one thing for me,' she whispered brokenly. 'At the . . . When she . . . When we fall down that dirty great hole together . . . Hold my hand, will you?'

'Oh, yes!'

He sobbed then. Just once. A tortured, racking sound – the sound of the forbidden.

Oh, Christ, Liz thought dismally, who'd be a man?

It was like having your right hand cut off. You kept reaching out to do things with it, but it wasn't there. And you could never get it back. Though your heart shrivelled every time it confronted the ugly, useless stump where once had been the best thing in your life, you had to bear it. Get used to it. Be brave.

Marcus was deeply aware that if he felt like this, Liz and Tom must be in hell; yet neither of them showed it. They were like two little kids whose high spirits had earned them a punishment from an adult they weren't quite sure of. They kept smiling, hoping he didn't mean it, that he'd change his mind and let them off with a caution. They seemed not to realise that the blow had already fallen.

Marcus watched Liz in wonderment, finding it difficult to take his eyes off her. He'd seen her growing thinner and older during the last few months of Callie's decline and had sometimes thought she'd go mad with the strain. Yet now that Callie was dead, all trace of anguish had gone.

The most curious thing was that she didn't look old any more. She looked very young and innocent, like a child. But the energy had gone out of her. When he'd come home from Bristol he'd found her sitting on the sofa in the drawing room; and she'd barely moved since then. She'd worn herself out. Even the simplest of tasks was too difficult, too strenuous. Marcus felt himself constantly overwhelmed by a desire to pick her up and rock her to sleep in his arms.

But she didn't shed a tear; and, after the funeral, when half the village came back to the house to pay their respects, she was quietly gracious: a neat, dignified little figure in a slim black dress. Not like Liz at all. Even her hair was tidy.

Most people stayed just long enough to have a drink, shake hands with everyone and murmur the appropriate words of sympathy; but some stayed to talk.

No one mentioned Callie. They talked of happier times and told funny stories; some of them reaching as far back as the First World War. Liz smiled and looked politely interested, but she didn't say anything until – as invariably happened – the Murray family was mentioned. Then, as if reaching out to grasp something she could understand, she said, 'How's James, now?'

'Oh . . .' Mrs Chislett nodded doubtfully. 'Not too bad. Give him another twelvemonth and he'll be back on his feet, I reckon. Mind, I can't say the same for that young 'un of his; and if I was James Murray I'd have summat on me conscience where she's concerned. Still, I'm *not* 'im. And thanks be to God for that.'

'Claudia's not doing too well, then?'

'Ah,' Mrs Chislett shook her head. 'Wild, impudent little hussy she's turned out, and all because . . . Well, it's no good to criticise. People do what they can, and if it ain't good enough, too bad. Cath's tearin' her hair out with worry over it, but what can she do? An old woman like that. Can't even *catch* the little perisher!'

Mrs Chislett's eyes brightened and she turned to look at Marcus, summing him up to see if it was safe to insult him. 'Reminds me of you, she do,' she said archly. 'Can't kick the dog that bit her, so she kicks the cat instead. But you was luckier.'

Marcus lowered his eyes. Callie's death ached in his chest: a pain he felt sure he would never be cured of; but Mrs Chislett was right. He'd been lucky. Had he lost his father – or his mother – when he was Claudia's age, he wouldn't have been content with kicking the cat. He'd have strangled it. Being thirteen was painful enough without adding bereavement to the agony.

'Boys!' Mrs Chislett continued scathingly. 'Yes, the boys is always luckier. They just knocks the windfalls off the tree. It's the girls has to bring 'em 'ome!'

Marcus's eyes widened with shock. He and Mrs Chislett had evidently been thinking of different things! A windfall was an illegitimate child, and he'd never (although not for want of trying) managed to knock one of *those* off the tree! But surely Claudia hadn't reached that stage already?

'She's too young for that sort of thing, isn't she?'

'Huh! Past a certain point, my lad, it ain't a question of age so much as of inclination. But that's not what I was saying. It's not what she's done, yet. It's what she's dang well going to do if someone don't catch her in time. It's a disgrace, that's what it is. No wonder women gen'rally lives longer'n men, for when the men are left they don't half make a ruddy hash of things!'

'But only if they're men like James,' Ben sneered softly.

'Ha!' Mrs Chislett's malicious gaze scooped up every man in the room before dumping him into the deep pit of her derision. 'That's what *you* thinks, Ben Saxon, but the proof of the puddin's in the eatin', and you never ate any yet! God grant you never do, neither.'

There was a stiff, pained silence. Mrs Chislett went too far, sometimes. She forgot herself. Either that, or she thought herself above the laws of courtesy which governed everyone else. In many ways she *was* immune, for there were few people in Larcombe who didn't live in dread of her sharp tongue and witch-like prescience. There were few people too who were not awed by the extraordinary goodness of the woman, which – paradoxically – shone all the brighter when she was at her most malicious. Marcus sometimes imagined that the angels of heaven would look like old Ma Chislett: fat, fierce and fearless, swiping the balls off every devil they came across with swords of burning gold.

She'd certainly taken a good, hard swipe at Ben's manhood. Telling him that he was no better than James Murray had put more starch in his smile than he knew what to do with. But it wasn't just that. She'd also called into question Tom's ability to cope with his grief – and that, damn it, was too much; if only because they all questioned it. He wasn't a man anyone thought of as being strong. He'd been second-best all his life. He'd never been master in his own house, never had anything to call his own – save Callie. And he'd lost Callie.

Mrs Chislett opened her black leather-cloth handbag, rummaged inside it and fetched out something small, which she hid in the palm of her hand. The bag snapped shut with a clunk, and she heaved herself out of her chair, her malice gone, a soft, motherly smile illuminating her hoary old face.

'Well, I must be leavin' you good folks to your sorrow. I'll put in a good word with the Almighty for you, Liz, my love, and Tom. May he bless and comfort you and bring some light to your darkness.'

She pressed the small thing into Liz's hand, saying softly, 'Tis dead, my love, but t'will last and stay pretty for as long as you needs it. And so will she, my love; so will she.'

Marcus couldn't see what the gift was, but he saw that it brought tears to Liz's eyes: the first tears, although he knew they would not be the last.

'Watch 'er,' Mrs Chislett hissed darkly as she left the house. 'It 'aven't come 'ome to 'er yet, and when it do you'll 'ave trouble.' She clumped off down the path. 'Yer, these irises wants splittin'.' And did a sudden about turn. 'I'd watch your Helen too, if I was you, Ben Saxon.'

His eyes widened with astonishment. 'Oh, Helen's all right.'

'No,' Mrs Chislett said. 'She'm just like the rest of us – half left; and 'er keeps her left hand behind 'er back so's us cassn't see it. But I'm tellin' you, you watch 'er.'

'Old witch,' Ben murmured when she'd disappeared through the gate. 'If we believed everything she said, we'd *all* be six feet under!'

Marcus shrugged and looked at his watch. It was gone three, and Tom would not be doing the milking today. 'I'll fetch the cows,' he said.

He didn't see the look Ben gave him; a strange glance: one part pity, one part triumph, three parts fear.

Marcus walked out across the fields, wondering what Mrs Chislett had meant about Helen, wondering when Liz would begin to cry, and how long it would take for the pain to ease. He barely noticed the long line of cows coming to meet him around the foot of Old Barrow, and when the phenomenon did make its mark, he thought, Some fool's left the gate open.

But the fool was Ellis, bringing the cows home. The same fool, in fact, who had driven them out after the morning's milking. He had, it was true, muttered something about taking Tom's place for a day or two, but Marcus hadn't expected him to overdo it!

'Hey, what's got into you?'

Ellis scowled and looked away. 'Old Ma Chislett. I can't stand that woman. She only goes to funerals to supplement her diet. Christ, did you see her packing those sandwiches away?'

He spoke hurriedly, his eyes never meeting Marcus's; and Marcus knew his brother too well. He was talking about Mrs Chislett, but he was thinking about something else. Callie, perhaps. Or, more probably, not Callie. You could break your neck to understand Ellis and still end up with nothing better than a broken neck.

So what was he thinking about? What was worrying him? Did he feel guilty? Yes, he probably did, because he'd scarcely been home at all during the past few months. He'd done nothing to help. And Marcus *could* understand that; for he, too, had wanted to forget Callie and pretend that nothing bad was happening at home. But he hadn't been able to do it. Not while he knew he could do something. Not while he felt he was needed.

He smiled wryly, admitting to himself that he'd needed to be needed. But now he was satisfied that he'd done all he could. The grief he felt was grief alone, untainted by guilt; although, should he want it, Ellis had a perfect excuse for once. His Finals were coming up, and after three years at college he'd need all the time he had left for study.

'I thought you'd be going back to London tonight,' Marcus said.

Ellis shrugged and stepped sideways to slap a bony, slow-moving rump. 'Yah! Hi-yup! When do you go back, Marc?'

'I've got a lecture in the morning, but I'll come home straight afterwards. See how things are. Ma Chislett seems to think Mother's more upset than she looks. Stands to reason, I suppose.'

Ellis nodded, but he wasn't really listening. It was as if they approached the English language from opposite ends of the spectrum; using the same words to mean totally different things.

'She keeps things pretty close to her chest,' Marcus went on. 'She never says much, does she?'

'She asks questions,' Ellis muttered. 'She's always asking bloody questions.'

'You don't have to answer them.'

'What am I supposed to do, then? Give my name, rank and number?'

'Can't you just be enigmatic?'

'Huh! That's your territory!'

Marcus smiled. 'Oh, I dunno,' he said cynically. 'You're a complete enigma to me.'

'Likewise. But so what? We're different, aren't we? We don't have to match like a pair of bloody socks! We don't have to be . . .' He sighed. 'Ah, well.'

Something had upset him. He rarely got excited about anything, rarely protested, argued or fought. It was one of the things Marcus disliked about him. The policy 'Anything for a quiet life' struck Marcus as being immoral. If you felt something was right, it was your duty to fight for it, even if you had to die in the attempt. The war had proved that, if nothing else.

But Ellis looked worried and angry, close to tears. No, there was no understanding him. He probably *was* upset about Callie and talking about other things merely to distract himself.

'Look,' Marcus said. 'Knock off if you like. I'll do – '

'No!'

Marcus blinked. No? Ellis never said no to the chance of

putting his feet up! 'It's all right,' he said. 'Ma Chislett's gone. You're safe.'

'No. Thanks. I . . . I said I'd do it.' He laughed shortly. 'I need the money.'

Ellis filled the mangers with cow-cake and the first dozen cows came in from the yard, hurrying now to get at their evening ration of goodies. Marcus washed the udders of the first pair and attached the milking machine clusters, moving on to wash the next two while Ellis set up the second machine. Even with Noddy helping in the dairy, it was a slow, laborious job which they could do in half the time if only Ben would invest in new machines.

'We need a new building,' Marcus said as the next four cows bustled in. 'If we had a couple of abreast parlours we could milk eight cows at once and be finished in half the time.'

'A couple?' Ellis scoffed. 'You're joking. We'd never get Dad to spend that kind of money; not when we can manage without it. It's a terrific risk . . .'

'Risk? Where's the risk?'

'Well, all that money . . .'

'Nonsense. The most important economy we can make is time. We should be aiming to save ten hours a day. That's one man's pay packet. We'd recoup the capital in a couple of years.'

They went on talking until the milking was finished, and when Ellis went off to take the cows back to pasture, he left Marcus a relatively happy man. There were always two sides to a coin . . . Perhaps, in losing Callie, he would find a brother?

The thought was more pleasant than he could have imagined possible. He'd written Ellis off, expected nothing from him, yet he wasn't really so bad. Yes, he was lazy; but perhaps that was only because Ben insisted on pushing him in the wrong direction. Even his college course had been thrust upon him – he'd wanted to do English and ended up doing Economics instead. Had Ben had it all his own way, Ellis would have gone to Agricultural College; but Ben rarely had it *all* his own way – just enough of it to take the pleasure out of life for everyone else.

And Ellis didn't have the strength to resist. All he could do in his own defence was to be stubborn, be lazy, refuse to cooperate; and even these tactics had limits while Ben held the purse strings. Things might be easier all round when he'd done his Finals and found a job in London. Then he could thumb his nose at Ben. He'd be free.

Marcus was late home for lunch the next day and was astonished, when he entered the house, to hear his brother's raised voice coming from the dining room. He paused, frowning. Why hadn't Ellis gone back to London? The funeral was over. His exams were almost on top of him – yet he was still here, arguing with Ben!

'No, Dad, no! That's not the point!'

'Well, what is the point?'

'You're looking at it from the wrong end! The best way to save money is to save *time*! An hour here, an hour there. If we could save ten hours a day – '

Marcus smiled and took a deep, cynical breath, tilting his head to one side to hear himself quoted in detail. 'Get it right,' he murmured.

And Ellis got it right, leaving out only one detail: that his ideas belonged to someone else. That didn't matter to Marcus except as a moral irritation. The important thing was to make the farm keep up with the times, which were changing a hell of a lot faster than Ben was.

'Well, I'll give it some thought,' Ben said. 'You're right

about the milking of course. I've been thinking that one out for years. But it's a question of investment, you see.'

'Yes, but if a new building costs, say, two thousand pounds, you'd get that back in a few years just on the strength of one man's wages!'

'You've really been thinking things through, haven't you?' Ben said admiringly. 'We'll make a farmer of you yet.'

Marcus decided it was time to make his presence felt. His grandmother had told him to bide his time and keep his own counsel, and that was precisely what he intended to do, but this opportunity was too good to resist! 'Hey, Ellis!' he called mischievously. 'Why don't you tell him your idea about the Ayrshires?'

'Ayrshires?'

'You know!' Marcus helped himself to some soup from the pot on the stove and strolled through to the dining room, as straight-faced as a hanging judge.

'Go on, Ellis. Tell him about the Ayrshires.'

Ellis just stared at his plate, which was understandable since he had no idea what Marcus was talking about.

'Well, I think you're right,' Marcus said. 'Friesians are better in virtually every respect but Dad'll never get rid of his Ayrshires. You're on a loser there, Ellis.'

'Get rid of the Ayrshires?' Ben laughed indignantly. 'No, no. That's going *too* far.'

'The trouble with you – ' Marcus turned to his brother, grinning encouragingly ' – is that you think of everything in terms of *economics*. What about tradition? If everyone goes over to Friesians we won't have any of the old breeds left.'

'Ha!' Ben sneered. 'And you're the one who's always saying we should be more efficient! You can't be traditional *and* efficient!' He turned back to Ellis. 'So you're interested in Friesians?'

'Er – ' Ellis frowned, but to Marcus's astonishment he rose to the challenge. 'Well, they *are* better, Dad. It's not just the extra milk. It's the value of the calves and barren cows. It seems a bit mad to hold on to the Ayrshires when you'd make twice as much out of Friesians.'

Ben laughed, his eyes travelling from Marcus to Ellis as if they were all sharing a pleasant little joke.

'All right,' he said. 'How about starting up a herd of your own, Ellis? I'll give you the capital to get started, and you can help pay for the new parlour out of your profits. How does that sound?'

Marcus froze. Only his eyes moved: once to the left to see Ellis squeezing his eyes shut, and once to the right to see Ben, smug and malicious, smirking his satisfaction. 'Hoist with your own petard, Marcus?' he enquired sweetly.

'*Ellis*?' Marcus snarled. 'What's going on?'

'I left college six months ago,' Ellis muttered. 'I've come home.'

Chapter Ten

Marcus walked into Larcombe village via Farrington Gurney, Marksbury, Keynsham and Whitchurch; a round trip of roughly fourteen miles; and he was still walking as fast when he crossed the cattle grid the second time as he had been the first.

His father hated him! He'd known it all his life; only sheer stupidity had led him to ignore the fact, pretend it wasn't true. Yet only a man who hated him could do this, today, now, before Callie was even cold in her grave!

'Hoist with your own petard . . .' Even in historic terms there was something viciously mocking about that phrase; and it sounded a good deal worse when it was true! Hoist with your own petard. Taken in your own trap. Ho-ho, shot yourself in the foot, didn't you, Sonny Jim?

Christ, what a fool! Why the hell hadn't he seen it coming? Ellis *had* been feeling guilty last night; although not about Callie. And he'd been feeling beaten, ashamed, hopeless. Given up college? In his final year? After all he'd said about wanting to make a life of his own, to have to come to Ben and admit *that*!

Well, now he'd made a failure of them all. He'd be a rotten farmer, and Marcus wouldn't raise a hand to help him. That was where Ben was wrong. He thought once Ellis had made his decision to stay, Marcus would fall in behind as Tom had done and they'd all live happily ever after, with everyone in his proper place and no harm done.

But Marcus would burn first. He'd lost the farm; and if that was the way Ben wanted it, that was the way it would be. Marcus would not play second fiddle to a man like Ellis. He wouldn't even play second to Ben. Not now. Not now and not ever again! Ben was strong only insofar as he failed to acknowledge his weaknesses, and only for as long as he could convince the opposition that he had none. But Marcus was no longer convinced. His father didn't merit all the respect Marcus had shown him, the . . . love.

Yes, love. He had loved Ben, done everything to please him. *Everything*. He'd formed his own character in the hope of pleasing him: he'd learned, he'd worked, he'd listened and emulated; and – oh, Christ! – he'd outstripped the bastard in everything except cruelty! Well, that could be changed. He had nothing to lose now. Callie and the farm were lost, and there was nothing left to keep him sweet.

He was just as angry when he crossed the cattle grid the second time as he had been the first; angry enough to beat his father to a pulp; and that wasn't cruelty so much as sheer stupidity. He had to calm down. He had to think. He needed to find a position of strength he could hold and never be moved from. And he didn't have such a position. He was dependent on Ben for everything, no matter which way he turned.

He turned into the woods and stood like a statue, head back, eyes closed, listening to the sound of his own heartbeat. No, he couldn't go home yet. His temper had always been his downfall, although, until today, he'd thought he'd got it licked. He hadn't. All he'd done was to learn it, the way sailors learned the Bristol Channel, steering around the treacherous sandbanks where shipwreck threatened. But sandbanks move. Lose your concentration and you hit them just the same. And there you are . . . wrecked.

Marcus's legs gave out suddenly and he sat down, resting his back against a tree. For a few moments his mind went blank; and his first thought, after that, surprised him, for it was not one of anger but of pity.

Poor Ellis . . . To be loved by a man like Ben must be worse than being hated by him. In fact, it was probably Ben's love which had ruined Ellis; and Ben's hatred . . . Yes, Ben's hatred which had made Marcus, such as he was.

He felt sick. Sick with disappointment, with grief. And, most of all, with self-knowledge. It was all his own fault. He'd deceived himself all these years. And for what? For the love of a man who hated him. For the respect of a man who despised him. The crazy thing was, he'd always known it; known it and pretended it wasn't true; known it and prayed that it might change – if only he *tried* hard enough. But no, that wasn't the crazy thing. The crazy thing was that even now he wanted to try again; to take his father by the throat and shake him and scream, 'I loved you! Why couldn't you love *me*?'

Marcus squeezed his eyes shut. When he opened them again he saw someone moving, deep in the woods, and shrank back, dreading the thought of a meeting. It was gone six, he'd been out for hours, and if anyone had come to look for him . . . No, he couldn't face anyone yet, not with any hope of keeping his temper.

The spot where his legs had chosen to take their rest was not the spot Marcus would have chosen, for the ground was thickly clothed with bramble and seedling beeches, but now he was glad of it, for if he'd reached the clearing he'd been aiming for he would have been seen. Now, hopefully, if he sat still, Helen (it was always Helen who sought him out) would go home disappointed, but with her ears unscorched by his venom.

No . . . it wasn't Helen. Then who? Christ, it was Claudia Murray, and she was aiming straight for him, looking straight at him!

No. No, she'd stopped and was looking about her, her eyes bright, her face animated and unaware. From Marcus's position she looked quite tall, though he guessed she was no more than five foot two or three. She was still a very pretty kid, but wild-looking, neglected. Her soft, silvery-blonde hair had grown down to her shoulders, shapeless, untidy and in desperate need of a comb.

But even as this thought crossed his mind, Claudia took a comb from her pocket, dragged it through her hair a few times and turned away, stooping to do something beyond his line of vision. When she straightened up again she was holding a large parcel, tied cross-wise with string. She looked around again, her head up, peering between the trees and sheltering leaves and again seeming to find Marcus, staring straight into his eyes before her gaze moved on and she decided she was alone.

She took off her sandals. From the parcel she took a pair of blue jeans, which she wriggled into with some difficulty. Then the dress came off.

Marcus caught his breath and found that he was grinning. Mmm, she *had* grown up! She was as thin as a wafer, but very much the right shape: 'broad where a broad should be broad', as the song had it.

The jeans had been shrunk to their limits and, in spite of having virtually no stomach to suck in, Claudia sucked, stretched herself upright, held her breath and fought with the zip until she was blue in the face. But Marcus wasn't exactly looking at her face. Although her breasts were small they responded very nicely to all this stretching and wriggling, and when the zip finally did its stuff, leaving Claudia gasping for breath . . . No, it was by no means the worst thing to have happened to Marcus that day.

A cheap white Sloppy Joe sweater was next out of the parcel and the covering up of Claudia's front view was amply compensated for when she bent over to pull on a pair of low-heeled pumps, giving him a charming view of her denim-clad rear. She rummaged again, and this time came up with a plastic sponge bag, full of cosmetics.

Marcus's eyes widened again – this time with horror – as she slapped the stuff on. She had a marvellous complexion, an all-over honey-colour, relieved by faint touches of pink, but she covered it all with thick pancake make-up in a ghastly shade of putty, streaking it over her throat so that her neck suddenly looked dirty. She applied lipstick and mascara and then twisted her hair into an elastic band, producing a jaunty little pony-tail which swung like a pendulum just level with the tips of her ears.

It was an amazing transformation. She'd aged from thirteen to eighteen in about five minutes – and God only knew what she intended to do with it now she'd got it! The only thing Marcus was sure of as she parcelled up her discarded clothing was that James and Cath Murray knew nothing about it. Claudia had left the house a little girl, and no doubt she'd return a few hours from now the same little girl – but who would she be in the meantime? And, more to the point, with whom?

The parcel – now containing her dress and discarded sandals – disappeared. Claudia jammed her thumbs into the front pockets of her jeans, gave her pony-tail an experimental twitch, and sauntered away, swinging her hips in a ridiculously expert fashion. Marcus's heart was racing again, although not with anger. Mrs Chislett had been right . . . Claudia was on the loose and hunting for trouble; the sort which came all too easily, like windfalls from a tree.

Marcus shrugged and massaged his calf-muscles, which were beginning to stiffen after their long march. Claudia

Murray was none of his business. He didn't care what she got up to.

Neither – a small voice suggested at the back of his mind – did anyone else.

He frowned. He stood up. He turned in a circle and shoved his hands in his pockets. A few minutes later he was racing down the drive, trying to cut her off.

But he'd left it too late. By the time he crossed the cattle grid she'd already met up with her friends: Diane Bridges, Eddie Tinknell and another boy whom Marcus didn't know. But Eddie was seventeen, and the chances were that his friend (a Cliff Richard look-alike with five pounds of Brylcreem in his hair) was roughly the same age – and rampant.

Marcus knew about rampant. He also knew about Watery Lane, which was where they appeared to be going. No one lived down Watery Lane. It was deeply secluded, wild and lovely, with grassy little hollows beside the stream just big enough for two to snuggle up in. In August, when the nights were drawing in and the stars at their brightest, you could walk down Watery Lane and hear, 'Hush! Someone's coming!' hissed from every hollow along the way.

Marcus sighed. She was only a kid. So was Diane Bridges; but that, somehow, was different. 'Simple village folk' like Noddy and Mrs Nod had simple ideas about morality. They deemed their daughters perfect until they came home pregnant, and then wondered where they'd gone wrong. But Claudia's family wasn't like that. If Madge hadn't died, if James had been in his right mind, if old Mrs Murray had even guessed what her granddaughter was up to, there'd be hell to pay.

He went back to the woods, to the clearing where Claudia had changed her clothes. Her parcel was stuffed into a hole between the roots of a tree. Marcus took it out, stared at it for a moment and smiled. Then he reached up and hid it in the fork of the tree.

Hunger forced Marcus to make a move for home several times during the next few hours, but he couldn't quite get there. The very thought of meeting his father – even passing him in silence on the stairs – made his heart pound with renewed rage. He began to think that only a fist-fight would cure him. A good, solid punch to the end of Ben's nose . . . And one in the stomach for luck.

If it could have ended there, he might have done it; but he knew it wouldn't end there. Marcus was not a hot-blooded fighter; once he began he went stone cold, taking an almost technical pleasure from the conflict. He wouldn't be satisfied with one punch or two. He'd be satisfied only when he'd won; and you couldn't win a fight with a man who'd rather die than admit defeat. All you could do with a man like that was get yourself hanged.

And so, rather against his inclination, Marcus found himself waiting for Claudia. He'd hidden her clothes on a whim born of his rage but as the evening grew older and the scent of the bluebells stronger, a soft, peaceful feeling came over him, and his fury seemed spent. It didn't matter. He'd lived in fear all his life of losing the farm, but he'd known in his heart that he *would* lose it, just because Ben had wanted it that way. And Ben had prepared him for the loss. He'd given him an alternative. Perhaps he'd never wanted him to accept the alternative, for without Marcus to back him up, Ellis would go broke and lose everything, given time.

And, given time, Marcus would take a first class degree and a PhD, get a job in pharmaceuticals, textiles, petrochemicals . . . In America, perhaps? Yes, perhaps. And by the time he was thirty, thirty-five, he could buy Ellis out

. . . Perhaps. All was not lost. It had just slipped a little way out of his grasp. And he hadn't lost his temper: ditto. That was something to be proud of. That was a strength he had held, and *would* hold from now on. The buggers wouldn't shift him from that.

It was almost dark when Claudia returned, crashing through the woods like a frightened steer, gasping for breath. It was half-past nine, and Marcus guessed she was about to miss her curfew, for she exhibited none of the caution which had marked her first disrobing. In fact, her sweater had come off and she was half way out of her jeans before she stopped running. The button flipped, the zip unzipped, the waist-band shimmied down to reveal – incongruously – a pair of navy-blue gym knickers and a luminous flash of thigh.

She hopped about on one leg, trying to yank the jeans off by the ankles, whispering, 'Oh, hell! Oh, damn! Oh *sugar*!' before giving up the attempt and sitting down among the bluebells.

Marcus grinned but held his peace until, with a frustrated little shriek, she hobbled herself: one leg off, one leg on. Then with his hands in his pockets, he sauntered out into the clearing.

'Good evening, Claudia.'

'*Shit*!' Claudia said.

Rage slammed against Marcus's chest like a hammer-blow, making him gasp. He wanted to kill her! Not because she had sworn at him, not even for the look of cold hatred he saw in her eyes, but just because he wanted to kill *someone*, and Claudia was there!

'What did you say?' he whispered.

'I said *shit*. That's what you *are*, isn't it?' She curled her lip, bared her teeth; and the rope of Marcus's temper frayed a little more, slipping beyond his control. Claudia had abandoned her attempt to escape her jeans and hadn't even tried to escape Marcus. She just sat there, arms folded contemptuously, facing him out with all the insolence of a street-corner whore.

'You *bitch*!' His eyes filled with blood, his ears with thunder; and although Claudia had been on the far side of the clearing – yards away – she was suddenly between his hands, and he was shaking her like a rat. There was no question of her escaping, protesting or retaliating. He was almost a foot taller than she was and ten times stronger, and this fact alone was enough to give him a surge of pleasure; for here was someone he *could* beat, and *wanted* to beat, if only because she hated him.

'Little slut!'

The thunder in his ears suddenly ceased, bringing his voice back to him, terrifying him with its fury. He turned cold and set her down, but his fingers seemed welded to her arms. He couldn't let go.

Claudia was crying. 'Let me go!' she wailed. 'Please!'

'Shut up!'

Dear God, he had to control himself! He had to stop. And one more word out of Claudia would be the end of both of them. He was still raging but he was ashamed of himself, too, not merely for exerting his strength on a kid half his size but for breaking the resolution he'd made only minutes ago to keep a hold on his temper!

'Please!' She twisted and writhed under the locked grip of his hands. 'You're hurting me!'

'Good.' But his fingers loosened a little and Claudia stood still, trembling and whimpering with shock.

'Do you know what happens to girls like you, Claudia?' he asked coldly.

'I didn't mean what I said! I was – '

'Shut up and listen! I know where you've been and who you've been with. I know what you've been up to, Claudia!'

'No! No, I didn't – '

'And if *I* know, you can bet your life a few other people know! Do you imagine they won't tell your father? Is that what you want? Hasn't he had enough trouble? Don't you care?'

He shook her again, less roughly than before; but again he felt a strange surge of pleasure. She was such a pretty thing . . . Delicate, fragile, soft – and almost naked, her skin glowing like moonlight in the shadows. And she was so small, so frightened now; her dark eyes bleak with a misery which he, if he chose, could relieve for a short while. He could soothe her. He could comfort her. He could do anything he liked with her.

'*No*, Marcus.'

His eyes widened. Claudia hadn't spoken; yet the voice was a girl's, as real as his own and defined with perfect clarity. He blinked and his rage left him. He released Claudia's arms and turned away, shaking with reaction.

'Get dressed,' he said quietly. 'Go home. And leave your glad rags behind. You won't be needing them again.'

'But they're Diane's!'

'Then I'll give them to her father. Perhaps that'll put a stop to her game as well as yours.'

Claudia was still crying, but he heard her scuffling around in the undergrowth; and then: 'Oh, God! Where are my clothes?'

Marcus had forgotten her clothes. He threw the parcel down from its hiding place, not looking at her. Not daring to look at her.

'Girls like you get a bad reputation, Claudia. They bring shame on their families and misery to themselves. What would your mother think of you? She'd break her heart – '

'She's *dead*!' Claudia wailed.

'That doesn't mean she can't see you!' He shivered, remembering the voice he had heard in his mind. Callie's voice.

'And it doesn't mean she doesn't care,' he added softly. 'You can't lie to the dead, Claudia. They *know*.'

Marcus went home through the garden to avoid disturbing the dogs. The hall light was on, but otherwise the house was in darkness; and he breathed a prayer of gratitude.

All he wanted now was peace – and something to eat. He was feeling slightly frayed at the edges after his run-in with Claudia. Frayed but triumphant. Frayed but relieved. She was only a kid. Nicely put together, of course; and, as Mrs Chislett had said, past a certain point in a girl's life, age didn't matter – unless a policeman caught you at it. Still, he would never have expected to be so aroused by a kid of thirteen, especially one named Claudia Murray! God, what a confusing day . . .

He tip-toed through to the kitchen, gasping with shock as Liz, looking small and ghostly in a long white nightdress, tip-toed out of it, clutching an empty tumbler. She gasped too, and then laughed softly. 'God, you scared me!' She touched his arm. 'You all right?'

'Yes. You?'

'Fine.'

Marcus noticed, even in near darkness, that the hand holding the tumbler had crept out of sight among the folds of her nightdress.

'Oh, well,' he said cynically. 'I suppose I was lying, too. Give me the glass. I know how you like it.'

She leaned backwards against the door-jamb, sighing. 'Oh, Marcus, what a rotten life.'

'Oh, Liz, what an understatement.'

She laughed again and gave him the glass. 'Neat, please,' she murmured. 'Will you have one?'

'Not while there's a full moon, thanks.'

'But there isn't.' She smiled, but her smile was wary, as if the idea of Marcus as werewolf wasn't all that far-fetched.

'Put the kettle on,' he said briskly.

They sat at the kitchen table in companionable silence while Marcus ploughed through the remains of a cold chicken pie, a stack of ham sandwiches and three mugs of coffee.

'You seem very calm,' Liz said at length.

'You seem very surprised.'

She smiled wanly. 'I am. I've never seen you so angry.'

'Who, me? I didn't say a word!'

'That's what I meant. I thought you were going to dispense with words completely and just kill someone. Ellis for preference.'

'Ellis?' Marcus frowned, suddenly realising that he hadn't been angry with his brother at all. 'No, funnily enough . . . No.'

Liz watched him. 'Makes a change,' she murmured suspiciously.

'Yes. It's been a day of revelations.' He blinked, remembering Claudia and pushing the thought away again. She had revealed more to him tonight than her body; but he wanted to deal with one thing at a time, sort it into some kind of order. 'I've been using Ellis as a whipping boy,' he said. 'But Dad's messed him up, too, hasn't he?'

'Too?' Liz wrinkled her nose and stared into her glass. 'I don't know, Marcus. I begin to think he hasn't messed *you* up at all.'

'That's what I'm beginning to think, too. You know, I suppose, that Ellis won't make a farmer? Ten years from now . . .'

'Hmm?' She finished her drink. 'Can I have another, or will you tell on me?'

She sounded tired and hopeless; and Marcus closed his eyes briefly, hating himself. Christ, how selfish could anyone get? For a short while, he'd completely forgotten Callie, yet they'd only buried her yesterday!

He took Liz's glass, refilled it from the decanter in the dining room and returned to find her sitting with her chin in her hands, staring into space.

'Liz.' He touched her shoulder and she turned into him, resting her head on his chest. She was crying.

'Liz, do you believe in an after-life?'

'Yes,' she sobbed. 'And no. Yes, because I want to believe she's . . . happy somewhere; and no, because it's too bloody good to be true!'

'Same here. But we don't know, and because we don't, we have to behave as if it *is* true, and that she's still with us, aware of us, caring about us . . . And watching us. She was with me tonight, Liz, I'm certain of it. I heard her voice. She kept me from doing something . . .' He sucked in a breath through his teeth. 'Something terrible.'

'Terrible? How terrible?'

Marcus laughed. 'You're too young to know.'

Liz's arms tightened around his waist. 'Oh, I wish I was! I feel so old, Marcus!'

He stroked her hair, gently fingering it clear of her eyes. 'Nonsense. You look about sixteen. Especially in that nightdress, with your hair loose.' He shut his eyes and would have moved away had Liz not been leaning on him. What the hell was he saying? What was he doing? What was he *thinking*? She was his aunt, not a girl! She was thirty-nine, not sixteen! But he couldn't turn away now. She needed him.

'Hey,' he said gently. 'Have some Horlicks. It'll do you

more good than this stuff. Just because it's called Teacher's doesn't make it educational, you know.'

Liz giggled and blew her nose. 'Don't ever leave home,' she whispered. 'I'd go mad without you. You make me laugh.'

'Oh, thanks.'

'And you give good advice.'

She sighed, sniffed and gave her whisky an apologetic glance. Then she stood up and poured it down the sink. 'If Callie's watching,' she said, 'she won't want to see me turning into a soak, will she?'

'No, she'll hate it. So shall I make you some Horlicks?'

'Cocoa. And tell me what you nearly did, but didn't, because my daughter was keeping her beady eye on you.'

'It was Claudia Murray.'

Liz's mouth dropped open. 'Marcus! You didn't!'

'No. I told you I didn't. But she was incredibly rude to me, which made me . . . incredibly angry. Mrs Chislett's right about that kid. She's gone off the rails.'

'But she's *always* been rude to you!' Liz laughed. 'I remember her throwing stones at you when she was just a tot!'

'Yes. But she threw stones because she was scared of me. She wasn't scared tonight. She was cold, brazen and vicious. She didn't give a damn.' He laughed bitterly. 'Poor kid. And it was the first time in her life she damn well *should* have been scared. I'd taken all day to work off my temper, and it didn't take much to set me off again. *And* I was starving. That didn't help.'

'So what happened?'

'I'm not really sure. I went mad for a moment. Everything went hazy.'

'*Marcus*?'

He laughed softly. Liz was thinking the worst, which meant, for once, that she wasn't thinking about Callie. Still, even to hold her interest it might be better not to mention that Claudia had been half naked at the time!

'I yelled at her,' he said. 'I don't remember what I said. And I shook her. If she'd been strong enough to retaliate, I'm fairly sure I would have slapped her; but it suddenly crossed my mind that I was using her the way I've used Ellis: as a whipping boy. I wanted to hit Dad, and Claudia just got in the way.'

Liz's mouth dropped open. 'And you say she wasn't *scared*?'

'Not at first. She changed her mind later.'

'Who could blame her?' Liz remarked hollowly.

'And she looked so sweet.' Marcus laughed again. 'I wanted to kiss it better, if you know what I mean. I couldn't 'elp meself, officer. It just come over me, sudden-like.'

Liz's eyes were as wide as saucers. 'And Callie stopped you?' she whispered.

'Yes.' He smiled and passed Liz her mug of cocoa. 'What did Mrs Chislett give you yesterday?'

'It – it's a little pressed violet in a silver frame. An old locket, I think, without the cover.' Liz gulped back a throatful of tears. 'Wasn't that good of her?'

'Very good. But she *is* very good. Underneath.'

'Like you,' Liz murmured. 'I do love you, Marcus.'

Marcus lowered his eyes. How did she mean that? However she meant it, the feeling was dangerously mutual. And he couldn't live with that. He couldn't handle it. Neither could Liz.

'Thank God someone does,' he said briskly. 'Hey, I'm still hungry. Is there any cake in the tin?'

Marcus did not go home again until his exams were over: an exercise in discretion which was successful only for as long as it lasted. He was still angry with his father, grieved about Callie and worried about Liz, but he thought he was managing to drive all these things from his mind, subduing them, learning patience.

Yet an hour after he'd slammed the last full stop into place on his last examination paper, he found that he was as angry, as grieved and as worried as ever. The thought of speaking to Ben made him feel sick. The thought of walking through the empty spaces of the house, where Callie had been, made him ache with misery. As for Liz . . . And Tom . . . Not to mention Ellis!

And there was nothing he could do about any of it, save wait – and hope. Have patience. Christ, *patience*! It was all very well to *know* that patience and wisdom were virtually synonymous; quite another to believe it! He didn't feel very wise. He felt helpless. And helplessness just made him feel angrier, sadder, more worried than ever.

He cleaned the flat, packed his things and went home, his teeth firmly gritted. He'd chosen to arrive soon after four, when he could be certain that the men would be busy with the milking, giving him time to settle in before he'd have to face them.

'Settling in' had always been important to him; and now that he came to think of it, it had been important for precisely the reason it was important now. For every member of the family (even poor Callie) had provoked different responses in him. They'd had different expectations of him, so that he never felt he could be completely himself with anyone. They broke him up into his component parts: gentle, violent, warm, cold . . . Loving and hating.

But the worst was over. He knew what to expect from Ben now, and although the knowledge was painful, it was at least *knowledge*, which was a good deal less painful than hope. No, he'd never ask anything of Ben again; he'd never be disappointed again; and perhaps that meant he *could* be himself from now on.

He found this thought strangely soothing; and his approach to Larcombe worked the usual magic on his spirits, so that, in spite of everything, he arrived home with a smile on his face – a smile which disappeared as soon as he opened the kitchen door.

The table was piled with unwashed crockery; the floor was dirty; and his mother was sitting among the wreckage, calmly smoking a cigarette.

'Oh, hello.' Her smile was the same as usual: rather vague, rather cool, but she did not look the same as usual. Her eyes were empty.

'What's going on?' Marcus asked frigidly.

'Nothing. Nothing at all. How were your exams?'

'Fine. Did you have lunch late?'

'No.' She sighed heavily. 'No. Dead on time. As usual.'

Marcus let his gaze drift pointedly over the mess. 'Then what's all this? It's gone four, Mother.'

'Hmm. Yes. Yes, I suppose it is.' She sighed again. 'Doesn't time fly?'

Marcus dumped his bags in the corner, rolled up his sleeves and began grimly to wash the dishes. 'Mother,' he said, 'you never smoke in the kitchen.'

'Not usually, no.'

'So what's different? What's changed? What the hell's wrong?'

'I'm tired, that's all.'

'Where's Liz?'

She shrugged and said nothing.

'Where's Liz?' Marcus insisted.

'I don't know. Probably out. Might be upstairs. Could be anywhere.'

'Did she have lunch?'

'No.'

'Did she help cook it?'

'No. She's grieving, Marcus. There's nothing to do with her except leave her alone.'

Marcus sighed. She was probably right, but the house was too big and the family too hungry for one woman to manage alone: especially when that woman was his mother. It wasn't that she wasn't competent, just that she hadn't much . . . Whatever it was: spirit, motivation, or perhaps just confidence. She was like Tom in a way: very good at cooperating, but no good at all at taking the lead. And what had Mrs Chislett said about her?

He turned back to the table to fetch the meat dish. 'You're grieving too, aren't you?' he asked quietly; and his mother averted her face and stared at the dresser.

'We all are,' she said sullenly. Then, her voice hardening: 'But only some of us are allowed to show it. She wasn't *my* daughter.'

'Did Liz say that?'

'No.' Helen stood up and snatched a teacloth from the Aga rail. Marcus had never known her to lose her temper; when she was angry she just snatched at things, flounced a little, slammed the occasional door.

He smiled. 'Let yourself go, Mother,' he teased gently. 'Say it. Get it off your chest.'

Helen snatched up a plate, gave it a cursory wipe and slammed it down on the table. 'Oh, leave me alone!' she said.

Liz was sitting at the top of Old Barrow, hugging her knees. She hadn't been crying but her eyes looked like Helen's eyes: empty and dull, and it wasn't until Marcus made the comparison that he realised how deeply his mother was grieving.

He sat down. He surveyed the view. He said nothing. After a while, Liz leaned against him and patted his hand. 'Thanks,' she murmured.

'For what?'

'Understanding.'

Marcus kept his peace, although he had a feeling it wouldn't last. Yes, he understood. He understood that Liz couldn't function any more; that all her energies were centred on herself, her loss, her grief, and that no one else existed for her. She was like James Murray which probably meant that he understood James Murray, too, and, for the first time in his life, truly pitied him. But that didn't make it right. People could exist in a vacuum for only so long; but it was long enough for those who supported them in the meantime to drop dead, go mad, wear themselves out – or just go off the rails as Claudia had done.

'My mother would have liked a daughter,' he said pensively. 'But she didn't. All she had was Callie. Callie was all Tom had, too.'

Liz jerked her head from his shoulder and turned to face him. Her eyes weren't empty any more. They were as sharp as needles.

'No,' she hissed. '*I* had Callie. She was a part of *me*!'

Marcus's heart began to thud: partly with anger – but mostly with fear. He had no answers to mother-love. They said it was different from any other kind, and since he would never be in a position to prove otherwise, he'd do better to keep his mouth shut and go home. But he almost hated her. What was so wonderful about her grief that she wanted to keep it to herself and let no one share it? And how dare she imply that *his* grief was nothing, Tom's nothing, Helen's – *nothing*?

He stood up and walked away, and was half-way down the hill before she screamed after him, 'No! Oh, Marcus! *Please*!'

He turned, but he made no move to go back. There seemed to be no point. As Helen had said, there was nothing to do with Liz except leave her alone.

'Don't leave me!' She was crying, stumbling downhill to join him. 'I – I've been waiting for you!'

'Waiting?'

She fell into his arms, sobbing like a child. 'You loved her too!'

'Liz . . .' He caught her by the elbows and gently pushed her away; but she clung to him, forcing herself closer.

'Stop,' he said quietly. 'Stop, Liz. Only one person loved her as you do, and that's her father.'

She drew away, her eyes wide now, wounded and bewildered. 'But I hate him,' she whispered.

'You hate everyone, Liz.' Again he turned away, but she caught his arm, clawing at it as if it were the proverbial last straw in wild, drowning sea.

'No,' she sobbed. 'I love *you*.'

He'd been half-expecting it, but it still shocked him rigid; if only because, until now, her feelings hadn't been entirely unreciprocated. They had grown too close, talked too intimately; and he'd needed her dependency on him, he'd needed her trust – and her love. But not this kind of love!

He shut his eyes and threw back his head, thinking of Callie, hearing her voice in the woods. And his own. *You can't lie to the dead.*

Yes, he had wanted Liz. But only . . . only in his fantasies. Then he could transform her, rejuvenate her, detach her from the realities of her life and make her perfect. And she wasn't perfect. She was more than twice his age. She was *old*.

He said nothing, but guessed that his feelings were written clearly in his eyes, for after staring at him a moment, Liz turned scarlet and hid her face in her hands.

'Liz . . . please.'

'Go away!'

She sat down and rocked herself back and forth, uttering a low, moaning sound deep in her throat. He desperately wanted to do as she'd said – go away, as far as he could get – but he didn't dare leave her now. Anything could happen. She could go mad, run amok, kill herself – and it was all his fault. *Shit*! Why couldn't he have left her alone?

He seemed to stand there for hours. Then, almost as if nothing had happened, Liz dragged her hands from her face and folded them gently in her lap.

'Well,' she said flatly, 'you've done it again.'

'Done what?'

She looked up at him and smiled wanly. 'I'm not really sure, but you made a lovely job of it. I think I'm all right now, if you want to go home.'

'I'd be happier if you came with me.'

She thought about it. 'Hmph,' she said at last. 'Your grandfather's right about you. You're like a bloody old sheepdog: never happy until all the lambs are in the fold.'

'There's nothing wrong with that, is there?'

She smiled bitterly. 'But I'm no lamb, am I? I'm mutton.'

Marcus sucked in his cheeks, took a deep breath. 'Not until you're dead,' he said grimly. 'And you're not dead, Liz. Callie is. You can't change that, however much you think about it.'

'No.' Liz adjusted the strap of her sandal with shaking fingers. She stood up and brushed the dust from her skirt.

Marcus offered her his arm, but she flinched and drew away, and they walked home with a yard of space between them.

It felt like a hundred miles.

Chapter Eleven

It was almost ten o'clock. Bats flittered in the shadows and a bird sang a sweet, rippling song somewhere nearby. But the peace of the churchyard had not soothed Daniel Murray's spirits. He gazed into his mother's cold, white marble face with deep resentment, hating her for deserting him in his hour of need. Hating her for *creating* his hour of need: an hour which seemed to stretch into the dark reaches of his future and contain nothing but grief.

He was going to end up like his father, after all. Bow-legged and bitter, ever railing against the cruelty of Fate.

He wept, letting the tears slide down his face unhindered. He hadn't a handkerchief, and was about to wipe his nose on his sleeve when the little picket gate creaked open at the foot of the churchyard steps.

Dreading a meeting with anyone alive (the dead at least didn't nag), Daniel slid a little further into the shadows, not even daring to sniff in case the intruder heard him. He was half expecting to see Claudia, but the head that appeared above the well of the steps was a dark one. A dark face set on a long, muscular neck and lean, square shoulders.

Daniel let out a sigh and felt his face turning pink with embarrassment. Of all the people in the world he didn't want to see at a moment like this, Marcus Saxon was the worst. Daniel couldn't imagine Marcus wiping his nose on his sleeve, or wearing shrunken grey flannels which flapped around his ankles like rags on a clothes line. Even when he was fetching the cows, Marcus always looked clean and neat; and tonight he looked even smarter than usual in cream cotton slacks and a soft, blue-checked shirt. He was carrying a bunch of white roses.

Callie. Her grave was still unmarked, but there was an old stone jug for the flowers. Marcus pulled out the dead ones, poured out the stale water and went to the stand-pipe behind the church to fill the jug for his roses. Then he stood for a few minutes, just looking at them, looking at Callie sleeping under the ground.

Mrs Chislett had said that Marcus had been devoted to his cousin, and Daniel could believe it; could imagine, too, that she had been devoted to him. He had always been very kind to Daniel, very warm, as if it had touched him to find one Murray among the bunch who didn't hold grudges for forty-odd years.

But they hadn't met very often, and not once since Madge had died thirteen months ago. Now they were both bereaved, although Daniel didn't suppose Callie's death could have left nearly so much havoc for the Saxons as his mother's had done for the Murrays.

It was impossible to appreciate a mother properly until she was dead. You just didn't notice all the things she did, let alone the things she didn't do. Like nag. Moan. Weep. Shriek. Slam doors. And forget to put salt in the potatoes.

Marcus moved suddenly, stooping to pick up the bunch of discarded flowers from Callie's grave and strolling down the grassy path to throw them on the rubbish heap. It was almost dark now. He hadn't seen Daniel and would fall over him if he didn't move.

Daniel moved. He drew his knees up to his chin, that was all, but the effect was electric.

'*Jesus Christ!*' Marcus rocked up on his toes, clutching his heart. The dead flowers flew around his head like autumn leaves, the dripping stems staining his shirt.

'Sorry,' Daniel murmured. 'I should have said something.'

Marcus blew out a long, relieved breath and laughed softly. 'Never mind. Shock's a terrific cure for hiccups.'

'Did you have hiccups?'

'No, but if I had I'd be cured.' He glanced to his left, his smile fading as he saw Madge's name on the white marble slab across the path.

'You all right?' he asked softly.

'Yes. Fine. Just . . . having a few words, you know, with . . .'

'Yes, I know. Me, too.'

'I'm sorry about Callie.'

'Thank you. She was a lovely kid. It's strange how the best people are the ones . . . They say the good die young. Seems an excellent reason for being thoroughly evil, doesn't it?'

'No,' Daniel said softly. 'It sounds like a perfect reason for being good.'

Marcus was silent. He stood for a moment looking down at Daniel's bent head, and then sat beside him, plucking a stem of long grass from a nearby grave and chewing it thoughtfully.

'Things pretty bad, then?' he asked.

'Mm.' Daniel averted his face to hide another rush of tears and then remembered that Marcus couldn't see him anyway: it was too dark. 'I leave school next Friday,' he murmured.

'Oh? How come?'

'I don't seem to have much choice. John's home for the summer – '

'What's he doing?'

'Engineering. Electrical. Manchester.'

'Long way from home,' Marcus remarked softly. 'Bristol's got a terrific engineering department.'

'Yes. But he wanted to get away. We've both felt a bit guilty about not wanting to take Murray's on, although Dad's never said anything about it. When Mum died – '

He bit his lip on the rest, feeling sadder than ever. It would be good to talk to someone, but Marcus wasn't the one. He was so calm and sophisticated, so superior; and he was, after all, the enemy. Not Daniel's enemy, but the enemy just the same.

Daniel laughed shortly. 'Oh, well. I suppose everyone's got problems. It's time I was going home, anyway.'

But he didn't get up.

Neither did Marcus. 'Get it off your chest if you'd like to. I wasn't doing anything.'

'You have to be up at the crack of dawn though, don't you?'

'No, I've given up farming . . . for a while, at least. That's why I came here: saying goodbye for a few months. I'm going away tomorrow. Paris, Rome, Florence . . . Doing the Grand Tour, my father calls it . . . I call it the Great Escape.'

'What are you escaping from?'

Marcus shrugged. 'Grief, I suppose.'

'You can't escape that,' Daniel murmured.

'Not my own, no. But I can cope with that. Other people's is harder to bear though, isn't it?'

A sigh escaped Daniel's lips. 'You're lucky,' he said softly. 'Oh, God, I'd love to . . . Well, you know. Escape.'

He felt Marcus's eyes on his face, but didn't look up. Envy burned in his chest; and although he knew it was envy, it felt exactly the same as grief. In that moment he understood how James felt about the Saxons. They were so strong, so confident, so – rich. When things got too much for them, they could just flit off to Paris, shake it off, forget it. They had the means to wake from their nightmares.

'I'll write to you, shall I?' Marcus offered.

Daniel smiled. 'Better not. My nan'd have a fit. She's not very good at minding her own business.'

'Hmm. Grandmothers are all the same. What were you saying about John?'

'John? Oh, only that he doesn't want to help Dad with the business. He's wanted to do engineering ever since he was little.' He shrugged. 'So it looks as if . . . I think I'll have to . . . Well, I've decided, anyway. It isn't just that Dad needs someone to help, it's – '

'Hmm?'

'Well, I don't see how I can put the work in for another two years. If I've passed my O-levels it'll be a miracle. My nan, you see, can't really cope. She does the books for Dad, writes all the letters, does the housework and cooking – and by the time I get home from school she's done for. So I can't *not* fetch the coal or wash the dishes, can I? It wouldn't be fair.'

'No . . .'

'And . . . my dad doesn't care much any more. If he doesn't have someone to back him up, I think he'll just let everything go. I suppose he's got a fair bit of capital, but I don't know. I know we're not rich. So what'll happen to us if he loses the business?'

'Think he could afford to get a good man in?' Marcus asked.

'God, d'you think I haven't thought of that? *I* don't want to be a market gardener, for Christ's sake! I want . . .'

He sighed heavily. No, there was no sense in thinking of that. Some people could do what they wanted with their lives. Marcus could. Daniel couldn't. There was no way around it, and no point in trying to find one.

'There aren't any good men,' he said. 'There've never been any.' He laughed bitterly. 'I think it might have something to do with Dad. He's never trusted anyone, and when you don't trust people they lose interest and go somewhere else. And now, of course, people don't need the work. Not this kind of work. It's hard, it's dirty, the hours are . . . Well, it's probably the same for you.'

'Yes,' Marcus said. 'But if we wanted a farm *manager*, someone to direct the whole operation, we could get one. Have you thought of that? Not someone local. A man with qualifications and experience, someone who wants a business of his own but hasn't the land or the capital to get started.' He paused and shook his head. 'No, that wouldn't work. If your father wouldn't trust him – '

'Oh, he doesn't care what happens now. I've done thousands of things for him, and he doesn't check. He doesn't even notice. And I don't really know what I'm doing. It doesn't mean anything to me. Even Claudia knows more about it than I do.'

He swallowed and closed his eyes. To spend the rest of his life doing something he hated? No, no. Oh, no.

There was something frantic in his voice when he spoke again. 'But how do you *get* a man like that? What do you do? Advertise?'

Marcus laughed and rolled flat on his back on the grass. '*Other* people advertise,' he said. '*We* just tell old Ma Chislett. Tell her, and I bet within a fortnight you'll have some chap ringing up to ask for an interview.'

He propped himself on his elbow and looked sideways into Daniel's face. 'Don't leave school, Daniel,' he advised softly. 'Life never turns out the way you expect, and things could change drastically in the next few years. Your father could sell up, for instance, and then you'd have nothing to fall back on, would you?'

'No,' Daniel whispered. 'I hadn't thought of that.'

'And tell Claudia to do the bloody washing up!'

Daniel stiffened and bit his lip. He spent virtually every waking moment worrying about Claudia, criticising Claudia, hating Claudia; but he didn't want anyone else to do it. Not even Marcus.

'She's only young,' he said defensively.

Marcus sat up and leaned forward to grasp Daniel's ankle, which he shook once and then released. 'Not young enough,' he said.

Daniel's heart began to thud. He turned his head, staring blindly into the shadows. 'What can I do?' he whispered. 'She won't listen to me. She just seems . . . She hates everyone, and I can understand that, Marcus. Sometimes I hate everyone, too. Even Mum. Sometimes I think . . . Sometimes I think she just got tired, and shook us all off because we were too much trouble. Mad, isn't it? My mum would have *died* rather than leave us like this!'

He laughed, stifling a sob. 'Oh, I know she didn't do it deliberately. I just – I just can't seem to stop blaming her! But Clo misses her, Marcus. She's lost without her.'

For a long while Marcus was silent, and Daniel thanked him in his heart, for he was near to breaking point again and needed time to recover.

'Have you talked to Mrs Chislett about it?' Marcus asked at last.

'About Claudia? Good God, no. She'd have it plastered all over the village in no time!'

'She's done that already. You've nothing to lose. Tell her. And if there's anything to be done, she'll help you do it.'

Marcus stood up, brushing the grass from his trousers, smoothing his hair, straightening his shirt. He bent to tousle Daniel's hair. 'And don't leave school. Promise.'

Daniel laughed, and immediately felt Marcus's fingers tighten on a thick lock of hair, tugging to hurt.

'*Promise*?'

'I can't! What if – ? *Hey*!' They were both laughing, but Marcus clearly meant to scalp him if he didn't promise; and there was something wonderful about that. It was the thing Daniel needed more than anything in the world: someone to care. 'Okay! Okay, I – *ouch*! I *promise*!'

Marcus released him and hurried away. His spine was as straight as a board, his head up, his shoulders set square; yet he walked as if he weighed nothing, his feet scarcely touching the ground. Daniel envied him that, for even before Madge had died he'd felt as if he walked with a burden on his shoulders. Then, the burden had been James. Now he seemed to be carrying everyone, everything, and it was a problem, sometimes, to summon strength enough to put one foot in front of the other, let alone keep his head up while he was doing it.

Marcus was half-way down the steps before he turned again, his face clearly lit by the moon. 'I can't stand people who break promises,' he said. 'And I'll be back in September, so watch it!'

It was crazy to have a nightmare about a colour but Claudia kept having it, and it was the kind of nightmare she couldn't forget when she woke up. It kept coming back at odd moments throughout the day, making her spine crawl, as if a goose had walked over her grave. Yet it was nothing! Just a strange, moving cloud of dirty yellow which covered her face and filled her mouth so that she couldn't even scream. That was the most awful thing about it: that she couldn't scream for help. She just had to suffer it. Alone.

She did everything alone these days, thanks to Marcus Saxon. He'd given Diane's jeans to Noddy Bridges, and Diane (little sneak!) had told her father that Claudia had left them in the woods. Mrs Nod had told Mrs Chislett;

Mrs Chislett had told Nan. And then all hell had broken loose. Claudia wasn't friends with Diane any more.

She hadn't liked her much, anyway. She was as thick as a plank. All she could talk about was film stars and boys. But she'd been company. She'd offered a few hours of escape from the dreariness of home. Now there was nothing. And all because of those bloody jeans!

But what was so wrong about wearing jeans? Claudia could, if she tried very hard, understand that it was wrong to wear make-up before you were sixteen, if only because Madge had told her it was. But Madge had never mentioned jeans. Jeans were one of Nan's silly ideas. She thought only 'tarts' wore jeans.

Claudia wasn't a tart! She wasn't a slut, either! Nor a dirty little slummock, nor a conniving, good-for-nothing little liar!

Well, yes, she'd told one or two (perhaps three or four) lies about that night, but what did they expect? The *truth*?

Yet even the truth wasn't worth all the trouble it had caused.

Do you know what happens to girls like you?

Christ! She hadn't even *kissed* Robert Baxter! They'd talked about his motorbike all night – the one he didn't have yet because he wasn't old enough. Claudia had been bored stiff, and would have gone home if she hadn't promised to wait for Diane.

The school bus crested the top of Larcombe hill and wound slowly downwards, its brakes squealing. It was the last day of term. Claudia had the entire summer holiday to look forward to. Eight weeks of Nan's company. Eight weeks of hell.

Going home . . . It was like falling into deep water, sinking into darkness. Madge wasn't there any more.

Claudia had ceased to look for her; but in the days when

she had looked – and been disappointed – a sick, empty feeling had overcome her as she'd clambered off the bus; and that feeling had remained with her. It didn't make her cry any more. It just made everything seem pointless, useless and ugly.

Diane Bridges had helped her to forget that, for a while. She'd brought some excitement into Claudia's life, made it feel thrilling, even a little dangerous. And when life was dangerous Claudia had wanted to come through it unscathed, she'd wanted to stay alive. Now she didn't. Even the old, creepy feeling she used to have when she crossed the bridge wasn't there any more. She didn't care.

Yet as Claudia approached the bridge, determinedly not caring, her step faltered and her large grey eyes widened in dismay. Diane Bridges and her sister Carol were standing in the passing place, and although they seemed oblivious to Claudia's approach she knew they were waiting for her.

Diane hadn't believed a word Claudia had said about Marcus Saxon. She thought Claudia had abandoned her jeans to the elements, and it had just been a stroke of luck that Marcus had 'found' them, and so 'kindly' returned them to Noddy.

'Thirty bloody bob them jeans cost our ma!' Diane had shrieked. 'And she ain't half so well-off as some ungrateful little snobs we could mention! Well, you can buy your own bloody jeans in future, Claudia Murray, because you ain't lending mine off *me* again!'

Stupid bitch. Common, ignorant little cow. And Carol was as bad. Carol was bigger, too . . .

Claudia settled her school satchel on her hip and sauntered over the bridge as if she hadn't noticed the waiting ambush. Diane giggled and covered her mouth with her hand. Carol leaned backwards against the parapet and casually began to whistle.

Claudia's heart thumped. She told herself they couldn't hurt her. She was beyond being hurt, now. She was numb. She didn't care.

'Hiya, Clo,' Carol said pleasantly.

'Hi.' Claudia managed a stiff-lipped smile, but she kept her eyes on Mrs Chislett's bedroom window on the far side of the bridge. As she came level with the girls, Diane fell into step beside her, leaving Carol behind.

'Want to forget it, then?' Diane smiled. 'Want to make friends?'

Claudia smiled with relief. And then, from behind her, Carol shrieked with laughter and knocked her hat sideways, over the parapet, into the river.

'Don't worry, Clo!' she chortled mockingly. 'I speck Marcus Saxon'll bring it back!'

Claudia walked on at the same steady pace, pretending not to notice that anything was amiss. But it felt even worse than being shaken and yelled at by Marcus Saxon. She'd been terrified then; but, in a strange sort of way, she'd enjoyed being terrified, and she'd thought about it since almost with longing.

He'd yelled at her, shaken her, almost lifted her off her feet; and there'd been nothing she could do to stop him. There'd been no point in being brave, no point trying to keep her head up and her nose in the air. It had been so easy to cry, to give in, to surrender. But it was the hardest thing in the world to pretend you didn't care!

'What the dickens d'you mean, it fell in the river?'

Catherine Murray's face was an all-over shade of pink, her faded blue eyes snapping with irritation. Her hands were wet, and she wiped them on her apron and snatched Claudia's hat from her hand.

'Look at it!'

Claudia looked at it from under insolently drooping eyelids, letting her gaze roam wearily to the kitchen floor, which – she noticed vaguely – wasn't all that clean.

'It'll dry out,' she offered dully.

'Yes! Dry out of shape and stinking of drains! Do you know how much these hats cost? Do you? No! And you care less! D'you think your father works and slaves just to keep you in new hats? And *look* at me when I'm speaking to you, or I'll give you such a flop . . . !'

Claudia raised her eyes and ground her molars together, trying to keep a grip on her temper. She knew that to hit one's grandmother was to go beyond the pale, but sometimes . . .

Hit her? She wanted to kill her – especially when she 'flopped' Claudia across the face with a wet dishcloth. It hurt. It also stank of cabbage, and usually came with a liberal helping of tea-leaves and shreds of wire wool. Had Claudia not already worked up an abiding hatred of the old woman, the wet dishcloth would have completed the job with no trouble at all.

'It fell in the river,' she said wearily. 'I couldn't help it, Nan. The wind – '

'Liar! Little liar! There's not a breath of wind!'

She made a lunge towards the draining board, and Claudia stepped backwards, colliding with the dropped shelf of the kitchen cabinet where a precariously balanced heap of dirty plates and mixing bowls had been waiting their turn at the sink.

They seemed to topple in slow motion, and although Claudia moved like lightning to catch them, they fell through her hands, bounced off her arms; and when all the crashing and splintering was over, she found her school uniform splattered with gravy and cake mixture, and Nan was there beside her, shrieking, 'Cat! Wicked little cat! You did that to spite me!'

Claudia stuck her fingers in her ears, squeezed her eyes shut and screamed. But while she was screaming her mind suddenly cleared of the suffocating yellow nightmare which had haunted her all day and she thought, quite dispassionately, This won't do. You can't go on like this.

And then she heard Marcus Saxon's voice, shaking with rage: *What would your mother think of you?*

Pig! Louse! Bastard! What did *he* know about anything? What did *he* care?

Claudia went on screaming: partly with temper, but mostly because it drowned out Nan's voice, the horrible nagging, the bleak, empty *lovelessness* of it all.

She screamed until her throat hurt. Then she stopped, swallowed, and heard something else. Cath Murray was leaning over the sink, hiding her face, and she was sobbing like a child.

Claudia stared at her grandmother's stooped, heaving shoulders and felt nothing. No pity. No regret. She couldn't have apologised to save her life.

But suddenly she understood. Nan was old. She couldn't help it. And Claudia was young. Too young to be left alone in the world without her mother. *She* couldn't help it, either.

Madge was dead. Absolutely, stone-cold *dead*, and nothing could bring her back, so it was of no earthly use to keep hoping.

Had she been hoping? Yes, and waiting. Letting everything hang, fall, break, until . . . Until the door should open and Madge, wearing her best camel hair coat, should stroll into the kitchen and gasp: 'What on earth's going on? Goodness, I've only to turn my back for five minutes – !'

She would never say that again. They were on their own: the old, the young, the helpless. And they had to manage, somehow, without her. Get used to it. Be brave.

'It's all right, Nan,' Claudia said flatly. 'Go and sit down. I'll clean it up.'

'So you should!' the old woman sobbed. 'I can't – I can't – Oh, God, I'm too old for this! I should be laid out in my grave, not slaving my guts out for a wicked, ungrateful – ! Oh, I wish I was dead!'

Daniel came in at the door. He was smiling, but as he registered the chaos his face crumpled and he closed his eyes. Claudia counted the times he'd come home from school to a scene like this and never once screamed to shut it out. All Daniel ever did was close his eyes, gather his strength. And then . . .

But he wouldn't clean up the mess this time!

What would your mother think of you?

Not much. So far. But one day, when this was over . . .

'It's all right, Daniel!' Claudia was crying now. 'We had . . . I knocked . . . But it's all right now. I'll clean it up. Take Nan . . . Sit down. I'll – ' She lifted her chin and dashed a hand through her tears, attempting to smile.

'I'll make us all a nice cup of tea, shall I?'

Chapter Twelve

The daughter Madge would have been proud of lived in the Murray household for two and a half days. They were days of calm, quiet optimism. Days of courtesy and kindness. Days when Claudia cleaned her room, washed and ironed her clothes, vacuumed the landing, the stairs and the best sitting room – and then spilled the contents of the dust-bag all over the kitchen floor.

She barely had time to contemplate this disaster before the corded hem of Cath Murray's wet dishcloth slashed violently across her face, accompanied by a stream of insults which changed Claudia from saint to raging demon in the space of three seconds.

She burst into tears. She kicked her feet through the heap of dust, spraying it all over the kitchen. She screamed, 'Shut up, shut up, you miserable old witch! I hate you! Oh, I hate you!'

She was trembling from head to heel, and although she knew that this was the time to make a run for it and have done, her legs were shaking too much to make it possible.

She had reached the end of her rope – perhaps the end of the world – and she knew that nothing she could do from now on would matter. She could break all the china, smash the furniture, shatter every window in the house and then – she didn't pause to wonder how – she'd die and it would be all over.

Her grandmother had turned very white, and her eyes were popping, her chin quivering with shock. But she wasn't beaten yet.

'You're mad!' she said, and the notion was not unpleasant. It seemed almost to confirm Claudia's idea that she could do anything she liked and not be held responsible. So the best Royal Albert tea service could go! Everything could just – *go*!

But her fingers had barely grasped the spout of the said Royal Albert tea-pot when the kitchen door flew open and John flew in from the yard.

'What – ?'

He didn't wait for an answer. He didn't even finish the question. He just tipped the sobbing Claudia over his shoulder and carried her from the room.

When he threw her down on the sofa a few seconds later, she was still holding the tea-pot. Its lid had fallen off, but otherwise it was intact, and although Claudia could barely see, think or breathe, she was strangely glad to discover she hadn't smashed it.

John crouched at her feet and prised her fingers from the spout before carefully placing it out of her reach. Then he sat beside her, gathered her in his arms and let her sob herself to exhaustion.

'I hate her!' she whispered at last.

'I know,' John sighed.

'Nothing I do ever pleases her! I c-cleaned my room. I hoo-hoo-hoovered – !' She sat up suddenly, waving her arms to indicate the spotless sitting room. 'Look! *I* did this! It took – took me all – all m-m-orning, and then – then she *hit* me!'

John sighed again. 'I know, Clo, but you've got to try and see things from her point of view.'

'I did! Look where it got me!'

'But, Clo, you've got to learn patience! Do you want to grow up like Dad, having everyone pity you because you can't control yourself?'

If anything else could have shut Claudia up and made her think, nothing could have done it better. She flopped back against the sofa cushions, her face suddenly pale.

'Clo, none of us wants to live without Mum. We all miss her, we all need her. But saying so doesn't help matters, it just makes them worse. And we can't afford to let that happen. You'll be home for eight weeks, and if you don't find a way . . .'

Again he sighed, filling his lungs, stretching his spine; but just at the point when he should have exhaled, he caught his breath and stared at his sister with wide, astonished eyes.

'What?' Claudia demanded suspiciously.

'Nothing.' He sat back and folded his arms, smugly smiling.

'Tell me!'

'What's it worth? If I can get you out of the house? Out from under Nan's feet? Away from the bloody hoo-hoo-hoover?'

A dawning of hope shone in Claudia's tear-swollen eyes.

'Come on, Clo. What's it worth?'

'What do you want?' she asked pathetically. 'I've only got ninepence.'

'It's worth more than that. But I'll let you off if you promise me something. Keep your temper, and if Nan goes for you again, just walk out, kick hell out of the compost bins, and don't come home again until you can come smiling. Promise me that, and I'll pay *you*.'

'You will? What for?'

'Promise?'

'Mmm.' Claudia scowled. John had been very different since his mother's death, and his first year at university had changed him even more. He was very much a man now: solemn and quiet, as if he carried all the cares of the world on his shoulders. But he was still a mere brother, and brothers were never completely trustworthy.

He grinned. '*Mmm*? That's not a promise.'

'Okay, I promise, but – '

'Come on, then.' He caught her hand and tugged her to her feet. 'Let's have a word with Daniel.'

A cloudburst on August Bank Holiday Monday had over-brimmed the river, sending ominous trickles of muddy yellow water into a few of Larcombe's cottages and turning James Murray's land into an unworkable marsh. But the water had receded, the sun had come out, and now, three weeks later, it looked as if the bean crop would be the best ever. They'd already sent almost a thousand pounds to market, and there were still plenty more to be picked.

But not today. Work was over for today, and Claudia, sitting with her back to a fence post on a patch of wasteland in the furthest corner of the property (where her grand-mother never came), basked quietly in the evening sun. The school holidays had worked out better than she could have imagined possible, thanks to John – and Daniel.

Daniel had turned a pale shade of green when John had suggested that he and Claudia change places, but after a few seconds' thought, he'd calmly handed over his hoe and walked back to the house to wash the kitchen floor. True, he wasn't mad keen on housework, and he resolutely refused to hang the washing on the line or do the ironing, but in other respects he'd turned out a better housekeeper than Nan had ever been.

And Claudia – to her amazement – was turning out to be a much better gardener than Daniel had ever been. She liked the work and didn't care how wet and muddy, or hot and sweaty she became in the process. She didn't even find it hard. John said it was because she was small: she didn't have to double her back as the boys did to hoe between the beans or pick caterpillars from the cabbages. As for planting out lettuce seedlings, she did that on her hands and knees; and although she came home filthy, she came home a good deal sooner than anyone else did. Her seedlings recovered sooner, too, and, when he'd noticed this, her father had produced a wistful little smile and said, 'Green thumbs. At last.'

It was the first time in her life that Claudia had felt truly fond of him. And although she could not forgive him his failures over the past eighteen months, she began to feel that they were over the worst, and beginning – like her lettuce seedlings – to grow again.

She'd become brown and fit. Almost happy. But would it last? In three weeks' time she and Daniel would be back at school, and soon after that John would return to university. Then where would they be? Dad couldn't manage without John. Nan couldn't manage without Daniel. It would be hell on skates all over again.

She wasn't certain when she noticed the man strolling between the beansticks: she'd thought at first he was John, and had taken no notice. But suddenly she realised that he was a stranger. Just strolling casually about the property, tasting the beans, inspecting the Brussels sprouts, poking the ground with the toe of his shoe.

She jumped to her feet, quite forgetting that she was wearing Daniel's old Boy Scout shorts (tied with string around the middle) and a Swiss cotton blouse which had gone ripe in several places and completely disappeared in others.

'Can I help you?' she called irritably, and the man slowly turned, and slowly smiled – and Claudia remembered her outfit and stepped hastily backwards, trying to hide her more disreputable bits behind a tall clump of willow-herb.

But he looked a nice sort of person. He was very clean, very slim, and should have been neat enough in his navy blue slacks and white Aertex shirt, but in fact there was a rather endearing scruffiness about him which, taking her own sartorial condition into account, made Claudia warm towards him instantly.

He was blond, but his hair needed cutting. His trousers were pressed into knife-edged creases, but he'd dragged them down over the hips slightly, so that they sagged at the knees. And he'd pulled his shirt on any old how and forgotten to tuck it in at the back.

'Hello,' he said. 'Are you the proprietor?'

Claudia laughed. 'Don't be silly. My father is.'

'Oh.' He nodded. He seemed very solemn, yet there was something about his mouth, something about his eyes (large, dark blue eyes, lashed with gold) as if he had a great well of laughter hidden inside him. 'So you must be Claudia.'

'Yes. How d'you know? Who are you?'

'Oh . . .' He scowled and looked up at the sky, as if trying to retrieve these details from the depths of his memory. 'Er – Chalcroft's the name. Alister Chalcroft. I'm – at least, she tells me I am – a distant relative of Mrs Chislett's.'

'Ugh.' Claudia's response was automatic. 'Poor you.'

He smiled. Just a little smile at first but it spread, slowly filling out the gaunt hollows of his cheeks, crinkling the corners of his eyes, breaking into a soft, almost caressing breath of laughter before fading again, as slowly and sweetly as it had begun. Claudia couldn't tell how old he was. Quite old. Perhaps even as old as thirty.

'What's the soil here?' he asked.

'Alkaline. Why?'

'Use much manure?'

'Loads. Dando's – that's the farm on the Bristol side – give us more than we want, really. And we make our own compost. Why?'

'How many work here?'

'Three at the moment, not counting the family. Why do you want to know?'

'Want to show me around?'

Claudia laughed. '*Why*?' she demanded.

'Oh . . . I'm just interested.'

He wandered off, and before she quite knew what she was about, Claudia had joined him and was telling him all she knew – feeling rather astonished to discover just how *much* she knew. When had she learned all this? She'd just absorbed it, she supposed, over the years of listening to her father's moans and groans; but still it surprised her and gave her a warm, pleasant feeling which almost verged on excitement. Not that knowledge of this sort actually mattered. It didn't mean she was *clever*. But – yes, it was fun.

Mr Chalcroft didn't interrupt; and, save for the fact that he asked some pretty astute questions when she ran out of things to tell him, gave the impression that market gardening had been a complete mystery to him until Claudia had consented to teach him the facts.

But those astute little questions began to embarrass her at last and she blushed and shrugged. 'I don't really know very much,' she said. 'If you're really interested, I'll – '

But Mr Chalcroft's eyes widened almost disapprovingly. 'You don't know much? Nonsense. How old are you?'

'Thirteen, but – '

'Are you planning to take over the business when you're old enough?'

Again Claudia laughed. 'Me? No! Who, *me*?'

'Why not you? From what I hear, your brothers aren't interested.'

'Yes,' she said. 'But I couldn't take over, could I? I'm a girl! I can't even drive the tractor!'

'Not yet, but you can learn.'

Claudia frowned. Something curious was happening inside her head as if little doors were opening, a few chinks of light beginning to gleam through the darkness. It felt rather good. But it was painful, too. She slammed the doors shut.

'Puh!' she scoffed. 'There's more to it than that! What about accounts, marketing . . . ?'

'You can learn,' Mr Chalcroft said calmly. 'You're a Grammar School girl, aren't you? You can learn anything. Think about it.'

He strolled off down the track towards the glasshouses. 'What's in these?'

'Tomatoes,' she replied distractedly. 'Cucumbers, melons and seedlings for succession. That one over there's mostly parsley.'

She stopped walking. She scowled, smiled, laughed and then scowled again, turning around in a frustrated little circle.

Take over the business? She dug the heels of her sandals into the black cinder track. No, it was a ridiculous idea. Market gardening was a man's job. It was hard and dirty, hot and . . . And she couldn't drive the lorry. She couldn't even reach the pedals. Anyway, Dad would have a fit!

'Melons?' Mr Chalcroft called. 'What variety?'

'Why are you so interested, anyway?' she demanded irritably.

'Hmm? Oh . . .'

He looked at his feet. 'I'm looking for a job.' He turned

his head, and that slow, sweet smile of his began to spread to the corners of his eyes. 'Think you could take me on?'

Mrs Chislett's back garden was twelve feet wide, fifty feet long and almost as tall, for it climbed the steep hill behind her cottage in a series of narrow terraces, each one stuffed to bursting with flowers, fruit and vegetables. She'd laid a little lawn on the highest terrace, with a wooden bench and a small rickety table to hold the tea-tray, and from here she could see right over her roof to the busy end of the village street, into Murray's yard and, between a thin spot in the woods, even manage to observe the comings and goings at Saxon's farm.

Daniel gazed about him in open-mouthed fascination as Mrs Chislett chortled smugly into her tea-cup.

'Ah!' she said. 'So now you knows! Don't you go tellin' nobody, mind, for I likes to make out I got second sight. But all I got really is second wind – you needs it to get up here in a hurry, I can tell you!'

'And no one knows?' Daniel grinned.

'Well, maybe they do, maybe they dussn't. They can look up, just as I can look down; yet still they do ask how I can see through stone walls. "Ah!" I says, "That's for me to know and you to wonder at!" It's only a bit of fun, though. I likes a bit of fun. We all likes a bit of fun, don't we? Now and then.'

She leaned sideways, lowering her voice to a whisper. 'Mind,' she said archly, 'I'm not the *top* of the hill, so I can look *up*, an' all. Through them roses, see, just behind us.'

Daniel twisted in his seat, but he saw only roses.

'Go on!' Mrs Chislett hissed. 'Make a bit of effort! Second sight ain't all tea and buns, Daniel! Stick your nose through!'

He blushed, but it seemed a good deal easier to do as

she said rather than tell her he disapproved of this sort of thing. And anyway, he was interested. Mrs Chislett's cottage was situated in the lowest part of the village; and it was the strangest thing to enter at her front door, right beside the bridge, and, a few minutes later, find himself half-way to heaven. He'd lost his bearings and now had no idea where he was in relation to the rest of the hill or of what he might find when he 'stuck his nose through the roses'.

He found a garden: a large one, not terraced, not even very steep, but gently sloping up towards the back of a large grey house which had once been painted white.

'Oh!' he gasped. 'It's Miss Fairfield's!' Then, emerging from his garland of flowers, 'Didn't she die?'

'Well, if she didn't there'll be trouble,' Mrs Chislett said glumly. 'They'm redecoratin' it. Pale cream, all through. She wouldn't like that. Shows up the dirt something fierce.'

'Who's redecorating it?'

'Her nephew and his wife. Nice people. Been livin' over Corston way. Got a daughter, your Claudia's age. He's one of these whatchyacologists in the Royal United. Women's doctor, type of thing. Got a Labrador bitch. Soppy old thing, she is. They'm gettin' her in at your Claudia's school, so I speck they'll be in the same class.'

'Who? The Labrador?'

'No! The daughter, you fool! Marian, her name is. Lovely-looking girl. A bit on the tall side. Shy. But I think she'm got a bit of the devil in her, so maybe her and your Claudia'll get on.'

She winked and patted the bench to invite Daniel back to his seat. 'How's she gettin' on with our Alister?'

Daniel sat down again, remembering his reason for being here. He'd come to thank Mrs Chislett for Alister. Thank her on his knees, if necessary, for although she'd taken six weeks, rather than the fortnight Marcus Saxon had predicted, she'd done it: she'd found him! Not only that, she was putting him up until he could find somewhere else to live; and a woman couldn't be more generous than that, even if she did say Alister was 'family'. (He was her granddaughter's husband's second cousin!)

'Getting on all right, are they?' the old woman persisted.

'Why?' Daniel teased. 'Don't you know?'

'No,' Mrs Chislett laughed. 'My second sight can't get past your ruddy packin' shed. And *he* never says. Close as a miser's purse, that 'un is. Takes after his ma. Tactful, she do call it.'

Daniel grinned. 'What do you call it?'

'Boring! Christian, mind. Very Christian. Never says an unkind word about a soul. But I dunno, Daniel. They say silence is golden, but what I say is . . . What I say is, you'd miss your own flamin' funeral before Alister Chalcroft'd trouble to tell 'ee you was dead!'

Daniel closed his eyes and smiled at the sun. 'Oh,' he said softly, 'Alister's all right. God, he can *work*, can't he?'

Mrs Chislett patted his hand. 'We can all work,' she said kindly. 'When we loves our work. Going back to school, then?'

'Mm!' Daniel's smile spread almost to the tips of his ears.

'Marcus'll be pleased.'

'Marcus?' Suddenly Daniel was wide awake. 'What d'you mean?'

'You know Marcus,' Mrs Chislett teased. 'Friend o'yourn. One o' them Saxon lads from up the farm. Remember?'

Daniel swallowed, closed his eyes and leaned back again, sighing. 'Did he tell you, then?' he asked after a while. 'About school?'

'Wrote I a letter from abroad. Said he'd told you to tell I, but if you never I was to look out for a man to help your dad. Very decent, I thought that was. He's a funny boy . . .'

'I like him,' Daniel murmured.

'Ah. I'm beginning to think I do, too, though I never thought to say it. He've got a way of lookin' down his nose at you, haven't he? A bit like your Claudia, in fact, though he've got more excuse.'

'Why has he?' Daniel was immediately on the defensive; yet as soon as his armour went up, Mrs Chislett knocked it down again with a hoot of derisive laughter.

'Why, 'cos he's bigger'n most of us, ain't he? Claudia ain't. I sometimes wonder how she manages it without breaking her neck. I s'pose there must be a trick to it . . .'

Mrs Chislett attempted to look down her nose at the tall fence post beside the bench. Her moustache quivered; and although Daniel still wasn't happy at hearing Claudia criticised, he laughed.

Mrs Chislett rearranged her features and folded her arms, staring down thoughtfully over her rooftop towards Murray's yard.

'Lonely little kiddie though, ain't she?' she said sadly. 'I was glad when she broke up with that Diane Bridges. Diane's too forward, by half. She'll come to grief one of these days, but you can't say nothing. They don't listen. I just wouldn't like to see your Claudia go the same way, for t'would break your poor mother's heart.'

'Yes, but she's calmed down a lot, Mrs Chislett. She seems happier since . . . Well, she seems to like being out of the house.'

Mrs Chislett smiled. 'I know, my love. Your nan don't understand kiddies. Never did. Not even her own. Some women are like that, and it's a crying shame for Claudia. Girls of her age needs a nice, cosy gossip now and then, especially when they'm lacking a mother and a sister. Otherwise they don't learn nothing, see, Daniel. They don't learn how to be women, and it ain't an easy thing to learn. There's a lot to it.'

Daniel smiled. 'Isn't she going to be a woman anyway?'

'Ah. But there's women and women, Daniel. There's women like Helen Saxon – female all through – and there's women like Phyllis Derby. Walks like a chap, talks like a chap, even smells like a chap if you'm stood downwind of her on a warm day. And why's that? Because she were brung up by her dad, that's why. No female example, see. No one to learn her.'

She swivelled her head around to look Daniel straight in the eye. 'That's what your Claudia wants,' she said sternly. 'Someone to learn her.'

Daniel's face crumpled with bewilderment. 'About what, though?'

'About *frocks*, you gurt lummox! Frocks and scent and keepin' your armpits nice! I can't recall when I last seen your Claudia in a nice frock! I can't even – now I come to think – recall when I last seen her *clean*!'

'Oh,' Daniel said hollowly.

Mrs Chislett smiled. 'So stick your nose through them roses again,' she said. 'And shout coo-ee. Marian Fairfield's the girl for you. And,' she added mischievously, 'I 'ope you'll both be very happy.'

Daniel turned a dark, beetroot red and jumped off the bench as if he'd been stung by a wasp. Two seconds later he was three terraces down, bellowing up the steps, 'I'll send Claudia over!'

Mrs Chislett chuckled to herself. 'Ah, well,' she murmured. 'P'raps he'm a late starter.'

Marian Fairfield was two months older than Claudia. She was five inches taller, and as dark as Claudia was fair, as calm and peaceful as Claudia was high-strung and defensive. Marian was an only child, her parents' pride, and for this reason alone Claudia was disposed to envy and dislike her; yet they hit it off in the moment they met, and were rarely separated afterwards.

They travelled on the bus together, sat in class together, travelled home together, talking non-stop. Marian brightened the dark places of Claudia's life. She made her feel loved, cherished and protected; and this last in spite of the fact that Marian hadn't an aggressive bone in her body. She just seemed to sail through life – five inches above Claudia's head – like an angel on a slow-moving cloud: sweetly smiling.

But they had been friends for the best part of two years before Claudia discovered just why she loved Marian so much. She was dusting the sitting room, and stopped for a moment to look out at Madge's beloved 'view of the village': the road and the river, the low stone wall on the far side, the little row of cottages and shops which backed on to the churchyard. And then she saw Marian coming out of Dingle's Hardware. She was wearing a white dress printed with pale flowers, and her long, dark hair was pulled into a single loose braid at the back. She turned in the doorway to say a last word to Mr Dingle, and there was something about the way she turned, the way her skirt flared against her knees . . .

Claudia frowned and stared; watching as Marian set off along the street, strolling as if she had all the time in the world, yet somehow purposeful and confident. She bent her head to speak to a small child. She raised her hand to wave to someone in the butcher's. She looked just like Madge . . .

Yet the next time they met (only ten minutes later), Claudia could see very little resemblance. Marian had a round face, sallow skin and soft, dark brown eyes. She didn't look like Madge at all. And yet, in all the ways that mattered, she was Madge all over again: safe and strong and stalwart, a star Claudia could follow and *know* where it would lead.

It seemed that it would lead Claudia to university, for Marian had no other end in view. And where Marian went, Claudia went. Even if it killed her.

'I think it'll kill me,' she confided glumly to Alister. 'If only I didn't need physics. I'm hopeless at physics, Ali.'

They were in the largest of the glasshouses, picking tomatoes for market; and although Claudia had scarcely grown at all during the past two years, and although she was wearing shorts and a cotton blouse, just as on the day when she'd first met Alister, she looked very different.

For one thing, the shorts were her own. For another, she was clean. Her pale, silky hair had grown almost to her waist, and she wore it in a single braid, just like Marian's. She was slim now, rather than thin. And, partly in an effort to match up to Marian, she held herself very straight, making the most of the few inches she had so that no one who guessed at her height ever guessed it right.

But it was in her face that Marian's influence was most evident. Claudia rarely looked calm, for her eyes and mouth were as expressive as they'd ever been. But the pinched, hollow-eyed look had gone, and she looked as healthy and as happy as any girl could whose future rested in the balance of examinations.

'What if you don't pass your physics next year?' Alister asked softly. 'It won't get any easier, you know.'

'Oh!' Claudia tossed her head. 'I'll face that when I come to it. No sense worrying.'

'Plenty of sense in planning, though, Clo. If you fail – '

'I won't fail!'

'No, of course not.' He disappeared behind a vast bush of tomato foliage. 'But what if you do, Clo? It'll come as a nasty shock if you don't think it out in advance.'

'I don't want to think about it!'

'Okay, Clo. Keep your hair on.' He smiled, but his smile quickly faded and he craned his neck to one side, watching anxiously as James Murray emerged from between the bean sticks, some distance away.

Claudia watched her father too, her heart sinking with disquiet. When Alister had first come to Murray's, her father had taken an overnight turn for the better and Claudia had immediately seen why. For Alister was strong. Alister was confident, calm and responsible: a shoulder to lean on, just as Madge had been. Alister never railed against the weather, or slugs, or white fly. He accepted them. He dealt with them. And, when they were dealt with, it was as if they had never been. James needed that. He needed a protective buffer between himself and the world.

But just recently he'd become very strange again, almost as he'd been at the beginning, when Madge had first been taken ill. Yet Claudia sensed that there was something different about this. She didn't know what, and almost suspected that it was because *she* had changed. She'd become more accepting, more forgiving. Yes, even more affectionate, for in spite of everything she loved her father and wished with all her heart that he could be happy.

He never would be. Sometimes he looked crazy, with wide, bewildered eyes and a faint, nervous tremor shaking his head, as if he was forever whispering, 'No, no, oh, no, not me!'

He even walked strangely: tilting his body forward, almost running along the straight cinder tracks, and then teetering to a halt as he reached the corners, as if his feet had been glued to the ground. It looked as if he'd fall flat on his face. But then suddenly he was off again and, save for the forward tilt of his body, he looked perfectly normal. Bow-legged and busy. Same as ever.

But Alister was still watching.

'Ali?' Claudia whispered. 'When I went to the theatre with the Fairfields the other night, we saw a man walking across the Centre, just like that. Doctor Fairfield said he . . . He said he was a drunk.'

Chapter Thirteen

Marian had been born on Friday the thirteenth of February at three minutes to midnight. The obstetrician had set his watch five minutes fast, and, to the exhausted Mrs Fairfield (who'd been in labour since the eleventh), he said, 'Congratulations, my dear! A Valentine's baby!'

But, bleary-eyed as she'd been at the time, Mrs Fairfield knew. And Marian knew. Even Claudia knew that Marian was three minutes older than her birth certificate claimed.

'But you're not unlucky,' Claudia said with a tinge of envy. 'Friday the thirteenth didn't affect you.'

'Not yet,' Marian said. 'But there's plenty of time. I'll probably go to prison for telling fibs on my birth certificate. And I can still fail all my O-levels . . .'

'Huh!' Claudia said. '*You* won't. *I* will.'

Both girls shuddered. Their 'mock' examinations were only three weeks distant, a prospect they couldn't bear thinking about, let alone talking about; and Claudia hastily turned the discussion back to its starting point.

'Perhaps that's why you're not interested in boys,' she suggested anxiously. 'Because you weren't really born on Valentine's Day.'

'Neither were you!'

'No . . . But I'm seven weeks younger than you, anyway. You'll be sixteen next month. If you don't fall in love soon, you'll be an old maid!'

'Mmm.' Marian frowned and thought about it. 'Well, I am *interested*,' she volunteered doubtfully. 'But I think I'd be too scared to *do* anything. Kissing, I mean, and . . . that sort of thing.'

'Yes, I'm exactly the same.'

Claudia and Marian were 'exactly the same' in every way that Claudia could contrive – or pretend. They wore the same brand of underwear, used the same baby shampoo (Marian was inclined to faint if the soap stung her eyes) and cleaned their brown school shoes with Cherry Blossom 'Oxblood' polish, because (in Marian's opinion) only common people used dark tan.

But Claudia was beginning to think that they weren't exactly the same after all. And, in spite of Marian's being two months older, Claudia was beginning to think her friend rather young. She couldn't *do* anything – except homework. She couldn't cook a meal, clean the house, iron a shirt. She couldn't tell the difference between lettuce seedlings and cabbage. She couldn't darn, knit, or cut a dress from a paper pattern. She couldn't even drive a tractor! (She could reach the pedals, though.) And she wasn't interested in boys.

Claudia was interested in boys. She was interested in them against her better judgement, for she knew they meant trouble – if only because they would break the uneasy peace which existed at home. Nan seemed to think Claudia could get pregnant if she just waved to a boy from the far end of the bridge, and she'd go mad if Claudia actually went *out* with one! But she wanted to go out with one. She wanted to know how it felt to be kissed. She didn't admit it, but she'd thought about it a good deal just recently – especially since she'd become so friendly with Mrs Chislett.

Perhaps 'friendly' was too strong a word, for the old woman still managed to put Claudia's back up from time to time; but she could be very kind, too. And, when it was directed somewhere other than at Claudia's indignant head, her outspoken honesty could be very helpful. No, Mrs Chislett was by no means all bad. And she understood things about Claudia which no one – not even Marian – had ever understood.

'What you want,' Mrs Chislett had said, 'is to get married young, Clo. Find someone strong to lean on. Someone nice. Put all your troubles behind you, my love, and raise up a nice little family of your own, that's the best.'

Claudia wasn't too sure about the 'family' part of it, but she'd been completely hooked by the bit in the middle: 'someone strong to lean on'. Oh, that sounded good! But how was she to find someone strong to lean on while Marian was always so 'backward in coming forward'?

'Want to know what I think, Marian?' Claudia volunteered cautiously. 'What I think is that if we could get over the first bit, where you have to sort of . . . *notice* them, the bit where you always whisper, "Oh, quick, Clo, look the other way!"'

'That's the worst bit,' Marian agreed gloomily. 'It's so embarrassing! It makes me feel like one of those women.'

'What women?'

'You know.' Marian blushed and giggled, and she said the next word without using her voice, just mouthing it: '*Prostitutes*.'

Claudia fell over backwards on to Marian's bed, howling with laughter. 'Prostitutes? Where on earth did you learn a big word like that, Marian Fairfield?'

Marian threw a pillow at her; but when Claudia came up for air, still giggling, she found her friend looking unusually solemn, even a little sad. 'Thing is,' she sighed, 'I can't do everything, Clo. My parents'll go mad if I don't pass my exams. And boys? Well, they . . . They're not all that good for your concentration, are they? But I am interested, Clo. Really. I quite like your Daniel – '

'You don't!'

'I do.' She smiled, pretending coyness. 'I think he's sweet.'

Claudia wrinkled her nose with disgust. '*Sweet*? You're mad!'

'No, I'm not. He *is* sweet. And there's someone else I like too, but I can't tell you who.'

'Why not?'

'You'll say I'm mad.'

'I will not!'

'You just did!'

'Yes.' Again Claudia wrinkled her nose. 'But Daniel's different. You can't be in love with him. His feet smell. So who else do you like?'

'Oh, he doesn't count. He's too old.' Marian took a deep, shivery breath. 'Mind you, I'm not saying he's *nice*. I'm definitely not saying *that*. But he *is* very good-looking, Clo.'

'*Who*?'

'Marcus Saxon.'

Claudia's mouth dropped open. She couldn't say a word, and Marian filled the silence with a hasty explanation.

'Mrs Saxon invited Mum and Dad over for drinks on New Year's Day.'

'You didn't tell me!'

'I thought it would upset you, especially after what you told me about . . . You know.' Again she spoke voicelessly. '*The woods*.'

Claudia looked at the floor. 'I haven't seen him since then,' she murmured. 'Except once or twice in his car. Do you really think he's good-looking? Diane Bridges always said he was.' Claudia's chin went up. 'But I'm blowed if *I* could ever see it!'

'That's because you hate him, I expect,' Marian said. 'But he is. His eyes are fantastic. I know they're very pale, but there's this thin black ring around the blue bits – '

Claudia looked at the ceiling and whispered, 'Boring, boring.'

Marian laughed. 'Oh, all right. But he was very *polite*, too! I kept looking at him, trying to imagine him yelling at you, Clo. But I couldn't. That is – ' She laughed nervously. 'I couldn't imagine you being rude enough to make him yell at you! I'd be terrified!'

Claudia shrugged and looked at the wall. She hadn't told Marian quite everything about that night. She hadn't told her that ever since, when things were bad at home and she couldn't sleep, she'd remembered Marcus shaking her, and pretended he was doing it again. Shaking and shaking her until she felt her mind emptying, her body weakening, and she was helpless to do anything except do as he said.

And then everything was easier, somehow. He took the responsibility away. He took the blame. And all the wrong things in the world were his fault, and she didn't have to think about them any more. Yes, Marcus Saxon had shaken her to sleep many a night when she might have cried instead . . .

She hadn't told Marian he'd called her a bitch. A little slut. But the memory still burned. He was *wrong*!

Claudia tilted her chin in the other direction, to stare at another wall. 'Did you speak to him?'

'Only to say hello and goodbye. And "thank you" when he gave me a drink. He talked to Dad, mostly. He's doing a PhD.'

'What's a PhD?'

'It's short for Doctor of Philosophy; but you don't have to know anything about philosophy to be one. It's just another degree.'

'Hmph!' Claudia said. 'Typical! Trust *him* to have two of everything!'

Marian and Claudia waited for the bus in silence and were more than half-way home before Marian spoke. 'Come on, Clo,' she encouraged softly. 'It mightn't be as bad as you think.'

'Oh, don't be so *stupid*!'

At the sound of her own voice, Claudia's eyes flew wide with horror. She'd never spoken to Marian so roughly before, and she regretted it instantly, her hand flying out to catch her friend's arm, to comfort and apologise. But before she could speak her throat filled with tears and she turned away, staring grimly from the window at the darkening February sky.

'Sorry,' she croaked at last. 'It's not your fault. But I know I've failed, Marian. I never could do bloody Physics. I don't understand it, and that's that.'

Her tone had a finality about it which matched her thoughts. She'd had plenty of time to think. The two-hour examination had occupied her mind for roughly thirty minutes and afterwards there'd been just a long, long silence, broken only by the horrible scratching of other girls' pens.

This was the end. She couldn't stay with Marian any longer, sit at the same desk, share the same homework, hate the same teachers. If you didn't pass Physics, you couldn't do sciences in the Sixth Form. And it wasn't fair! Claudia had been top of her class in Biology two terms running, and she'd always done pretty well at Chemistry. But without Physics she was nothing. She'd hit a brick wall. There was no way over it, no way round, no way through. She wanted to die.

By the time the bus drew into Larcombe it was almost

dark and beginning to rain. It had rained every day for weeks, and the river was as high as it could get without flooding. The dull roar of the fast-flowing torrent, the yellow gleam of the three dismal streetlights, and the lowering, rain-filled sky, all combined with Claudia's depression to bring that old, crushing sense of misery and hopelessness which had haunted her for so long after her mother's death. She stumbled off the bus, and stood with her face upturned to the drizzle, biting back a howl of anguish.

Nothing had changed! She'd lost Madge, and now she was losing Marian, too! They'd still be friends, but it would never be the same again. Whatever happened now, they'd be following different paths, travelling in different directions. Claudia would be alone! No one to hold her hand. No one to keep the nightmares away . . .

'Come on, Clo. We'll get soaked.'

'Everything looks yellow,' Claudia whispered.

'No, it doesn't. It's just grey and wet. Look on the bright side, Clo. It's half term next week. It's my birthday. My party!'

'Oh, God,' Claudia wailed. 'I wish *I'd* been born on Friday the thirteenth!'

They parted on the far side of the bridge: Marian turning left to haul her way home up the steep, winding hill of Skipper's Lane, and Claudia turning right along the Woodley Road, beside the darkly dripping hem of the woods.

Just as she came level with the entrance to Saxons' drive, she heard a man's voice, slightly raised, demanding irritably, 'Give up?'

Then Daniel's voice: 'Christ, I don't know! Do you think I want to ?'

Claudia stopped in her tracks to listen for more; but the voices were suddenly lowered and, since the voice of the river refused to follow suit, she could hear nothing more enlightening than the occasional word, detached from its meaning. But she knew who the other man was. It was Marcus Saxon, and he was quarrelling with Daniel! God, what if it turned into a fight? To the best of Claudia's knowledge, Daniel had never fought with anyone in his life! He didn't know how!

' – pushed me this far – ' Daniel said, and Marcus let out a bark of derisive laughter.

'Pushed you? Oh, no.' He said something else, and then: 'But if you give up now, I'll wring your bloody neck. It's not worth – '

Claudia did not care what it was worth, she'd heard enough, and if Marcus Saxon laid a hand on her brother, he'd wish he was dead three times over!

This new development had almost driven Claudia's Physics exam from her mind, but the strain of it had made its mark on her nerves, so that when she stepped forward to make her presence known, she was quivering all over, her dark eyes blazing with rage.

But the scene she found was not the one she had expected. Marcus and Daniel weren't facing each other out, with bulging neck muscles and clenched fists, but leaning back against Marcus's car, which was parked across the cattle grid, facing downhill. They were each wearing a raincoat: Daniel's his outgrown school Burberry with the lapels curling up; Marcus's an elegant beige trenchcoat which looked as if it had never been worn before. The contrast was sickening. It made Claudia feel worse than ever. A failure. A victim. That Burberry should have been in the charity box years ago, and if Madge hadn't died . . .

'That's not fair,' Daniel said. 'You can't say my family's not worth – '

'No!' Claudia's voice throbbed with rage, broke with tears. 'How dare you say that! How dare you!'

She dropped her satchel and flew to the rescue, her fists raised for combat. 'You leave my brother alone!'

Marcus said, 'Whoops,' and retreated a little way up the drive just as Daniel, murmuring, 'Bloody hell,' stepped out into Claudia's path and turned her aside.

'All right, Clo,' he said. 'Go home. It's all right.'

'I'm not going home without you!' To her horror, she realised she was crying, and could only hope that in the dark shelter of the woods, Marcus couldn't see it. But he'd hear it in her voice if she said anything else. He'd know! Oh, God, how she hated him! Why couldn't he leave them alone?

She turned away, brushing the tears from her face as she stooped to retrieve her satchel. Then she stood waiting, tapping her foot.

Daniel shrugged. Marcus turned on his heel to open the car door. Whatever their quarrel had been about, it was over. For the moment.

'Come on, Clo.' Daniel put his hand on her elbow and steered her into the shelter of the trees as Marcus drove past them.

He stopped to glance to his right, then left, his eyes connecting with Claudia's for a moment before he winked and drove away.

'Bastard,' she muttered.

'Stop it, Clo.'

'Well, he is! I hate him! And if he'd touched you – !'

'Don't be silly. We were just talking.'

Daniel sounded almost as dismal as Claudia felt: depressed, irritable, and likely to blow up at the least provocation.

'Oh, come *on*, Clo!' he snapped. 'Let's go home!'

*

Murray's packing shed had been built at right-angles to the house, just inside the gate. At half-past four in the afternoon the doors were wide open and the lorry backed inside to be loaded up for the next day's trip to market.

'Come in here for a minute,' Daniel said quietly. 'I want to talk to you.'

'About Marcus?'

'No.'

'What then?'

Daniel's eyes flashed. 'Come *on*, will you? For God's sake, Claudia, why do you have to turn everything into a bloody argument?'

Chastened, she followed him into the shed, where Alister and poor Timmy Marsh were busy heaving sacks of carrots, swedes and spring cabbages into the lorry.

In spite of his powerfully muscled shoulders, Alister had always seemed too thin and rather gaunt. He looked even more haggard than usual as he turned his head to watch Claudia go by. But still he smiled at her, and she wanly returned his smile, her eyes stinging with tears of gratitude. No matter how busy he was – how tired, cold and harassed – when Claudia came on the scene, Alister smiled. It made so much difference!

'Hi, Ali.'

'Clo.' He stooped to heave another sack up into Timmy's arms. Then, brushing his hands on the seat of his jeans, he said slowly, 'Think you can manage for ten minutes, Tim?'

Timmy nodded, equally slowly. 'Yeah. I fink so. I just – I just got to liff 'em up, and – and – '

'Atta boy,' Alister said. 'Couldn't manage without you, Tim.'

And that was true, Claudia thought sadly as she trailed after Daniel to the far end of the shed. Her father had done very little work this winter, but Timmy was as slow as cold treacle, both mentally and physically, and although he was over thirty, he still ran home crying to his mother if anyone said a cross word to him.

It was hard not to be cross when Timmy hoed up half an acre of cabbage seedlings in the dreamy belief that they were sow-thistles; but, as Alister said, although Timmy caused ten per cent damage, he also managed fifty per cent useful work, so they'd still be forty per cent worse off if they sacked him.

God, what a state to get into! What a come-down! Murray's had employed twenty men when Claudia's grandfather was a boy! Now there were just Alister, Timmy, and whoever else happened to be desperate for a pay-packet until something better cropped up.

Daniel had thrown himself down on one of the donkey benches at the far end of the shed and seemed to be falling asleep when Claudia joined him. But Alister was right behind her. She'd thought he was going outside, but he leaned against the wall, folded his arms, kicked Daniel's foot and said, 'Well?'

'What? Oh . . . yes.' Daniel sighed. 'Clo? You know . . . You know Dad's been a bit strange, just lately?'

'Yes.'

'And you know we thought he was, well . . . drinking?'

Claudia bit her lip. 'Yes.'

'Well, he wasn't. He's ill. He's got – ' He jumped. Alister had kicked him again.

'Ah!' Daniel nodded. 'Right. Tact, right?'

'Might help,' Alister murmured.

'Well, you see, Clo. It's like this. Dad might have to give up work. Not yet. Not completely. But . . .'

'But if we can't think of some way out of it,' Alister said gently, 'he'll have to sell up, Clo. I can't manage single-handed. You can see that, can't you?'

Claudia's eyes closed down almost of their own accord. All she could see was a nightmare cloud of dirty yellow; all she could hear was the roar of the river as it sped past the end of the packing shed.

'Is he going to die?' she whispered.

'No!' Both men spoke at once. Alister's arm encircled her shoulders. 'No,' he said. 'It's not that serious, Clo. It just affects his balance a bit and makes him a bit shaky. He won't be able to drive the lorry any more, or do any of the delicate work. That's all. It definitely won't kill him. And it's not painful.'

'But he's breaking his heart, Clo.' Daniel jerked his head in the direction of the house. 'So's Nan. We'd have had to sell up after Mum died if Nan hadn't kept things going, made Dad keep going. But she's old, Clo. She can't take any more. Neither can Dad.'

'No,' Claudia said bleakly. 'Oh, Daniel, why must we be so unlucky? What did we *do*?'

Daniel smiled hopelessly. 'I've often wondered that. I think it's because we're too afraid of losing anything. But I think . . . I think perhaps . . . Learning to lose is the only . . .'

He swallowed and closed his eyes, leaning back against the shed wall in an attitude of complete relaxation. But as Claudia watched him, a tiny chain of tears, like jewels, seeped from under his lashes and she caught his hand, rubbing it frantically.

'Oh, Daniel, don't! Don't cry! Please!

She was sobbing her heart out for she knew exactly what he'd been trying to say. And she knew, now, what he and Marcus had been talking about. *If you give up now, I'll wring your neck.*

'Daniel!' she cried. 'Marcus was right! He was right! You mustn't give up! It's not fair! John didn't give up! Why should you?'

Daniel leaned forward to hide his face in his hands.

'Because there's no one left, Clo,' he said wearily. 'I've got no choice.'

Everything was yellow. Claudia seemed to be drowning in it. She couldn't breathe; and although she felt a scream rising, she couldn't scream!

And then Timmy came behind her and, in his deep, mournful voice, said pleadingly, 'It ain't my fault, is it, Mr Chalcroft? I never did it, did I? I never made 'er cry?'

'No, no, Tim. It's not your fault. You go home, now, there's a good lad.'

His voice was calm, soothing, utterly gentle; and Claudia turned to him, and saw through her tears his soft blue eyes, his slow, sweet smile.

Are you planning to take over the business when you're older?

It was as if a floodlight had been switched on. The yellow nightmare had gone; and, with the aid of a severely sodden handkerchief, Claudia's tears soon went the same way.

She caught Daniel's head in her hands and shook it. 'You're not the last!' she grinned. 'I am! And guess what, Daniel? I failed Physics!'

'You?' James Murray gasped.

'You?' His mother repeated incredulously. 'Don't be ridiculous, Claudia! You can't! You're a girl! Tell her, Alister!'

Alister chuckled softly. 'You're a girl, Clo.'

Cath Murray turned rather pink. 'Hmph,' she said. 'She's only saying it to get out of the housework. Tell her, James! Good God, she's only fifteen!'

'Sixteen in April,' Claudia muttered.

'She can't drive the lorry! She can't lift! She doesn't know – '

'Ah, well,' James murmured doubtfully. 'She *knows* enough, Mother. And she's a good little worker . . .'

'Huh! Not when there's any ironing to be done, she's not!'

James turned his head to stare thoughtfully into Alister's face.

'It means you'd have to do all the driving. You realise that, do you?'

'Yes, but I can manage that, all right. It's everything else. If Claudia could do the books, the paperwork, the glasshouses . . .'

'Oh.' Cath eased herself back from the edge of her chair. 'Well, that's a bit *different*. She could manage *that*!'

Now James turned to his daughter, his eyes wide with the look of sad bewilderment which, she realised now, was a part of his illness, not a reflection of his state of mind.

'Do you really want to, Clo?' he asked. 'You were going to be a doctor with Marian the last I heard.'

Claudia could only shrug. 'I didn't stand a chance. Not without Physics.'

'Well,' Cath said, 'I told you that! I told you you'd never pull it off. You were never the scholar your brothers were. But no. You wouldn't listen. You had to copy Marian!'

Claudia ground her molars together, swallowing more swear words than she'd realised she knew. But she met Alister's eyes. And Alister smiled.

'You're right, Mrs Murray,' he said briskly. 'Claudia's worked damn hard to get through these exams, and she's done very well to fail only one of them. Okay, she can't be a doctor, but she can still go to university, still have a career like her brothers.'

'Career?' the old woman scoffed. 'Nonsense! She's a girl! She'll only get married and let it all go to waste! No, she might just as well stay at home, as you say. And do the books.'

Claudia had been warned in advance of this discussion to keep her mouth shut and let Ali do the talking; but the effort of staying silent was almost throttling her. *She's a girl!* Nan made it sound much the same as being a slug! Contrary old bat!

'No.' James spoke from the depths of the sofa. 'No, Mother. If she stays here she'll do it properly or not at all. Alister won't let her do anything beyond her strength, but apart from that, she can learn the business from the bottom up and do everything – *not* just the books. Either that or she'll stay on at school and go to college, if that's what she wants.'

'And then what?' Cath demanded angrily. 'What'll happen to us while she swans around at college for years on end, spending money we can't afford?'

'We'll sell up.'

'We can't!'

'We can.' His eyes grew even wider, sadder and more bewildered than ever. 'I sometimes wish I'd done it years ago.'

'But Daniel's going away!' Cath wailed. 'And if *she* – ' She pointed an accusing finger at Claudia's averted face. 'If *she's* working all hours on the ground, who'll help *me*? I can't do everything, James! It's too much! I'm too old!'

'We'll get a woman in,' James said grimly.

And he burst into tears.

'Well, that goes back to your grandad,' Mrs Chislett muttered scornfully. 'Silly old bugger. Beggin' your pardon, Claudia, but he *was*. Turn a bit to the window, my love.'

It was Valentine's Day. Claudia was standing on Mrs Chislett's kitchen table, having the hem of her party dress pinned up.

'That business with your poor Uncle Jim turned your

granfer's mind, I reckon,' Mrs Chislett went on. 'Before that, your place was open house, just like everyone else's. But afterwards, the gates slammed shut and nobody got past 'em.

'I remember one winter . . . Cor, that were a terrible winter! We had floods the one day and a freeze-up the next! Well, as you know, your house ain't never been flooded, but after the thaw come, you had a burst pipe up in your loft and the water took down your nan's bedroom ceiling. But would your grandad have a man in to fix it? Not him! No one could cross *his* threshold, see *his* bits, poke his nose in where it weren't wanted! So your nan lived four months – four *months*, mark you! – without no water, no toilet, no flamin' ceilin' and mildew everywhere she turned, just waiting for Albert to have time to fix it! That's what he were like, see, Claudia. And your father's the same. The thought of havin' an outsider cleanin' his house, makin' his bed, scrubbin' his bath – it's like askin' him to strip off naked in the high street!'

'But I *didn't* ask him, Mrs Chislett!'

'Just as well, too, or he'd never have come round to it. He did it for you, I reckon, my love. Not for your nan. He knows as well as I do . . . No, keep my mouth shut. You made a lovely job of this frock, Claudia, and you looks lovely in it. This dark blue suits you. Mind, you got your mother's touch with a needle. Pity you didn't have her build, too. I seen stouter-lookin' legs struttin' on the roof at nestin' time.'

'Oh, *don't*!' Claudia wailed. Then, making an attempt to clamber off the table: 'I'm not going! I don't want to! I've *always* hated parties!'

'Rubbish! Not going? You got to go! You made this lovely frock, had your hair done – I'm not keen on it, mind.'

Mrs Chislett squinted upwards to inspect the hairstyle

again. 'Looks like a stick of candy-floss, piled up on top of your head like that. But that's fashion for you. If you didn't look as daft as everyone else, you'd just feel daft, wouldn't you, my love?'

'That's the end,' Claudia muttered. 'I'm *definitely* not going now.'

Mrs Chislett laughed. 'Of course you will! Marian'd break her heart if you let her down now! She'm a good deal more shyer than what *you* are, Claudia! *She* never bin down Watery Lane!'

'Ooh! That's not fair! That was years ago!'

'Never mind how long ago it was. At least you knows which end of a boy is which, my girl, which is more'n can be said for poor Marian. If you ain't there to back her up, it'll be a disaster – start to finish!'

Claudia closed her eyes and took a deep, quivering breath. 'I think it'll be that anyway,' she whispered.

Two of the boys were Marian's cousins, and most of the others were their friends: a bright, polite, smartly dressed crowd who seemed to have been told in advance that if they wanted a good time they'd have to invent it for themselves.

At the few formal parties Claudia had attended in the past, the girls had stood at one end of the room, flouncing and giggling and generally making an exhibition of themselves, while the boys had stood at the other end, ignoring all provocation. But nothing like that happened at Marian's party. The boys arrived. One of them changed the record. And the next minute, everyone was dancing.

'But I can't dance!' The boy who was dragging Claudia forcibly across the room did not look back; but when he reached the spot he'd been aiming for he whirled on his heel, tugged her into his arms, jiggled her a little and then spun her around.

'There!' he yelled over the clamour of 'Jailhouse Rock'. 'That's all there is to it! What's your name?'

'What?'

'What's your name?'

'Claudia Murray!'

'I'm Steve! Come on then, Mary! Let yourself go!'

When the party was over and Claudia was at home in bed, her nerves still jangling with the excitement of it all, she decided that if Steve had got her name right, it wouldn't have worked. She'd have gone on being shy. Gone on protesting she couldn't dance. But when a boy called you Mary, nothing else mattered.

Half-way through the evening, Claudia met Steve again in the kitchen. His tie was loose, his face pink and glossy from exertion, and he was pouring a glass of cider for another boy. But his eyes lit up when Claudia appeared. 'Whooh!' he said. 'You've changed since I saw you last!'

'Have I?'

'Who's your little friend, Steve?'

The other boy was taller, older, infinitely better-looking. Claudia blushed and ducked her head, suddenly feeling shy again.

'Belle of the ball,' Steve said firmly. 'Neil Priest, may I introduce Miss – sorry, I've forgotten your name.'

'Claudia Murray.'

'Oh! Really? Oh, right – Miss Claudia Murray, belle of the ball. May I introduce – ?'

'Shut up, Steve.' Neil laughed. He took Claudia's hand. He led her away, towards the music, and she saw her reflection in the hall mirror: slim and pretty, flushed and smiling.

Her candy-floss hair had toppled towards the back of her head and soft, curling tendrils had escaped the hairdresser's scaffolding of pins and shiny lacquer to frame her face in a cloud of gold.

When Neil slid his arm around her waist to guide her on to the dance floor, she laughed out loud with the wonder of it all. Belle of the ball! Oh, just wait until she told Mrs Chislett this!

The music had changed from rock to 'smooch'. Neil gathered her close, then stepped even closer, rocking her in his arms. He smiled into her eyes. He touched her hair with his lips.

And far away, somewhere in the background, Elvis was sleepily murmuring, 'You're so young . . . and beautiful . . .'

Chapter Fourteen

'I'll have nothing to do with you,' James Murray told his daughter. 'As far as I'm concerned, Clo, you don't work here.' Then, seeing the shock registering on Claudia's face, he smiled uncertainly and added, 'We'll only end up quarrelling, love. Don't want that, do we?'

This was the longest speech James Murray had made since he'd first agreed to let Claudia join the business; and, as she realised what he meant, she felt a sudden urge to put her arms around him and stroke him like a puppy.

He'd changed so much in the past few years, but his illness had changed him even more; and only the smallest part of the change was physical. His speech had become slower and more slurred, his eyes more staring, and the slight tremor of his head and hands was more obvious than before. But something else had happened. He'd given up the fight. Fate had finally nailed him down, and he seemed almost glad of it, almost happy. He couldn't fight Parkinson's Disease. He couldn't run away from it. And he seemed to have faced that fact as he had faced nothing else in his life.

The urge became too strong to resist. Claudia wrapped

her arms around his neck and kissed the bald patch over his brow. 'I do love you, Dad.'

James gently pushed her away, averting his face. 'Hmm,' he said gruffly. 'Well, never mind that. You do a good job out there and do as Ali tells you. That'll be enough for me.'

Claudia was certain she could do a good job; and, since Ali had never told her to do anything she didn't want to do, she turned up for her first day's work grinning all over her face.

'Right, boss,' she said. 'Where do I start?'

Alister bit back a smile and pretended to have something in his eye. 'Er – ' he said. 'You can start by cleaning out the office.'

'*What*?'

'From now on, Clo, this business is going to be run like clockwork. It's going to be efficient, organised, and above all profit-making. This place will be yours one day. *You'll* be the boss.' His smile escaped from its confines to become a smug, all-consuming grin. 'So you'll need to know how to run the office, won't you? Clear it out, Clo.'

'*And*,' Claudia reported woefully to Mrs Chislett when she visited her the next evening, 'he's making me go to evening classes! Typing and accounts! City and Guilds Horticulture! I won't have any time left to see Neil!'

'Oh,' Mrs Chislett remarked dourly, 'I expect you'll manage.' After a silence which lasted no more than three seconds, she said, 'Yer, Claudia, you heard what's been goin' on up Saxons' lately?'

'No,' Claudia turned away, shrugging. 'I don't take any interest in *their* business.'

'Oh, no, of course you don't.' Mrs Chislett was folding her laundry, damping it down for the iron. She began to hum a medley from *My Fair Lady*, which Claudia knew was intended as a personal insult.

Neil and his parents had taken her to see the show at the Bristol Hippodrome. The men were wearing bow ties and dinner jackets, Mrs Priest a chinchilla stole, Claudia her first long evening dress. She'd breezed into the theatre feeling like a million dollars – and found a coach trip from Larcombe W.I. lined up in the foyer, shouting, 'Yer! Ooh! Look! There's Claudia Murray! Ooh, Claudia, don't *you* look nice! Out with the nobs tonight, are you, my love?'

She hadn't known where to put herself. She'd blushed like a beet and cut them all dead.

Mrs Chislett was in no hurry to let her forget it.

'Ohh!' Claudia groaned. 'All right! Tell me about the Saxons!'

Mrs Chislett smirked. 'Ellis've gone!'

'Gone? Gone where?'

'Nobody knows. Just upped and left. He hadn't been happy, mind. You could see it in him. And Tom's none too well – heart trouble it looks like. It've put Ben Saxon in a terrible fix.'

'Good,' Claudia said crisply. Then, after a moment's thought, 'Why has it?'

'Well, they can't get the labour, see, Claudia. They got Noddy, they got Little Georgie and they got that young lad from up over – ' She jerked her head towards the Bath Road. 'You know. What's-his-name. His mother was a Tinknell. So what's that, if we leaves Tom out?'

Mrs Chislett did a quick count on her fingers. 'Four, counting Ben – and the lad's not up to much. Nearly ran hisself over with the tractor, t'other day. Got off it to open a gate, forgot to put the brake on, and it chased right after him!'

Mrs Chislett laughed. 'No, I shouldn't laugh,' she said thoughtfully. 'It could have mangled him.'

But Claudia, too, was counting on her fingers. 'That's five, not four. You didn't count Marcus.'

'Marcus? *Marcus*? Where *you* been the last few years? Marcus don't do nothing. Haven't raised a hand up there, not since Ellis come home, just after – Yes, he come home when Callie died, didn't he? So when was that? Three years? Or four, is it? No, Marcus don't do nothing. Won't neither.'

'Why?'

'Ah. Well. That's the puzzlin' thing, see, Claudia. I ain't quite worked that one out, for he never wanted to do nothing else but farming. *He* never wanted no fancy education. *He* never wanted to go to college. And now the little blighter won't come back!'

Mrs Chislett sighed. 'I dunno. The world's gone mad and God only knows where it'll end. Atom bombs, space ships . . . *Wickedness*, that's all it is.' She sighed. 'I got a feelin' that's what Marcus is up to, an' all,' she added thoughtfully.

Claudia's eyes brightened. 'What? Space ships?' she crowed gleefully. 'Oh, good, they're sending him to the moon!'

'Oh, well, if you're goin' to be awkward.' Mrs Chislett thrust two corners of a large white sheet into Claudia's hands. 'Give me a hand folding this, will you? *Every juke – and earl – and peer wuz yer –*'

Claudia ground her teeth and tried not to listen. She had grown fonder of Mrs Chislett than she cared to admit, but she was still scared of her, too. The old bat was always *right*, in this case as well as in a few thousand others. Claudia *had* been ashamed of the W.I., her mother's old friends. And the worst thing about it was that if Madge had lived, she'd have been there with them. Not wearing a headscarf admittedly, and not yelling her head off as if she was at a rugby match, but there. Claudia couldn't have snubbed her. She wouldn't have wanted to. But she shouldn't have snubbed Mrs Chislett, either.

'Okay,' she said briskly. 'You're right. I was wrong. I just didn't know what to do, that's all. I didn't mean to hurt you.'

Mrs Chislett's face softened. 'That's all right, my love. It was our fault, really, callin' attention to you like that. You was bound to be embarrassed.'

Claudia blushed. She had long ago ceased to notice Mrs Chislett's moustache, her watery eyes, the jowls which quivered when she walked; but now she looked again, saw them all, and knew that they didn't matter. It was how you were inside that mattered; and, under the skin, Mrs Chislett was a fine-looking woman.

Claudia snatched the carefully folded sheet from Mrs Chislett's hands, brandished it like a bullfighter's cloak and stamped her feet in a rather dubious attempt at the flamenco.

'The rain in Spain falls mainly in the plain,' she sang, sticking her nose in the air, just as she had done at the theatre. 'I think she's got it! By George, she's *got* it!'

Mrs Chislett laughed. 'Ah, you got it, all right,' she said. 'Bein' in love suits you, I reckon, Claudia. You'm pretty as a picture when you laughs. Your ma'd be proud of you, my love.'

Claudia sat down suddenly, her eyes stinging with grateful tears. 'Thanks,' she croaked. 'Tell that to Nan, will you?'

Neil's new, blue Morris Oxford purred in at the tall, wrought iron gates, and crunched sweetly along the gravel drive to his own front door. It was a lovely old house, built of the local honey-coloured stone, with a view which stretched away for miles, down to the shores of Blagdon Lake. The drive was edged with wide beds of Michaelmas daises, Japanese anemones and chrysanthemums, with here and there a few arching stems of late pink roses.

As always when she visited Neil's home, Claudia felt the cares of the world lifting from her shoulders. Nan and her eternal complaints no longer existed. James's trembling hands were a dream she'd almost forgotten. Even Daniel's departure for London no longer mattered so much; even though, yesterday, she'd cried her eyes out to see him go. And he hadn't looked back. He hadn't even waved.

'Too upset, I imagine,' Alister had said comfortingly as the train disappeared into the distance.

But Claudia knew better. Daniel hadn't been upset. He'd been glad to go. For the past week, while he'd packed his things, he'd been like a dog digging feverishly for a bone: his eyes glazed over with passion for the new life he'd worked so hard to win. Why the hell should he be sad? He'd won through. He'd escaped. And left his little sister to carry the entire can of worms . . .

But it didn't matter now. And, until ten o'clock tonight, it wouldn't matter again. She had Neil. She had his house, his garden, his beautiful view. And, best of all, she had his parents.

The front door flew open almost before the car had stopped, and Neil's father ran down the shallow curving steps, flinging his arms wide. 'Here she is! Here's our little angel!'

He caught her, hugged her, set her away from him to inspect her outfit (the best part of a month's salary in Jolly's summer sale), and smiled his approval. 'Mm! Gorgeous!' He turned to encourage his wife down the steps. 'Look at her, Esme! Isn't she gorgeous?' Then he closed his eyes and pursed up his mouth. 'Where's my kiss?'

Claudia giggled. She wasn't too keen on this bit, innocent though it must be with both Neil and Mrs Priest smiling benignly on. They knew that Mr Priest's regulation kiss was intended to make her laugh, to make her feel loved and welcome. But he always managed to wet her lips; and, try as she might to dispel the thought, she invariably *did* think it was like kissing a tom-cat's back end.

Mrs Priest hugged her more gently and brushed her cheek with softly painted lips. 'How are you, darling? Come in, come in. We were just about to have sherry in the conservatory, weren't we, Charles?'

'We were. We are. Neil, old son, fetch the tray of nibbles from the kitchen, will you?'

'Where,' Mrs Priest whispered as they passed through the carpeted shadows of the hall, 'did you get that suit, Clo? It's – mmm! I've been looking for something like that for years! But it wouldn't look nearly as good on me. You don't know how lucky you are not to have *hips*.'

This wasn't true. Every time she saw Mrs Priest from behind, Claudia knew precisely how lucky she was not to have hips. Yet Mrs Priest wasn't fat all over. She had a small head, a long, thin neck and legs like Betty Grable's. But her hips were her ruination and couldn't be denied.

Claudia was still trying to think of a way to deny them when Mr Priest, carrying a tray of sherry glasses, bustled into the conservatory behind her. Then he was showing her to a chair, holding it gently at the back of her knees, stooping to plant yet another kiss on the top of her head. 'What kind of a week have you had, angel? Alister been giving you hell?'

She'd known them just eight months. Since a week after Marian's party. And it had been love at first sight, all round. Claudia could scarcely believe it, let alone understand it. No one had ever loved her like this. And now, all of a sudden, there were three of them at it! All at once!

She was still only sixteen yet they treated her like a woman of twenty-three; someone who *knew* things, who *understood* things. The first time she'd met them, feeling shy, ungainly and not a day older than eight and a half, she'd said something (completely by accident) which had made them laugh.

'Ohh,' Mr Priest had murmured archly. 'Well, done, Neil, old son. If a girl can make you laugh, she can make you happy. And when she's as beautiful as *this* girl . . . !'

Before Claudia quite knew where she was, she'd been marked down as a wit, a raconteur. Now they sat gazing at her with bright, scandalised eyes, waiting for the latest episode in the continuing tale of 'Murray's Market Gardens'. It didn't seem to matter what she said: if she said it in a certain way, they laughed; and it was the most wonderful feeling. It was like being rescued from a dark place: being caught up and carried away, flown so far above the realities of life that they became . . . just a story.

It was hard, while she visited the Priests, even for Claudia to believe that the circumstances of her life were real. That she lived in a house where no one laughed. Where no one kissed, touched or held hands. Mr and Mrs Priest were always holding hands, twining their fingers together quite casually, as if it were the most natural thing in the world. And Neil was always holding Claudia's hand. He'd kiss it, too, not caring who might see, and smile, and remark upon it.

'Ahh, look at our little love-birds, Esme. Aren't they sweet?'

'Less of the "little", Dad. I'm bigger than you, remember.'

Neil was five feet ten. His mother was five feet seven. Mr Priest was an inch shorter again, and – Claudia suspected – painfully conscious of the fact. She also suspected that part of his delight in 'his little angel' was that she was three inches shorter than he was. He liked tucking her under his arm as they walked in to lunch. He liked looking down at her, tilting her chin with his thumb to make her look up to him.

The house was always immaculate, always cool and sweet

and smelling of lavender. The table was always set with the best silver, the best china and crystal, snow white napery, blood red wine.

Except for the most special occasions at Marian's house, Claudia hadn't seen vegetables served from their own dish since Madge had died, and God only knew what had happened to the pastry forks.

Oh, *this* was real! This was right! Claudia knew she would never rest, never be happy, until she could find such a reality for herself. And keep it. But for *ever*, next time!

It was January. It was dark and freezing hard. The lorry had been loaded, Timmy had gone home, and Claudia, held loosely in Alister's arms, was trying to disentangle the toggles of her duffle coat from the toggles of his. Her release obtained, she stamped her foot, turned her back on him and gave the wall a good, hard kick.

'Christ!' she said angrily. 'I'll be eighteen in April! If I can't do it at my age, I'll never learn!' She kicked the wall again. 'I feel such a fool!'

'Nonsense. Just because you feel a fool there's no need to act like one. Try once more. Come on.'

'No! It's no good! I can't do it!'

'Yes, you can. Look, Clo. Let's try it in the living room, where it's warmer. Your father won't mind.'

'Nan will! You know what she's like! She thinks anything I do is immoral, ever since – '

Alister laughed softly. Mrs Chislett had told him about Watery Lane.

'Come on, Clo.' He caught her hand and pulled her gently into his arms. 'Try again. Relax. *Relax*, will you? Good girl. Now – *one*, two, three; *one*, two, three. Da, da, de-da . . .'

They shuffled around the packing shed floor for another ten minutes before Claudia began to feel she was getting the hang of it; and then, all of a sudden, it became quite easy, as if she'd known how to waltz all her life. 'Hey,' she murmured.

'Now, up on your toes, Clo.' Alister's loose, coaxing grip suddenly tightened around her waist, forcing her to lean backwards. She giggled and he whirled her away, singing the tune.

'Da, da, de-da . . . Da, da, de-da . . . My goodness, Miss Murray, you dance like a dream!'

'I'm doing it!' Claudia squealed. 'Ali!'

''Course you are. Told you you could, didn't I?'

'Oh, thanks, Ali! Thanks!' She broke away, panting slightly. 'Now all I've got to do is tell Nan what time I'm coming home tomorrow night. She'll go mad. She thinks *everyone* who stays out after ten o'clock comes home pregnant!'

Alister smiled and looked at her under his eyebrows. 'Keep your temper,' he advised softly. 'The way I see it, she only goes mad if you go mad first.'

There was some truth in that, and Claudia recognised it; but it wasn't all true. Nan wasn't like Mrs Chislett. She looked a good deal better on the outside, but inside . . . Inside, Nan was a lot like James, flailing her fists at everything in sight just in case it should hit her first. And she didn't forgive. She didn't forget. Every time there was a new conflict, she remembered all the old ones. Fibs, sulks, and tantrums so old they'd gone mouldy. The Royal Albert tea-pot . . . Watery Lane.

The crazy thing was, Claudia could scarcely remember a thing about Watery Lane! She couldn't even remember the boy she'd gone with. Someone from Woodley. Or was it Chelworth? No, the only thing she could remember about that night was its aftermath.

Marcus Saxon. The memory still made her blush. She'd had no clothes on! And now, or so Mrs Chislett said, he was going to America. Or perhaps he was already there. The thought made her feel a little empty, much as she'd felt last year when Mr Saxon had cut down the oak tree in Long Meadow. It had been dying anyway. Like Marcus, it had been of no use to anyone; but it had been there for so long . . . A part of the landscape, a part of Claudia's life. For months afterwards she'd felt a sad little pang when she'd looked over the fields to find it gone.

She hadn't seen Marcus as often as she'd seen the oak tree, of course, but in a way she hadn't seen the oak tree, either. You didn't really look at things which had been there for ever. You just knew they were there. She'd known Marcus was there. And now she knew he wasn't, it felt . . . strange.

Claudia breezed into the kitchen, pinning a smile into place for her meeting with Cath Murray.

'Hi, Nan.'

Cath Murray didn't smile. 'Where the dickens have you been?' she snapped. 'The dinner's ruined. I slave all the hours God sends to put a decent meal on the table – '

'Ali's been teaching me to waltz.' Claudia took off her coat, lifted the lid from one of the saucepans on the stove and peered inside. 'It's not ruined,' she said brightly. 'Smells terrific. Have you laid the table, or shall I do it?'

'Hmph!'

'Can *you* waltz, Nan?'

'Waltz? Of course I can't waltz! Waltz? A woman who can barely drag herself around for the pain? But no. You don't think of that, do you? You think only of yourself.'

'That's not fair!'

'Oh, isn't it just? And what do *you* want to go waltzing for, I'd like to know? A girl of your age. Gadding about to dances. Riding about in cars with the boys!'

'Just one boy, Nan,' Claudia said levelly.

'Hm! So *you* say! It's a disgrace, that's what it is. When I was your age it wasn't allowed. We had to stay at home, do as we were told, help in the house – '

'Oh, come on, Nan! You've *got* help in the house!'

'Help! Huh! That Hilda Marsh doesn't know what dirt looks like! I have to follow her around, pointing it out! No wonder her Timmy's peculiar – you can see where he took it from. And you're as bad. I'd just got this kitchen tidy, and now look at it! Wellies, coats . . .'

'It's just *one* coat, Nan!' Claudia snatched it up and marched out to hang it up, remembering just at the last moment not to slam the door. She still had to tell Nan about tomorrow night. She had to keep her sweet; or, at least, try to *get* her sweet. But even that was doomed to failure. Nan hadn't much sense, but she wasn't entirely daft, either. The minute Claudia turned helpful she sneered, 'Oh, yes, and what do *you* want?'

Supper was long over before Claudia at last plucked up courage to broach the subject.

'Nan, I thought since I'd be home pretty late from the dance tomorrow – '

'What dance?'

'Oh, Nan! The dance I've been talking about ever since Christmas! The dance at the Country Club, tomorrow night! The dance I was learning to waltz for!' She took a deep breath. *She only goes mad if you go mad first.* 'You know,' she said sweetly. 'You helped me shorten my dress for it.'

'Hm! Call that a dress? Going half-naked, that's what I call it. Showing yourself off like a hussy. Catching your death. Taffeta? At this time of year? You ought to have your head read!'

Claudia bit back the caustic remark that she'd never heard of flannelette ball gowns and instead said reasonably,

'Scoop necks are in fashion, Nan. Everyone wears them. I'd look an idiot going to the biggest dance of the year in a warm skirt and blouse, wouldn't I?'

'Hm! I'd rather look an idiot than a trollop! You're just asking for trouble, that's what you're doing! And if you find it, Claudia! If you bring a windfall home here! Breaking your father's heart – ! Well, you'll be out in the street, that's where you'll be. Don't say you weren't warned!'

'Oh, Nan! It's a dance, not an orgy!'

'Dance? Huh! I'm amazed at your father for letting you go where we don't know anyone, with no one to keep an eye – '

'Nan, Mr and Mrs Priest are coming with us. And you can't get more respectable than the Country Club! It's a dinner dance! The tickets were – '

She hesitated. The tickets had cost almost as much as a week's housekeeping, and Nan was always saying the Priests had more money than sense. No, best get back to the big one. The killer.

She stretched a bright, affectionate smile across her face. 'Nan,' she began coaxingly. 'It's half-past seven for eight, and the dinner won't finish until half-past nine, so . . .'

When Claudia had finished speaking, there was a short, incredulous silence. Then, '*One o'clock*?' Cath Murray howled, 'Over my dead body!'

The dinner tasted like ashes. The draught on Claudia's bare shoulders felt like ice. Her smile hurt. Her heart ached. Neil hadn't spoken to her for the past two hours.

His parents seemed not to have noticed. Either that or they were pretending it wasn't happening. Claudia was grateful for their tact but at the same time, if Mr Priest called her his little angel just once more . . . twice at the very *most* . . . She'd kick him.

She had been aided in this decision by Neil's cousin Caroline, a large, supercilious girl with a nose like a carrot who sucked in her cheeks every time Mr Priest spoke to Claudia, as if she thought he was lowering himself. She'd also made some unpleasant remarks about Claudia's job, which had made Neil crosser than ever.

'Murray's is a *business*, Caroline! Claudia's a *business-woman*! She works in an *office*!'

Had he been on speaking terms with her, Claudia might have pretended he'd been jumping to her defence; but it would have been just pretence. Neil couldn't bear the thought of Claudia getting her hands dirty, driving the tractor or mixing with 'rough-necks' at St Nicholas Market. In fact, she'd been to the market with Alister on only three occasions, just to see how it worked, but she hadn't seen any rough-necks there. Market gardeners were respectable businessmen, as were the merchants who bought up their produce, but Neil seemed to think that anyone who did business at five o'clock in the morning was up to something shady.

God, this was deadly! The band had been playing for ten minutes already, and there were still only four couples on the floor.

Neil stood up suddenly. 'Dance?' he offered distantly, and although Claudia had a nasty feeling that this was a quick-step (Alister had only had time to teach her the waltz), she decided she'd rather be kicked black and blue than be bored to death.

'I can't do the quick-step,' she laughed nervously as they took the floor.

'Neither can I.'

He couldn't waltz, either. He just walked the floor in a large circle, steering Claudia around as if she were a small bicycle with a bent front wheel.

'You're just making it worse,' she advised gently. 'I know

you think it was hardly worth coming if I have to be home at eleven – '

'You're nearly eighteen, for God's sake! Why do you have to do everything your granny says? Why can't you – ?'

'You know why, Neil. My father's ill. If he gets upset he trembles more, and then he can't do anything. You can't ask me to do that to him.'

'But you aren't doing it to him! It's her! Why is it *your* responsibility, for crying out loud? You're only seventeen!'

'I was nearly eighteen a minute ago,' Claudia muttered bitterly. 'Look, we've only got an hour, Neil. Why don't you try to enjoy it, instead of moaning all night? You're spoiling it for your parents, too.'

'Oh, *I'm* spoiling it, am I? I thought it was you!'

They went back to their table. Caroline's boyfriend, David, was picking a hole in the tablecloth with his thumbnail. Mrs Priest was watching Mr Priest dancing with Caroline and, for want of something better to do, Claudia followed her example. They were dancing very close. Mr Priest was stroking Caroline's bottom with the palm of his hand.

Claudia swallowed and glanced quickly towards Neil's mother, who smiled and said brightly, 'Isn't Caroline's frock lovely? No good for me, of course, with my hips. *Entirely* too clingy.'

The band leader announced a Paul Jones, and a sudden buzz of excitement filled the ballroom. Neil immediately livened up, which didn't please Claudia in the least. When the music stopped, he'd get a chance to dance with someone else; and Claudia would be *forced* to dance with someone else. She found herself praying that it wouldn't be Mr Priest.

Everyone was laughing. It looked as if it might turn out to be a wonderful dance after all, but it was already twenty-past ten. She'd have to leave as soon as the Paul Jones was over. She laughed, but her eyes had misted over with self-pitying tears, and the whirling ring of prospective partners blurred into a jagged mountain range of white shirt fronts, black waistcoats, bow ties.

The music stopped. Claudia stepped forward, going up on her toes to meet the tall man opposite her. She laid her hand in his, felt his arm circle her waist. It was a process which was completed by momentum rather than choice, and horror had dawned in Claudia's face before she could step backwards again. But he didn't let go.

'You turn up in the most surprising places, Claudia.'

Her face scorching with humiliation (he meant the woods, the bastard!), Claudia hissed, 'So do you! I thought you were in America!'

'I changed my mind.' He laughed softly. 'If you don't want your toes crushed, stop struggling, will you? It'll be over in a minute.'

'Thank God for small mercies,' Claudia muttered.

But he was right. She'd only make a fool of herself if she ran away. She attempted to put her nose in the air, but it barely cleared the line of his shoulder. He smelled of cinnamon and lemons.

'Why did you change your mind?' she demanded.

'To annoy you,' he sneered softly. 'Why else?'

'Huh! I couldn't care less!'

Marcus grinned. 'You look very pretty with your clothes on, you know. You should wear them more often.'

'*Ooh* . . . I *hate* you!'

He laughed. His arm tightened around her waist to sweep her around in an expert turn. She had no idea what dance this was. It wasn't a waltz. But her feet seemed to be doing all the right things, even if her brain wasn't. It felt like a rice pudding in too hot an oven. Scalding, seething, boiling over.

'Who've you come with?' Marcus asked now. 'One of your many boyfriends?'

'Shut up,' Claudia said.

'Ever the little lady.' His grip on her hand loosened, making Claudia miserably conscious that her palms were sweating. And not just her palms . . .

'I hear your father's not well, Claudia. I'm sorry. Really.'

'Thank you.' She ground the courtesy through gritted teeth.

'And you're planning to take over the business?'

'*So*? What's wrong with that?'

'Nothing.' He grinned. 'I think it's very brave of you. And Mrs Chislett says you passed your driving test. Er – can you reach the pedals in the lorry yet?'

Claudia didn't reply. She closed her eyes, vaguely resolving that she'd never tell Mrs Chislett anything ever again; but it didn't really matter. Nothing mattered. She felt rather odd. The hot, seething sensation in her head had stilled and grown cold. Very cold. She felt . . .

Her eyes widened with horror. 'Oh!' she breathed frantically. 'I'm going to be sick!'

Neil put her into the car as if she was made of cut glass. Mr Priest folded her into the travel rug, brushing her breasts with furtive, lingering hands. 'Poor little angel.'

'I'm all right now,' she snapped. 'Really. Thank you.'

For the moment, she thought grimly. It was already ten-past eleven. Nan was going to kill her.

But, thanks to Marcus Saxon, at least she hadn't been sick. He'd helped her to a chair, pushed her head between her knees and kept it there until the worst had passed. God, what an embarrassment!

'No,' he'd said when she'd been strong enough to protest that she was perfectly well again, 'you're running a fever. Probably 'flu. You'd better go home. Shall I take you?'

'No!'

And then Neil had turned up, with Mr and Mrs Priest close behind, and it was all over. Marcus had put in a brief, rather curt, 'medical report' and disappeared into the crowd. But before he disappeared, Claudia had become aware of a strange contrast between him and the Priests. She still wasn't sure what it was, but it hadn't felt good. And it still didn't. Oh, why did they have to make such a *fuss*?

'Now you look after her, Neil, old son. Drive carefully and don't jostle her about. And make sure you tell Mrs Murray she's ill. We don't want anything happening to our little angel now, do we?'

They were half-way home before Neil stopped asking, 'How do you feel? All right now? You aren't going to be sick?'

Claudia thought he was worrying about his expensive mohair travel rug but after a few moments' silence, he said softly, 'I'm sorry I was cross, Clo. It's just – I'd been so looking forward to it. I'd made . . . plans, and suddenly it was no good. There wasn't time.'

'Time for what?'

'Oh, I was going to wait for the smooch towards the end, when they dim the lights and it gets all romantic. And then . . .'

Claudia smiled wanly. 'What?'

'And then . . . ask you to marry me. And give you this.'

He turned into Murray's yard with only one hand on the wheel. With the other he handed her a small leather box.

Claudia stared at the ring in silence. It was a sapphire, as big as the nail on her little finger: the sort of ring she'd pointed out as a joke, never imagining it could really happen.

She was amazed at herself for not feeling thrilled. For just feeling . . . flat. Yet this was what she'd wanted. Someone strong to lean on.

'Well, Clo?'

Claudia blinked. She gave herself a mental shake.

'Oh, yes!' she managed at last. 'Thank you.'

Neil kissed her, hard and long. He seemed to have forgotten she was ill. But Claudia hadn't. She felt awful.

Chapter Fifteen

It was May, and Claudia had bought a new summer outfit: a short A-line dress and matching jacket in fuchsia pink linen which should have knocked Neil's eyes out if only for the unprecedented amount of leg it revealed. But he came in through the back door in a hurry, kissing her cheek and shoving her aside simultaneously: 'Quick, has your dad got the cricket on?'

Claudia shrugged and followed him through to the sitting room, but his eyes were already glued to the television, his shoulders hunched, his hips squirming as if he, rather than Freddie Trueman, was doing his darnedest to bowl Australia out of the First Test.

'Come on, come on, come on,' Neil muttered. 'Get the blighter out this time!'

Claudia ran her tongue over her teeth. She examined her engagement ring. This time next year, if she played her cards right, she could be doing this all over again – and for ever – watching Neil watching someone else playing cricket. She'd have to have sex with him, too. And darn his socks. She couldn't say which one of these prospects appalled her most, and surely that was wrong? There should be a difference, shouldn't there? He twitched his nose, too. It drove Claudia mad. Every time he did it she wanted to hit him.

She smoothed her skirt and sat down, observing him covertly under lowered lashes. She still thought him good-looking, but she'd never liked his jaw, which was fleshier than the rest of his body. It made him look fat, and he wasn't fat – just very well-built.

I'm sorry, Neil, she rehearsed mentally. I don't want to hurt you, but I can't possibly live with your jaw for the rest of my life.

No, it wasn't a good enough reason. There were no good reasons for not marrying him, except that she didn't want to. But what else was there? Who else was there? As everyone had informed her when they'd got engaged, she couldn't have done better.

'And he's a proper gentleman,' Mrs Chislett had informed her in hushed, dark, warning tones. 'The sort what'll take no for an answer – *just as long as no's the answer you gives 'un*.'

Claudia often wondered how so many of the village girls managed to get into trouble with Mrs Chislett watching every move they made; although it wasn't Mrs Chislett and it wasn't Nan who'd kept her knees stuck together all this time. It wasn't Marcus Saxon, either, but he'd certainly had more to do with it than Claudia liked to admit.

What would your mother think of you?

He'd probably ruined her for life. If the day ever came when she really wanted to let herself go, she wouldn't be able to manage it anyway. How could she, with Madge always there, making remarks from the ether? Steady on, Clo! I might be dead, but I'm not blind yet, madam!

It was true: her mother had always intervened when Neil was at his most insistent; but Claudia knew she was nothing more than a symbol of her own conscience. And an excuse, because she really didn't want to have sex with Neil. The idea revolted her. It seemed crude, ugly, embarrassing and unnatural, like torture.

But Mrs Chislett had been right. Neil did know how to take no for an answer – up to a point. It was usually a long way past the point at which Claudia said no, and it often reached the point at which she bit, kicked or punched him. But when he backed off, gasping, to wipe the sweat from his neck, it was always to say that she was right; that a woman who wasn't a virgin on her wedding night wasn't worth marrying and that he'd have no respect for her if she gave in too easily. So why did he keep begging her to give in? And if all he cared about was her virginity, what would happen to the rest of her on Day Two of the honeymoon? Claudia had a suspicion that the rest of her would disappear. With her virginity up the spout, darning his socks would be all she'd be good for.

Claudia sighed heavily, wondering if she'd have felt differently if he'd had a nicer jaw. Alister had the sort of jaw Claudia liked. It went all the way round, from ear to ear; a clear, clean line. He had nice hands, too. Slim and agile and gentle. He had to gather himself to do anything rough or violent, while Neil had to gather himself to do anything delicate.

It had been a long time before Claudia had noticed this, and she'd noticed it when, by coincidence, she'd watched both men – on the same day but in different places – change an electrical plug. Alister had done it with his fingers. Neil had done it with his entire body, every muscle tensing as he manipulated the tiny screws into place. Claudia had found the difference acutely distressing. It had worried her; made her wonder what would happen to Neil when he lost control of all those tightly clenched muscles. It would be like having sex with a bulldozer.

Yet she loved him. Apart from Marian, there was no one in the world who knew so much about her. She'd told him everything (almost everything) and, in a way, it had been like locking the important parts of herself – all the sorrows which had made and marked her – into a little cash box which Neil had then put away, somewhere safe. She'd felt as if he'd relieved her of the responsibility for these things, taken the pain of them away; and she'd been glad of it, for she hadn't wanted them.

Yes, she'd have to marry him. Leaving out all the questions of love, jawlines and bulldozers, breaking it off would cause such mayhem elsewhere. Nan would go mad. Just as she'd given up calling Claudia a hussy and begun to treat her like a human being . . . And Neil's parents would go mad. They had it all worked out: the house, the mortgage, the grandchildren. But worst of all, if she finished with Neil, Claudia would go mad. There wasn't much to do in Larcombe if you didn't have a boyfriend, and new ones didn't just fall off the trees. After more than two years of being taken out regularly, having all her spare time accounted for, being one half of a whole, it would feel like dying to end it all now – or at best like being stranded in a desert. She wouldn't even be able to rely on Marian to fill the gaps, for now that Marian had fallen in love at long last, she'd be no company at all.

Marian! In *love*! And she made it seem the same as spying for M.I.5!

'What's his name?'

'Oh . . .'

'What's he look like?'

'Well . . .'

'How old is he?'

'Er . . .'

Claudia was beginning to think he was called Egbert, and that he was short, fat, balding and forty-five!

'Clo? Hey, Clo!' Neil snapped his fingers under her nose.

'Hmm? Oh, sorry. I was miles away. Did we win?'

'Win? It's only the first day! We haven't got started yet!'

Neil threw an 'Oh, isn't she pitiful?' look at James, who blushed and shrugged and turned away, pretending to be interested in something outside the window.

Claudia lifted her chin and gazed narrowly at her father, realising that he was the only one who would be glad if she finished with Neil, simply because marrying him would end her involvement in the business. That had been taken for granted from the beginning, and Claudia hadn't thought to argue with it, until now. Of course she couldn't go on working once she'd had children, but until then there didn't seem to be any good reason why not. Neil said only poor men allowed their wives to go out to work, and he wasn't poor. He could give her everything she needed; and, as long as she was reasonable about it, everything she wanted, too. But she both needed and wanted to help her father with the business.

'So!' Neil said now. 'Where would you like to go?'

Claudia stood up, assuming a model-girl's pose to show off her new outfit. 'Well,' she said, 'since I'm all dressed up . . .'

'Yes, very nice,' Neil said automatically.

'Is that all you can say?' Claudia laughed.

'No, it's nice. Skirt's a bit short though. Where shall we go?'

'How about the jazz club?'

'The jazz club? On a lovely evening like this? It'll be as hot as the hobs of hell. No, let's go to The Swan. We can sit by the river and – ' He took her arm, the decision made. 'Goodnight, Mr Murray. And talk,' he concluded, not waiting for James to reply.

'That skirt *is* too short,' Neil complained as Claudia took her seat in the car.

'Not short enough,' she replied acidly. 'Ever heard of fashion? Ever heard of paying compliments to a woman who's just spent two hours dressing up for you?'

'As long as it's just for me.'

'Meaning?'

'Meaning that, in a public place, everyone else gets an eyeful too. Is that what you want?'

'What do *you* want?' Claudia demanded irritably. 'For everyone to wonder why you're engaged to a frump?'

Claudia seethed quietly, trying to imagine how she would look if Neil had the choosing of her clothes. She guessed she'd look a lot like Neil's mother who, ever conscious of her barn-door hips, modelled herself on the Queen Mother: horsey headscarves, doggy tweeds, thirty-denier stockings and well-polished brogues. There wasn't much point in being a woman if you dressed like that.

On warm, summer evenings, everyone who was anyone ended up at The Swan, which was the only pub for miles around to have thought of putting some tables outside, on the lawn beside the river. But Claudia didn't like it. 'Everyone who was anyone', in these parts, meant the arrogant little nobs from Young Farmers and Young Conservatives: red faces, loud voices, silly jokes and braying laughter. None of them seemed to have a care in the world, and it made Claudia feel unaccountably angry, especially when, looking about her, she discovered that she couldn't pick Neil out from the crowd. His parents had held his hand and smoothed his path from the minute he was born; and they were still doing it. They'd do it for Claudia, too (especially the holding hands bit), when she married him. She'd never have to make a single decision for herself, ever again.

And that was what she wanted. Making decisions was too difficult, too painful. She wanted to be picked up and swept along, to have all the decisions taken from her. She wanted to marry Neil as soon as possible, to get it over with, to make it irrevocable – before her freedom to make decisions led her to do something irrevocably stupid.

They walked along the side of the pub, to the crowded gardens at the rear. Neil left her there, saying hurriedly, 'Quick, you grab that table while I get – '

He went inside to get the drinks, leaving Claudia – as he always left her just when it mattered – feeling small and shy and inadequate, wondering if her dress was, after all, too short. As far as she could tell, there wasn't another girl in the place who had yet dared to bare her knees. That was the trouble with reading *Vogue*. It was always years ahead of the local fashions . . .

Her eyes misting with embarrassment, Claudia put her nose in the air and sauntered coolly towards the empty table on the river bank, feeling agonisingly certain that everyone was staring at her legs, just as Neil had warned. Oh, why did she always try to be different? She invariably ended up regretting it, wishing she could melt into the background with everyone else!

'Not speaking to me, Clo?'

'Marian!' Sheer relief made Claudia laugh. 'God, am I glad to see you! I feel such a twit!'

'Why? You look fabulous! That colour's perfect on you!'

'Is it? Honest? Isn't it too short, though? Neil said – ' She sat down, her eyes suddenly widening as she realised that, since Marian would not have come here alone, she must be with the mysterious Mr Right. Whoever he was, he'd done wonders for Marian's complexion! She looked lovely. She'd even done her hair differently!

'God, Marian, you look marvellous!'

'Do I?' Marian blushed and lowered her eyes.

'So, where is he?' Claudia grinned.

'At the bar.' Marian took a deep, nervous breath and bit her lip. 'I don't think you'll like him, Clo. He's not really your type.'

Claudia laughed again. 'Is that a polite way of telling me to get lost?'

'No! No, of course not. It's just . . . Well, if you don't like him, you won't . . . I mean, you will be nice to him, won't you?'

'Of course I will! What do you take me for, for heaven's sake?'

She smiled teasingly, and then more sympathetically, for Marian did indeed look very nervous. Perhaps Claudia's guesses had been right first time round. Perhaps he *was* short, fat, balding and forty-five. But what if he was? Marian wasn't the type to fall in love with someone who wasn't nice underneath: kind, well-mannered and honest. So who cared if he was ugly? Marian did, evidently . . .

'Look,' Claudia said kindly, 'I'll grab another table and leave you to get on with it.' She winked and gave Marian's hand a reassuring pat; but just as she stood up to go, Neil arrived with the drinks – and sat down.

'Marian! What a nice surprise! Hey, what are you drinking? I'll go – '

'No, no. I'm just – ' Blushing, Marian turned her head, looking for her escort.

Claudia followed her gaze, at the same time saying hurriedly, 'Come on, Neil. We'll sit somewhere else. Marian doesn't want us elbowing in on her date.' Then, equally hurriedly, she sat down again, blushing uncomfortably. 'Christ,' she muttered, 'Marcus Saxon! What the hell's *he* doing here?' And she met Marian's eyes just as they closed in a despairing, embarrassed grimace. '*Marian*?' she hissed.

She looked up again, staring, outraged, at Marian's 'short, fat, ugly' boyfriend. He had fought clear of the crush by the door, and was now standing quite still, staring at

Claudia; not with outrage as much as with a malign amusement.

'I don't believe this,' she muttered. She could hear Neil, somewhere in the background, laughing his bewilderment.

'What's going on, girls? Was it something I said? Marian? Clo? What's going on?'

Claudia wanted to hit him. Suddenly, and for no good reason that she could think of, she was ashamed of Neil. She wanted to drown him, or at best hide him under the table and kick him to silence.

Short, ugly, balding . . . Oh, dear God. Hate him as she did, there was no denying the fact that Marcus Saxon was not . . . ugly. And he wasn't short, either. He was probably no taller than most of the other men near the door but he looked taller, just because he held himself so well. He was dressed as many of the other men were dressed in black, close-fitting jeans, a loose cotton shirt and narrow tie, but the others all looked like second-rate pop singers. Marcus looked like a Spanish dancer: cool, elegant and as hard as nails. But what the hell was he doing with Marian?

Claudia glared at her and stood up, preparing to leave. 'Well, thanks for warning me, chum,' she said bitterly. 'Come on, Neil.'

She realised that she was trembling with shock; but Neil evidently didn't, for he stayed where he was, still stupidly laughing. 'Why? Where are we going? What's going on?'

'Nothing's going on! I want to go, that's all!'

'But there aren't any tables left! We can stay here, can't we. Marian won't mind, will you, Marian?'

'No, of course not.' She turned pleading eyes to Claudia's face. 'You promised,' she added faintly.

Claudia closed her eyes, wishing she could disappear. She hadn't felt so angry in years, and was amazed to find that it felt exactly the same as it used to do: the quaking knees, the pounding heart, the volcanic churning of too many emotions all attacking her at once, fighting for a way out. And she couldn't let them out. She couldn't tear Neil apart with her fingernails. She couldn't scream at Marian, call her a traitor, spit in her face. And, most of all, she couldn't run away from Marcus Saxon.

She sat down again and stared, as if mesmerised by it, at the stained wooden table. Marcus's hands came into view, slim and brown and long-fingered, holding two glasses of cider.

'Hello, Claudia.'

She flicked a glance towards his face and found it too soon, for he was leaning forward, his pale, laughing eyes skimming over her to rest on the hem of her dress, her thighs, her knees. 'How nice you look,' he added softly.

Claudia's face flamed. So much for fashion! In future, she'd wear tweed and well-polished brogues, and to hell with femininity!

'Thank you,' she murmured frigidly, but Marcus was already doing his country gentleman act, extending a hand across the table, introducing himself to Neil. 'Marcus Saxon,' he said. 'We met once before, didn't we, at the club? Marian says you're in publishing.'

Neil twitched his nose: twice to the left, once to the right, as if he'd shoved a pea up his nostril and was trying to dislodge it. 'Well, printing, to be more exact,' he said smugly. 'But we handle most of the major London publishers, of course.'

Claudia leaned her chin on her hand and stared at the river, pretending she wasn't with him. Why did he always have to *boast*? And what did he have to boast *about*? If he'd once bothered to mention that his father had set up the business, made it work, made it prosper, it wouldn't have been so bad. But it was all 'I, me, mine,' – and all to make certain that Marcus knew how important he was, how wealthy he was, where he lived, what car he drove. Any other man would be quick to compete, to make a list of his own assets, but not Marcus. Marcus just listened, summing it all up; and even to Claudia's ears it didn't amount to much.

She met Marian's eyes across the table and saw her lips frame the word, 'Please?' and at the same time she remembered Alister saying, 'Just because you feel a fool, there's no need to act like one.'

Quite right, too. She was a grown-up woman now, a responsible engaged-to-be-married woman. Soon she would be Neil's wife, have a house of her own, children . . . She'd be her mother all over again: calm, firm, capable and optimistic. But what was the optimistic view of this situation? That Marcus was being polite, civil, taking an interest in Neil's business. Typically, though, Neil hadn't even bothered to ask what Marcus's business was.

She smiled and patted Neil's arm. 'Marcus is a farmer,' she said brightly, and before she could lose her nerve, turned her smile in Marcus's direction, not looking at him so much as at his left ear, which was so much less threatening than the rest of him. 'Have you started haymaking yet?'

'No, not yet.'

Encouraged, Claudia laughed. 'But the weather's so good. What happened to "Make hay while the sun shines"?'

'The sun sometimes shines in February, too,' he smiled.

'What's that supposed to mean?'

'Have you harvested your runner beans yet?'

'No, we've only just planted them out. They're not ready until – oh!' She blushed. Just because you feel a fool, there's no need to act like one. But what if you couldn't help it?

'But how – ' Marian interjected desperately ' – do you know when the grass is ready? I mean, it's obvious with beans, isn't it? But grass is just grass.'

Marcus laughed and slid his arm around Marian's

shoulder, but he kept his eyes on Claudia. 'How do you know when beans are ready?'

Claudia opened her mouth and shut it again. It wasn't that she didn't know the answer, just that she couldn't describe it. It was something you judged with your eyes and your hands, not with words. 'I just do,' she stammered at last. 'They look right, that's all. And they feel . . . right.'

'But there are signs, aren't there?' Marcus prompted softly. 'The flesh – ' He lingered over the word, testing it with the tip of his tongue ' – feels firmer, cooler, more silky. And you can feel the seeds swelling in the pods. Isn't that so?' He grinned and widened his eyes, demanding a reply.

'Yes, but – '

'But perfection is critical. Only experience can tell you when anything is *exactly* ripe for the picking.'

Claudia swallowed. Was he talking about beans? He sounded as if he was talking about beans, but he looked as if he was talking about something else. Or was he just teasing, telling her she didn't know her own business?

'I certainly have enough experience to know that!' she snapped.

Marcus grinned again. 'Yes,' he said. 'I'm sure you do.'

He had begun to knead the point of Marian's shoulder with his thumb; a gentle, circular motion which set Claudia's teeth on edge. And she was trembling again, finding it difficult to catch her breath. Oh, God, how she hated him!

'It's the same with grass,' Marcus went on smoothly. 'There's a certain point, just before the seed sets, when it's at its most nutritious. But it's too sappy then, which means it might go mouldy in the bales, so you wait a little longer. After that, if the sun shines, you make hay as fast as you can.'

'What if the sun doesn't shine?' Marian asked.

'Hard luck. People whose lives depend on nature have to learn to live with it. Don't we . . . Claudia?'

Just the way he said her name seemed contemptuous, mocking. Most people, when they bothered to say her name in full, said 'Clawdja'. Marcus said 'Claw-dear', emphasising the latter syllable so that it almost sounded like an endearment. And Neil seemed to have noticed it, for he suddenly caught Claudia's hand, holding it against his chest to show off her engagement ring.

'She won't be depending on nature much longer,' he announced proudly. 'She'll be depending on me.'

'Ah, yes.' Marcus smiled. 'I'd forgotten. Congratulations, Neil. Congratulations, Claudia. Will you be leaving the firm when you get married?'

'Yes, of course.'

'Of course?'

'Well,' Neil laughed, 'she certainly can't go on working! We have to get our priorities right, don't we, Clo?'

Marcus looked mildly astonished. 'Oh . . . isn't Murray's one of your priorities, Claudia? I thought you meant to take it over. Your father's still not well, I understand.'

Again Neil laughed. 'Hey, Marcus! We've already been through all this! Whose side are you on?'

'Oh, I'm all for women staying at home, of course, but only if it suits them. And I can't quite see Claudia in a frilly pinafore.' He frowned as if he was trying to picture it, and although Marian and Neil laughed, Claudia didn't. He was right, he was right, the bastard! A pinafore? Dear God . . .

'Will Alister stay once you've gone?' Marcus asked more seriously.

'Stay? Of course he'll stay. What do you mean?'

'Only that the job will be more difficult to do single-handed. And he's well qualified. He has ideas. Mrs Chislett says he'd like to set up on his own some time – and who could blame him? If a man has to work himself to death, he might as well do it for himself.'

'He doesn't work himself to death!'

'Only because you're carrying half the load, surely?'

'Hey,' Neil laughed. 'Stop it, you two! This is too nice an evening to be talking about work. Another drink, Marian? Marcus?'

Neil had scarcely moved away to fetch their drinks when Marcus drew Marian closer and whispered something in her ear. She laughed and pretended to hit him, and he caught her wrist, smiled into her eyes. Claudia couldn't bear it. Any fool could see what he was up to! If he'd worn a placard around his neck, saying 'Love 'em and leave 'em, it couldn't have been more obvious! And Marian thought he was Mr Right!

'I think I'll take a look at the swans,' she murmured weakly, but she was half-way to the river before she remembered her short skirt. Damn them! Now they'd be laughing about that, too!

She felt very cold inside, sick and fluttery and scared; but most of all embarrassed, as if she'd been showing off more than her knees. Marcus always had that effect on her, ever since he'd watched her taking her clothes off in the woods. Years ago. But she was so different now! Why couldn't he give her credit for being different?

And what had he said to Marian about Neil? Whatever it was, it hadn't been pleasant. Nothing he'd said had been pleasant. He'd implied that she was leaving her father in the lurch. He'd even implied that Alister . . . But that was probably true. Alister did like her, and there was a chance he wouldn't want to stay at Murray's once she was married. And then James *would* be left in the lurch!

'Clo! Hey, Clo! Drinks!'

Claudia closed her eyes. It was typical of Neil to shout, to draw attention to himself – and to her. She walked a little further along the river bank, trying to get a grip of herself so that she could go back smiling. A group of boys at one of the nearby tables grinned as she passed, and one of them said kindly, 'Don't do it, love. Whoever he is, he's not worth it.'

Claudia scowled and walked back the way she had come. What had he meant? Whatever he'd meant, he was right! Neil wasn't worth it. Her father would have to give up the business if she wasn't there, and it would finish him, she knew it would!

'Clo?' Neil came to meet her, scowling impatiently. 'What on earth's the matter with you? Why did you go off on your own like that? Marcus said you were having one of your little tantrums! What did he mean? You said you hardly knew him when we met him at the club, yet he seems to know more about you than I do! What's going on? And what's all this about Alister? What did he mean, he wouldn't stay at Murray's without you? Alister doesn't *fancy* you, does he?'

'No!' Claudia jerked her elbow clear of his grasp and turned to go back to the table. Neil tugged her to face him again, and with a cry of irritation Claudia pushed him away, realising too late that he'd been standing much nearer to the river than she'd thought.

She clapped a hand to her mouth as he fell – almost in slow motion – into the river's green, scummy depths. His yell of dismay was cut off with a gulp as his head went under, his hair floating upwards, like pondweed, before following him down to the bottom. Everyone who had seen it laughed out loud, cheering, jeering, asking for an encore. And it *was* funny . . . Even Claudia laughed: a nervous, embarrassed little giggle which verged upon tears.

Neil floundered to the surface, his eyes squeezed shut, his mouth gaping, his face streaming with muddy water. Claudia giggled again, and reached out to pull him ashore; but at the same moment Marcus arrived, tugging her clear of the bank with a none too gentle hand. He was laughing his head off.

'You little brat!' he gasped incredulously. 'Wouldn't it have been simpler just to give him his ring back?'

'I didn't do it deliberately! It was an accident!'

'Ha!' he scoffed. 'Come on, Neil, grab my hand. What's the water like?'

Most of the other men crowded around to help, shouting encouragement as Neil slithered up the bank. Claudia crept back to Marian, half hoping that if she could just sit down, finish her drink and chat about the weather, everything else would go away. But one look at Marian's face crushed the hope at its source.

'Don't look at me like that!' Claudia howled. 'It was an accident!'

'Accident?' Marian repeated scornfully.

'It was!'

'Yes, perhaps it was, but if you hadn't walked off in a temper – '

'I wasn't in a temper! I was trying to be tactful, leaving you and Lover-boy to get on with your petting in private!'

'Quite!' Marian showed her teeth. 'I've always suspected it, and now I know! You're jealous!'

Claudia's mouth fell open with astonishment. 'Jealous? You mean of you and that – and *him*? Are you *mad*? He's been trying to cause trouble all night, and he's bloody well succeeded, too! All that stuff about Alister! As if I'd look twice at Alister, for God's sake! But that's what he wanted Neil to think, and he did! That's why – '

She sat down, her knees quaking again. How could Marian turn on her like this? And why? It wasn't fair, and it damn well wasn't true! *Jealous*! Of all the nerve!

'I think you're the one who's jealous,' she said angrily. 'Jealous of me and Neil! And you've every cause to be, because if you think Marcus is in love with you, you've got another think coming! He's had more girls than you've had hot dinners!'

She'd almost forgotten about Neil. Marian was more important. She *loved* Marian! Marian was her friend! But not any more!

'And don't,' she concluded vengefully, 'come running to me when he ditches you, Marian Fairfield! You've been warned!'

Save for the squelch of Neil's foot on the accelerator, it was a silent drive home. Although he'd managed to laugh it off at the pub, he was furious. Neil didn't have much of a sense of humour when he was the butt of the joke; and, to be fair to him, falling into a river, fully clothed, wasn't much of a joke. Claudia wouldn't have blamed him if he'd called off their engagement on the spot. The awful thing was, she wouldn't have cared much, either.

They were in the middle of Larcombe bridge before Neil dared to speak. 'I could kill you,' he said.

'I can't say I blame you,' Claudia sighed. 'But it was an accident. I didn't realise you were so close to the edge.'

'That doesn't make it any better! You're too damn handy with those fists of yours. I hadn't thought about it before, but – Do you know what Marcus said? Do you know what he said?'

'No. Surprise me,' Claudia said frigidly.

'He said if he had the handling of you, he'd give you a damn good hiding! I'm tempted, Clo! I'm really tempted! And why shouldn't I be? You made me look a bloody idiot!'

'Hmm,' Claudia murmured.

'And what do you mean by that?'

'Nothing. But just because you feel an idiot doesn't mean you have to act like one! I'm sorry you fell – '

'I didn't *fall*!'

'Okay. I'm sorry I pushed you. But if you're really

tempted to take Marcus Saxon's advice, I wish you'd damn well drowned! He's a skunk!'

'Oh, you'd be sure to say *that*, wouldn't you? Just because you didn't charm his socks off with that disgusting little dress of yours! He had a good look though, didn't he? *And* you enjoyed it! Blushing and squirming like a little . . .'

'That's enough!' Claudia snapped. 'Don't say another word, because when it comes to exchanging insults, Neil, I've been saving a few for you! Want to listen – for a few hours?'

'Yes! Why not, while we're at it? Come on, let's hear the truth for once!'

He was so busy glaring at her, he almost hit the gatepost at the entrance to Murray's yard, and his sudden avoidance tactics, followed by a wild squeal of brakes, shocked them both to silence.

As the car slid to a halt, Claudia took a deep breath and closed her eyes. This was the end, and it felt marvellous! She was free!

'Well?' Neil demanded. 'Out with it! What are all these insults you've been saving up for me?'

Claudia smiled. She took off her ring, set it carefully on his knee and opened the car door. 'I'll let you wonder about them,' she said sweetly. 'Goodbye.'

Chapter Sixteen

'It was the best exit line I've ever done,' Claudia said. She was sitting on the staging in one of the glasshouses, idly watching the struggles of a small fly which was drowning in her coffee. She hadn't told Alister everything. Just the easy bit, the best bit: that she'd given Neil his ring back.

'And now, you're regretting it?' Alister asked softly.

'No. Well, yes and no. It feels strange. Insecure, I mean. I hate feeling insecure. But that's why I was marrying him, you see, for the security, and that's wrong, isn't it?'

'Possibly, but when you come down to it that's why most people get married.'

'Even men?'

'Especially men. So you're regretting the security. Anything else?'

'The company, I suppose. Having somewhere to go, someone to go with. I haven't really enjoyed Neil's company for – oh, ages. But it was better than nothing.'

'Never mind, Clo. There's still Marian. She'll be glad you've got more time for her, won't she?'

Claudia lifted her chin and stared silently at a spider's web in the roof, heaving a sigh. 'No,' she said.

'No? Why?'

'It's a bit complicated. She – she just . . . Well, I'm not really sure what happened, to tell the truth. We had a bit of a row. And it's upset me a lot more than breaking up with Neil has, because . . . Well, I don't know why. She – he – That is – I mean *we* . . .'

She shook her head irritably. 'I can't explain.'

Alister laughed softly. 'Let me know when you've worked it out.'

Claudia thought she'd never work it out, if only because she was too angry to think about it for longer than ten seconds at a time. Yet she had thought about it – against her will – for three days and as many virtually sleepless nights.

She wished she could talk to Alister about it, but she didn't dare until she *had* worked it out. He was a funny chap; the sort of person you could trust with your life: gentle, kind, generous and utterly reliable. But he didn't tell lies and wouldn't listen to them, which made talking to him about something like this virtually impossible. Everything Claudia wanted to say was a lie, simply because she didn't know what the truth was. She *hated* Marian . . . but only because she'd loved her so much! She felt betrayed and bitter, as if something ugly had invaded her soul.

Jealous! Nothing Marian could have said would have hurt more. Had it been true, Claudia could have borne it, but it *wasn't* true! The very thought was obscene; but to have Marian, of all people, accuse her of it! It was intolerable! It woke her up in the dark reaches of the night, making her groan with frustrated rage.

But she scarcely gave Neil a thought. He'd rung a few times, saying, 'Look, we have to talk,' but it was as if a stranger was speaking to her. It sounded almost presumptuous; as if she'd met him just once, in a crowded room, and absently given him her phone number.

'There's no point,' she'd said. 'There's nothing to talk about.'

'Of course there is! We were engaged last week, for Christ's sake! We were going to get married! What about *my* feelings? And how am I supposed to explain to people? Everyone's asking where you are, and I don't know what to tell them!'

'Tell them it's over.'

'But it's not! Not for me! And what about my parents? They're devastated!'

Claudia could only shrug. She might have sympathised had Neil claimed to be devastated, but he sounded more irritated than hurt; and the 'feelings' he demanded she consider weren't feelings at all. He just didn't know how to face his friends at the club.

Her own family had reacted much as she'd expected. Cath had called her a fool and added bitterly, 'You'll regret it, my girl, and when you do, you needn't look to me for sympathy!'

James had just shrugged. 'Probably for the best, love.' But it was this little endearment, so rarely used now, which told Claudia how he really felt.

Daniel, when he phoned a week later, made no comment at all, which was typical of him. He just listened and then asked, 'How do you feel?'

'I don't feel anything. I'm not sorry, if that's what you mean.'

'And what does Marian think of it?'

'I wouldn't know,' Claudia said stiffly. 'She's got a new boyfriend.'

'Oh? Anyone we know?'

'No,' Claudia said. But Daniel was insistent, which meant that she had to lie in her teeth to put him off and she was trembling when she put the phone down.

She had never been so glad to see Alister who, for reasons Claudia couldn't imagine, was waiting for her outside the kitchen door.

'Oh, hello, Ali. I thought you'd gone home.'

'I had. I forgot my jacket.' But he'd retrieved his jacket now, and was carrying it over his shoulder. He looked tousled, hot and grubby, but unusually attractive, for the sun had bleached pale streaks into his hair, tanned his skin to reddish-gold and made his denim blue eyes seem darker and brighter than usual. He wasn't the sort of man to make a girl's heart beat faster, but there were times when the urge to cuddle him made Claudia stand very still, biting her lip on a grin.

'You look as if you've just done something very wicked, Clo.'

'Do I? I can't think why. I've just washed the dishes.'

'Ah, well. That's life.' He raised a hand in farewell and strolled lazily towards the gate.

'Bye,' Claudia said wonderingly. 'Have a nice evening.'

Alister stopped and half turned, looking at her over his shoulder. 'Thanks. You too. What are you doing? Feel like a drink later?'

So that was why he'd come back! And just in the nick of time, for if she'd had to spend another evening washing her hair and doing her nails, she'd have gone mad with frustration. 'I'd love to,' she laughed. 'What took you so long?'

Alister gave her a thoughtful look under his eyebrows, then: 'Wisdom,' he smiled. 'Pick you up at eight.' He walked a little further and turned again. 'Just a drink. Nothing fancy.'

Claudia had heard that line before and trusted it no further than she could throw a hundredweight of beetroot. 'Nothing fancy' meant different things to different people, and the only way around it was to wear something plain and unassuming which would make everyone else feel overdressed. Claudia chose a dark blue cotton dress, its length discreetly middle-knee, and added a string of plain white beads to make it seem more summery. With a pair of white ear-rings tucked away in her bag, she decided she was fit for anything, short of Royalty, and, with any luck, Alister didn't know any of them.

In the event they drove to a pub which, as the crow flew, was little more than three miles distant from Larcombe; but Claudia had never heard of it, let alone been there before. It turned out that no one else – save a few very local farm labourers – had heard of it either, for these few farm labourers were the only customers there: solid, balding, red-faced old men who looked up and grinned as Claudia came in and said, 'Ahh!'

It wasn't a remark she could ignore. There was no escaping it, and no point in trying, for Alister, when she glanced at him, was grinning too.

'Ahh?' she echoed warily.

'Ah!' Alister said. 'I've brought you to a den of vice, Clo.'

Claudia could almost believe him, for the pub was certainly the dirtiest she'd ever seen: stained dark brown by the nicotine of half a century with a dusty board floor, a few blackened oak settles and a terrible stench of spilled beer and pig manure. 'Ever played table skittles?' Alister's eyes widened mischievously. 'For money?'

'No. I've never even heard of table skittles. What is it?'

'Ah!' All three of the men stood up, rubbing their hands. 'Come on over 'ere, m'dear, an' us'll show 'ee!'

The game was a glorified version of Shove-ha'penny, requiring only a little skill and not even much luck (with only a ha'penny to lose at each try); but Claudia had enough competitive spirit to want to win, and not so much that she minded losing. In fact, she didn't care what happened, as long as it was fun.

'That's the way to do it, m'dear! One more like that, and us'll be hard put to pay the rent! Oy, Pete, look at the blush on 'er! Look at 'er laugh! 'Ave 'ee ever seen anything handsomer than she?'

By the time the pub closed, Claudia's face and ribs were aching with laughter, and she was weak with a feeling of ease and well-being such as she'd never known before. Alister put his arm around her as they strolled back to the car, and that felt easy too, safe and warm and comfortable. She took a deep breath of sweet, hay-scented air.

'Oh, Ali, I've never had so much fun. Did you know it would be like that?'

'No. I just hoped it would.'

'But it's such a dirty little hole, and they were just . . . Well, they were just old men!'

'The secret of relaxation, Clo. Nothing to live up to, no one to impress, no rugs to spill your drinks over. I can't think of anything better – once in a while.' He smiled. 'We'll go to the Ritz next time, okay?'

The car was parked in a gateway, with a steep hillside beyond it, dipping down and away to the west, where, even at half-past-ten, the sky was still light – a pale, translucent green – and the newly mown hay seemed to radiate a glow of its own. There were thick hedges and towering elm trees almost black against the dusk; and, high in the sky where the afterglow of sunset faded to blue, a single star.

'Venus,' Alister said thoughtfully.

'Oh, this is lovely,' Claudia sighed. 'Look at it, Ali. We're so lucky.'

'Lucky? You're at least ninepence poorer than when you went in!'

'Tenpence. And it was worth every brass farthing.'

'I'm glad. Does this mean you've sorted out your problems?'

'No. It means I haven't got any. I'm glad about Neil, Alister. I knew all along I'd done the right thing, but I couldn't say I was really glad about it until tonight. When I first knew him, he seemed so special – he and his family, I mean. They were so . . . I don't know how to explain it except to say that nothing ever went wrong for them. Everything was so smooth, so dignified and elegant. The house was always spotless, the meals always served on time – and no one ever seemed to make any effort. It just happened that way. I thought they were perfect – at first. And I thought that if I married Neil, everything would be perfect for me, too.'

'But?'

'But . . . I'm not like them, Ali. Neil and I . . . Well, he'd never had any trouble in his life. He seemed a bit shallow.' She laughed suddenly. 'Perhaps it's something to do with our jobs. He's interested in surfaces, making them look good, while I'm . . .'

'Always digging holes in them,' Alister finished dryly.

Claudia's mouth pursed on a giggle. 'I dug a hole in the river,' she confessed wickedly. 'With Neil.'

'Hmm?'

'I pushed him in. It was an accident. I wasn't really angry with him, but . . . Yes, I was. But under the surface. Feelings can get so confusing, can't they?'

'Only if you let them. Don't you ever ask yourself why you feel as you do? Really analyse it? Why, for instance, do you suddenly feel glad you finished with Neil?'

'Because he wasn't the right man for me.'

'You knew that before. What's been so different about tonight?'

Claudia bit her lip and turned back to look at the view. Oh, God. What kind of hole had she dug for herself now? She didn't want to lead Alister up the garden path, make him think he was special. He wasn't special. He was just Ali, in exactly the same way that Daniel was just Daniel. He even looked like Daniel at times: rumpled and scruffy, as if keeping a grip on the ordinary routines of life – like combing his hair – was a complication he would rather do without. She did love him, of course, but everyone loved Ali; it was impossible not to. Children loved him. Dogs and cats loved him. James loved him. Even Nan loved him. But that was different . . .

'I suppose it was as you just said,' she answered carefully at last. 'Relaxation. Not having to make any effort. With Neil I was always having to make an effort. With you . . . Well, I know you so well, there's no need.'

'That's not the reason,' Alister said softly. 'The reason is that I know *you* so well. There's no point in pretending to be anything you're not, because I won't be fooled. That's why it was fun, Clo, because you could be yourself.'

'You mean that with everyone else I'm a phoney!'

'No. Just that you haven't enough confidence in yourself to relax, to do what you want to do, say what you want to say.' He caught her hand and squeezed it approvingly. 'And you're lovely when you relax, Clo.'

'Am I?' In spite of herself, Claudia blushed. Ali wasn't the type to pay compliments unless he really meant them; which somehow made his very rare offerings all the more pleasurable. When Alister said she was lovely, she *felt* lovely. 'Thanks,' she grinned. 'I'll try to relax more often!'

'We ought to bring Marian here, you know. She'd love it. Remember what you said about Neil calming you down? Do you still think he did?'

Claudia sighed. 'Yes, I suppose so. He . . . made me want to control myself, anyway. I never really lost my temper with him, and that's really saying something when you think I was going out with him for two years. I certainly *wanted* to lose it, lots of times.'

Alister was silent for a while, tipping his head back to watch the stars emerge against the darkening sky. 'Is controlling yourself the same as being calm?' he asked at last. 'You've always said Marian's calm, but I don't think she is. I think she's controlled, and that when she lets rip –'

'Oh,' Claudia groaned. 'Don't let's talk about *her*.'

'Why not? You're the only friend she's ever had, Clo. The only real friend *you've* ever had, present company excepted. She needs you.'

'Huh! She should have thought of that before she . . .'

'Hmm?'

'Nothing.'

'All right, Clo. Forget it. It's just . . .' He shrugged and smiled, shaking his car keys. 'Home, modom?'

'Just what?' Claudia prompted reluctantly.

'Well, just what I was saying, really. That she's too controlled. Her parents ask too much of her.'

'True.'

'They've tried to make her into something she's not, and as you discovered with Neil, that's not comfortable. It's like being confined in too small a space; there's no room for development, no room to spread out and express your nature.'

He stretched his spine, opened his shoulders, spread his arms wide; a slow, graceful movement which beautifully conjured an image of unfettered growth. When he relaxed again, he turned in his seat to peer at Claudia through the gloom. 'You realised you didn't love Neil before it was too late, but Marian's never going to realise she doesn't love her parents, is she? She'll just go on and on trying to please them until she . . . Well, until her roots smash the pot. Where will she be then, Clo, without you?'

Claudia stared at her hands for a long, tense moment. 'She's going out with Marcus,' she whispered.

'Oh,' Alister said. 'I see.' And his voice hardened, as if he hated Marcus almost as much as Claudia did. Claudia's eyes widened, not so much with surprise at his tone, but because it had given her a small stab of pain, which felt almost like jealousy.

'Do you – ?' Claudia began tentatively. 'I mean . . . Have you got a soft spot for Marian?'

Alister laughed. 'No, I haven't got a soft spot for Marian.' He started the engine and put the car into gear, laughing again. 'Come on, let's go home and get some sleep. With any luck, you might even wake up – eventually.'

'What's that supposed to mean?'

'Just that you've got a blind spot for soft spots, Clo.'

Claudia swallowed, hoping he wouldn't tell her where his soft spot really lay. And she realised with regret that she could never go out with him again. She did love him, but not in the way he wanted to be loved; and if she started something romantic, how could she finish it if it didn't work out? They had to go on working together, and it would be agony for both of them if something went wrong. No, Alister was too valuable, both as a friend and a colleague, to be considered as a lover. God, why did life have to be so complicated?

Claudia woke from a nightmare soon after five – a nightmare so vivid, it forced her out of bed to check that it wasn't true.

And it wasn't true. The glasshouses hadn't been smashed, and Claudia was heartily relieved to see them still standing and more or less intact. But she wasn't surprised that she'd dreamt of their destruction. They were a perennial worry and expense but it was usually in winter that they suffered most damage and severe gales and hail storms could keep Claudia awake at night as nothing else could.

As dreams so often did, this one faded very quickly and was almost forgotten before Claudia had finished dressing.

But she still felt threatened, as if it had been an omen of something; perhaps even an omen of her father's eternal nightmare, that the entire business would be washed out by floods. This had happened at least twice since Claudia's great-grandfather had started the business eighty years ago, but a major flood had never happened in James's lifetime. He'd lost the strip of land nearest the road a few times; and he'd lost a few of the glasshouses to high winds; but he'd never lost *everything*.

It made Claudia shudder to think what her grandfather and great-grandfather had gone through after a total wash-out: having to start again from scratch, with almost no capital, no machinery, nothing to help them save the terrible threat of destitution. It was no wonder, when you came down to it, that James was a worrier! Floods . . .

It didn't bear thinking about, and was, anyway, rather hard to imagine now, for in spite of heavy rain throughout most of March and April, the sun had put in an appearance nearly every day since then. But floods *had* been known to happen in June. And in August. And at virtually every other time of the year. Was it an omen?

Claudia tapped the barometer as soon as she went downstairs. It didn't even quiver. She gave it a good hard thump with her knuckles, but the marker remained steady: set fair.

Her dream – and the fear of it – forgotten, Claudia sat in the kitchen with her usual breakfast, two cups of strong black coffee, and finished the crossword her father had begun the evening before. He never finished a crossword these days, not because he couldn't work out the clues but because he couldn't write them down: a pencil was too delicate a tool for his eternally trembling hands. Soon, if his health got any worse, he wouldn't be able to feed himself, or even dress himself . . .

Claudia rested her elbows on the table and jammed her

thumbnail between her teeth, staring grimly at the wall. She couldn't believe that she'd seriously considered leaving her father, and for Neil of all people! But even if he'd been Robert Mitchum, she shouldn't have considered it! She hadn't 'considered' it; she'd just blindly followed where she'd been led, wanting to follow, wanting . . . What the hell *had* she wanted? A life free of pain, decisions, worry and responsibility. Some hope.

But the business was a major responsibility; and the welfare of aged and sick relatives a heavy burden to carry. Who could blame her for wanting to shrug them off? Nobody *had* blamed her, of course. Even John had said she shouldn't be expected to give up her chance of marriage for the sake of the business. If she'd been a man, he'd said, it would have been different; but girls needed to be looked after, they needed to have children, they couldn't be expected to take on men's responsibilities. He'd been very sweet about it, not at all patronising, but now, as she remembered it, Claudia's scowl deepened. Not *patronising*? She must have been mad, taking all that without sparing a thought for the implications. And the implications were . . . that she was an idiot, or at best no more useful and reliable than a child!

And that wasn't true. James had worked hardly at all during the past year, and although Ali had done the important bits, such as taking the produce to market every morning, he certainly hadn't done everything! Yet the profits had gone up – *sailed* up! They were using more land, exploiting more markets, growing more produce than ever before. Yet no one had given Claudia the slightest credit for it. No one had expected anything of her except that she get married, have children, take her rightful place in the world as an obedient little housewife. The awful thing was that *she* hadn't expected anything more of herself, either. In fact, the only person who had ever questioned her had been . . . Marcus.

Raising her eyes to heaven, Claudia laughed softly. Him! Always him! But then, unlike the rest of the village busybodies, he didn't care about conventions. All Cath and John and Mrs Chislett – and perhaps even Daniel – had wanted was to get her respectably married before she could disgrace them with a nameless 'little windfall'. Huh, if only they knew!

The sun warmed her back, changing her mood, filling her with energy. It was a perfect morning, and even at half-past six, when Claudia made her first inspection of the glasshouses, the temperature inside was climbing towards eighty. She opened the doors, opened the ventilators, drew down the shades and soaked the cinder paths with water to increase the humidity. The tomatoes were already beginning to change colour, and the scent of the leaves was delicious. Another week and the first crop would be going to market, at early season prices. It was perfect weather for growing things.

She discovered later that morning that it was perfect weather for hay-making too. The distant but distinctive sound of a tractor's mowing blades drew her eyes to the southern slopes of Saxons' hill, and suddenly an image of her dream came back to her. It hadn't been about flooding . . . It had been about Marian.

'Ali?' she said faintly. 'Do you ever have dreams?'

'Only when I'm asleep, Clo. Why?'

'Do you think dreams can tell you things? Warn you, I mean, of something that might be going to happen?'

'No.' He followed her gaze, watching with her as the tractor made a circuitous tour of the hayfield, the mower leaving soft swathes of jade-coloured grass in its wake.

'So what was this dream of yours?'

'I'm not really sure. I can't remember. Little bits just keep coming back to me. The glasshouses were all smashed, and I thought we'd been flooded, but now I think it was about Marian.'

Alister smiled. 'Then it probably was. Marian and the glasshouses . . . Your security again, perhaps? And, to answer your question, I don't think dreams tell you anything you don't already know, or haven't already worried about. Have you been worrying about Marian?'

'No. Just missing her and feeling angry. It seems such a betrayal, Ali. She knows how much I hate him, and – '

'And?' Alister prompted gently.

'I keep thinking about . . . Well, yes, I suppose I have been worrying. She's just not the type to . . . You know.'

'I know what you mean. I'm not sure you're right, though. He might be just what she needs. If you'd allow yourself to look on the bright side, for a moment . . . He's intelligent, independent, lively, experienced.'

'But that's the whole point!' Claudia wailed. 'She's *not* experienced, Alister! He'll eat her for breakfast!'

'I meant experienced in life, Clo.' He smiled. 'Not sex. I've had some experience too, but I'm not eating *you* for breakfast, am I?'

'I'm not as gullible as she is!'

'Aren't you?' His eyes crinkled teasingly. 'I'm not so sure about that. Pride ever goeth before a fall, Clo.' He turned away, grinning. 'Don't worry. She'll work it out. And, feeling the way you do about Marcus, you're in no position to advise her, are you?'

Much to Claudia's irritation, Alister walked away, forcing her to follow after him. 'Make up your mind!' she snapped. 'You were telling me only last night that she needed a friend!'

'Well, yes. But there are friends and friends. If she's in love with him, she'll hardly want you breathing disapproval all over her, will she? She'll want to tell you how handsome he is, how clever he is, how kind – '

'*Kind*?' It was almost a shriek.

Alister whirled on his heel, and continued to talk backwards down the track, his face lit up with laughter. 'So you agree he's handsome and clever?'

Claudia almost stamped her foot with frustration. 'Don't laugh at me! I'm serious, you fool!'

Alister stood still and stared at her for a moment, his smile fading. 'Oh, no, you're not, Clo. If you seriously cared about Marian, you'd go on caring for her, whoever else she loved. Did she ever tell you she thought Neil a bit of an oaf?'

'No!' she gasped. 'Is that what she told you?'

'Of course not. She'd be too loyal to tell me. But I'm not blind.' He turned away to hide another grin. 'I leave all that side of things to you.'

Feeling as if she'd been slapped, Claudia stood very still, watching as Alister disappeared behind the last of the glasshouses. She supposed he was right – on all counts. Even her hatred of Marcus was a kind of blindness, for when you came down to it he'd never done very much to deserve it – except laugh at her – and Alister did that, too. But she didn't hate Alister. In fact, she was finding him increasingly fascinating. She even began to feel that she liked him more than . . . No. She'd worked all that out last night, been fairly clear-sighted for once, and Alister was ***definitely*** off-limits.

As was her usual practice, Claudia bathed and changed her clothes straight after lunch and spent the afternoon in the office, keeping the paperwork in check. She had learned to enjoy this side of the business almost as much as she enjoyed the outdoor work and realised that it was just as important. She felt safer in the office, too. She could order it, which was more than could be said for the other things on which Murray & Son depended. Pests, diseases and the weather – she just had to learn to live with those and do as they dictated – but in the office, Claudia was boss. Calm, not controlled. *In* control. It felt good.

It usually felt good, but this afternoon it didn't. The magic she usually conjured with a bath, a clean outfit and a business-like spray of perfume hadn't worked this time. She felt nervous and distracted, unable to concentrate. She kept thinking about Marian.

Alister came in at three o'clock, carrying a tray of tea and biscuits. 'I've been making eyes at your nan,' he explained. 'But it was a waste of time. She's immune to my charms.'

'She's immune to anyone's charms,' Claudia muttered. 'If you wanted cake, why didn't you ask for it?'

'Oh, I was very obvious. I stared at the cake tin, drooled, panted and burst into tears when she doled out four Rich Teas as usual. But she didn't notice. Perhaps she needs new glasses.'

'Hmm,' Claudia said grimly. 'She's just lazy. The cake tin's further away from the tea-pot than the biscuit barrel.'

Alister's eyes widened disapprovingly. 'Now, now.'

'Well, it's true. She doesn't do anything any more. No one does anything. It's lucky *I'm* organised, or we'd be living in total chaos!' With this, she yanked a freshly typed letter from the typewriter, slapped it into the 'out' tray and knocked everything flying. Files, letters, tea, biscuits and a large box of paper clips made a wide, glittering arc across the office floor as they fell, accompanied by the smash of breaking china and a loud 'ping' as a teaspoon bounced off the side of the filing cabinet.

'I'll see to it,' Alister murmured. 'Sit still and count to ten . . . *thousand*, very slowly.'

Claudia closed her eyes and clenched her fists. 'One,' she said grimly. 'Huh! It's a good thing *I'm* organised!'

'Two, three,' Alister intoned solemnly. He was crawling over the floor, salvaging documents from leafy pools of tea.

'Total chaos! God, I'm such an embarrassment!'

'No, you're not, Clo.'

'I am! I've got no – no – no . . . I've got no – no – '

'Vocabulary?'

'Dignity!'

'Nonsense. Why, at this very moment you look exactly like Queen Victoria.' He tipped his head to one side to look at her more closely. 'Sort of boot-faced,' he added thoughtfully.

Claudia laughed, her eyes stinging with grateful tears. 'Oh, Ali, what would I do without you? I'd go mad.'

For a moment Alister seemed to freeze; then, as if to himself, 'Appreciation, at last. Play your cards right, my boy, and you might get some cake out of this.'

Grinning, Claudia looked away. 'Ali,' she murmured thoughtfully, 'if I fetch you more tea and some *cake*, would you finish clearing up for me? I – I want to go and see Marian, and if I don't go now I'll run out of courage.'

He sat back on his heels, his eyes narrowing suspiciously. 'How much cake?' he demanded.

Although Marian lived barely half a mile away, Claudia drove there to get it over with sooner. During her chaotic afternoon, she'd planned her approach fifty times over, but it wasn't until she actually drove out of Murray's gateway that she realised she'd have to apologise. She'd said some pretty rotten things to poor Marian. But so what? Marian hadn't exactly been the soul of courtesy, either! She'd started it! It was she who ought to be apologising, not Claudia!

With twenty yards of her journey accomplished, Claudia slid to a halt, gripping the steering wheel until her knuckles whitened as a new onset of rage overtook her. Oh, this was stupid! She was about to make a bloody fool of herself again! She might just as well turn round and go home!

No. She'd been building up to this all day, had virtually wrecked the office for it! And there was no point in being angry. She wanted to see Marian. She wanted to make it right between them. Therefore . . .

'Hi,' she whispered. 'Sorry I was rotten to you. How's things?'

That was okay. It didn't sound like grovelling. She could do it, just as long as she didn't blush. Just as long as Marian cooperated. Just as long as . . . But Marcus *wouldn't* be there. That was why Claudia – or her dream! – had chosen today, because he was haymaking, and would go on haymaking until it grew dark. If the weather held good, he'd be at it all week, and Marian would be lonely . . . Just ripe for the picking.

Miss Derby was weeding her front garden. Claudia smiled and waved, and her smile felt good. She kept smiling, rocketing up the hill at top speed before the brightness of her smile could fade. But it disappeared the moment she reached Marian's house. The drive was empty of cars, the garage doors shut; no dogs ran to bark a welcome. They were out!

No, Claudia reasoned nervously. Doctor Fairfield was out, and perhaps Mrs Fairfield was out, but Marian might still be in. She had to be, if only because Claudia knew she'd never be able to bring herself to do this again!

She rang the doorbell and received some immediate encouragement as the two Jack Russell pups threw themselves at the far side of the door, yapping furiously. This was a good sign. When everyone was out, the dogs were usually shut up in the rear scullery, where they couldn't do so much damage to the paintwork.

'Shut up,' she said sternly. 'It's only me.'

The dogs went on barking, but no one yelled at them. No one came. Claudia sighed and was just turning away when the dogs fell silent. She waited. Suddenly, from the direction of the staircase, she heard a series of bumps and crashes, a thin cry, and then the concerted whimperings of the two dogs, now coming from the other end of the hall. Without much hope, Claudia tried the door knob, almost kicking herself when she found the door swinging open at her touch. The dogs rushed towards her, yapping and panting, and then led her further down the hall, where Marian lay, her head on the rug, her legs sprawled uncomfortably over the lower steps of the stairs.

'Marian! Dear God, are you all right?'

Marian was not all right. She was barely conscious and her right arm lay at an unnatural angle beside her head, looking suspiciously as if it was broken. Her face was white, with a bluish tinge, and her eyes and lips were badly swollen, as if she'd been crying for days.

Claudia knelt down, elbowing the fussing dogs aside to stroke Marian's hair back from her face. 'Marian! It's Clo!'

Marian's eyes opened slightly and then closed again. 'Clo,' she croaked. 'Fell down.'

'I know! Marian, where's your father?'

'Gam, gam . . . gone.' And while Claudia was frantically trying to work this out Marian added feebly, 'Burm-am.'

'Birmingham? Oh, no!' She stood up, turned in a circle and crouched again to squeeze Marian's shoulder. She was shaking all over, knowing that she must keep calm and think clearly, yet feeling she'd snap in half with the effort.

'Marian,' she said, 'they've gone to your grandmother's? When will they be home? Tonight?'

Marian's eyes opened again. And closed. She said nothing.

'Tomorrow?'

'Uh,' Marian said. 'Clo . . . ? Slib tabs. Took . . . *Ambulance*.'

'*Sleeping tablets*?'

'Please.'

Claudia understood; but she didn't believe what she'd understood. Marian had taken sleeping tablets? To kill herself?

Claudia eyed the telephone as if it would explode at her touch. She'd never dialled 999 in her life, but Marian was injured, perhaps dying; and, without the slightest knowledge of first aid, Claudia couldn't help her. She picked up the phone, took a deep breath and dialled.

It was three hours before Claudia drove away from the hospital, knowing that Marian was safe – or at least not going to die. She had jumped to a few rather obvious conclusions while she'd waited for the ambulance to arrive; and Marian, only feebly struggling for coherence, had said nothing to change her mind.

Why should a girl of eighteen want to kill herself? There was only one reason. More than anyone else in the village, Marian had lived on a knife-edge of adult expectation, always striving to please her parents, always sacrificing her own wishes to theirs. The Fairfields counted among the most respected and respectable of Larcombe's families; kind, good, generous people who, although 'newcomers', had quickly woven themselves into the starched warp of village life. In many ways, Mrs Fairfield had taken Madge's place in the community, but she was tougher than Madge had ever been. Claudia had often thought it was the difference between a woman who had three children and a woman who had only one. Everything was focused on Marian. Everything was expected of Marian. Marian must not fail.

During the three hours while Claudia had waited, pacing the floor, while the doctors pumped Marian's stomach, set her broken arm and, finally, 'made her comfortable' in a quiet side ward until her parents could come to fetch her, Claudia had plucked up courage time and time again to ask the only question which needed an answer. 'Is she pregnant?' But she couldn't face it. She couldn't bear to know that Marian was expecting Marcus Saxon's child. It was enough to know that he had left her.

'I've phoned your parents, Marian! They're coming back tonight!'

'Uh . . .'

'Is there anyone else? Should I ring . . . Marcus?'

'No . . . no.' A wan smile touched her mouth. 'Not Marcus.' The smile widened painfully, making her dry, colourless lips stick to her teeth. 'Hot dinners, Clo . . .'

It was the last thing she said before she fell asleep, and Claudia wept, imagining that she'd somehow conjured Marian's fate in so cruelly predicting it. If she hadn't predicted it, hadn't quarrelled with Marian, if Claudia had only been there to help . . . But how *could* she have helped? Nothing, save a back-street abortionist (and Claudia didn't even know any back streets, let alone any abortionists) could help a girl who was pregnant!

Other things were reputed to do the trick, but Claudia had heard of girls who'd tried them all and still had their babies seven or eight months later. There were burning douches of raw Dettol, massive doses of laxatives, scalding baths, whole bottles of gin drunk by the tumblerful. Then you hurled yourself downstairs, praying, as you fell, that you'd have a miscarriage when you hit the bottom. Was that what Marian had done, using sleeping tablets instead of gin to lend her courage for the fall?

And now what? If Marian had been pregnant, the chances were that she was still pregnant: her education wasted, her career finished, her parents' hopes for her eternally blighted. Marian, of all people!

They'd been expecting it of Claudia for years, warning her, scolding her, telling her she was 'asking for it'; and she hadn't even *touched* it!

But no one had warned Marian. They'd thought she was safe!

Claudia had begun the drive home from Bristol feeling cold, calm and deeply chastened. Now, with six miles of her journey still to be accomplished and with a dozen other thoughts jostling for her notice (she must go back to the Fairfields', feed the dogs and check that the house was locked), she began to seethe with a growing indignation.

Marian would be disgraced! She'd be sent away to one of her remote relatives for the essential 'long holiday'. Why this was considered necessary Claudia had never fathomed, for as soon as a girl disappeared from the village for longer than a fortnight, everyone began saying, 'Here, I haven't seen Marian Fairfield for a while. Not poorly, is she?'

And then someone else would shake her head, purse her lips and whisper, 'Long holiday.'

You couldn't escape it. The shame went with you, wherever you went, and waited, narrow-eyed, for you to come home again: with your windfall, if the boy could be blackmailed into marrying you; or without it, if he happened to be Marcus Saxon.

Dear God, it was Sibyl Blake all over again! Nothing had changed! Forty years had gone by and nothing had changed! And, oh, it wasn't fair! It wasn't right! Why should Marian bear all the disgrace, suffer all the pain, lose everything she held dear (including her baby), while he – the bastard! – just carried on haymaking as if it had nothing at all to do with him?

Haymaking! And beans! He hadn't been talking about *beans*! He'd been talking about seduction, shame and sodding suicide! Ripe for the picking? She'd give him ripe for the picking! She'd kill him!

Chapter Seventeen

Had anyone asked what Marcus was thinking as he cleared the remnant of last year's hay from the barn, he would have said, 'Nothing,' for his thoughts were of the vague, almost abstract kind which hours of solitude are inclined to produce. He heartily disliked haymaking, which, even leaving out the complexities of weather, timing, and a few dozen other variables, was one of the hottest, dirtiest, most tedious jobs in the farming calendar; and it made his back ache as nothing else could.

He heard the roar of a car's engine on the drive, and stepped out of the barn to take a look, his heart leaping with astonishment as Claudia Murray's little Triumph, throwing up a great cloud of dust, skidded to a halt just outside.

Claudia always managed to astonish him. Every time he saw her he felt himself needing time to recover; and he'd never quite understood why this should be. He fancied her, of course, but that wasn't the reason. He'd fancied dozens of girls, and none of them had managed to stop his breath the way Claudia did. Perhaps it was because she was unavailable? No . . . Marcus had often sensed that his more lusty feelings towards her did not fall upon completely barren ground; the difficulty was only to find her in a receptive mood – which was the same as saying that the difficulty with touching the moon was that it was too high up. The damn thing would *never* come down.

Marcus straightened his aching spine and took a deep, relaxing breath, as Claudia leapt out of her car and slammed the door. She looked furious – and gorgeous. Her skin was tanned, her hair sun-bleached and slightly damp at the roots, her grey eyes huge and blazing like beacons. And she had perfect legs. Although she was so tiny, they were long, slender, and exquisitely proportioned. Summer-bare and summer-brown, their conformation was somehow emphasised, the delicate hollows of ankle and knee (and thigh: he'd caught a glimpse as she'd jumped from the car) giving him a terrible temptation to . . . Yes, well. Perhaps later, when the moon fell down.

'Good evening, Claudia,' he said dryly. 'Lost your way?'

'No! I've just come from the hospital!'

Marcus immediately thought of the day he'd left Clifton, almost exactly six years ago: the day Claudia's mother had died. Claudia had been raging then, too; and, in a way, she'd never stopped raging. Could she bear another loss?

'Your father?' he frowned.

'What?' She seemed almost to reel with surprise, her eyebrows flying up before descending again in a scowl of fury. 'No!' she snapped. 'Marian! And she was nearly dead, thanks to you!'

Marcus blinked. It was little wonder he always felt astonished by Claudia. She did and said the most amazing things. He hadn't seen Marian for weeks; in fact since that extraordinary night at The Swan. So what was all this about?

'Well, you needn't think you're getting away with it this time!' Claudia went on furiously. 'You can damn well marry her, because if you don't – if you don't – '

Her eyes, as they always did when she lost her temper, seemed to go out of focus; flickering and darting as if in search of something she could never find. Marcus was fascinated. Marry Marian? What on earth was the girl talking about?

'Well, you just *will* marry her!' Claudia gasped. 'Because it isn't fair, it isn't right, and it shouldn't be legal, and if I had my way, I'd kill you! She'd never even *done* it before *you* – !'

It was lucky she'd run out of words again, because Marcus's brain was beginning to scramble and he needed a moment to straighten it out. He hadn't touched Marian, and neither had anyone else as far as he knew; but something, very clearly, was wrong.

'Are you telling me Marian's pregnant?' he asked hollowly, but he was smiling: partly with nervousness; partly because he'd imagined himself as the Archangel Gabriel, impregnating Marian with a brush of his wings; and partly because, if Marian *was* pregnant, Claudia would have hysterics when she discovered who the real father was.

But he shouldn't have smiled. Claudia didn't like it. 'You bastard!' she shrieked. 'You know she is! That's why you left her!' And her hand flew up, claws bared, to slash at his face.

Marcus caught her wrist – it was a good deal easier than catching a gnat – and then the other one, which was easier still. Why were women always so slow? And why did they always express surprise that men were faster? Claudia was shocked rigid to have been put out of action without landing a single blow. But she was thinking, too, and he could read her thoughts as clearly as if they were printed on her forehead. Now I'll kick him.

'Don't,' he advised softly.

Rather to his surprise, Claudia didn't; but her face, which had been flushed with rage, suddenly drained of colour. She bared her teeth, shocking Marcus all over again. He even felt a little frightened on her behalf. Didn't she know that by losing control of herself, she lost control of everything? She was too damn small to be picking fights with men twice her size. One day she'd choose the wrong man, and get her delicate little neck broken – or worse.

'Let – me – go!'

'Now why should I do that?' Marcus asked reasonably. 'You'll try to claw me again, and I'll have to stop you again, and we'll be back where we started – like this.'

And this, in its way, was by no means unpleasant, for Claudia wasn't fighting now. She seemed to be gathering strength for another onslaught, and was beginning to quiver with the effort. Marcus tightened his grip, and then, more by instinct than design, snatched her against him. She gasped then stood perfectly still, her face averted, her eyes shut.

'Let me go,' she whispered. 'I want to go home.'

Marcus couldn't help it – he laughed out loud. Not just for the ease of his victory, but for the scent of her hair, the lightness of her body, the soft, satiny skin on the insides of her wrists. He wanted to catch her up in his arms and swing her around; and, when she was dizzy enough . . . God, what had happened to his backache?

'You want to go *home*?' he mocked. 'Why? You came here to tell me something, didn't you?'

'What the hell do you care? Let me go!'

'I'm not letting you go until you calm down. I don't want a fight, Claudia. I'm bigger than you. One of us – naming no names – could get hurt.'

'Are you *threatening* me?'

She sounded quite indignant, and Marcus laughed again, not wholly believing that any of this was happening. She was like the Red Queen in 'Alice'. Almost logical, but not noticeably sane.

'No,' Marcus said. 'Are you threatening me?'

Claudia said nothing. He tilted his head to watch her reaction which, like everything else about her, touched him almost to tears. The scowl, the down-turned mouth which meant that she wasn't beaten yet; then the frustrated pout which meant that perhaps she was; then her face clearing, her eyebrows lifting with disdain as she prepared to change tactics. Marcus wasn't keen to know where that might lead them.

He took a step backwards, bending his knees to get a clearer view of her face. Yes, he'd won the first round. She looked wary now, as if she, too, had begun to calculate their differences in height and weight and realised she'd bitten off more than she could chew. He could afford to be generous. He needed to be. He didn't want her to run off yet. She'd given him the only interesting few moments in an otherwise rotten day.

'About Marian,' he prompted cautiously. He released one of her hands and indicated the piled up hay bales at the far end of the barn. 'Shall we sit down?' He let go her other hand, and immediately felt bereft. 'Please,' he added softly.

Claudia put her nose in the air and strolled slowly across the barn: bored, aloof, altogether too good to care. And she sat down exactly as she had done when she'd taken sick at the Country Club: as if her knees had given way. She was still trembling.

'Claudia.' He sat down beside her, but at a respectable distance so that he shouldn't give way to his feelings and hold her hand.

'Could you just wait a moment?' she demanded hurriedly.

She straightened her shoulders, blinked, took a series of deep breaths, bit her lip, and then, by force of will rather than inclination, relaxed.

'Better?'

She lifted her chin and gazed determinedly into the far corner of the barn. 'Yes,' she said at last.

Marcus almost laughed again, but decided that it was probably more than his life was worth.

'I went out with Marian three times,' he explained quietly. 'And, except in the most casual of ways, I didn't touch her. *No.*' He pressed down on the air with the flat of his hand, silencing her protests. 'Let me finish. We went out for a drink on each occasion, and she spent most of the time talking about someone else. I didn't mind, because that had been the object of the exercise. She wanted to talk, and the man in question was a mutual friend. If she *is* pregnant . . .'

He frowned, not believing it; but if Claudia had come from the hospital, if Marian . . . No, he couldn't believe it. 'Are you sure?' he asked softly.

Claudia's face had lost its colour again. She said nothing.

'Tell me what happened.'

Her eyes widened, lost focus, skimmed his face, his shoulders, his hands. 'No!' she gasped. 'She told me! She said she was in love with you and . . .'

'With me? Or just with *someone*?'

'With you!'

Marcus shook his head. 'No.'

'She took sleeping tablets,' Claudia whispered. 'It *was* you. I know it was!'

'But do you know for certain that she's pregnant? I can't believe it, Claudia. She hadn't seen this other chap since – oh, months ago. And I didn't touch her. I couldn't, wouldn't. For one thing she's not my type, and for another she's in love with someone else.'

Claudia frowned, hesitated. 'And he won't marry her?' she asked faintly at last.

Marcus bit back a sigh of relief. She believed him. 'If she's expecting his baby, I think he will, yes.'

'Then why did she try to kill herself?'

'I don't know, Claudia. She's been depressed about a number of things – her exams, this chap . . .'

'But who *is* he?' she wailed. 'Why didn't she tell me? At The Swan, she – she let me believe it was you!'

Now, to Marcus's horror, she began to cry, tensing her shoulders, searching her pocket for a handkerchief. 'She's my friend!' she wailed softly. 'We've never had secrets from each other!'

Marcus didn't know what to say. It was all too complicated. If only to comfort her he would have liked to tell what he knew; but it didn't amount to much and it seemed that at least half of it – in the light of recent developments – was guesswork. Marian had clearly had reasons for not confiding in Claudia. He wasn't certain what they were, and knew too little – both of Marian and Claudia – to guess at them. Torn loyalties, perhaps. Or perhaps it was just Claudia's dangerous tendency to jump to all the wrong conclusions.

He averted his gaze while Claudia blew her nose and made an attempt to reclaim her dignity. Not that she'd really lost it. Although he always seemed to catch her at her most embarrassing moments, he'd never thought less of her, never felt that she was less worthy of his respect. It could be just his imagination, of course, but she'd always seemed the type who could survive anything, however terrible, and still come out fighting.

God, she was a funny girl . . . She was carrying responsibilities a woman twice her age could have been excused for balking at. She worked like a horse, looked like an angel and behaved like a . . . like a schizophrenic fairy: turning everyone into donkeys at every move she made! He still hadn't recovered from seeing her push Neil into the river. Every time he thought of it, it made him smile.

He smiled now, watching covertly as Claudia stroked the

tears from her face with her knuckles, like a child. It was a touching little gesture, and breathtakingly erotic; not only because it made her seem so vulnerable, but because it made her seem so strong. And she was quite calm now. She'd even stopped shaking.

'Okay?' Marcus asked softly.

'Yes.' She smiled; a mere courtesy, for there was no matching warmth in her eyes. 'Sorry. I was a bit strung up. I – I wrecked the office earlier. I'd been telling Alister how organised I was, and then I knocked everything, including a tray of tea, all over the floor.'

She had addressed all this to the topmost corner of the barn, but now she looked at Marcus, shyly, almost pleadingly, as if, like him, she'd realised that for the first time in her life she was being civil to him, and that everything would be lost if he didn't respond in kind. And she hadn't just been civil, she'd been self-critical, self-mocking – almost inviting him to laugh at her. A gift? Or a test? Or . . . something else?

'Well, that's life,' he smiled. 'Just when you think you've got it tamed, it jumps up and bites you. Is Marian all right now? Do you know?'

'Yes. The doctor at the hospital said she just had to sleep it off. She'll be a bit sick tomorrow, but otherwise . . . Oh!' Her eyes widened. 'She's broken her arm.'

'Good God. How?'

'She fell downstairs. I – I thought she'd thrown herself, but now I don't know.'

She looked chastened and bewildered, as if being left in ignorance of Marian's secrets had completely undermined her. Marcus wanted to cuddle her and kiss it all better. But it seemed safer to change the subject.

He glanced approvingly at her unadorned left hand. 'I see you broke it off with Neil.'

'Yes.'

'I'm glad.'

'So am I.'

'It wouldn't have worked.'

Claudia smiled wanly. 'No.'

'What made you decide?' He risked another grin. 'The river?'

'In a way.' She averted her eyes. 'I think it was you, though, mostly.'

Marcus blinked and caught his breath, but before he could question her she went on quickly, 'It was what you said about my father. And Alister. I suddenly realised that the business would probably fold if I left, and Neil wouldn't let me go on working, especially at that.'

'That?'

'Market gardening.'

'Sorry. I don't quite – '

'Well . . . He didn't say, but I always suspected that in Neil's opinion it's only one step up from road mending. He always told people I just did the business side of it.' She pulled her mouth down at the corners, but her eyes were bright with an unholy mischief. 'Company director,' she murmured.

Marcus roared with laughter, his heart almost bursting with excitement when Claudia laughed too, throwing her head back to expose the delicate, creamy shaft of her throat. She looked wonderful. Except at a distance, with someone else, he'd never seen her laughing, and it was a complete transformation. It was as if, until now, he'd perceived her in only two dimensions, almost as a cliché: 'the village wildcat'. Now she became solid, occupying a whole space rather than just a surface. She was like an unexpected parcel from an unknown source, provoking an almost irresistible urge to tear off her wrappers.

A tense silence fell. She would go soon. Marcus imagined her going as the snapping of a finely spun thread, so fragile and delicately wrought that it might never be repaired.

'No,' he said quickly. 'You wouldn't have been happy with Neil. You aren't – ' He had been going to say 'polite enough', which was hardly calculated to prolong her visit.

'Aren't what?'

'Hypocrite enough.'

Her eyes tipped up to meet his, sparking with merriment, and his heart clenched like a fist, making him dizzy.

'Oh, well, in that case,' she grinned, 'I'd better be honest. It was the frilly pinny, really.'

'The what?'

'You said you couldn't quite see me in a frilly pinafore. It seemed to sum everything up, that's all. You hadn't said anything I didn't already know, but you . . . Well, I suppose you clarified it.'

She looked at her hands. They were a little paler than her arms and very well kept: the nails filed to short, pearly ovals.

'You haven't the hands of a road mender.'

'No, I wear gloves. Dad's got a thing about blood poisoning, since Grandad . . . you know.'

It was as if they were both waiting for something to happen, marking the time with words, like people at a railway station who, even while dreading to say goodbye, still wish the train would move and put them out of their misery.

'I must go,' Claudia said. 'I'm sorry about . . . I'm sorry.' She stood up, blushing.

It seemed very natural to rest his arm on her shoulder as they walked to the door. It seemed natural until he did it, and then it seemed almost magical for Claudia didn't shrug him off – she simply stopped walking, stopped breathing, as if, mesmerised by stage-fright, she'd forgotten all her lines. Marcus curled his fingers around the warm skin of her arm, and she turned, very slightly, towards him, lowering her eyes.

Marcus felt his heart thud, constrict, and seem to stop beating before it began again, more loudly than before. What was she doing? Why had she stopped? Christ, she looked so beautiful, so passive and still, as if she was just waiting for him to . . .

It was like catching a butterfly. Every move Marcus made was slow, controlled: every breath he took so shallow it made his head spin. He stroked a finger over the soft down of her cheek and closed his eyes, terrified that when he opened them again she'd have flown away. He cupped his hands under her chin, touched her mouth with his mouth and slowly withdrew, knowing that the look of wide-eyed horror on her face was reflected in his own.

'Claudia?' he breathed.

Everything about her was unexpected, startling and strange. He'd known she was small, but when his hands strayed to her waist he touched empty air. Her waist was narrower than he remembered, more tiny than his eyes had judged it to be. He had often admired the soft swell of her hips, but when his hands followed their curve, it was deeper, softer, exquisitely feminine.

'Oh, God,' he groaned softly. 'Claudia?'

But when she would have spoken he was afraid. He silenced her with his mouth and trapped her in his arms; and she leapt in his arms, towards him, not away.

They knelt on the floor in a rosy beam of late sunlight. Marcus held her shoulders, kneading them with his fingers as if to break her trance. But he spoke like a hypnotist, offering escape with words which his voice and his eyes denied.

'Are you sure you want to go, Claudia?'

She was breathing through her mouth. Her skin was

flushed, damp and slightly grubby, streaked with hay dust. She smelled of musk.

Marcus closed his eyes. 'Don't go,' he whispered. He gathered her against him, cradling her head with his hand.

It was like touching the moon.

'I want to look at you.' He'd hoisted a few bales clear of the heap, making a wide, sheltered bed in the centre – dusky, dusty, sweet and warm. 'May I?'

He had never spoken to a woman like this. The teasing, masterful approach had always worked pretty well in the past, and he had no idea why this should be different. But it was very different. He was afraid of her; afraid of doing a single thing wrong; afraid not only of losing the ultimate prize but of missing a single step along the way. He wanted everything first, and then he wanted everything at last, and then he wanted everything again – until he died of it.

'You *are* looking at me.' Her voice was dry, husky and hesitant, as if she was fainting with thirst.

'All of you,' he whispered.

She said nothing, but her hand strayed to the top button of her dress, defensively at first, then gently fingering it as if she couldn't quite recall how to unfasten it.

Marcus swallowed. 'Let me.'

The buttons began at the shoulder and went all the way down. Ten buttons. Large enough to manipulate without fumbling, numerous enough to prolong the suspense to a delicious degree. And he missed nothing. The golden line of her collar bone, the dewy hollow of her throat, the gilded plane of her chest fading to shell pink where her breasts parted, nestling softly in white lace.

He smiled and left the task half finished to sip at her mouth, to drink from her eyes. They had darkened and seemed bigger than ever, but her expression was calm, half smiling, as if, although fascinated by the progress they had made, she still wasn't certain it was happening. Her uncertainty only added to the tension – and the pleasure – for when Claudia was unsure, she was dangerous. She could cry 'Stop' at any moment and punch hell out of him. Marcus held his breath and, with his eyes on her face, undid another button.

Claudia tipped her head to one side, reached out, withdrew, reached out again and pressed her fingers, very gently, to the base of his throat. He gasped, and closed his eyes, arching his spine as though he'd touched a live wire. Claudia retreated. Marcus caught her hand and kissed her palm. 'Touch me,' he murmured. She unfastened his shirt, her fingers shaking. Marcus leaned over her, shadowing her with his shoulders. 'Hold me.'

He was careful not to rest his weight on her. He was careful of his hands, lest in his eagerness he grab or push or pull. He mustn't frighten her; she mustn't feel compelled – except by her own desire. Of all the women in the world, Claudia must come to him freely and without hesitation. There must never be a moment when she regretted this or wished it hadn't happened. Yet the need to imprison her was great, almost frightening in its intensity. He wanted her!

The dress had gone. Claudia lay on her back, staring up at his chest as if at a starry sky. She licked her lips and Marcus stooped lower, presenting his nipple to her mouth. She tasted it, and Marcus groaned, tasting heaven.

'Claudia!'

'Yes?'

He laughed and drew away. 'Don't rush me.' He stroked her face, her throat, ran a finger between her breasts and his palm over her belly. He tweaked the ribbons of her petticoat. 'Look,' he chided softly. 'I still can't see all of you.'

She cooled immediately, her face pinching with fright. 'What if somebody comes?'

'No one will come. The men have gone. Dad's out. No one will come.'

'Your mother?'

'No. No one. I promise.'

The tension left her by slow degrees. She closed her eyes, and Marcus waited, using the time to slide one of the ribbons clear of her shoulder, lifting it with his finger, observing the contrast of brown skin, white satin and purple shadow as if memorising it for a painting. She was thin enough to allow the bone to gleam at the point of her shoulder, but her arms were firm and strong, the skin taut, and as smooth as warm milk poured from a pitcher.

'Take it off?' Marcus whispered.

Naked at last, Claudia shuddered, and he held her in his arms to hide her. He rocked her. He stroked her hair. 'There,' he murmured. 'Don't be shy.'

He smiled and rubbed her nose. He kissed her eyes. He laid her down.

God, she was beautiful! Her breasts were small, but full and rounded, the skin blue-pink and as lustrous as the inside of sea-shells. Her nipples were as rosy as her cheeks, but even her shyness was a delight. He was touched by it, and felt as honoured by it as if he were the first living mortal ever to see, ever to touch, ever to come near her.

'Claudia?'

She peeped at him from under her eyelashes. 'Yes?'

'I'm shy, too, you know.'

She thought about it, a little smile coming and going at the corners of her mouth. 'Are you?'

Her smile broadened deliciously, and she put her arms around his neck and drew him down.

With his weight on his knees, Marcus kissed and stroked her from her mouth to her thighs, easing her legs apart. She was wet, the scent of her like incense.

'All right, baby?'

She said nothing.

This was it: the long, dark journey into light. He pushed and she gasped, her eyes flying wide. She was tight, tense; but he'd waited too long. If he couldn't have her now, he'd die!

'Relax,' he murmured urgently.

It was the last word he said before he drowned.

Although Marcus and his father still quarrelled, they had established a system which kept things civilised and their emotions always at one remove. They never discussed personal matters. They never swore at one another. In times of absolute desperation, Ben swore at one of the labourers instead; but Marcus prided himself on his self-control. The angrier he was, the quieter and more courteous he became; and he'd discovered that this virtue, like many others, reaped its own reward, for his courtesy won more arguments than rage had ever done.

But Marcus had more than one kind of rage. There was the kind which courtesy consumed, and used to his advantage, and the kind which, subdued by courtesy, consumed and used him: burning in his guts like a cancer. In such a rage he understood sadists and murderers. In such a rage he frightened himself witless, knowing that his self-control, like an unexploded bomb, needed only the faintest of vibrations to blow it sky high. Until Claudia, only Ben had made him so angry. No, not even Ben had made him so angry.

He *hadn't* raped her!

He hadn't known she was a virgin! The thought hadn't even crossed his mind! She'd been going out with Neil for years, had been engaged to him, for Christ's sake! And, even if it had occurred to him, he'd have deemed it impossible that she would choose him, of all people, to be the first. Why not Neil? Why not anyone? But not him! Not him!

She'd done it deliberately. It had been some sort of twisted revenge, with only one motive: to do the worst thing she could possibly do to him – accuse him of rape.

Rape! *Him*! And to *her*!

But twelve hours later, as he drove the cows in for milking, with his teeth gritted so hard he thought they would shatter in his mouth, he could have raped, strangled her and chopped her up for rat bait. Why hadn't she said anything? It was an unwritten law, a principle of courtesy (not to mention self-defence!) that a virgin should announce her condition, ask for special consideration, crave leniency! If Claudia had spoken, he'd have left her alone. Well, perhaps not. Almost certainly not – for he'd never wanted anyone so much. But he wouldn't have hurt her. He would never have hurt her. And then she . . . could not have hurt him.

But she'd crushed a part of his soul he hadn't even known existed; something small, fragile and, above all things, essential, like one of the tiny glands in the brain whose power goes unnoticed until it stops working. Then, suddenly . . .

His rage would fade. Today or tomorrow, next week or next year, his heart would stop racing, his stomach stop churning, his thoughts be ordered again. But he'd never be the same. He'd never get over this. He'd loved her! And oh, he hated her now!

He couldn't believe it had happened. Had she done it deliberately, or been as shocked as he was? She'd been as shocked as he was, surely, for how could she have faked such a scream? But it had been too late to stop. He'd heard her screaming as if they were existing in two worlds, as remote as the earth was from the moon; and he hated himself for that. He hated himself, but he hated Claudia more.

Rape! It hadn't been rape! He'd *loved* her!

The long dark journey into light . . . He'd thought he'd be dazzled by it, transformed and re-born; but it had been like drowning, being swept up by horrors and sucked into cold, strangling depths. His needs had brooked no refusal, had gone where he'd led them; but Claudia had been far away, her screams changing to sobs which had broken his heart. He'd never get over it. Never.

He skipped breakfast and went straight out to the hayfields, turning the grass he had mown the day before. He went back to the yard, hitched up the mower and was on his way out to the top pasture when Ben flagged him down. Marcus stopped, but the very thought of having to speak made him feel sick. He sent his father a cold, forbidding stare, and took bitter satisfaction from seeing it properly interpreted. Ben turned aside, looking at his feet.

Gritting his teeth, Marcus thrust the gear stick forward and drove out of the yard at speed, wondering how he'd ever be able to go home again. He was a danger and a threat to anyone who approached him. He'd gone wild inside, and the wildness was too close to the surface, looking for any excuse to break out.

Last night he'd thought he'd got himself tamed. He'd thought (yet again) that he'd reached the top rung of that bloody ladder, where you stepped into another world and found that everything was right. She had been . . . He had thought . . . Jesus, it had been like a revelation: all his vague feelings about her over the years condensing into pure knowledge. That this was the one. That this was the girl he had known without knowing, waited for without longing, looked for without searching. The one he could cherish all his life and never tire of. And she hadn't said a word . . .

But *he* had spoken! He had asked her and asked her, every step of the way! Until the end. And then it was too late. She was too tight, and he too heavy. He too big, and she too small. He couldn't stop!

Marcus drew the tractor to a halt in the middle of the field he had mown, staring zombie-like at the distant, purple haze of the surrounding hills. He closed his eyes and his body shimmered with pain, every part of it: muscle, gut, nerve and bone.

He should have known. She'd been so shy, so hesitant. But he'd thought it was just . . . He'd imagined she'd felt as he felt: amazed and wondering, stunned by the depths of her feelings for a man she'd thought she hated.

But he'd never hated *her*! She'd always been . . . He'd always cared about her. He'd watched her from a distance, absorbing the pleasure she gave him without even recognising it. The way she walked, the distant sound of her laughter, the remote events of her life; they'd entered his bloodstream by a kind of osmosis, so that he'd known her without knowing it, known everything – except the most important thing of all.

He would never forgive her.

Chapter Eighteen

Claudia explained her swollen eyes and her misery with a muted tale of Marian's 'accident'. No one doubted her. They seemed to take it for granted that the shock had been enough to turn her to mash; and even Cath managed a word of sympathy: 'Hush, hush. You take things too much to heart, Clo,' before adding caustically, 'Huh, you'll learn what trouble is before you're much older, my girl.'

'I thought she was dead!' Claudia protested. 'Isn't that trouble enough, for crying out loud?'

But then she remembered Marcus telling her she wasn't a hypocrite, and the shame of it almost felled her where she stood, for she didn't care if Marian was dead or alive. If it hadn't been for Marian, none of it would have happened.

You're jealous! Yes, that was where it had begun. And now it had ended. Everything had ended.

Flames of shame swept over her in great, engulfing waves, making her halt in her tracks, gasping with shock. She'd never known anything like it. Not even when Madge had died. For that had been a cold, drowning pain; the pain of disbelief. She'd felt cheated and beaten, innocent and bereft. And then she'd been angry, raging, hating everyone and wishing all the mothers in the world could die, all the daughters in the world suffer as she was suffering.

But she hadn't been ashamed! And she couldn't bear the shame! She couldn't carry it. It would kill her!

She hadn't slept. She'd been up at four, preparing the day's meals, washing the kitchen floor. Save for the wild treadmill of her thoughts, she was aware of only one thing about herself: that she had tunnel vision and could look neither right nor left. It was as if, when she turned her head, she would see Marcus standing there, shaking with fury.

I wish you were dead.

She wished he'd killed her, then they'd both be out of their misery.

Somehow, she ploughed through the entire day with her eyes downcast, moving so fast she began to feel she'd drop with exhaustion. Alister didn't try to stop her. After the first anxious enquiry he left her alone; but as the hours went by she found that she was longing for him to stop her. Longing for him to stop *it*, before it drove her mad.

At lunchtime she went to her room, stripped off her clothes and stared at herself in the mirror. Her body was still the same. Nothing had changed save for the two purple bruises on her shoulders where Marcus had shaken her; shaken her and wept.

'No! No! No! I *loved* you!'

It was true. He had loved her. And she had loved him, knowing from the minute he caught her wrists that Marian had been right: she'd been jealous; she'd wanted him, and had taken the first excuse she could find to seek him out. It was the only reason she'd tried to hit him, so that he would touch her, hold her . . .

No good to say now that she hadn't known. She'd known and denied it, and believed her own lies. Cheap. Cheap. That was what he would tell himself, that she'd thrown herself at him, like a cheap little slut. *Asking* for it. *Panting* for it. It was true.

The only excuse she had was that she hadn't known precisely what she was panting *for*. No one had told her it would be like that! She knew only one girl who had done it and been prepared to talk about it; and it hadn't been a *bit* like that! But then, Diane Bridges was hardly . . . Well, Diane Bridges was *natural*. She took it all for granted, chewing a lump of gum all the while. 'Yeah, it was all right. Nothing to it, really. We went to the pictures after.'

Claudia hadn't expected to go to the pictures afterwards. But she had at least expected it to be possible. She hadn't expected it to hurt!

She closed her eyes and bowed her head, aching with shame. She knew it was all her own fault, that she should have told him. Why hadn't she? Partly because it had seemed such a crude thing to say in a situation where words of any kind seemed superfluous. It had all been so fragile: a tense, breathless thing which words could so easily have broken. She'd just wanted to see, to feel, to hear him, to learn everything that had been hidden through all the years she'd known him – without knowing him.

And she'd wanted to . . . surprise him! She'd wanted to lie in his arms when it was over, talking at last, reminding him of that day in the woods when, without even realising it, she'd decided to save herself for him, to prove that she wasn't as he'd thought her. But she'd been crying too much to speak, and he was too angry to listen.

'Why didn't you tell me? You fool! You stupid little bitch!'

She'd deserved worse than that. She'd wanted him so much, and had never thought . . . No, that wasn't true. How could she not think of babies, of getting pregnant, of being shamed, when that was the reason she'd gone there in the first place? But she'd thought of it, and let it drift away with his voice. She'd thought of it,and let it drown in his eyes. And when he'd touched her . . .

He had touched every part of her, so beautifully; but the touch she remembered most clearly was the first. Just his arm resting lightly on her shoulder, as if they were the best of friends and had always been so. Yet the response it had wrought in her had had little to do with friendship. A terrible, beautiful feeling, it had begun in her toes and rocketed through her entire body, pinning her to the spot. She would remember that feeling for the rest of her life: his arm on her shoulder; just that.

Afterwards, it had been like a ritual of prayer. An act of faith, of absolute trust. 'No one will come. No one.'

Not even an unwanted child. It was as if they were beyond nature. As if in so hallowed a place, nature couldn't intrude. Perhaps this was how it happened for everyone. This was the thing which reduced Mrs Chislett to naught. In a hallowed place, among the faithful, the devil and all his works are simply forgotten. Until the preacher cries, 'You'll burn!' Until the high priest murmurs, 'All right, baby?'

So simple. But he might just as well have cried, 'You'll burn,' for it had had precisely the same effect. Baby! If he'd said it two seconds earlier she'd have been out and running. But he'd come down on her in the same instant; in the instant that she'd shut him out. Had he cut her in half with an axe it couldn't have hurt more. She'd screamed, fully believing that he would leave her, take the pain away; and it was as if the world had caved in when he didn't.

The trust had all gone, just crumbled to dust; and she'd remembered she hated him, and that he hated her. She'd remembered how she'd come there, threatening to kill him, accusing him of this very thing; and she'd remembered his response: 'I'm bigger than you. One of us could get hurt!'

Panic. Terror. And pain. And memories which weren't her own – of Luke Saxon and Sibyl Blake. How could she blame herself for thinking it was the same, that it had been just a cruel, vengeful trick to punish and torment her? But oh, she blamed herself for saying it, without even once looking at his face! 'You raped me!' Even then she could scarcely bear to look. A glance through her tears, merely, but she'd known at once that she was wrong.

'No! No! No! I *loved* you!'

But she'd been beside herself, sobbing her heart out, and his grief had only made it worse. That was the shame! That was the agony! She'd have given anything to buy the words back, but they were already carved in stone on his face and could never be reclaimed.

Oh, dear God, if a baby came out of this she'd strangle it at birth! She'd never tell him! She would never go near him again.

She ground to a halt in the late afternoon, creeping away to the furthest corner of the property where her mother's long-abandoned bee-hives and an old wooden bench had been left to rot. She kept saying they'd clear this patch – almost an acre of wasted ground – but they'd never got around to it. Would they ever, now?

Claudia sat on the bench and cried, without passion or energy, just letting the tears fall. She felt she was dying; that all of her past and all of her future had been swallowed up, and that nothing remained of her except pain. Not *that* pain. Excruciating as it had been, eternal as it had seemed, it was over and had no consequence now except as the begetter of *this* pain, which she couldn't endure for another day, another hour.

She wished she was dead; and she *would* die, she *would* die! They couldn't make her live through another day like this!

'Oh, no.' The voice came out of nowhere; a sick, sweet,

cloying voice, full of threat. 'Oh, no, Claudia, it's not as easy as all that. Think of your father. Think . . . Think of Uncle Jim.'

Her body turning ice cold, Claudia thought of Uncle Jim, knowing that he had suffered this – this and twice this, fifty times this – and endured it. No, they didn't let you escape. And her father . . . He'd screamed too, when Madge had died. He'd said he couldn't bear it. Yet six years later he was still bearing it; and worse. The days passed: long, empty stretches of grief and loneliness, sorrow and pain; and you lived every one of them. There was no escape.

Something hardened in Claudia at that moment. The panic began to fade, and she sat very quietly, with her eyes closed, knowing she'd never be the same again.

'Clo?' The sun was setting, and Alister was just a silhouette against a rose and violet sky. 'Are you asleep, Clo?'

'No, just thinking.'

He came closer, standing beside her with his hands in his pockets. He smelled very nice; and without looking at him Claudia knew he'd been home, had bathed and changed his clothes. But a glance to her left told her that he had changed for something special: he was wearing a suit. 'Going out, Ali?'

'Been. Thought I'd just check . . . On the tomatoes, before I went home.'

Claudia bowed her head. 'Oh,' she whispered. 'They're almost ripe . . . for the picking.' She turned to him. 'Oh, Ali, I'm so miserable! Don't go home yet!'

'I wasn't planning to.' He stroked her hair, pushing her head down to rest against his thigh. And then they were quiet, listening to the swallows twittering overhead.

'She's all right,' Alister said softly at last. 'That's where

I've been, Clo: to the Fairfields', and she's all right. She's still a bit woozy, but she's perfectly sensible, and she's grateful – very grateful to you. Clo, you saved her life! Can't you think of that, instead of blaming yourself for quarrelling with her?'

He crouched beside her and looked earnestly into her eyes, and Claudia hadn't the heart to tell him that his efforts had all been wasted. Marian . . . As if she mattered.

'Will you go to see her tomorrow?'

Claudia turned away. 'I don't know, Ali. I'm . . . a bit confused.'

He smiled. 'A bit? What do you do when it's serious?'

To her amazement, Claudia laughed feebly. 'God, Ali, don't make me laugh . . . I've got a crashing headache.'

'Come back to the house, and we'll have some nice, warm aspirins together, shall we?'

'Sounds lovely.' She stood up and immediately sat down again, hiding her face in her hands. He was so good to her. And she didn't deserve it, not any of it! God, if he knew what she'd done, he'd never speak to her again! He'd give his notice! He'd hate her!

'Clo, that's enough. Stop it. You'll make yourself ill, and you know I can't manage without you. Just a day of it was bad enough.'

'I worked all day!' Claudia sobbed. 'You didn't have to manage without me!'

'I wasn't talking about work, Clo.' He sat astride the bench, holding her while she cried. 'You've got the worst temper of any girl I've ever met, but this was the first day since I've known you that you didn't smile – or make me smile. And I don't want another day like it, Clo. It's bad for my nerves.' He'd said all this very softly. Now, in a fading falsetto, he added, 'I have very *sensitive* nerves.'

Again Claudia laughed, pushing him away to blow her

nose. 'You've got nerves like an ox,' she chided wistfully. 'Oh, I wish I was like you, Ali. You seem to know . . . You always seem to know what to *do*.'

'Bravado,' he said modestly. 'I'm a jelly inside.'

'Really?'

'Yes, sometimes. When there's nothing I can do, when I feel helpless, as I do now. I sometimes think we're all the same inside. We're all lonely, all wishing . . . for something or other.'

Claudia watched his face, realising suddenly that it was a very beautiful face even though almost every feature – save for his jaw – was imperfect. But there was something deeper. A spiritual beauty which nothing could ever spoil.

'Have you ever been hurt?' she whispered.

'Yes. Many times.'

'And . . . Did you know what to do about it? How to cope with it? Did you know how you'd get through tomorrow?'

'No. I just knew I'd have to.'

'But some . . . people . . .'

'If you mean Marian, she just had a funny half hour, Clo. By the time you found her, she *knew* she had to get through tomorrow; and the important thing is, she wanted to. The door never closes, you see. We just sometimes think it has.'

He pulled her to her feet and slid his arm around her waist to support her. It felt good: infinitely comforting. *He* would never hurt her. And the door never closes . . .

Merely to give credence to the state she'd been in over Marian, Claudia went to see her the next evening, taking a bunch of pink roses and a clutch of magazines. She had no idea what to say. On the one hand she felt very old, wizened and hopeless; and on the other she felt like a small child, still quivering from a punishment and not yet forgiven.

Either way, it seemed wisest to keep her mouth shut and let things happen as they might. Ask no questions. Tell no – as few lies as possible.

Marian was in the garden, sitting on the low wall which edged the fish pond, with her arm in a sling. When she saw Claudia, her eyes filled with tears. 'Oh, Clo,' she whispered.

Claudia smiled stiffly. 'I brought you . . .' She laid her gifts on the wall. 'How's the arm?'

'Fine. It doesn't even hurt.' They were silent, looking anywhere but at each other's face. 'Did you walk up?' Marian asked at last.

'No. Feeling lazy.' Feeling scared, she added silently. In fact she was wondering if she'd ever be able to walk anywhere again. In the car she was safe. In the car, she couldn't meet anyone, couldn't be challenged, inspected, attacked. The car was like a snail's shell, protecting her from a world full of thrushes.

'I – I owe you an explanation,' Marian said, 'but I don't know where to start. It wasn't – '

'It's all right,' Claudia said hurriedly. 'There's no need to tell me anything. Wait until you feel better.'

'But I need to tell you!' Marian wailed. 'Marcus was here!'

Claudia sat down very suddenly, knowing that she'd turned white. Her stomach felt like a block of ice, its contents freezing. She wanted to be sick, to run away, to push Marian backwards into thc pond and hold her under; but she couldn't move, not even to blink.

'I didn't mean to hurt you,' Marian groaned. 'It was just . . . Well, I didn't know anything! I still don't, and it seemed so wrong to tell you, when . . . Oh, God, I don't know where to start, Clo! With Marcus . . . I honestly thought you were deceiving yourself with all this feud business, and that if you could just face up to it . . . But I was wrong, and I'm sorry. If I'd known . . .'

'Known?' It was a murmur, barely audible even to herself. He'd told! Now the door really had closed.

'Oh, Clo.' Marian took her hand. 'Don't look at me like that. It just never occurred to me that you'd jump to that conclusion! It should have, I know, but – '

Claudia closed her eyes. Perhaps, in a minute or two, she'd find strength enough to walk out of here; but until then . . .

'What conclusion?' she muttered.

'That Marcus and I – that he'd – that I was pregnant! God, he was so angry with me.'

'With you?'

'For leading you up the garden path, for letting you believe . . . But I didn't do it deliberately, Clo! I thought I was being discreet!'

Claudia produced a dry, humourless little chuckle. 'And what did he say about me?' she sneered softly. 'Come on, Marian. Don't be *discreet*.'

Marian turned scarlet and looked away. 'You hate me, don't you?' she said flatly.

With great weariness Claudia thought about it, and realised that for the first time in her life she didn't hate anyone. Except herself. But she didn't love anyone either. Except Marcus. The pointlessness of it, the sheer waste of it, should have been enough to make her weep; but she couldn't even do that. She'd wept herself dry. There was nothing left.

'No,' she said wearily. 'I don't hate you.'

'Marcus said – '

The sound of his name was an agony; but it was an agony Claudia wanted to suffer. Whatever he had said, she wanted to hear it, to know, once and for all, that there was no hope. Then she'd be able to cope with it.

'He said,' Marian went on gruffly, 'he hoped I wouldn't

put our friendship – yours and mine – under that sort of strain again, because if you came near him again . . . Oh, Clo, I'm so sorry!'

'If I came near him again?' Claudia whispered.

'He'd kill you. He said he didn't have to take that kind of insult from anyone, least of all you.'

Claudia had thought she was as cold as anyone could get without losing consciousness, but now she turned even colder. That sort of insult? *You raped me*! Dear God, he'd told Marian *that*?

'I told him you'd only said it for my sake, Clo, that you'd genuinely thought I was pregnant. After all, he's got a reputation for that sort of thing. It isn't true, of course. I don't expect you to believe it, Clo, but he's too much of a gentleman to leave a girl up the creek like that. I suppose that's why he was so furious . . .'

Claudia took a deep, warming breath and pretended to examine the roses she'd brought. Too much of a gentleman . . . Yes, he was too much of a gentleman. He hadn't told.

She reflected dully: 'I couldn't think of any other reason you'd want to kill yourself.'

There was a long silence. Then, very softly, Marian said, 'It's Daniel, Clo.'

The restaurant claimed to be Italian, but it served only steaks and omelettes and otherwise upheld its claim with an excess of raffia-clad Chianti bottles and large, misty photographs of the Coliseum.

It was the sort of place Neil had scoffed at, calling its impoverished patrons 'little plebs'. Claudia thought she must be recovering if she could feel angry at the thought. Alister was no pleb! And his manners were far better than Neil's, for all that Neil thought himself so suave! With Neil, she'd always felt like someone who'd been allowed to tag along, just in case he needed someone to talk to when he'd finished being sniffy with the waiters.

'So what's all this about Daniel?' Alister encouraged softly when the waiter (having been courteously thanked) had disappeared into the dark maw of the kitchens.

Claudia sighed heavily. 'She's been in love with him for years, ever since she first came to the village; but he didn't notice her until he came home last Christmas. He took her out a few times. But *I* didn't know!'

Alister laughed. 'Is that what's upset you? That you weren't consulted?'

'No! It would have been nice to be trusted, but I can see her point. I probably would have said something to Daniel and made it all . . .' She widened her eyes. 'Well, I don't see how I could have made it *more* difficult!'

'So what is the difficulty? Aren't her feelings reciprocated?'

'I don't know that either,' Claudia said. 'He took her out. He kissed her. He wrote to her twice, phoned her once and hasn't been in touch since. She got desperate and wrote him a long, passionate letter, telling him everything. And he didn't reply. That's it.'

'That's it?' Alister frowned. 'But she tried to kill herself!'

'Yes.' She lowered her eyes.

'Do you understand that, Clo?'

'Yes.'

'Can you explain it?'

'She – she felt humiliated. She'd exposed herself.'

'By writing this letter?'

'Yes, but not just that. She'd also confided in . . . Marcus.'

'Ah.' Ali's voice hardened. 'I wondered where he fitted into the picture! And he took advantage of the confidence to take advantage of her?'

'No.' Claudia found herself suffering tunnel vision again.

She seemed incapable of raising her eyes from her plate, where a large slice of tutti-frutti ice-cream was slowly melting. 'But there's something else I didn't know. Daniel and Marcus are friends. They've been writing to each other, Marian said, ever since Mum died. That's why Marian . . . She wanted to know if Daniel had ever said anything, if she had anything to hope for. Marcus didn't know. He said Daniel only ever told him about veterinary school, but she said . . . She said he was very kind, and she wanted someone to be kind, someone who knew Daniel and wouldn't – wouldn't interfere.'

Tears sprang to her eyes, and at the same moment Alister reached across the table and took her hand. 'It's all right, Clo.'

Claudia hated herself. She was misleading him, letting him think all the wrong things, being a hypocrite of the worst kind. But what else could she do?'

'Clo. It's all right, love.'

'Yes,' Claudia said quickly. 'I know. I would have interfered. I couldn't have resisted asking Daniel how he felt about Marian, which would have led . . . Well, anyway, I think I understand why she kept quiet about it. But – '

'But Marcus interfered anyway?'

'No, he didn't. But he did what you do sometimes and told the truth. He said she'd have to toughen up and stop wearing her heart on her sleeve, which made her feel she'd made a fool of herself twice over. It was too . . . much.' At last she looked up, her eyes burning. 'It's so easy for men, Ali! You can say what you feel, ask girls to go out with you, ask them for anything you want! We just have to wait. And if we don't . . . you call us fools, cheap little – '

'No,' Alister said softly. 'We wait too, Clo, and live in fear of rejection. We even cry ourselves to sleep, just as you do. But *we're* not allowed to admit it.'

Claudia closed her eyes, knowing that he was talking

about himself, and that he had waited for her, never daring rejection, humiliation and hurt by declaring his feelings. But she didn't imagine Alister crying himself to sleep over her. She remembered Marcus, weeping with rage. 'No! No! No! I *loved* you!'

'Ali?' she whispered. 'Could you forgive anyone who hurt you enough to make you cry?'

'No,' Alister said.

Claudia was in the public library, furtively searching for a simple manual of obstetrics, when she saw Marcus again. Three weeks had gone by since she'd wept him out of her life, but the tears had begun again, more than a week ago, when her period had failed to materialise. It had begun to rain on the same day, and had scarcely stopped since; but Marcus had finished haymaking and, save for his tan which could just as easily have been acquired in Bermuda, he looked as if he'd never been near a farm in his life.

She had seen him walking in town before, and always been amazed at how different he looked, for unlike most country people he dressed for town, as if hoping to merge with the background. If that was what he hoped, he must have been disappointed, for he did it too well. Today he was wearing a light cotton trench coat over his suit, and even with his face glistening with rain, he looked beautiful. He spoke to the librarian, a tall, slim girl whose long, red-gold hair rippled down her back like a river at sunset; and she smiled and directed him to the index files in the centre of the library hall.

Her heart hammering, Claudia ducked behind the shelves just as his head came up. She had managed to park the car just outside and hadn't got wet, but she felt like a drowned rat, soaked to the skin by her own distress, almost dismembered by the violence of her reaction to him. More than anything in the world she wanted to hide; but she was expecting his baby! She had to know if . . . She had to know!

She swallowed and stroked her hair. She took a book at random, not noticing its title or comprehending a word of the single paragraph she read. But she read it three times over, trying to compose her features into the bland, vague smile of someone who is reading a book, in a library, and has no thoughts beyond it.

It was with this smile that she walked towards Marcus, her face raised, her gaze drifting casually over the shelves until it would have seemed unnatural not to look at him, he at her. He did look; an automatic smile touching the corners of his mouth before it froze, died, and he turned away, his pale eyes hooded with aversion.

Claudia walked on, blind and deaf; turning her vague smile on the librarian while her book was stamped. She went to her car, even managed to chuckle an apology when her umbrella tangled with someone else's as she searched her bag for her car keys.

Six miles out of town she realised that she'd driven through the crowded centre of Bath without seeing a thing. She swore, hit the brakes and pulled into a lay-by, biting her knuckles to keep herself from screaming. A thousand thoughts, each one more nightmarish than the last, tumbled in on her. He hated her, and she was expecting his baby! If she could have gone to him! But she was alone. She couldn't even tell Marian it was his child. *His* child!

Afterwards she had no idea how long she'd sat there. It felt like an eternity and might have been hours – or just minutes – but at the end of it, with a whoosh of speed which made Claudia's car rock where it stood, Marcus drove by in his father's Alvis, disappearing around the next bend almost before she'd recognised it. But he must have recognised her car, stranded in a layby in the rain! He hadn't stopped. He hadn't even slowed down. *'I wish you were dead.'*

He'd meant it. He'd *meant* it. . .

She began to cry, groaning aloud the only words that offered any hope of comfort. 'Alister, Alister. Oh, God, I want Alister!'

He had gone to market at five o'clock that morning and taken the rest of the day off to clean the cottage for a visit from his mother.

'She's coming to spring-clean,' he'd murmured ruefully. 'But you know what she's like. She'll kill me if it needs cleaning.'

Claudia wasn't sure when Mrs Chalcroft was due to arrive, and could only pray it wasn't yet. Babies could be three weeks premature without too many people raising an eyebrow, but more than that . . .

It stopped raining just as she turned into Hoppers Lane and almost immediately the clouds tore open, letting the sun shine through: wide columns of radiance which turned the landscape to a patchwork of light and shade. She was in no mood to appreciate the beauty of it until she rounded the last bend and saw Alister's cottage shining in a spotlight of its own, warm, bright and welcoming, with a thin spiral of woodsmoke issuing from the chimney.

'Oh, please,' she prayed. 'Please, God, help me!'

But when she stopped the car at the garden gate, she hadn't the courage to get out. This was her last hope, and she was desperate – which probably meant that it was no hope at all. She'd known him so long . . . and didn't really know him at all. Perhaps he looked at every woman the way he looked at her, making everyone feel loved, cared for, special. If she made a fool of herself again . . .

He came to meet her as she walked up the path, and she smiled stiffly, averting her eyes.

'Clo? What are you doing here?'

He stood aside to show her through the door. 'You came at the right moment. I've just put the kettle on.'

'Is your mother here?'

'No, tomorrow. Tea or coffee?'

'Coffee. Please.'

Alister walked into the kitchen crabwise, with one eyebrow up, one down and a quizzical smile pulling his mouth to one side. 'Say something,' he ordered suspiciously.

'The room looks nice.'

Alister groped for the cups, laughing with bewilderment. 'Say something else. Your face is all . . . I can't read it.'

Claudia swallowed. Thank God for that, she thought grimly. She summoned a shy smile to her face and looked at her feet. 'It's a bit difficult,' she said.

They sat at the table by the window. Claudia stared into her coffee cup. Alister stared at Claudia.

'Go on,' he said. 'Try me.'

'It was what you said . . . About waiting.'

'Waiting?'

'I said that girls have to wait, and you said men wait too, and I was just wondering . . . If they're both waiting for the same thing, when does anything – happen?'

She closed her eyes, opening them again only when she was sure they could reveal nothing. Alister had pressed his palms together, his fingers to his lips; but his eyes, too, were unreadable.

'Who are you talking about?' he asked softly.

'You. It's so hard to tell . . . You're so nice to everyone, Ali. I can't tell how you feel, and it's – driving me mad.'

She felt sick. She looked at him with shame in her eyes, real shame, and for so many reasons she couldn't have counted them all.

Alister crouched at her feet and took her hands, letting them rest softly in his palms. 'If you can't tell how I feel,' he said gently, 'you're dafter than I took you for, Clo.'

'Sometimes,' she croaked, 'I think I know. But . . .'

The tension was killing her. She let out her breath with a shudder, squeezing his hands to give herself strength for the lie – the hypocrisy – of her life.

'I've been a bit confused,' she murmured. 'I suppose I had a crush on you when you first . . . But you . . . you were so grown up. You were twenty-four, Ali! I thought you'd be married before I was old enough to . . . But I always wanted . . . I always wanted to know how you felt about me!'

Alister's face was scarcely recognisable: all the craggy lines and sharp angles softening, warming, his eyes glowing with happiness.

'Clo, I love you,' he said sweetly. 'I always have. Surely you knew?'

'But . . . *that* kind of love, Ali? You've known me since I was a little girl! Do you really *want* me?'

'Oh, yes.' Alister lowered his eyes. 'I wanted you when you were a little girl, too,' he confessed softly. 'Which is why I know so much about waiting, Clo. I waited for you to be legal, then I waited for you to get rid of Neil, and then . . . I just waited.'

Claudia smiled and closed her eyes, thanking God. But Ali still hadn't kissed her. And they had to get a lot further than that before the day was over!

'Ali,' she prompted breathlessly.

'Yes, Clo?' He seemed mesmerised, drunk with wonderment; and Claudia knew how he felt, knew what he was doing. He was trying to know her with his eyes, trying to learn everything which had been hidden for all the years he'd known her – without knowing her. And Claudia wanted to blind him, to put his eyes out so that he should never know. Alister, who never told lies! Alister, who wouldn't listen to them!

'I love you,' she whispered. 'Oh, please, Ali, kiss me!'

Chapter Nineteen

As soon as the hay was gathered Marcus spread the shorn, dead-looking grass with manure. As soon as that job was completed the rain came; and, when that was over, the grass was green again. Seven of the Friesians calved. None of the calvings produced complications. All the calves were heifers, and there were two sets of twins.

Farming never went as smoothly as this: the sun and the rain coming just when they were needed, the vet made redundant, the stock multiplying like flies. It felt decidedly spooky. Ben, as astonished as Marcus was by their protracted run of good luck, looked at his son from the corner of his eye. 'Sold your soul to the devil, Marcus?'

It was a joke. Marcus knew it was a joke; but later, when he was alone, Ben's remark drifted back into his mind and stayed there for a long time. For if a man's soul was – as he'd always assumed – the central core of his feelings, he didn't have a soul any more. He looked inside himself, searching for something which meant anything. He found nothing except pride; and pride was almost worse than nothing if it was all a man had. It was cold. It was hard. And it didn't say much.

Marcus had been aware of not saying much during the

weeks which had followed his parting from Claudia; but he'd kept quiet for a good reason – to save the family from his wrath. And it had worked. After a few days of watching him and waiting for him to explode, the family had turned their attention elsewhere, and seemed to have stopped wondering what had happened to him.

But Liz and his mother had lowered their eyes and stepped aside when they'd met Marcus in a doorway. And Ben, instead of arguing the toss over every decision they made, had given way to Marcus's views with barely a murmur of dissent. Marcus had known, then, that they'd been afraid of him, and had been grateful; for he'd been afraid, too. Not so much of hurting them – although that had been a big part of it – but of letting loose something which might tear *him* apart.

That fear had gone. He no longer felt that he was made of fragile tissue, liable to break at the merest touch. He felt now that he was made of toughened glass, capable of enduring all manner of rough treatment without feeling the strain. But the women still stood aside when they met him in a doorway; and, if he spoke to them, they smiled over his shoulder, not wanting – or not daring – to meet his eyes.

He knew he had to do something about that. He knew he must change it. But he didn't know how. Not saying much had become a habit. It had almost become an obsession, after the manner of a child refusing to step on the pavement cracks, 'just in case'.

Just in case the earth should blow up. Just in case the sky should fall down. Just in case Claudia Murray should escape the dark, airless box he'd locked her in, and come to torment him again.

Something had gone wrong with his watch. He had bathed and dressed for a meeting with a friend in Bristol, not realising that he was more than an hour early until he heard the hall clock striking six.

'My watch is gaining,' he muttered irritably.

'Did you get it wet, darling?'

'It's supposed to be waterproof. Damn. What do I do now? All dressed up and nowhere to go.'

His mother sent him a cautious smile. 'Where *were* you going?'

'Dinner with Doug Hammond. Didn't I tell you?'

'You told me you wouldn't be home.' She tilted her head to one side. 'You never tell me where you're going.'

Marcus felt one of his silences descending. He shook it off and smiled instead, widening his eyes to tease her. 'There's no need to worry. I'm twenty-four, Mother. Quite a big boy, now.'

Helen blushed and looked at his tie. 'I'm not worried,' she said. 'Just nosey.'

'Oh!'

He laughed, and it felt good. His mother laughed, and that felt even better.

'Oh, well, in that case, what do you want to know?'

'Is Doug living in Bristol now?'

'No, still in London. But his sister – Kay – remember Kay? We stayed with her in Florence, the year Callie died. She's teaching at the university next term. Bought a house in Bristol. Somewhere in Redland, I think Doug said.'

Helen's smile pursed knowingly. '*Doug* said? Haven't you seen Kay lately, then?'

'*No*, Mother.' He grinned. 'I think I'll go, before your imagination gets the better of you.'

But he was still an hour ahead of time; and the thought of having to kill time – either at home or in Bristol – appalled him. He had always led a strictly organised life, and this had been more true of him recently than ever before. Except at busy times, he worked a twelve-hour day. Then he read, worked at his desk or went out for the evening. But he never had time to kill. He didn't want time to kill. Just the thought of it frightened him.

He kissed his mother, saying distractedly, 'I imagine I'll be late. Leave the hall light on, will you? I'll come in through the garden.'

'Right ho. Give my love to Douglas. And Kay.'

'I will.'

'Umm . . . if you aren't in a hurry . . . ?'

'Yes?' He turned, grateful for the distraction.

'Any hope of your taking the charity box to Mrs Chislett? She's got a jumble sale coming up soon, and I promised . . . But I haven't had time. Drop it in as you pass?'

Marcus felt his smile cooling. Except from the safety of the car or the cattle truck, he had not shown his face in the village for weeks lest he bump into Claudia, and Mrs Chislett was almost as bad. He already feared that her X-ray eyes might have penetrated the thick stone walls of the old barn; or at least that she'd seen Claudia arrive – and not leave until three hours later. And when Mrs Chislett added up two and two, the damn woman never made five. It was four every time. Spot on.

Not, of course, that he cared about Claudia's reputation. He just couldn't stand the thought of Mrs Chislett asking questions, or at best making oblique remarks to see how he'd react. Under normal circumstances Marcus could be certain of keeping his feelings hidden behind his smile; but Claudia Murray was no 'normal circumstance'. She'd ripped him apart, and the wounds . . . Oh, damn her to hell!

'Oh, well, never mind, darling.'

Helen's voice seemed to falter, and Marcus became aware that his smile had not merely cooled but disappeared entirely, setting his face into a cold, staring mask. God, it came to something when his own mother was terrified to speak to him!

He managed another smile. 'Charity box? Oh, yes, of course. Where is it?'

The 'charity box' turned out to be three large cardboard cartons, and, when he turned up at Mrs Chislett's front door ten minutes later, Marcus's face was so well hidden by the load that he was amazed to hear her gasp, 'Ooh, look who it ain't! Marcus Saxon, come back from the blimmin' dead!'

He lowered the cartons a few inches and glared at her over the edge of the top one. 'How did you know it was me?'

'Ah! That's for me to know and thee to wonder at, my lad.'

But he barely heard her reply. He'd noticed her nose, which, like her eyelids, was too bright a pink and glistening with moisture. Mrs Chislett crying? The only time Mrs Chislett cried was at weddings! And floods, of course – but that was mostly temper.

'Er,' he said hesitantly. 'Jumble sale. My mother said to be careful with the top one. It's jam, and the raspberry didn't set all that well.'

'Jam! Oh, that was good of her! Put it in the front room, Marcus. Mind where you puts your feet, though. Our Veronica's had kittens, and the dang things gets in every blimmin' where.'

Marcus coughed to disguise a snort of laughter. *Veronica*! What a name to call a cat!

'What are you calling the kittens?' he asked solemnly.

'Pests! If I didn't hate that blessed river so much, I'd drown the dratted things! You got a minute? I just brewed a pot and . . . And I had a letter from Daniel Murray you might like to – ' She hurried away to the kitchen, but not before Marcus saw her glasses mist over and her nose flush to crimson.

'Bad news?' he asked anxiously. And then, 'Oh *sh* . . . !' as he hit his forehead on the kitchen door lintel.

Mrs Chislett laughed tearfully. 'You always does that!' she said. 'You always nearly *says* that, as well! Yer, you'm lookin' very smart, tonight. Goin' somewhere nice?'

Marcus laughed. Tears or no tears, she could never keep her curiosity down!

'Bad news?' he prompted firmly.

'Oh . . . Daniel, you mean? No, not *bad* exactly, but he mentions Marian, and I wondered . . .'

She passed the letter over but it contained very little that Marcus did not already know. Daniel was in love but he still had four years to wait to be qualified and earning his way, and the Fairfields would never let Marian wed an impoverished student.

'I think he's right.' Marcus passed the letter back. 'It's hard on Marian, of course, especially after . . .'

No, better not mention Marian's little 'accident'. Daniel evidently knew nothing of it, and if Mrs Chislett (by a miracle) had failed to root out the cause of it, she was best kept in ignorance a little longer.

'But,' he went on, 'he can't ask her to wait, can he? If he wasn't in London it would be different, but when can he see her? Love letters have their merits, I suppose, but if that's all they can share . . . No, she'll meet someone else. Eventually.' He sighed, thinking of himself.

Mrs Chislett poured the tea, and Marcus winced. He disliked tea at the best of times; but at the best of times it emerged from the pot in a pale gold stream, not the near-black colour of last year's silage.

'Trouble is,' Mrs Chislett went on briskly as she handed him his cup, 'I got this feelin' about Marian. She'm a *swan* sorta girl, if you know what I mean. Mates for life, like. And, call me a fool, but I reckon she'm beginnin' to pine. She looks blimmin' awful, any road. I'd be worried sick if she was mine. No, Daniel's making a big mistake. If he loves the girl, he should up an' tell her so. Yes, they'll have a hard time of it, but not near so hard together as alone. Trouble *makes* people, Marcus, but pinin' kills 'em. On the inside, sorta thing. They looks alive, but they ain't. That's my opinion, any road.'

Marcus swallowed. He stirred his tea. *They looks alive, but they ain't* . . . God, she chose her words well!

But it wouldn't kill *him*, damn it! Claudia Murray wasn't the only fish in the sea, and by no means the best! Oh, she was bright and brave and beautiful; but so were thousands of other girls, most of whom he could have for the taking. Kay Hammond, for instance. Yes, he could have Kay. At the drop of a hat, with a snap of his fingers. She'd wanted him for years . . .

He shrugged. 'Nonsense,' he said. 'Marian won't die of it. Come on, cheer up. It's not like you to get maudlin.'

'Maud – ? Oh! Oh, no, my love. I weren't cryin' over Marian! It's our Alister. He'd only gone out of here two minutes afore you come in. He's gettin' – married.'

Marcus's eyebrows went up. He scarcely knew Alister, but he knew of his reputation. It made him out to be a cross between Superman and St George, for the man had reclaimed Murray's from near-ruin – and almost killed himself in the process. Whenever Marcus had seen him in the village, he'd looked a wreck: rumpled and haggard, his feet barely clearing the ground for weariness. Marcus had sometimes wondered if the man was mad, for he gave himself no time to make a life of his own. And Murray's wasn't his. It didn't merit the dedication he'd given it. *Unless* . . .

'Married?' Marcus asked faintly.

Tears once more filled Mrs Chislett's eyes and she poked a corner of her apron under her glasses to wipe the mist away.

'Register office,' she muttered, in much the same tone that she might have muttered 'Dartmoor Prison'.

'Oh, I never thought to see the day! Our Alister . . . As good, as kind, as straight, as sensible . . . *Trustworthy*! And now this! After all I done! I couldn't have tried harder if she'd been me own, and now he've brought her down to the level of – ! No, keep my mouth shut.'

She closed her eyes. She shook her head. 'But oh, dear, oh, dear . . . I never for a moment *thought* – ! You expect it of some men – you'd be daft not to. *You*, for instance! I wouldn've turned a hair if 'twas you! But not our Alister!'

Marcus was beginning to feel sick. *Him*, for instance! But who else did Alister know? Who else did Mrs Chislett care so much about?

No, it couldn't be true! Two months ago (nine weeks, two days . . .) she'd been a virgin! She *couldn't* be expecting Alister's child!

'Who – ?' he murmured dizzily. 'Who's the – er – ?'

'Why, Claudia, of course, you daft lummox! What's wrong with you? Educated up to the eyeballs and can't see – ! No, shut your mouth, Mariah, for *you* never seen it comin' either! Fool! Damn fool!'

She blew her nose. She took her glasses off and polished them furiously.

'I wanted her to get away,' she said wistfully. 'Make a life of her own and be happy, not get herself stuck with . . . Damn it all, she should never have called it off with that Neil Priest! Nice boy, he was, see. Good family. Plenty of money. And it's not just the business she'm stuck with now, see, Marcus. And it's not just her little windfall. She'll love it, see. She'll be a good mother to it. And Alister – '

Mrs Chislett bit back a sob. 'He'll make a lovely father.

But, oh, Marcus, I wanted her to get away! Madge didn't *never* want that kid to get stuck . . .'

'Stuck?' Marcus prompted weakly.

'Well, think of it! Cath Murray: vindictive old . . . No, shut my mouth. But *she's* never going to pop off quiet, Marcus, not before she's ninety. And look at James! He were never an easy man, and now he's took bad he ain't going to get no easier, is he? Give him five years, ten at the outside, and he'll be a complete blimmin' invalid, wanting feedin', dressin', nursin', night and day! And Claudia carryin' the whole wretched load of it, babies an' all! It's a blimmin' crime, that's what it is! And while I don't say nothin' against the boys . . . They'm out of it! They'm safe!' She shook her head, her mouth tightening angrily. '*Men*! I'm disappointed, Marcus. Disappointed in our Alister.'

She sighed and added hurriedly, 'That's just between you and me, mind! Don't you go passin' it on!'

Passing out seemed a more likely prospect for Marcus at that moment. How had she managed it? Gone straight from him to Alister to cover her tracks? He couldn't believe it! It wasn't possible! Or had she faked her virginity, faked her screams . . . ? Christ, he wished he'd strangled her!

'Yer,' Mrs Chislett said, and her voice was suddenly sharp with suspicion. 'You all right, Marcus? You gone all white round the gills!'

After a long struggle, he managed to smile. 'I think it's the tea,' he murmured apologetically. 'You didn't, by any chance, drown the kittens in it, did you?'

Marcus had not seen Doug Hammond for more than a year yet when they shook hands and clapped each other's shoulders, it was just like old times. Clifton, Paris, Florence. and Kay, of course. But Marcus had not seen Kay since

Doug's graduation, three years earlier, and now he scarcely recognised her. Her long, dark brown hair had been cut to the tips of her ears (Marcus's first thought was that it looked like a coal scuttle); her elegant, rather conventional clothes thrown away and replaced by a . . . What? A sort of dish cloth, knitted from string. The holes were larger than the stitches and . . . Was it *true* she had nothing on underneath? The hem of the skirt cleared her knees by a good six inches. So did her long white boots.

'Good God . . .'

She laughed. 'Don't you like it?'

'I don't know. It's . . . Is it really you?' He aimed a tentative finger at one of the holes near her midriff and she smacked his hand away, laughing, her brown eyes dancing with pleasure.

'Cheek! This is what they're wearing in London now, Marcus. What are they wearing in Larcombe?'

'Er . . . Wellies. Pinnies. Cardies.' He closed his eyes briefly. But Claudia had always been one step ahead of Larcombe. Always smart. Always fashionable . . .

'Hey.' Doug steered him to a bar stool. 'Don't take it so hard, old son. Look at it from my point of view: I'm *related* to her! Now, what'll you have?'

'Whisky. A double. Neat.'

They laughed, but Marcus meant it. Kay's transformation had shocked him; and after Mrs Chislett's bombshell he wasn't certain he could take any more.

But after two whiskies he felt much better. Claudia was of no significance: a silly little country girl he had laid in the hay. And Kay was beginning to grow on him. She looked good, and she had a wonderful figure: tall and willowy with wide hip-bones, slanting thighs, a belly as flat as a board. And the clothes . . . The clothes were . . . They were interesting, anyway!

'So,' Doug asked as they waited for the first course to

arrive. 'How did you pull it off, Marcus? Ellis left. And then?'

Marcus shrugged. 'Nothing. I just went home one weekend, and there he was – gone. Dad said, "He's gone," and I said, "Oh, tough," and then I went back to the flat. I didn't really want Saxons – '

'Oh, come *on*!'

'It's true. I told you I'd been offered this junior lectureship at Berkeley? Well, it seemed a good idea. Fresh fields, pastures new. Money. Sunshine. Surfing. Not to mention the T-birds. And the other birds, of course.'

He slanted a smile in the direction of Kay's slender thighs and caught a glimpse of something more intimate in pale pink lace. So she *was* wearing something underneath! Thank God for that!

He blinked and stared in some confusion at the artichokes the waiter had placed before him. 'Er – where was I?'

'Back at the flat, you lying sod, pretending you didn't want Saxons!'

Marcus laughed. 'Okay, I wanted it. But not on Dad's terms. At least . . .'

'*Yes*?'

Marcus laughed again. 'I think I've worked him out. If I tell him what I want, he turns the screw. So I didn't say anything – except about this job I'd been offered. It took him the best part of a year, but he came round in the end – and, of course, he thinks he got what *he* wanted, which makes everything a good deal easier. But it's legal. Ellis gets a percentage; the rest is mine. At least, it will be, when Dad retires.'

'And you're happy?'

Marcus swallowed a long draught of wine. 'As Larry,' he said.

*

He was mildly disappointed when Kay turned up at Saxons' dressed fairly sensibly in slim white jeans, stout leather boots and a sweater. He'd rather enjoyed the thought of Ben keeling over at the sight of one of her mini skirts. But he was disappointed, and had to make do with criticising her colour scheme.

'White? On a farm? You'll get filthy!'

'Oh!' Kay laughed. 'I thought you'd invited me to lunch, not to muck out the pigsties!' She slotted her hand through his arm and swung on it, smiling teasingly. 'Any road, gaffer,' she added in a phoney Somerset drawl, 'I don't z'pose you've come acrawz it yet, but they'm gone and invented Persil zince you wuz a lad!'

'Very funny.' He smacked her rump, remembering too late that her hide was a good deal more sensitive than a Friesian's. 'Sorry,' he grinned when she yelped. 'My hand slipped.'

Kay laughed again, but her eyes said something else. A brief, bewildered spark which pierced Marcus's armour for a moment. She was right, of course. He had changed; and although in her opinion it was not for the better, Marcus greatly preferred it. Not caring was easy. It didn't hurt. And, as long as you kept smiling and remembered your manners, other people's pain was their own business.

Helen had met Kay just once, when Marcus and Doug were still at Clifton, but the two women greeted each other like old friends – and immediately began talking about clothes. Marcus was forgotten, and rather than hang around *looking* forgotten, he went straight out again and spent the next hour helping Noddy to strip down the milking machines.

Ben wandered through on his way to lunch, and exhibited astonishment to see Marcus there.

'I thought you had guests.'

'Hm. She's talking hemlines with Mother.' He stood up

to wash his hands. 'I can't quite see Mother in a mini skirt, but I suppose we'll get used to it.'

'No.' Ben shook his head. 'We won't.'

Kay was helping to serve the meal when they arrived back in the kitchen, her white jeans neatly draped with a tea towel.

Liz was giggling, 'It's all right for you two, with your long legs! I haven't even *got* ten inches above the knee!'

'You must have!'

'I haven't! Look!' And the lunch was abandoned while Kay measured Liz's legs with a wooden spoon.

Marcus sighed.

Ben said, 'Have we come to the wrong house?' and turned to go out again.

'Oh, dear,' Helen murmured. 'Ben, you know Kay, don't you? She's leading us astray, darling.'

'Yes, I noticed.' He grinned and shook Kay's hand. 'Good to see you again, Kay.' Then, suddenly noticing the near-empty wine bottle in the centre of the table, 'Hey, what's this?'

'That's what I meant about being led astray,' Helen smiled. 'What did *you* mean?'

Marcus might just as well not have been there, but Kay did consent to throw him a wink half-way through lunch. He didn't return the compliment. She'd entertained Olivia with tales of her year's studies in Florence, wrung a history of the farm out of Ben, consulted Liz about the proposed lay-out of her little garden in Redland and discussed the control of rheumatism and angina with Edward and Tom respectively.

Marcus couldn't think of a thing he wanted to say to her.

The thought depressed him. She was one of the most intelligent women he knew, and certainly one of the most beautiful. She was marvellous in bed, irrepressibly cheerful, smart, well-bred, wealthy – and what else? Oh, yes, she'd done the one thing no other girl had ever done: taken on his family and charmed the socks off them, one and all. So why was he so bored?

He leaned back in his chair and stared morosely into his coffee. He was bored because he wanted to be bored. He wanted her to notice that he was bored. He wanted to offend her, hurt her, wipe that irrepressibly cheerful bloody grin off her face.

But, damn it, he *liked* her!

He stared at his plate, trying to work it out. She was his best friend's sister. They'd known and liked each other for years. Why the hell should he want to hurt her, or, for that matter, hurt anyone?

It was the whipping-boy syndrome again, he supposed. Can't kick the dog that bit you, so you kicks the cat instead.

But why kick the poor, innocent cat every time? Why not the real culprit?

Because he was too angry. Murderously angry. If Claudia was expecting Alister's baby, Marcus was a Dutchman! And Alister was a bloody fool. Fathering another man's child? Ha! And a Saxon's child at that! The village would laugh him to his grave!

Kay wanted to walk the 'rolling acres', and didn't seem to care that a trip around Saxon's with all its ups, downs, ins, outs, woods, ponds and coppices, would carry them the best part of twelve miles. Marcus agreed to the walk, but he began it in the least convenient quarter – the woods – and then, deciding he wanted some mints to suck on the way round, he took an unscheduled detour through the village.

He lifted Kay over the fence just outside Murray's yard, and didn't let her go until he'd kissed her. He slid his arm around her waist. He looked into her eyes and told her she was beautiful.

'Hey,' she demanded suspiciously. 'What's come over you? You were a bear with a sore head five minutes ago!'

'I was jealous,' he murmured. 'Couldn't wait to get you alone.'

'So why are we traipsing about in public? Quick!' She tried to push him back into the woods. 'Let's find a heap of fallen leaves!'

She had a deliciously dirty laugh which encouraged Marcus to lean closer and whisper something deliciously dirty in her ear. They made a handsome sight. They were both dark, both tall, both laughing. And only a fool could have failed to guess what was on both their minds.

'This is Miss Derby's cottage,' Marcus said, pulling Kay to a halt at the gate – still in full view of Murray's. 'Miss Derby is a wonderful gardener, as you can see from the copious amounts of our horse manure she's spread over every damn thing in the garden. But just look at those purple chrysanthemums!'

Kay giggled. 'They're Michaelmas daisies, you cretin!'

'Wasn't that what I said? And this is the bridge. Fifteenth century. Its been here since the fifteenth – er . . .' He tapped the stonework with his fist. 'Rock solid. Lovely bit of masonry, that.'

Kay was laughing. He picked her up, sat her on the parapet and kissed her soundly. He was praying that Mrs Chislett would emerge from her cottage and catch them at it before she began putting two and two together again. White about the gills? Just for a cup of stewed tea?

The grocer-cum-baker shop was crammed with Saturday afternoon shoppers. Kay was mesmerised, her brown eyes dancing with excitement. 'Hey, what's that fantastic smell?' she whispered. 'Like dark red wine. Burgundy. No, port!'

'Ice lollies. They make them themselves, in little moulds. They don't sell wine here.'

'But they bake bread, don't they? I can smell bread! And

cheese, and tea! Oh, Marcus, it's lovely! I haven't seen a shop like this since – '

'And poor Mrs Chislett's breakin' her heart over it, Muriel.'

The voice was soft, secret, and as penetrating as sharp nails hit by a hammer.

'Well, she feels a bit responsible, I s'pose. It was her brought him here in the first place, see; and when you comes down to it . . . Well, you can't help *wondering*, can you? It didn't seem natural – all the work he've put in over the years for a place not even his own.'

'But he'll come out of it smellin' of roses, just you watch. It's the girls what suffer. Every time. Poor little kiddie. She've had nothin' but trouble since the day poor Madge – '

'And don't she look *dreadful*! What is she? Three months gone?'

Marcus gritted his teeth, caught Kay's wrist and dragged her outside.

'Hey!'

'Come on! We could stand in that queue all day!'

And he marched off, leaving her behind; his swift, spring-heeled stride beating out the rhythm of his thoughts. *Four* months gone, *four* months gone!

Olivia and Edward's sitting room overlooked the largest of the yards, where Edward could supervise the work and pretend that he was still a part of it. Marcus often spent his evenings here, quietly reading, while the old people were in the drawing room, catching up with the rest of the family. Or sometimes he just sat, staring into the fire, wondering what had happened to his life.

He was almost twenty-five. At eighteen, and looking forward to 'things working out', he'd planned to be married by now, with the next generation of Saxons already on the way. And it *was* on the way if his guess was proved right. If his guess was proved right, Claudia would produce a dark-haired, blue-eyed baby on March 17th, or as near as made no difference. He'd marked the place in the farm journal: just a pencilled C in the margin, June 17th.

His feelings were still as mixed as ever. When he thought of that dark-haired, blue-eyed baby, his heart swelled with . . . He wasn't sure what it swelled with. Pride? Love? Rage? Yes, still rage. Yet, at the same time, he longed for Claudia to thwart his expectations and produce a blond, grey-eyed baby a whole month later. Yes, that was what he wanted. For if it was Alister's child Marcus could put this whole lousy year behind him; just forget it and begin again.

But the thought of Claudia's having *his* child tormented him. For if it *was* his child then Claudia had cheated, lied and connived to a degree which was too appalling to contemplate. He couldn't believe – didn't want to believe – that she was capable of that. Yet he knew she was capable of it, if only because she'd had no choice. He had given her no choice. And even if he had, how could she have married him? A Saxon! Her father would have died before he'd have given his consent. He'd have thrown her out. Had her stoned in the street . . .

The distant ring of the telephone interrupted his thoughts, and he stood up and replenished the fire, half expecting to be called out to retrieve some sheep, mend a fence.

He heard brisk footsteps in the passageway and was already reaching for his sweater when Liz poked her nose around the door. Her eyes were bright with excitement but she was biting her lip, uncertain of the reception she'd receive.

'Hi. You busy?'

'No, but I suppose I'm about to be. Who rang?'

'Ellis!'

'Oh.' Marcus sat down again.

'And you'll never guess! He's pregnant!'

Marcus closed his eyes. 'You're right,' he said coldly. 'I would never have guessed that. How did he manage it? Single-handed, or with a little help from his friends?'

Liz laughed and sat down in Olivia's chair opposite. 'Her name's Gloria – '

'Oh, God.'

'He calls her Glo.'

'He would.'

'Listen, you beast!' Liz reached out to slap his knee. Marcus hadn't seen her look so animated since . . . Oh, months before Callie's death. Now Ellis was bringing a new life into the world, and suddenly Liz was alive again.

'Is he going to marry her?'

'Of course he is! He's thrilled to bits! They want to have the wedding in Larcombe church.'

'Church? They can't! She's pregnant!'

'So what? No one knows. And she's an orphan, poor dear, so there's no one on her side to arrange it. Oh *please*, Marcus? I love weddings, and your mother – '

Marcus went rigid with shock. *Please, Marcus*? What the hell did she mean by that? Was she – ? Were they all – ? Dear God, this was terrible!

He laughed nervously. 'You aren't asking my permission, are you?'

'No . . . No, it's just . . . Well, actually, Ellis said he'd only come if you were happy about it. He said you'd had your nose put out of joint once too often, which is true, of course. And . . . And . . .'

'And?' Marcus asked wearily.

'And you've been so miserable just lately, Marcus.'

Liz's eyes filled with tears. She looked at her hands, then at the wall.

'He's my brother,' Marcus said stiffly. 'Of course he must get married here, if that's what he wants.'

'Yippee!' She flung her arms around his shoulders, kissed his ear and was off, shouting for Helen; but ten minutes later, just as Marcus was thinking he should join the others, make himself sociable, *try*, she came back again, bearing a tray of coffee and a plate of macaroons.

She looked so happy. So young again, although she'd never gained weight – indeed, she'd lost more in the sad, struggling years after Callie's death. She wasn't sad any more. She'd pulled through; and, oddly enough, it was the onset of Tom's heart trouble which had helped her most. She'd talked him through his terrors, laughed him out of them. Now that he was no longer terrified, she cosseted and fussed him like a mother hen; and Tom was lapping it up, making the most of it, enjoying every minute of being loved, even if he'd needed to revert to his childhood to get it!

'What is it?' Marcus teased now. 'Surely you don't want to be a great-aunt, at your tender age?'

Her eyes widened. 'Oh! I hadn't thought of that! And Helen will be a granny!' She grinned. 'Oh, and fancy someone calling your father "grandad"! Doesn't bear thinking about, does it?'

'But he's pleased?'

'Yes, of course he is. More little farmers for the Saxon line! What could be better?'

Her smile faded. 'What happened with Kay, Marcus? We haven't seen her for weeks.'

'Nothing happened.'

'But?'

'But nothing. In fact . . . Once lambing's over, at the end of March . . .'

He frowned. Yes, why not? Once 'lambing' was over, what else would he have to wait for? And since Ellis was already producing the next generation of Saxons, it was high time Marcus slotted some more 'little farmers' into the line. *His* children had first claim on Saxons now, not Ellis's!

Anyway, what did love matter? As long as a woman could run the house, raise the children and entertain her husband through the long winter nights . . . Yes, what the hell did love matter?

Chapter Twenty

Claudia shivered and stared at Marian with an expression which verged upon hatred. But she seemed to have gone beyond hatred, gone beyond feeling anything except sick. Tired. Hopeless. Oh, yes, and ashamed. But she was getting used to that, adapting to it. It was like having a sprained ankle. At first you thought you'd never walk again. Then you learned to limp, and it was only when you forgot to dot-and-carry-one that the agony returned.

Yet the agonies Claudia suffered most were not her own. They were her father's, her brother's, Alister's. And now Marian's. And yet, try as she might, she couldn't drum up much sympathy for Marian. The girl was pathetic. She didn't know what trouble was.

So Daniel had ditched her. She'd flunked her exams. She couldn't follow in Daddy's footsteps and do medicine after all. So what? Had her parents screamed at her, hit her, threatened to throw her out in the street? No, they damn well hadn't! They'd said, 'Never mind, darling. Go to bed early. Be a nurse, instead.'

Claudia took a deep breath. She stood up and reached for her coat, which wouldn't do up any more.

'Okay,' she said flatly. 'See you sometime.'

'Claudia!' Marian burst into tears. 'Oh, Claudia, please understand!'

'I do understand, Marian. I understand perfectly. You can't possibly come to my wedding if Daniel's going to be there too. It would be *entirely* too painful for you.' She produced a brittle smile. 'And we can hardly claim it'll be the wedding of the year, can we? You won't be missing much.'

'Oh, *Clo*!'

Claudia clenched her teeth and walked out, grimly reciting Shakespeare. It was a habit she'd always envied her mother, who'd claimed that Shakespeare had an answer for everything. Not if you could only quote *Hamlet*. *A Midsummer Night's Dream* and *Henry the Fourth Part One*, he didn't; but even they had their merits . . . 'Or to take arms against a sea of troubles, and by opposing, end them.'

No, he was wrong there. Opposing the bloody things just made them worse, made them multiply like rabbits.

'To die, to sleep no more.' (That was better . . .)

'And, by a sleep, to say we end the heart ache – '

Claudia sat in her car in the Fairfields' drive, staring at the dashboard, but instead seeing the painted iron headrest and starched white pillows of a hospital bed. Her mother's face . . .

She won't die! She won't die, will she, John? She will get better, won't she?

Claudia screwed her eyes shut, thumped the steering wheel with both fists and screamed, 'Bitch! Bitch! Bitch!'

Marcus had said that just because Madge was dead it didn't mean she didn't care. But he was wrong! She *didn't* care, and why the hell should she? *She* was all right, playing her harp, floating around on her bloody silver cloud, while her poor little darling daughter . . .

'Not so little,' Claudia muttered. She stroked her palm

over her thickening waistline and smiled grimly down at the barely discernible (but oh, so obvious!) bulge.

'It's all your fault,' she said. 'Your mother hates you, baby. How do you like that?'

This was the first time she'd spoken to the bulge which was Marcus Saxon's child. It was the first time she'd faced the fact that it was, indeed, a child, rather than some hideous, anti-social disease she'd picked up in Saxon's barn: something veterinary, like swine fever.

'Swine fever,' she whispered. 'Oh, I caught that, all right!'

Again she stroked her belly. 'No, it wasn't your fault, Fred. You were too young to know.'

They said – she'd heard it countless times – that Saxon offspring always looked like Saxons. They had very strong genes.

(Jeans! Ha! Nan had been right about jeans, after all! They could get you into trouble even five years after you'd taken the damn things off!)

Yes, the Saxons had very strong genes. Black hair, blue eyes . . . Even Liz Saxon, who was as different from Tom as chalk from cheese, had produced a tall, dark, blue-eyed child. And while little Fred could be as tall and blue-eyed as he liked (Ali was five-foot-ten; Ali had blue eyes), dark he must not be; for after this radiant summer both Claudia and Alister had hair as pale as thistledown, and two blondes do *not* – however hard they try – make a brunette.

'To die, to sleep no more . . .'

No, no! That was no good! She should have killed herself months ago. It was too late now. She'd told too many lies, made too many promises, caused too much pain for too many people. If she died now . . . God, how could she *ever* die without burning in hell?

No, she couldn't die. But she *must* tell Ali she couldn't

marry him tomorrow. Tell him she didn't love him. Tell him about Marcus . . . and Marcus's baby. And then . . . Well, then, whatever else happened, she wouldn't go to hell.

But she'd thought something similar every day for weeks. And every time she thought it she felt – just for a moment – like a bird flying out from a darkened cage.

But her flight lasted only a few moments before Marcus shot her down again. And the name inscribed on his bullet was . . . Fred. Because of Fred, she had to marry Alister tomorrow. Because of Fred, she had to say she loved him. Because of Fred she could never be free again. She must swim in the sea of troubles until she drowned.

Smocks were in fashion. That smocks were in fashion was a stroke of good fortune so ironic that it made Claudia cry. She couldn't be married in church. She couldn't be married in white. She couldn't be married in love. But she could be married in *fashion*!

And virtually in secret, for although everyone knew when she'd be married, where she'd be married and to whom, virtually no one would attend.

Mrs Chalcroft couldn't come because she was having her gallstones removed; James couldn't come because he wouldn't be seen in public, staggering and trembling like a drunk; Cath wouldn't come because she'd disowned her granddaughter (the feeling was mutual); and Marian wouldn't come because Daniel would be there.

Daniel and John. Oh, and Alister, of course. That was all; and it was all that was necessary for a register office wedding. A bride, a groom, two witnesses, five minutes. It was almost as quick – and as final – as dropping dead; but without the relief of getting away from it all afterwards.

John had hired a large, luxurious wedding car, with a

uniformed chauffeur. It was good of him. Better than she deserved, as her grandmother had been quick to point out. 'Silly waste of money! You'll just attract attention! Oh, but she'll like that, won't she? Letting everyone see the shame she's brought on us, the ruin!'

But John, bless his heart, had stood his ground. And James, in an unprecedented display of support for his daughter, had snapped irritably, 'Everyone knows, anyway, Mother! Don't keep on!'

Cath hadn't spoken since, except in bitter monosyllables. She'd scarcely moved from her room. She'd gone on strike.

Since then, James had been unfailingly supportive, almost ridiculously kind; and Claudia, although touched by his kindness, had begun to wonder if his mind had completely gone at last. He'd never argued with his mother before. No matter what she did, what she said, James had kept out of the way and let her get on with it. Now, suddenly, he was biting back; and although Claudia appreciated it . . .

'I think there's something wrong with him, Ali. I think the shock's been too much. He's never been like this before.'

Alister scratched his chin. He laughed softly. 'Are you afraid of your nan, Clo?'

'No, not really. She just drives me mad. She's so . . . malicious! I sometimes think she does it for fun.'

Alister laughed shortly. 'You're probably right. But you and I know what a good mother is, Clo. Your father doesn't. Your nan's the only mother he's ever had, and he's as scared of her now as he was when he was six.'

'*Scared*? No!'

'I think so. When was the first time he spoke up for you?'

'God, I don't know! It's all a blur!'

'It was when I said we'd live at the cottage. She said, "Good riddance!" and he said, "Over my dead body! They'll live here!"'

'He needs support, Clo. He needs someone to stand by him. He isn't strong enough to cope with her alone.'

'But I've always been here!'

'You were a child. Now, as a soon-to-be married woman, with a husband to defend her . . . Well, he's safe, Clo. Your father's the kind of man who always sides with the strongest. Your mother first. Now, you and me. And don't despise him for that, Clo. It's too late to despise him. He can't change himself.'

'But he *has* changed! Before Mum died – !'

'Hmm?'

'Oh . . .' Claudia murmured. 'You mean Mum was the boss? All the time?'

'Every step of the way, Clo. Women usually are.'

Claudia got up at four on the day of her wedding to clean the house, prepare breakfast and put in two hours' work in the glasshouses. For Alister, too, it was business as usual. He arrived at four-thirty, had a quick cup of coffee and then went off to market, grinning all over his face.

The only thing which marked the day out as being different from any other was that Claudia sighed, gasped and quivered throughout; and was still gasping, sighing and quivering when John handed her into the wedding car at ten o'clock.

'You look gorgeous,' he said. 'Calm down, Clo.'

'Has Daniel gone to get Ali?'

'Yes. He went hours ago. Everything's all right.'

They were half-way through Bristol before John spoke again. 'You do love him, don't you, Clo?'

Claudia swallowed. 'Yes, of course!'

'And you do realise that a register office wedding is just as binding as the church kind? You don't make your vows to God, but they're vows just the same. It's final, Clo. You know that?'

Claudia blinked violently. 'Isn't it a bit late for this sort of thing?'

'No. "Too late" is when we're on our way back. If you want to change your mind, now's the time to do it. And, if you change your mind, I'll stick by you, Clo. So will Daniel. We both like Ali, you know we do, but – '

'It isn't true what they – what Nan said about him, John! He didn't – '

She closed her eyes, feeling the flames of hell burning her face, melting her carefully applied make-up. Of all the things she'd done to Ali, ruining his reputation was the worst. She was probably the only true 'fallen woman' ever to have walked Larcombe's streets – and the only one who hadn't been soundly derided for it. Ali had taken all the flak, the cold, sideways glances, the lowered voices which were never quite low enough; while Claudia had been given nothing but sympathy, smiles and mawkish encouragement. They thought she'd been *had*! Poor, innocent, motherless little kid, led astray by the big, bad, money-grabbing wolf! Ali, a *wolf*!

She lowered her voice to save the chauffeur's ears from a scorching. 'He didn't seduce me to get his hands on the business, John! God, if he'd intended to do that, he'd have done it when I was going out with Neil. But he never said a word – not a word – until weeks after I'd called off the engagement. You don't believe . . .'

'No, no. We just want you to be happy, Clo. That's all.'

Claudia closed her eyes and folded her hands in her lap. 'I will be happy,' she gasped faintly. 'We'll both be happy.'

But her folded hands clenched into hard little fists as she added silently, Until little Fred Saxon comes along.

Her smock, perfectly tailored in pale pink crêpe, with a little hat to match, was off-set by creamy leather shoes, a tiny spray of cream roses and the single string of pearls which James had given her for her eighteenth birthday. It was not the outfit she had planned to wear at her wedding, and the only thing in its favour was that it had turned out a good deal cheaper than the five acres of white lace she *had* planned to wear.

She felt decidedly under-dressed, decidedly over-pregnant; and was astonished, when John handed her out of the car, to hear the little crowd of professional wedding-watchers outside the register office gasp, '*Oooh*! Aw, don't she look *lovely*?'

Claudia blushed and grabbed John's hand.

'Lovely,' he murmured. 'Head up, Clo. *Smile*.'

Claudia put her head up. Claudia smiled.

And when she came out again, ten minutes later, she was laughing: covered in confusion and confetti; for Marian was there, her hand firmly grasping Daniel's. And the Fairfields were there with Mrs Chislett. And James was there. Staggering and trembling, blushing and weeping, but *there*!

Claudia couldn't stop kissing him. She had a feeling she was meant to be kissing Alister instead, but he didn't seem to mind.

'I couldn't tell you I'd be coming,' James explained tearfully. 'Just in case I . . . Well, you know what I'm like, love. Wasn't sure I'd make it, one way and another. But I'm glad I did. You be good to him now, won't you, Clo? Make him happy.'

'Oh, yes!' Claudia said.

Daniel had gone to see Marian almost as soon as Claudia had left her, the day before. He'd gone to tear her off a strip for letting Claudia down, but had got no further than, 'Now, look here, Marian,' before asking her to marry him. They'd still have to wait years before they could marry, but they were happy, wishing Claudia happiness, telling her to love Alister to bits.

'Oh, I will!' she laughed.

If it kills me, she added silently.

But it seemed to take no effort at all. Even six weeks after the wedding, Alister was still grinning from ear to ear, singing in the bath, cracking silly jokes and generally behaving like a love-sick teenager.

Claudia's only difficulty was to match his mood: smile for smile, song for song, joke for joke. And it was a great difficulty, for his very blissfulness seemed to be drowning her in horrors. He was a wonderful man: a sweet, kind, wise, gentle man who, it seemed, only had to catch sight of his rapidly expanding wife to overflow with pleasure. His eyes glowed. His chest swelled. His arms opened wide to hold her –

'How's my little darling?'

– and to stroke the growing mound of her belly –

'And how's our little Fred?'

Claudia had read somewhere that if an expectant mother had positive thoughts about her baby, he would turn out better than if she worried about him. So she spent every minute she could spare thinking, Be blond, Fred. Be blond for your mother, will you, darling? Be blond, blond, blond!

But if she managed to persuade Fred, she did not convince herself; and at least a half-dozen times a day she locked herself in the bathroom, just for the luxury of looking miserable, feeling miserable, giving in to the nightmare which was a dark, blue-eyed Fred. The nightmare which was Alister, with heartbreak in his eyes.

What would he do? What would he say? Claudia couldn't imagine – didn't dare to imagine – either his doings or his sayings; but she could imagine how he'd look, and that was enough. Once when she thought of it, she groaned out loud; and two seconds later Cath was hammering at the door, shouting, 'Claudia! Claudia! Are you all right in there?'

'Yes, fine,' Claudia said. Under her breath she added, 'Why? Does your tea need stirring?'

Cath had kindly promoted the respectably married Claudia to 'lady of the house'; an honour which, although graciously and gratefully accepted, had its drawbacks. For once she'd decided to opt out, Cath had pinned a sweet, grandmotherly smile to her face and never so much as washed a cup after that.

Timmy's mother still came in three mornings a week to do the rough work and the ironing; but Mrs Marsh was not very bright, and unless she was watched she had a tendency to clean the middles and leave the corners alone. Claudia often found herself doing the work a second time: moving the beds to find drifts of fluff underneath, shifting the wardrobes to dust behind them.

She told herself she was doing it for Alister: making him comfortable, making him happy, if only for the few months he had left before disaster struck. But Alister didn't give a damn about fluff. He told her to slow down in case she damaged the baby. *His* baby. Then Claudia admitted to herself that she hadn't been evicting fluff; she'd been trying to evict Fred: *Marcus's* baby.

But Fred was as tough as his genes. He lay in Claudia's belly like a sultan on a couch, smugly smiling. And, in the rare, brief moments when Claudia forgot he was there, he kicked her.

Then, with Christmas only a few days away, Claudia's terrors suddenly faded. Fred had turned blond overnight. Blond, tiny and fragile; a little, helpless thing whom Claudia must love, cherish and protect. She began to drink more milk. She began to knit.

They had a real family Christmas: the sort of Christmas Cath had never had time, spirit, or energy to produce.

Alister invited his mother to stay for a few days and, after meeting her train, bought a Christmas tree so tall it had to have its head chopped off before it would fit in the sitting room.

John came home, bringing his fiancée, Laura: a vivacious little character with dark, curly hair. And Daniel came, dividing his time (rather unequally) between Marian's house and Murray's.

Claudia had grown accustomed to having no help in the kitchen and was astonished when Laura, Marian and Mrs Chalcroft pushed her into a chair and did everything for her. Dishes were washed, floors scrubbed, capons stuffed and mince pies baked as if by magic. And although they all kept protesting, 'Take it easy, Clo. You're *pregnant*!' it didn't hurt a bit. Fred was a *blond*.

Fred was a girl. A tiny, skinny, wrinkled girl with a purple face and no fingernails.

Claudia had laboured for thirty hours to deliver her and was so glad to be rid of her at last, so glad to know she was all right, she didn't think to ask what colour her hair was. For a few minutes, while she struggled to get her breath back, her mind became a total blank. She cared about nothing, wanted nothing except to fall asleep and stay that way for the next month; but they wouldn't let her. They stitched her up, washed her, combed her hair – and, when they'd cleaned up the baby, they laid the little, mewling bundle in Claudia's arms and told her to say hello to her daughter.

'Hello,' Claudia whispered. And the little, purple, wrinkled child opened her mouth – and sighed.

Nothing had prepared Claudia for this. This sigh. It said so much. It knew so much. It was as though in this first hour of her life, Claudia's daughter had foreseen all the years of her life: years of sorrow, of error and loss. Years of searching, and hiding. Years of poverty, pain . . . Perhaps even war.

Claudia's eyes were wide with wonderment, blinded by tears. 'Oh,' she breathed softly. 'Oh, no. Not yet, my darling, and not for a long, long time. Nothing will hurt you while your mother's alive. *Nothing* will hurt you.'

She closed her eyes and became, for a moment, another woman, cradling another tiny life in her arms. *Nothing will hurt you while your mother's alive* . . .

'Oh,' she whispered. 'Oh, Mum!'

It was as if a crushing weight had been lifted from her heart. The years of blame and unconfessed hatred, the years of abandonment and betrayal. She had known all along that Madge hadn't died on purpose; *known*, yet believed something else. But now she knew the truth. Madge hadn't simply gone away; she'd been taken by force, mown down by an army. For nothing else would have beaten her. Nothing else *could* have dragged her from the child she had held in her arms.

Claudia gazed adoringly into her baby's face, at her tiny, pursed-up mouth, her pearl-bead nose, her dark, feathery brows. And the lashes which curled and glistened on her cheek were black . . .

Claudia eased back the thin, towelling shawl which covered her daughter's head. Her hair was black.

But somehow it didn't matter. It didn't matter what happened now. Claudia could lie, cheat, steal. She could do murder to keep her child safe. And if she burned in hell for that? Too bad. Madge had had dark hair. The baby took after her grandmother!

'You can come in now, Father! They're all clean and tidy for you!'

Alister came in at a rush, his hair standing up like a cockscomb, his face running with tears. He halted at the foot of the bed, and Claudia smiled, realising that the first thing she wanted to say to him was, 'Tuck your shirt in at the back'.

He came to her on tip-toe, not sparing a glance for the baby. His eyes were for Claudia, his thoughts for Claudia, his hands (trembling like James's) just for Claudia.

'Oh,' he groaned when at last he'd gathered her in his arms. 'Don't ever put me through that again, Clo! I thought you were dying!'

The same thought had crossed Claudia's mind, more than once; but she was glad she'd been in the middle of it, not locked, as Ali had been locked, out in the corridor all night, helplessly listening to her screams. She pitied him more than she could bear. To have suffered all that, for a child not his own. To have suffered all that, for a lie.

She stroked his hair, smoothing it gently into place. She stroked the tears from his eyes. 'There,' she said softly. 'There.'

He kissed her hand. He kissed her mouth and her eyes. And at last he turned to look at the baby.

Claudia stilled and watched him, her heart aching with pity. But she wasn't afraid any more. Whatever happened now, she would deal with it. Somehow.

Ali bent over the little creature, tracing his finger along the folded edge of the shawl, pausing at the little fringe of black hair, following the feathery line of her tiny, dark brows and the glistening curl of her lashes.

Claudia's daughter stirred, yawned, smacked her lips and sank away again, nestling into sleep.

'God,' Alister's mouth hung open for a moment. Then he grinned. 'She looks just like my dad!'

Claudia closed her eyes to hide her tears. But she couldn't hide her laughter. 'Oh, Ali,' she said, 'I do love you!'

It was ten to six in the morning. The first of April. All Fools' Day.

Chapter Twenty-One

Boiled breakfast eggs, in the Saxon household, were usually brought to the table in a large wooden bowl so that the family could help themselves; but that morning Liz had honoured everyone with an egg in an egg-cup.

No one noticed. Not, anyway, until – with a fierce swipe of his spoon – Ben took the top off his egg and found nothing inside.

'What the – ?'

'April fool!'

'Ooh,' Ben murmured. 'You wicked little . . .'

Marcus poked his finger through his empty breakfast. 'How old are you, Liz? Twelve next birthday?'

She sat back, wrinkling her nose. 'You're a lot of old miseries. You're no fun at all. It took me hours to blow all those eggs!'

'So who's the April fool?' Ben demanded smugly. 'What's for breakfast?'

'Nothing.'

'Tom, control your wife.'

'What, on an empty stomach? You're joking!'

Then they laughed; and Liz relented and brought in the omelettes; but her little joke had upset Marcus a little. She wasn't right about the family being miseries; but they didn't like to be made fools of, and he was as bad as the rest of them. They hadn't laughed until they'd smacked Liz down. Then *she* had laughed, and Marcus had loved her for it. Humility again?

The telephone rang and Helen hurried to answer it.

'Saxon's.' She always answered in the same flat, hopeless tone of voice: as though she expected the bailiffs to be at the other end, telling her she'd been rendered homeless.

But it was Mrs Chislett. Helen held the receiver at arm's length until everyone could hear the ear-splitting gabble which emerged.

'I wonder who that could be,' Olivia murmured caustically.

'Oh, splendid,' they heard Helen say. 'Oh, how dreadful. Oh, I'm so sorry. Yes, marvellous. Well, I *am* glad. Do tell her . . . No, don't, of course, but you know what I mean.'

'Hmph!' Olivia said. 'As long as someone does!'

Helen was smiling when she returned.

'She's moving to Glasgow?' Ben guessed wickedly.

'No, darling.'

'Shame. What then?'

'Claudia Murray – Chalcroft, I mean – has had her baby. Two weeks prem'. A little girl. Six o'clock this morning. Mother and baby doing well.'

Marcus froze. Then, just in case anyone should notice, he said, 'Any more coffee in the pot, Dad?'

'Thirty hours in labour, poor girl!'

'I thought she'd have problems. She's smaller than I am across the hips, and I had trouble enough, God knows. They say it's related to the size of your feet, don't they?'

Marcus stirred his coffee. 'Your feet?' he echoed faintly.

'The size of your pelvis, I mean. If you've got small feet, you'll have a small pelvis.'

Marcus swallowed a lump from his throat. Claudia's feet had been tiny. And was the baby two weeks premature or two weeks late? He still didn't know. Perhaps he would never know. *April fool*.

'Five pounds two ounces!' Helen said smugly now. 'Alister's over the moon. He says she looks like his father! Quite dark, apparently, but of course that could be Madge. Madge was dark.'

'I thought his father was dead,' Olivia said. Then, tilting her head to one side, 'But that's dark enough, I suppose.'

'They're calling her Sophy Madelaine. Isn't that pretty? I don't know what the Sophy's for, but Madelaine was Madge's name, wasn't it?'

'Yes,' Ben said sadly. 'Lovely name, Madelaine.'

'Not that babies really look like anyone when they're first born. You just look for resemblances, don't you? Everyone said Callie looked like me until she was three months old, and then – '

'Then she improved,' Tom smiled.

'But she's all right?' Liz asked hurriedly now. (She could never talk about Callie for long.) 'The baby, I mean. No problems?'

'No, she's perfect. No fingernails yet, but I think that's fairly normal with prem' babies. Marcus was the same.'

'What colour eyes?' Marcus's voice was carefully off-hand, so carefully off-hand that no one heard him and they went on to discuss prams, colic and nappy-rash, leaving him stranded in his ignorance.

Nine months, two weeks he'd waited for this, and still he didn't know if he was a father!

He wandered out into the hall. He stared for long, thoughtful moments at the telephone. He shrugged. He sighed. He dialled Kay's number.

*

'Put your heels down,' Marcus ordered irritably. 'Put your hands down, will you? I thought you said you could ride!'

Kay laughed. 'Shut up, Marcus. Tudor's not complaining.'

'That's not the point.'

'So what is the point? Aesthetics?'

'Morality! If you know how to ride properly, it's sheer bloody vandalism to make a mess of it!'

'Morality, eh? Okay, your reverence, suck this for a moral problem. If you know how to be sweet, why be sour? Why does everyone have to do things your way? Why can't you just enjoy the sunshine and the company and keep your complaints to yourself?'

Marcus noticed she hadn't even attempted to put her heels down. Stubborn little cat. Well, she'd be sorry when they reached the top of Old Barrow and Tudor realised they'd be going down the other side. He wasn't accustomed to long treks. Half an hour each way was all Helen ever gave him, and Tudor had an alarm clock for a brain. The minute the bell rang he headed for home; and if Kay didn't take charge she'd be going downhill rather quicker than she'd expected. Head over heels. On her own.

'Okay,' he said mildly. 'Let's go back, shall we?'

'No, I want to see the view from the top.'

'You've seen the view from the top. We walked up last week.'

'So? I want to see it again!'

They rode on, Kay pointing out all the pretty things they saw on the way. But when Marcus saw an untrimmed hedge, 'exploding' (as Kay put it) with white blossom, he didn't think it pretty at all. It might have been pretty in the woods, where trees were meant to grow tall and straggly; but not in one of his hedges.

'Hmm,' he said thoughtfully. 'That'll have to be cut down.'

'Ooh,' Kay breathed. 'You're a cruel bastard, aren't you?'

He was amazed. What had he done now, for Christ's sake? 'No,' he said wonderingly. 'Why cruel? A hedge isn't meant to grow – '

'Of course it is! It wouldn't grow if nature didn't intend it to grow! Why do you want to cut it down? It's lovely!'

'But nature didn't put it there. *We* put it there. It's meant to be a fence, not an oil-painting.'

'So? It's still a fence!'

'Not a very good one. When trees grow tall they thicken at the top and thin out at the base, which makes them practically useless as a barrier. If that hedge is left to grow the sheep'll get through it.'

'You're such a philistine,' Kay scoffed.

'I'm a farmer. Anyway, wasn't it a maxim of the Bauhaus that beauty follows function?'

'They were talking about design, not nature!'

'So am I. Farms are designed – '

'Huh! With no help from God, I suppose?'

'Is it your theory that the design of a wooden table has no help from God? Yes, a farm is designed with help from God but it's still a design, made by man to fulfil a certain function.'

Kay swung around in her saddle to point out one of the neater hedges, almost devoid of blossom. 'You think that's a better design than – ' she swung around again – 'that?'

'Yes, it's doing the job it was meant to do, and doing it *properly*.'

'Doing as it's told, you mean?'

Marcus took a breath through gritted teeth. 'If you say so.'

Kay grinned; but, like Marcus, she was inclined to grin when she was deadly serious; not levelling her eyes as he did, but tossing her head as if to say, 'Get out of my hair'.

Marcus shrugged. On his own territory he expected things to be in their proper place (including Kay's heels!) and why the hell not? He wouldn't tell Kay how to go about *her* business! He knew a fair bit about Art History, but Kay was an expert. He could *ask* her about Botticelli or Leonardo, but it would be a presumption to try to *tell* her.

They rode up the steep sides of Old Barrow in silence. Marcus would have gone straight up but with Kay's safety to worry about he followed the winding sheep paths which, over the ages, had carved the hill into graduated tiers, like an Aztec pyramid. It was an easy ride; but with Kay finding it difficult enough to make keeping her peace essential, Marcus had plenty of time to think.

He wanted to marry her. He wanted to marry her because he wanted a family; not because he was in love, and not – as he was beginning to discover – that he thought Kay would make a good wife for him. Farming was his life which meant that, for the rest of his life (if he was lucky), he would be on his own territory, demanding that things be in their place, fulfilling their proper function.

No, he couldn't marry Kay, they were too alike, and good marriages depended on two people's differences as much as upon their similarities. It was like a jigsaw puzzle. The pieces each had to be a part of the same picture, but if they were all the same shape they wouldn't fit together. Then, all you could achieve by trying to make them fit, was to break them.

Given time – and marriage gave one a great deal of time – he would break Kay as Ben . . .

Marcus caught his breath as the thought struck him. Then, smiling, he rejected it out of hand. No, Ben hadn't broken Helen. But Helen wasn't like Kay. Helen was cooperative!

They reached the top of the hill and rested there for a

while, looking at the view which stretched for more than twenty miles in every direction, even as far as the Welsh mountains, over the Severn.

'Does a view have function?' Kay asked brightly.

'Yes.'

'What is it?'

Marcus smiled, letting her go. 'It pleases you.'

Like most farms, Saxon's had been compelled to grow cereal crops during the war but most of the land was unsuitable for grain and, as soon as he could Ben had reverted to sheep, pigs and dairying – and a period of autumnal ease instead of the frenzied rush of harvesting.

Autumn was holiday time; but in recent years, save for a few token days out, the holidays (except for Marcus) hadn't materialised. Ben and Tom were content to stay home, and their wives just carried on as usual. Marcus had scarcely noticed this, let alone thought to question it. Now, chiefly because he intended to take three weeks off and was feeling guilty about it, he did.

'Time you and Mother had a holiday, isn't it, Dad?'

Ben blinked with astonishment. 'Hmm? No . . . I don't seem to need holidays nowadays. Strange beds and funny food . . . No, as long as things ease off for a few months and there's time to put my feet up . . .'

'But Mother carries on just as usual, Dad. She doesn't get an easy time.'

'Nonsense. I take her out.'

Marcus smiled and made a carefully timed exit. He was beginning to get his father's measure – and his own. They would neither of them be told what to do. But a few words, discreetly planted . . . A few travel brochures left littering the drawing room . . .

Nothing more was said, but three weeks later Ben and

Helen drove down to the South of France; and, when they came back, Tom and Liz had a few weeks in the Isle of Wight. Then Marcus, without a trace of guilt left to spoil his holiday, flew off to New York and a leisurely tour of the New England states. One of his university friends was now working in Boston, and they travelled together through the hot, New England fall in an open-topped Chevy, wearing Bermuda shorts, dark glasses, and wide, satisfied smiles.

Marcus saw no reason to call home until two days before he was due to fly back, and then only because Ben had offered to meet him at Heathrow.

Tom had suffered a heart attack two weeks earlier. The turves were already settling on his grave before Marcus arrived home again.

For a few weeks afterwards Marcus seemed to be searching for his uncle everywhere – and finding him nowhere. The farm had changed to compensate for his illness. They'd invested in new machinery, found new methods of working, so that when Tom was feeling rough and wanted a few days off, he wouldn't be too badly missed. And now he wasn't missed at all. It was as if he'd never existed.

Yet he'd lived and worked on the farm all his life; had seemed to be essential to it. Now, remembering Olivia's theory about humility, Marcus knew she was right. One termite had been stepped on, and it had made no difference at all.

So what had been the point of Tom's life? Fifty years of learning, laughing, loving, working? It couldn't just go! It couldn't just disappear down the drain, like so much dirty water! All the agony Tom had suffered with Callie. With Liz. And God only knew what else! But he needn't have bothered. He needn't have cared.

Even Liz seemed to have picked up the pieces and gone

on as normal. Ben said she'd sobbed like a child for two days before the funeral and sat in silence for two days after it. Then, almost as if someone had flicked a switch to set her into motion again, she'd cleaned the house from top to bottom, packed all Tom's clothes in the charity box and just given them away!

One day it would happen to them all. They would cease to exist and the world go on as if they'd *never* existed. It would happen to Marcus! Some woman would pack up his clothes in the charity box and just give them away.

The thought of it appalled him. He felt sure that, had Callie lived, Tom couldn't have disappeared so completely. Perhaps they *were* all termites; but what was the point of termites, except to raise more termites? Without his offspring, Tom was nothing. He'd lost his hope (if hope he'd ever had) of immortality.

Marcus did not intend the same thing to happen to him.

'I could've believed it of our Diane,' Noddy Bridges said mournfully. 'She were always a touch forward with the lads, our Diane was. Or even our Carol. Our Carol had her wild side.'

He and Marcus were stripping down the milking machines, sterilising every part before reassembling them for the afternoon's milking.

'But our Irene.' Noddy shook his head. 'Hand that spanner over, will you, Marcus? We was proud of our Irene: passin' for the Grammar, gettin' all them fancy O-levels and a nice little job in an office. Our Prilly always said she weren't rightly ours. Too good for the likes of us, she said. Said she'd end up marryin' gentry and never speak to us no more.'

Marcus smiled and said nothing. Noddy wasn't the type to bare his soul, and that he was doing so indicated a great depth of suffering. Yes, he'd been proud of his little Irene. And now she'd got herself into trouble in the back seat of some man's car. She didn't even know his name.

'Met the bugger at some dance in Bristol. Swep' her off her feet, she said he did. Mixed gin with her Babycham's more like it, the bugger! A blue Vauxhall Victor he had. Next time I sees a blue Vauxhall Victor, I'll haul the bugger out and strangle the bugger, and never bloody mind if 'tis the right 'un!'

Now, to Marcus's horror, Noddy bowed his head and wept. 'I dunno what to do, damn it all! Prilly's all for throwin' her out! She've beat her and shook her till the poor kid's dizzy, her face all swole up like a marrer! An' where's the bloody sense in it? It don't put the bloody clock back, do it?'

'No,' Marcus said kindly.

'Won't be the first windfall in Larcombe! Won't be the last! So what the bloody hell's the point of it all? It's the bloody women's fault, that's what 'tis! Mariah Chislett and all them old bitches! Sanctimonious old hypocrites! Just 'cos they never strayed – never got *caught* strayin's more like it – they calls down shame on them that do! And it ain't bloody right! It ain't bloody Christian! Throwin' our Irene out, four months gone! That's plain bloody cruel! And where's that bloody spanner got to *now*?'

Marcus gave Noddy the spanner. As for the rest, it was of no use to reply. If he agreed, Noddy would then feel obliged to defend his wife from his own charge of cruelty, and there was no earthly point in disagreeing. Cruel? It was barbarous!

Irene was no beauty, none of the Bridges girls was, but when Marcus imagined that poor kid's face, 'all swole up like a marrer', he felt a strong inclination to do something similar to Mrs Nod, and see how *she* liked it.

But when Noddy had cycled home for his lunch, Marcus

realised that the swollen face he'd imagined had been Claudia's, not Irene's.

Dear God, had they beaten Claudia? Had they threatened to throw her out? The thought sickened him; and it was no comfort at all to remember that she'd had Alister to protect her, Alister to help her, Alister to marry her and father the child.

Whose child? *Whose* child?

Marcus had never laid eyes on it, but if it had turned out anything like Ellis's twins, who had 'Saxon' virtually stamped on their foreheads, Claudia would, by this time, be having a very hard time with poor Alister.

Sophy was what? Eight months old? Old enough for her genes to be showing through with a vengeance, old enough to let even a blind man wonder where she'd come from! But if Sophy *was* Marcus's child, he need never see her to know the truth. The whole county would know it! They'd shout it from their doorsteps! And Claudia, God damn her, would never dare show her face in the village again!

The house was strangely quiet when he went indoors for lunch. No sign of Liz and Helen. No sign of Ben. But the table was laid as usual, and there was a fine (in fact, agonising) aroma of steak and kidney pie wafting through the house.

The drawing room was deserted. Olivia's sitting room likewise. Where the hell was everybody? He went through to the passageway outside Liz's room, and heard her voice – firm, clear and rather cutting, as it had been ever since Tom's death.

'It wasn't you I married, Ben. I married your brother, "till death do us part". And it did.'

'Yes, but *Helen* –'

'I didn't marry Helen, either.'

'But surely you care about her? You've been together now for – '

'Twenty years. And if you must take your quotes from the Music Hall, don't give me the next line from that particular song, because I'll have to tell you it's not true. Yes, I'm fond of Helen, but her welfare is her business, your business and your sons'. It isn't mine.'

'But *your* welfare – ?'

'Is not your concern.'

'Tom appointed me his executor – '

'And you've executed. There's no more to be done. There's no more to be said. You have no *say*, Ben. My duty was to Tom. Now, like that very nice cognac you bought on the ferry, I'm duty-free.'

There was a split second's silence. Then Ben said angrily, 'Had your positions been reversed, Helen would never have done this to you!'

Marcus still had no idea what they were talking about; but he knew emotional blackmail when he heard it, and he wanted to hear no more.

'Where is everybody?' he called cheerfully. 'Liz? Mother? Anyone at home?'

He stuck his head around the door, fully expecting to find just Liz and Ben in the room; but they were all there, sitting around as if at a seance, grim and silent, watching their feet.

'What's wrong?' Marcus asked.

For a while, no one answered. Then Liz stood up, squared her shoulders and said brightly, 'I'm leaving, Marcus. Rattling my chains . . . But leaving.'

Leaving! Nothing she could have said could have shocked him more; and yet he should have expected it, he should have known! Rattling her chains . . . Christ, what a condemnation! But she was right. He knew she was. She'd had a rotten life, and she had to take what chances she had to find a better one.

But how could they live without her? Ben was right, too! How would Helen cope? How would any of them cope? Liz was the light and the life of the house. Without her it would be empty!

'Well, Marcus?'

'Where are you going?' he whispered.

'To a bungalow in Chelworth. A *little* bungalow, with just enough room for me and my dog – when I can get a dog. And we both – ' she added defiantly ' – intend to eat out of tins!'

Marcus smiled. 'Not the same one, I hope?'

Tears flooded Liz's eyes. 'You understand?'

'Yes. Of course.'

'Then kindly – k-kindly – e-explain it to the others, because – '

And she walked from the room. Head up, shoulders back. Forty-five next birthday.

Every year, as Marcus's birthday approached, Ben asked, 'What can I give you for your birthday, Marcus?'

And every year, Marcus answered, 'A new car, please, Dad. Just a Jaguar. Nothing fancy.'

But the joke ran out of steam. Just before his twenty-sixth birthday, Marcus bought himself a Mercedes sports car; and, to his father's usual question replied, 'Damn! You're too late.'

Ben gave him a cheque (as he always did), and Marcus spent it (as he always did) at the January sales, replenishing his wardrobe.

He had just completed his shopping and was hurrying down Milsom Street on his way back to the car when he saw a girl he recognised going into the Old Bond Street restaurant. She looked marvellous. Her black fur hat and black, swirling cape certainly did more for her than her customary outfit of sensible skirt and demure little blouse.

Denise Robinson. The only girl he'd wanted at university who hadn't fallen at his feet. She'd just looked at him a lot, with her cool, green, frankly assessing eyes never once betraying what she really thought. Everyone had said she was unusual. Her looks alone had set her apart from the crowd. A tiny, white, heart-shaped face, with frizzy, carrot-red hair which blazed about her head like a furnace. And the clothes! Everyone said she'd inherited them from a maiden aunt. They were good; but so prissy, so neat, so conventional. And now here she was, dressed up to the nines . . . Had the eternal virgin given in at last?

He'd meant to turn into Quiet Street. Now, deciding suddenly that he was dying of thirst, he crossed the road and stood for a moment outside the restaurant, checking that she was alone. She was; and, to make everything easier still, she seemed to have taken the last free table.

Marcus went inside. He pretended to search for another table, pretended he hadn't recognised her. At last he said aloofly, 'May I – ?' And before she could reply, 'Good God! Denise! May I?'

She smiled and blushed. 'Yes. Yes, of course.'

He said nothing more. He waited.

'How are you?' she asked brightly.

'Very well. How are you?'

'Cold. I loathe winter.'

'You seem well protected.' He cast an admiring glance at the fur hat, which did wonders for her pale, redhead's complexion. 'And how did you like Moscow?'

She laughed. 'Still the same, then, Marcus?'

'The same?'

'Oh, that's how you always did it. An obscure compliment, a gentle tease. Keep 'em on their toes. Keep 'em wondering. You had it all taped, didn't you?'

Marcus blinked. He felt rather hurt. And even more hurt when he realised how right she was.

'Well,' he smiled, 'a man has to have a technique. He can't just blunder into these things. *Obscure* compliments? Well, I'm sorry about that. You look terrific. You look stunning. Is that frank enough for you?'

Denise burst out laughing. 'Thanks.'

'As for the gentle tease . . . Why did you wear those appalling clothes, anyway? Brutal enough?' He grinned. 'Are you a masochist by any chance?'

'No.' The waitress came and they both ordered coffee. 'I just prefer to be straightforward. And, since you ask, I wore those appalling clothes to fend off patronising bastards like you.'

'*Patronising*?'

'God's gift to women. I hear, from those who succumbed, that you were almost worth the sacrifice. But – '

The coffee arrived. And Marcus, in his confusion forgetting the rule of a lifetime, forgot to thank the waitress. Denise did it for him. Rather thoroughly.

'But – ' she went on calmly ' – I never wanted to join any man's harem. All you wanted was sex. I wanted love. I wanted to be the *only* one. And now I am.'

She stripped off her gloves, smiled and plopped a single cube of sugar into her coffee. She was wearing a wedding ring.

Marcus laughed. 'Oh, hell. Congratulations. Who's the lucky man?'

'No one you know. We live not far from you, actually. Chelworth. Just over the bridge on the Farrington side.'

Marcus stared glumly into his coffee. Patronising? Yes, in a way, he *had* thought himself God's gift to women; and now it seemed he was getting his come-uppance. Since

Claudia . . . God, everything dated from Claudia! Before Claudia, he'd thought he had the pick of the bunch. And since Claudia . . .

There had been no one since. No one who mattered.

'You're wrong,' he said flatly. 'It wasn't just sex.'

Denise smiled. 'Convince me.'

'Well, it was sex only insofar as I didn't *find* love, but I was hoping to find it. Had I found it . . .'

'Yes?'

Had he found it, she would have been the only one. She *was* the only one. Oh, God, this was crazy. He wanted to be married, he wanted to have children! But only Claudia would do . . .

He smiled. 'Well, never mind. I have to go pretty soon. Can I give you a lift home, or would that be patronising too?'

'No,' Denise smiled and seemed to forgive him. 'That would be very kind.'

Marcus had parked in Kingsmead Square. It was a short enough walk, but Denise was hampered by high-heeled boots, a clutch of paper carriers and a stiff, icy wind, which blew her cape open every time she let it go. Marcus relieved her of her parcels and offered her his arm.

As they set off again, he saw a woman with a pushchair crossing the road in front of the Theatre Royal. His heart missed a beat, and he held Denise's arm more firmly, gathering her closer as though to shelter her from the cold.

'Cheer up,' he teased faintly. 'It's sixty degrees below in Siberia.'

Her teeth chattered. 'God, how does anyone survive sixty below?'

'Quite briefly, I should think.'

She laughed. He laughed. But he felt as if he was dying; as if someone had pulled out a plug from his heart, letting all the life drain away.

The child in the pushchair was warmly wrapped against the cold, dressed in a white corduroy eskimo suit which covered everything but her face. Her nose was a little red cherry, her cheeks a wild flush of roses. And, as Sophy approached, sped along by her still unsuspecting mother, she clapped her warmly mittened hands together and cried, 'Whee!'

Marcus didn't know what to do. He wanted to die. But, more than anything else in the world, he wanted to push Denise under a bus. Since those last terrible moments with Claudia, this was the most terrible moment of his life, the most private, the most special; and, because Denise was with him, he must just let it walk by.

Then, as if prompted by his need, Sophy kicked off the thick woollen rug which had covered her legs; and, just as Claudia looked up and recognised him, the pushchair slammed to a halt, its wheels immobilised by knitting.

Claudia blushed scarlet and stooped to untangle it; but her gloved hands were trembling . . .

'Allow me.' He stooped, smiling up at Denise. 'Won't be a moment.'

Two moments, three, and all the time he was looking at Sophy, smiling at her, memorising every feature of her sweet little face.

There was barely a month between her and Ellis's twins, and they could have been triplets. The same straight, feathery brows, the same dark, curling lashes. But Sophy's eyes weren't Saxon eyes; they were Marcus's own: pale blue, palest blue; like a clear, wintry sky viewed through ice.

Chapter Twenty-Two

Claudia woke up, screaming, to tear the suffocating yellow from her face; but she was still suffocating, still screaming – until Alister tore the blankets clear and pulled her into his arms.

'Ssh, ssh . . .' His chest shook with comforting laughter and Claudia clung to him, sobbing with relief.

'Ssh, it was only a dream. You were all tangled up in the blankets, you dope. Here, want a hanky?'

Claudia blew her nose, and then, as Alister groped for the light switch, she gasped, 'No, don't. Not yet.'

'Oh, right.'

Claudia shivered, partly with remembered horror and partly with cold, huddling closer to Alister's warm, solid chest while he straightened the blankets around her. She'd had the yellow nightmare so many times since they'd been married, he knew it almost as well as she did. He knew that if he switched on the light straight afterwards it could stay with her for days.

'Anything special worrying you?' he asked.

'No.'

'Sure? You've looked a bit wan for a few weeks now, Clo.'

Ever since she'd met Marcus in Bath . . . Ever since he'd smiled and said, 'You have a beautiful baby, Claudia. And doesn't she look like her father? You must be very proud.'

'Wan?' she murmured now. 'Have I? I feel okay. It's just winter, I expect. There's nothing much to look forward to once Christmas is over.'

Alister chuckled softly. 'Nothing to look forward to? And you a market gardener, born and bred? Spring has sprung in the glasshouses, Clo. There's plenty to look forward to out there. Why don't you come back, love? Housekeeping doesn't suit you. It just gets you down.'

'But it still has to be done, Ali. And there's Sophy . . .'

'Sophy's no trouble. Sophy's an angel. Like her mother.'

Claudia wept. 'You're so good to me, Ali, and I – '

He laughed again. 'And all you can do is keep me awake all night. No!' as she recoiled. 'Just teasing. The alarm was about to go off anyway; it's almost four. Fancy a cup of tea before I go forth to earn my keep?'

He hopped out of bed as if the prospect of 'going forth' into the freezing mists of a February morning was slightly more pleasant than a luxury cruise to Tahiti. But Claudia sank back against the pillows, her eyes shadowed with weariness.

She was being eaten alive by anxiety: secrets, lies and terrors she dared not share with a living soul. It was like having a rats' nest inside her, a huge family of the little fiends: their long, obscene tails knotted together just under her heart, their teeth and claws tearing her apart as they fought for their release. And each one of them had a name.

She thought she'd managed to strangle the one called Marcus, or at least to render him unconscious. She hadn't seen him except at a distance. She'd scarcely heard his name, for Marian never mentioned him now, and Claudia had learned to keep herself to herself in the village. For the past eighteen months it had been as if she and Marcus Saxon existed on separate planets, rather than laying their heads to rest on pillows . . . On pillows barely half a mile distant from each other.

She'd forgotten what he looked like. Forgotten the sound of his voice. No, she hadn't forgotten . . . And although Sophy's eyes were his eyes, Sophy's were as round as pennies, as warm as sunshine, glowing with an innocence which tore at Claudia's heart. Perhaps one day, when her mother's sins had caught up with her at last, Sophy's eyes would become as cool, as cruel and as knowing as her father's . . .

'You must be very *proud*.'

If he'd stripped her naked and whipped her through the city, Claudia couldn't have been more ashamed. The pain of it had taken the strength from her legs so that, had she not been holding Sophy's pushchair, she would have fallen down and begged for mercy. The cold gleam in his eyes had told her he demanded nothing less; but the woman he was with had saved them both from such extremes. Her presence had strengthened the thin wisp of dignity Claudia still possessed and perhaps reminded Marcus that he was still 'a gentleman'.

Claudia curled into a ball, hugging her stomach. He knew everything. He knew everything she'd done, and he despised her utterly. She'd tried many times to conjure her old hatred of Marcus, knowing it would give her strength; but it wasn't there any more. She was afraid of him now in exactly the same way she was afraid of God, depending on his wisdom to save her from the pit. To save Sophy . . .

'Oh, Sophy,' she wailed softly, and it was as though she had moved into another phase of hell: the next rung down; a little nearer the fire. It was just a matter of waiting, now. It had always been just a matter of waiting. You couldn't give birth to a child with Marcus Saxon's eyes without *someone* noticing, *someone* talking! The next person to recognise the colour of Sophy's eyes would knock the ladder out from under. And then – ?

Claudia took a deep breath. She could scarcely imagine what would happen next. Chaos. Madness. Agony. But after *that* – ? She was ready for the worst. She'd saved some money and – thanks to Alister's evening classes in typing and accounts – had the means to get a job, as many miles from Larcombe as she could get.

It didn't matter how many, or how dreadful the problems she had to face once she'd escaped Ali's grief, for his grief would be the worst thing of all. She felt she couldn't face it, yet knew she must. And if, when she died, she burned in all the flames of hell for all eternity, they wouldn't, couldn't hurt her as much as that poor man's sorrow.

Since he and Claudia had brought Murray's up to scratch, he now had his pick of willing workers – untrained but as keen as mustard – who came for their year's 'work experience' before going on to Horticultural College. Ali was happy, he was radiant, and it wasn't just the business that had made him happy. It was Sophy. *His* baby, *his* daughter, *his* darling. He adored her. He took every opportunity he could to hold her, feed her, cuddle her. He even (to Cath's disgust) changed her nappies.

Claudia had never met a man who was so sure of himself: sure enough of himself to render any sort of assertiveness redundant. He never bragged, never boasted. But he totted up the score every night, lying in bed with his hands crossed behind his head.

'Got the lorry fixed, Clo. Sorted out the business with Palmer's – our letters had crossed in the post, so it wasn't a problem. Andy managed to plough that piece behind the glasshouses, so *that's* a good job jobbed. And Sophy's tooth came through. It's been a pretty good day, all things considered, and thank God for that.'

He rarely mentioned the many things that went wrong.

This was his evening prayer: as modest and unassuming as everything else about him. Just, 'Thank God for that,' before he turned to gather Claudia in his arms and kiss her goodnight – or hello.

He was, and had always been, a generous and thoughtful lover. She'd heard from other women that sex was a 'nasty five minutes to ruin the day'; but Ali's lovemaking was like a glass of mulled wine which she sipped in blissful luxury and drained to its dregs, sighing, 'Ohh . . . Ali,' before she fell asleep.

But he never said, 'I love you,' never asked Claudia if she loved him. It seemed that these things were taken for granted. They were certainties, not open to doubt; and, in a way, Claudia did not doubt them. She loved him. She had always loved him. And now she loved him more. More and more every day. Yet the thought of loving him sickened her, for loving him made the thought of grieving him – and leaving him – more terrible than she could bear.

There were no amends she could make. It would be like apologising to a man she had murdered; promising not to do it again. But somehow she felt she must comfort him now, for the pain he would suffer later; and with this thought in mind, she dragged herself out of bed and went down to make the tea.

Ali was disappointed. 'Oh! I was going to bring it up!'

'You do quite enough, without waiting on me.'

He smiled sadly. 'Why shouldn't I wait on you? You're always waiting on me. You try too hard. You're wearing yourself out. The house is spotless, you cook like a dream, you wash my socks, iron my wellies . . .' He drummed his fingers on the Rayburn, waiting for the kettle to boil. 'If I'd wanted to marry a doormat, I wouldn't have married you, Clo.'

Claudia swallowed uncomfortably. 'A doormat?'

'No, that's not the right word. But marriage is about sharing, and we don't share. You give and I take, and I don't find it all that comfortable, Clo. I don't have time to compensate the way most husbands do. Up at four, in bed by nine . . . No theatres, no dances, no holidays. And I can't afford to buy you diamonds.'

'I don't want diamonds! All I want . . .'

'Hmm?'

'I just want to make you happy!'

'Then think of a way to get back into the business, Clo. It's not half as much fun without you. And you're not half as much fun being a housewife as you were being a market gardener. You hate housework. You always did. And it shows.'

'Oh.'

Ali put his hands on her shoulders and smiled into her eyes. 'I'm not criticising. You're doing a wonderful job, Clo. It's just that I want to make you happy, too, and you aren't giving me a chance.'

Upstairs, the rhythmic creaking of cot-bars announced that Sophy was awake and as Claudia went upstairs to fetch her, she allowed herself a wry smile.

Knifed in the back by her own good intentions . . . Surely there wasn't another man in the world who'd opt for 'sharing' instead of having his wellies ironed? Any other man would think he'd died and gone to heaven!

She paused outside the door of Sophy's nursery, suddenly overwhelmed by a feeling of ironic retribution.

If she'd married a drunk, a lout, a miser, she could at least have told herself he *deserved* the trouble she would cause him; but Ali deserved none of it.

If God had wanted to punish her for marrying a man under false pretences, he couldn't have devised anything worse. Damn it to hell, she'd married a *saint* under false pretences!

It rained through most of March. Then it snowed, thawed and froze. Timmy's mother fell on the ice and broke her arm, leaving Claudia to clean the middles, as well as the corners, of a house which seemed to get bigger and more depressing every day.

Mr Foley, a stranger who, with his wife and two small children, had recently moved into one of the cottages on the Bath Road, overtook the gritting lorry on his way to work. His ancient Ford Anglia, one of the first to be produced after the war, ended up on its side in Miss Derby's front garden.

He was alive when she ran to Mrs Chislett's to call for the ambulance. When she came back, he was dead.

The village took it hard. Larcombe didn't care much for strangers and the Foleys had come out of nowhere, without so much as a by-your-leave. They'd lived in the village for almost a year without anyone giving them more than a cool 'good morning'; but now the doors were thrown open and comfort flowed out.

'Too dang late!' Mrs Chislett raged (with shame). 'But late's better than never, Claudia. No good sayin' we'm sorry. Make amends, that's what we got to do now – though how we'm going to do it, heaven knows. How's that poor woman going to live? Her youngest is barely out of his pram so a job's not on the cards. Not unless . . .'

Her eyes narrowing, she gave little Sophy a penetrating stare; a stare which froze Claudia's blood in her veins, making her dizzy with terror.

'Saxons,' Mrs Chislett went on thoughtfully, and Claudia sagged against the back of her chair, her eyes closing. The game was up. This was it. She knew what would come next: Mrs Chislett was not the sort to beat about the bush.

'Does Alister know? Better tell him then, hadn't you, my love? Before someone *else* do.'

But Mrs Chislett said nothing of the sort. 'I'd have asked Saxons to take her on. Helen's been finding it hard, keeping that place going without Liz there to help out, but Irene Bridges beat us to it.'

'Irene – ?' Claudia croaked.

'Yes! Didn't you hear? Gone up there to live, she has; her and her little windfall. Called him Tony. Tony Bridges. Got quite a nice ring to it, that, hasn't it? But Mrs Nod wouldn't keep him. She wanted him took for adoption, but Irene wouldn't agree, and I can't say I blame her, shame or no shame. It was Marcus's idea, by all accounts. Ben wasn't so keen. But she've settled in lovely, and she works like a little demon, Helen says. Mind, she were always quick on her feet, young Irene.' She smiled, puckering her mouth with cheerful malice. 'It was just on her back she didn't move so fast!'

'Pity about Hilda Marsh's arm,' she added thoughtfully. 'This is a big house to keep going on your own, with a baby to tend to and your dad so poor-to-middlin'. And I don't suppose your nan helps you out a lot?'

'Nan?' Claudia echoed faintly. Her bones seemed to have turned to mash. Saved again! But how many more times could she hope to be saved before the axe fell?

'No, I thought not. Cath were always – no, keep my mouth shut. But you're wearing yourself out, Clo. You'm as pale as a blimmin' ghost. And where's the sense of killin' yourself? You don't get thanked for it. The more you do, the more you may. People just takes advantage.'

'Ali doesn't!'

Claudia spoke more sharply than she'd intended, but she

hadn't yet forgiven the village for running him down so cruelly. Ali hadn't cared and he seemed to have forgotten it now, but Claudia wouldn't forget. Marrying her to get his hands on the business! As if he would!

'Well,' Mrs Chislett said doubtfully, 'be that as it may, Claudia. These compound fractures takes months to mend, you know, especially in a woman Hilda's age.' She lowered her voice to a dreadful whisper. 'The bone poked right out through her skin! Ooh, I'd have fainted if 'twas me!'

Claudia already felt like fainting although this had little to do with Hilda Marsh's bones.

'Shall I have a word with Mrs Foley, then? Her kiddies could come down with her, see, and it'd be company for your Sophy, wouldn't it?'

Again Mrs Chislett subjected the child to that thoughtful, narrow-eyed stare. 'Aw, bless her. Reminds me of you, she do, when you were that age. Come on then, my darlin'. Come to Auntie Chislett, poppet!'

Sophy, who until then had been happily tottering towards the old woman, now changed direction to hide her face in Claudia's lap. But even as she thanked God for Sophy's shyness, she cursed him in her heart. He was like a cat, playing with a mouse: catching her in his paw, letting her go. And he could keep it up for years yet! Sophy might be five, six, ten or sixteen before, with a peremptory flash of her eyes or a heart-melting smile, she showed off her strong Saxon genes for everyone to see. But it would come. It would come . . .

'My mother never had help in the house,' she remembered guiltily. 'And she had three babies.'

'Yes, but it weren't such a big house then, Claudia. And there's another thing: it never looked like it was killin' her – not until it killed her. You don't want Sophy left like you was left, now do you?'

And, leaving this shaft to rankle in Claudia's bosom, Mrs Chislett said, 'Think it over,' and departed.

Mrs Foley's grief was quiet, quick, ferocious and, apparently, inexhaustible. Claudia had never seen a woman who could work so hard and make so little fuss about it. No instructions were necessary. And all she asked was a play-pen to stow the children in while she worked.

She began in Sophy's room, achieving in twenty minutes what Claudia would have taken an hour to do: the cot stripped and re-made, the furniture dusted, the paintwork wiped, the lino mopped and the rugs shaken.

Claudia ran ahead of her, making beds, tidying up; but no matter how fast she worked Mrs Foley always overtook her, leaving only a faint scent of lavender polish in her wake. She said very little, except to the children. She was very sweet with the children. But when Mrs Foley put them in their play-pen they sat there and played. And when she put them down to sleep they lay there and slept.

After two weeks, she said, 'Are you happy with my work, Mrs Chalcroft?'

'Happy?' Claudia laughed. 'No! You've rendered me useless!'

'You'd prefer to be out with your husband though, wouldn't you?'

'Yes, but – '

'I'll see to Sophy. She'll be quite happy, playing with my two.'

Claudia had already discovered this. Sophy was just fourteen months old – and in love with little Andrew Foley, aged sixteen months. Claudia was redundant. And jealous. And wise enough to shrug off her jealousy to join Alister at last.

And it was strange: as soon as she turned her back on

the house and her face to the land, she began to feel safe again. There was nothing very beautiful about Murray's at this time of year. The glasshouses were bursting at the seams with plants, but save for an acre or two of bright spring greens, only the ragged remnants of the winter crops still stood in the ground. Everything else was ploughed up, the dark ochre soil slowly warming as the days lengthened.

Claudia's eyes brightened at the sight. Her heart was soothed, her mind totally absorbed by the strange, compelling magic of making things grow. She left the house every morning just as Mrs Foley arrived, and when she went home again, four hours later, it was as if no time had passed. Four hours were like so many minutes, and what could a woman *do* in four minutes? She wanted more!

'Mrs Foley,' Alister said smugly, 'also wants more. We can afford it, Clo. Ask her to stay longer.'

'But Sophy – '

'Sophy's fine. Sophy's happy. Sophy's thriving.'

It was true. Every time she approached the house, Claudia could see Sophy and her little boyfriend toddling about on the lawn, bashing hell out of one another with their teddy bears, shouting, laughing, and occasionally being separated by Mary Foley's gentle hand. James had been assigned to keep an eye on them. He sat in a deckchair, wearing a battered straw hat, listening to the cricket on a tiny transistor radio. He was happy, too.

Claudia considered her position. Since being relieved of the responsibilities of house, business and family, Cath Murray had slipped back into her old routine. She was seventy-seven, as fit as a flea, always moaning about her arthritis but still sprinting up the post office steps on pension day. The house was immaculate. And, save for one small, surviving worm of disquiet which she tried never to think about, Claudia was . . . happy.

'Well, Clo?' Alister turned her into his arms. He nuzzled

her ear; and Claudia slipped her arms around him, holding him tightly. His chest was as solid as a rock, his arms as brown, gnarled and warm as seasoned oak. Since he'd first stepped into her life, he'd brought peace, healing, laughter and love; not just for Claudia but for everyone. John was married and living his own life, untroubled by any duty to his family. Daniel was living in his idea of heaven and James was content. All because of Alister.

'I love you,' she murmured. 'Oh, Ali, I do love you!'

'Hey, what's brought this on?'

'I don't know. Happiness, I think.' She laughed tearfully. 'I hate being happy. It makes me feel so insecure!'

'Why?'

'Oh . . . just in case I lose it.'

'Oh,' he said flatly. 'Well, you probably will if you don't give me a hand in the office. It's chaos in there. I can't find anything. For all I know, we're about to go bankrupt.'

Claudia laughed. And she asked Mary Foley to stay all day.

At three, Sophy Chalcroft was two inches taller than Andrew Foley, and her hair had lightened from black to brown, with a hint of auburn where the sun caught it. It was as straight as a die, as fine as silk, and Claudia had styled it in a long, page-boy bob, with a heavy fringe to guard her pale, betraying eyes.

Sophy had style. She was as slim as a reed, as dainty as a daisy. She'd copied her mother's way of walking – head up, shoulders back – and her impossible little trick of looking down at everyone, regardless of their size. But she had none of Claudia's defensiveness. The village was still laughing about the time she'd said to the butcher, 'I won't speak to you today, Mr Burns. I'm in one of my moods.'

Sophy didn't have moods. Claudia did. They came upon

her without warning: the cruel cat's paw of God, snatching her back from her illusions of escape and holding her down so that she could barely move for terror. All she could do was to plod through it and pray; plod through it and smile and hope no one would notice. But Alister noticed. Alister couldn't help noticing, for it was he who rescued her from her fight with the blankets every night; he who kept her safe from the yellow nightmare; he who invented the saving phrase, 'Don't bother Mummy now, darling. She's in one of her moods.'

Alister thought the moods and the nightmares were all connected with her mother's death: an everlasting fear of sudden, devastating loss. And he was right, in a way. Had Claudia never lost Madge, never lost Marcus . . . Perhaps then she wouldn't have known what it was to lose everything – and not known how to fear it. But she'd have given the whole world to be twelve again, screaming at the roadside for her mother. For that agony had been no agony at all compared with this. Madge's death had not been Claudia's fault. She had committed no sin. She had told no lies.

Now the whole world hung on the thin, fragile thread of Claudia's lies. A breath of wind could snap it. And after that? When a cat played with a mouse, the mouse rarely came out of it alive; although it wasn't usually the cat that killed it. The mouse died of shock. It died of too many escapes. Too many entrapments. Too many 'moods'.

But Claudia was not in one of her moods on the morning of her twenty-second birthday. She felt marvellous. The sun shining, the sky blue, the trees in leaf, the daffodils in bloom. And Claudia was pregnant. With *Alister's* child. Oh, the relief! He couldn't leave her now. Even if he found out about Sophy, he couldn't leave her now!

It was seven o'clock, Saturday morning. Claudia had been up since five. She'd bathed and washed her hair.

Bathed and dressed Sophy. And now Claudia was preparing breakfast – a special one – for Alister.

Sophy was sitting on the draining board, her favourite perch, for from here she could see everything – the kitchen, the yard, the glasshouses and beyond. It had been a warm, mild spring and Claudia had spent the past week planting out the first outdoor lettuces, the first summer cabbages, the peas. And they'd all put their roots down and begun to grow. It was going to be a wonderful year.

'*How* old are you?' Sophy asked for the fifteenth time that day.

'Twenty-two.'

'That's very old, isn't it?'

'Oh, ancient,' Claudia laughed.

With her preparations for breakfast completed (it was no good cooking it until she heard the lorry come back from the market), Claudia made coffee and sat down to read the paper.

'Mummy?'

'Hmm?'

'Why do lambs jump up and down?'

'Oh, because they're happy, I should think.'

Saxons had moved the sheep with their lambs into Long Meadow only yesterday, and Sophy and Andrew had spent the best part of a day watching them through the fence.

'Aren't their mummies happy, too?'

'Hmm?'

'Their mummies don't jump up and down. They just eat.'

'Well, it's a very responsible job, being a mummy. We have to keep our strength up, you know.'

'Does lettuces keep your strength up?'

'Hmm?'

Sophy asked questions a mile a minute, every minute, from dawn to dusk. It was impossible to answer them all.

Impossible even to listen to them all if you wanted to get anything else done. But Claudia's brain seemed to have developed a filtering mechanism which swallowed all the unimportant questions and threw up the others two seconds later, with 'URGENT' stamped in red at the top.

'*Lettuces*?'

She jumped up and flew to the window, her face paling with dismay. The sheep were in! Dozens of them: up to their knees in the soft, yellow earth, up to their necks in Claudia's seedlings!

'Oh, Jesus wept!' she howled.

'Why did he, Mummy?'

The filter swallowed that one without trace.

Claudia clapped her hand to her mouth and spun around the kitchen like a bee with one wing, buzzing with confusion. 'Oh, my God. Oh, my God . . .'

What the hell could she do? It was no good trying to get them out on her own. Sheep knew no discipline, had no sense; they'd just scatter over the entire thirty acres, leaving mayhem in their wake! The only way to get them out . . .

She ran into the hall, quivering in every fibre. She stared at the telephone and her ashen face turned to fire. She had to ring the Saxons! She had to tell them to . . . Tell him to . . . She couldn't! Oh, God, she couldn't! But the sheep were wrecking everything, destroying months of work! Alister would die!

Clenching her teeth, Claudia picked up the receiver. She put it down again. She didn't know the number.

Claudia was still trying to recall where 'S' came in the alphabet when Alister came home and found her crouching on the stairs snatching her way through the telephone directory with wild, fluttering hands. She was still muttering, 'Oh, my God, oh, my God.'

'What's up?'

'Sheep! They're all over! Eating everything!'

'Oh, my God.'

'Will you phone them, Ali? I – I *can't*!'

Claudia barely noticed the sideways look Alister gave her then; but she noticed the next one.

Marcus and Noddy Bridges arrived within minutes, speeding across the bumpy ground of Long Meadow in a brand new Land-Rover with two sheepdogs racing along-side. Claudia saw Marcus step over the broken fence, wearing (it seemed) the same set of clothes he'd been wearing four years ago; before . . . Before she'd helped him to take them off. Slim khaki-coloured trousers, brown leather boots and a soft checked shirt. Oh, God, he was so beautiful!

She turned away, her face burning, her stomach heaving with nausea.

'I'll go out,' Alister said flatly.

'And me!' Sophy shouted. 'And me, Daddy!'

'*No*!' Claudia almost screamed it, catching Sophy in her arms, pressing her close.

Alister's eyes widened with disapproval. 'Don't be silly, Clo.'

'The dogs!'

'Are trained and under control.' He took Sophy's hand. 'Come on, sweetheart. You can tell the nice Mr Saxon he's going to pay us some damages.'

'What's damages, Daddy?'

'Pennies. Lots of 'em. Come on.'

Claudia felt she was being sliced through the middle with a blunt hacksaw. If she made too much fuss Ali might suspect something; but if he took Sophy out there, if he saw her with Marcus, he'd *know*!

'It'll be so muddy!' she protested feebly. 'I've only just put that dress on her!'

Alister pursed his mouth and gave her the second

sideways look. She had no idea what it meant. She didn't dare wonder what it meant. But it almost killed her. Oh, if only there'd been time to tell him about the baby!

Her teeth chattering, Claudia stood at the window watching her husband stride towards her lover; her lover turn to greet him with a smile. Ali picked Sophy up to keep her from the mud, standing for a moment to point out the black and white streaks which were the speeding dogs, snowy lambs leaping over their mothers' backs, ewes streaming like a yellow river towards the gap in the fence, their unearthly bleating combining to a thunderous roar.

Beside herself and in spite of herself, Claudia crept in pursuit of her beloved family, keeping herself hidden between the glasshouses until the sheep were far away and she heard at last the companionable rumble of male voices; the sweet, excited piping of Sophy's six hundredth question of the day.

'Don't your dogs understand English?'

'Yes, but they can't hear my voice when the sheep are making all that din. They can hear a whistle easily.'

'Because it sounds higher?'

There was silence. Then Marcus said, 'She's bright, isn't she?'

Claudia stepped clear of the last of the glasshouses. She saw Alister bumping Sophy higher in his arms, saw Marcus reaching out to tickle her chin, his smile soft with wonderment.

'How old are you, Sophy?'

'I don't know. How old am I, Daddy?'

'Dope! You're three! You had a birthday last week, didn't you?'

'And Mummy's got one today! But she's *very* old.'

The men laughed, and then Marcus caught sight of Claudia and his smile died. He turned away to repeat his apologies to Alister, murmuring something about insurance and getting in touch.

'I'll be off, then. Goodbye, Sophy. Be good.'

And he strode away, his spine like a ramrod, his shoulders set square. He didn't look back.

Chapter Twenty-Three

Liz's bungalow was called 'Sunnyside' but Marcus had rechristened it 'England's Glory', because it was the size of a matchbox.

Liz loved it; and because she loved it and was happy there, Marcus found himself visiting her more frequently than his early feelings of claustrophobia had led him to expect. He still felt claustrophobic when she let him into the tiny hallway, which barely accommodated the two of them; but once he'd cleared that obstacle and entered the bright, chintzy little sitting room with its huge, plate-glass window, he could sit down and relax. And talk.

He talked as he'd never talked before. He told Liz everything, leaving out only the names. Claudia became 'the woman', Sophy 'the child', Alister 'the husband'. And Marcus, for the first time in his life, became a man with no armour, no power, no answers.

'She's so beautiful, Liz! And she's *my* daughter! *My* child! I spend half my life making plans for her. I want to love her, educate her, give her everything! And I've only got near her twice! He said . . . she's learning to read. She's growing, she's changing – *without* me!'

'Do you still love her mother?' Liz asked sadly.

'Love her? I hate her. But oh, Liz, I ache for her. Every time I look at another woman, I see *her*, I want *her*, and no one else means anything to me. Nothing.'

'That's hate?' Liz smiled.

'Ohh . . . What's the difference? I loved Dad until I discovered I hated him. And then I stopped loving him.' He smiled wanly. 'I stopped hating him, too. I keep telling myself that all this will resolve itself in the same way, but I get so confused! It – it doesn't seem to be anyone's fault. There's no one to blame. And yet – I seem to need to blame someone, and she just fits the bill. She's told so many lies, and yet even that – I can't blame her for that! She had no choice!'

'You're sure her husband doesn't know?'

'If he does,' Marcus breathed wonderingly, 'he's a saint. No, he can't know. He adores that kid. When he looked at her . . . I wanted to snatch her out of his arms, hold her next to my face, let him see! But it isn't his fault, poor devil, and he's . . . I scarcely know him, but if I had to choose another man to father my child, he'd probably be the one I'd choose. But I dream of killing him, Liz. Every day of my life, I dream of killing him.' He laughed and added hoarsely, 'And it's killing me.'

'What about her feelings? This woman? What does she feel for you now?'

'She's afraid of me. She knows I could tell him; tell everyone.'

'But you won't?'

'I want to.' Marcus clenched his fists. 'Oh, I *want* to.'

Liz stroked his hair. 'But you won't,' she repeated firmly.

'No.' He spoke without emphasis. Without conviction. Without belief in his own helplessness.

Liz took his face in her hands, forcing him to meet her eyes. 'You won't,' she said. 'There's already enough tragedy in the world, Marcus, without your creating more of it. You'll ruin them. Not just the girl and her husband – '

'I know! Do you think I don't know? I *know* my daughter's happier with him than she could be with me if I took her from him! Damn it to hell, that's what *hurts*!'

But Liz was relentless. 'Take her from him?' she echoed sternly. 'You can't *take* her, Marcus. She may be your daughter but you have no legal claims on her at all. And if you think that woman would deign to spit on you after you'd ruined their lives, you've got another think coming. She'd see you in hell first.'

Marcus bowed his head. He closed his eyes. 'I know that, too,' he said.

He had known Sarah Lisle for years without knowing her name. Without knowing anything about her except that she was pleasant and softly spoken. And beautiful, although her beauty was not of the kind to hit a man between the eyes. It was of the sort which only gradually becomes apparent, emerging out of darkness, like the dawn.

The first time he'd noticed her had been the first time she'd worn her hair loose. Until then, she'd been just an ordinary girl, working quietly behind the desk at the Public Library. A face. A blouse. A pair of hands. He hadn't even observed that she wore her hair in some kind of bun at the back of her head. She could have been bald for all he'd known – or cared.

And then one day (Marcus remembered it very clearly, for Claudia had been in the library that day, too), Sarah had run out of hairpins, or patience, or both; and the sight of her hair had taken his breath away. She could never in her life have had it cut, for it poured down her back like molten gold; hanging straight to her waist, then waving deliciously to the tops of her thighs. Sit-upon hair. Fairy-tale hair. It was the sort of hair men dreamed of brushing until it crackled.

'Rapunzel, Rapunzel,' he'd murmured. 'Let your hair down.'

But she'd taken not a blind bit of notice: just smiled vaguely and handed his tickets over. He'd had to cook up some enquiry about the index files before she'd consent to acknowledge him.

She'd worn her hair up after that, and he hadn't, anyway, been in the mood for courtship games. He'd forgotten her. He'd forgotten the library, too; preferring, now that he was prosperous enough, to buy all the books he needed.

He might never have seen Sarah Lisle again had she not cannoned into him one morning at the corner of Abbey Green. She raced out of the little dairy there, carrying a small carton of eggs in one hand and a loaded shopping basket in the other. Something had to give, and the eggs did. The box flew through the air, landing (miraculously intact) about six feet away; and then – like a small child quietly wetting its pants – it oozed its contents all over the cobbles.

Sarah, doing a brilliant imitation of the mad March Hare, glanced at her watch, at the eggs, at her watch. She stared wildly at Marcus. Her hands were fluttering in panic, her eyes widening, blinking, widening again. They were large, long eyes. Strange eyes. A pale, tawny gold which almost matched her hair.

'I'm sorry,' Marcus said kindly. 'I'm afraid I wasn't – '

'No.' Her voice fluttered like her hands. 'My fault. It's just that my bus – and the eggs.' She stared helplessly into the shop as someone else went in. 'There's such a queue in there!'

Had Marcus been in the same predicament he'd have damned the eggs and gone for the bus. But Sarah seemed incapable of making any decision at all. She just hovered on the spot, juggling her priorities, and Marcus had a feeling she'd still be hovering and juggling when hell froze over.

'Which bus? What time's the next one?'

'Not for two hours.'

'And where are you going?'

'Woodley. No! Larcombe! That is, I live at Woodley, but the bus – '

'I get the picture. And I'm going to Larcombe, so if you want to go back for more eggs and you'd like a lift – ?'

She stopped panicking. She looked at him properly, and a smile came and went, revealing a wide, sensuous mouth and near perfect teeth.

'Do I know you?' she asked doubtfully. 'Yes, I do . . . Don't I?'

'Library. Marcus Saxon.' He offered her his hand. 'And you're Rapunzel, aren't you?'

'Er – well, Sarah Lisle.' The smile came again and stayed a little longer. 'Oh, yes, I remember. But you haven't been in for ages, have you?'

Tiny freckles over her cheekbones were suddenly overcome by a soft flush of pink. 'Er – well, I don't really know . . .' She glanced again at her watch. 'But I've missed my bus, now.'

Marcus grinned. 'So?'

He'd never had much to do with scatty women before this, and he found it rather charming. She *was* beautiful. But save for her extraordinary hair, it was a beauty which was hard to analyse. Her skin was the colour of ivory, silkily opaque; and her eyes, her lashes, her hair, were all of the same tawny gold. Her cheekbones were too high, her mouth too wide. She looked rather hungry, like a sleek lioness on the prowl for an antelope.

But she couldn't catch a bus, let alone an antelope. And she hadn't a clue how to catch a man! Perhaps she didn't want to catch one. Or was it just that she didn't want to catch *him*?

Marcus sighed heavily. He couldn't have Claudia. He had to forget her. And how better to forget her than with a challenge like Sarah Lisle? Woodley, too. It was virtually on the doorstep . . .

Sarah had moved only recently from her childhood home in Keynsham to a stately-looking cottage not far from the Woodley bridge. She lived with her aunt, a woman whom Marcus imagined as being small, plump and adoring. Sarah called her 'Annan', a name carried over from early childhood, when she'd been unable to wrap her tongue around the name, 'Aunt Hannah'.

Both Sarah's parents had died of tuberculosis; her mother very early when Sarah was only three, her father seven years later. Sarah could scarcely remember him, for he'd spent the best part of those years in Ham Green sanatorium, for ever 'getting better' and not quite making it.

In her teenage years Sarah too had fallen foul of the disease; but by that time it was no longer a killer, and after a couple of years on the appropriate drugs she'd made a complete recovery. But the illness had come at the wrong time for her education, and she was not, as Marcus had at first thought, a qualified librarian. She worked at the library the way other girls worked in shops, as a shelf filler and general clerk.

This bothered him at first. His happier relationships with women had never been just a matter of sex. He'd been brought up to hold education in high esteem. Other people's erudition had always excited him, and his 'art-versus-science' discussions with Kay (when she wasn't being stubborn) counted among the high spots of his life, if only because they'd shunted him into learning enough about her subject to win some of the arguments.

His bookshelves were now almost as well stocked with art history as with any other subject, and although he'd never quite won through to the intellectual point of it all, the process of learning had enriched his life immeasurably.

But Sarah was by no means ignorant. She knew who Kandinsky was and could describe his style. She knew who Giotto was, and Fra Angelico. She also knew about Gallileo, the Curies and Sir Humphrey Davy. She'd read Coleridge, Wordsworth, Shakespeare and Chaucer. She had no deep knowledge of anything, but she knew a little about everything under the sun.

And she still wanted to learn. Marcus liked that about her. She wanted to learn all he could teach her – except (but this was surely temporary!) about sex. She was twenty-four years old and still, very determinedly, a virgin. The cosy Aunt Hannah had told her to save it for her wedding night.

Marcus was certain he could persuade Sarah otherwise, given time; and, oddly, he didn't really mind how much time it took. She was good company. Not particularly animated and not especially exciting, but his self-confidence had taken a beating over the past few years and he was happy now just to be soothed.

Sarah could be very soothing. The scattiness he'd noticed in her at first was not one of her dominant features. Indecisiveness was, but so too was a willingness to have all her decisions made for her. When Marcus said 'turn left' she turned left, and he almost loved her for that. It was only when he said (in the appropriate manner) 'take your clothes off and lie down' that she turned stubborn.

Yet he felt certain she was fighting herself, not him; and he knew enough of the rigours of internal warfare to guess that Sarah would soon lose the fight. Her animal instincts were not far beneath the surface. Her skin rippled like a horse's flank when he stroked it. And sometimes, when he gazed steadily into her eyes, murmuring his (until now) failsafe persuasions, her long, tawny eyes would close down with blissful languor, her mouth soften, her body arch yearningly towards him.

But he could never get the next bit right! Whatever he did or said next was wasted on her; and within seconds she'd jerked upright, straightened her clothes, consulted her March Hare's watch and gasped, 'Oh, Marcus, it's late! Annan'll kill me!'

Not, Marcus was inclined to think grimly, before I kill Annan.

But that was before he met her.

Since his college days Marcus had never been any good at burning the candle at both ends, and he rarely saw Sarah more than twice in a week. However fit a man was (and Marcus was as fit as any man), farming was punishing enough to seek out his weaknesses, and the rod it used to break his back was the milk lorry. The milk lorry arrived at seven-thirty (give or take two minutes) every day of the year, and no farmer worth his salt would keep the lorry waiting.

While Tom had been alive, he and Ben (and, later, Marcus) had taken it in turns to get up at four for the morning milking. But Ben was now fast pushing sixty and although he remained fit, Marcus dearly wanted him to remain fit and taking an active part in the farm. If anything happened to Ben now, Marcus would be up a gum tree, for Ellis would never come back to farming. Gloria had finally pushed him into a decent job in the City, and – lo and behold – Ellis loved it.

So, for the good of his father's health, Marcus did five 'earlies' a week and Ben did two – as widely spaced as seven days could make them.

Even on his two nights off, Marcus was usually in bed long before midnight to be up again at six. At other times he hit the sack immediately after the nine o'clock News; and he enjoyed these evenings at home more now than ever before. If only he'd had a wife to share them . . .

Sometimes, in his madder moments, he thought he'd like to marry Irene Bridges, whose arrival at Saxon's (with baby Tony) had enlivened the household beyond belief. Her Grammar School education had only marginally improved Irene's grammar, and had done nothing to polish her social skills; but she was bright, funny, warm and affectionate, and her gratitude to the family for saving her and the baby 'from a fate worse than deaf' seemed inexhaustible.

She'd been desperately shy at first: a pale, rather lumpy shadow who'd tried to disappear into the woodwork when one of the men (especially Marcus) had appeared on the scene. Now she was as cheeky as she'd ever been. And as noisy. She sang, teased, joked, and laughed as Marcus had never seen anyone laugh, collapsing into the nearest chair and giving herself up to hilarity with everything she'd got. Shrieks, tears, giggles, roars. Even if you'd missed the joke which had set her off, it was impossible not to laugh too. She even made Olivia laugh, and that was a sight for sore eyes!

Little Tony Bridges was another joy. Save for a barely discernible crest of gingery hair, he was as bald as a coot and as soft and white as unbaked dough. But, as a small baby, he'd scarcely ever murmured except to burp – as required – after meals, or to gurgle his appreciation when anyone tickled him. But he was tickled, cuddled and played with more than any baby had a right to expect, and had Marcus ever doubted his need for children, Tony would have swept those doubts away with a single trusting smile.

'Doin' anything in the next five minutes, Marcus?'

'Not as far as I know.'

'Grab a load of our Tone then, will you, while I make up his cot?'

'Grabbing a load of our Tone' was always a pleasure, for the child fitted snugly into the crook of Marcus's arm, and sat there so contentedly, watching in fascination while Marcus talked to him and tickled his toes. There was something immensely satisfying in holding a life so small, so innocent and dependent. It brought out the most gentle side of Marcus's nature – the side which Callie had nurtured – and it was, without question, the side of himself he liked best.

It was interesting to compare his own baby-handling technique with that of the rest of the family. Edward nursed 'our Tone' as if he were made of spun glass, Ben more as if he'd been packed with gelignite, and Helen with a gentle, cooing efficiency which bored the kid rigid and put him to sleep faster than anything else could. But it was Olivia's responses which surprised Marcus most. She was crazy about the kid; couldn't get enough of him.

'Hello, hello, hello. Where's that little smile, hmm? Where's that little smile for Grandma? Where's that – little – *smile*?'

God only knew how Tony felt about it, but Marcus could never stay in the same room for fear of laughing. He'd grown accustomed to Olivia's hard, crusty shell, and it was strange to discover she was all strawberry jelly underneath.

'Grandma? Did you talk to me like that when I was a baby?'

'No. Never touched you. You were a brat.'

'Tony'll be a brat too.'

'No, he won't. No, he won't. You won't, will you, precious? No – you – *won't*.'

But he would. Olivia knew he would. She only had to look at Ellis's twins to know he would; and as soon as babies turned into brats, Olivia went back to normal: quelling the little terrors with a glassy flash of her eyes.

Perhaps out of cruelty or perhaps in his wisdom, Marcus decided to invite Sarah to lunch at Saxon's while the whole gang was there: Ellis and Gloria; Simon and Stephen (the terrible twins) and their six-month-old sister Lucy; the two-year-old Tony (who, having skidded around the house on his behind for the past fourteen months, had only just learned to walk); Irene Bridges, grandparents and great-grandparents; 'Old Uncle Tom Cobbley and all'.

The house, packed to the rafters with old, young and middling, was exactly the way Marcus wanted it. And if Sarah couldn't handle it? If Sarah couldn't handle it, she could save her precious virginity for someone else!

Afterwards he wasn't sure whether she'd passed the test or not. She hadn't passed it in the way he'd hoped; but on the other hand he couldn't fault her. He had observed her very carefully throughout but it had been rather like watching a statue of the Virgin being carried through a Carnival parade.

Gloria was into breast feeding in public. The twins were into baring their bottoms, ditto. Ellis, after suffering four years of total blackout, had suddenly remembered who was boss (Gloria), and gone into open rebellion – with Ben on his side. (It had something to do with the new contraceptive pill, although with everyone yelling at once it was hard to discover who was for it and who against.) Irene, in the middle of one of her giggling fits, had knocked a large pot of soup off the Aga and scalded herself horribly. She'd screamed horribly, too; and Marcus, stuck for a better remedy, had dragged her out to the dairy and turned the hose on her.

Within seconds she'd been laughing like a drain. 'Gerroff! Gerroff, you fool! You're bloody drownin' I!'

'Drowning *me*!' Marcus had roared. 'Get it right, woman!'

'I *ain't* drownin' you! You're drownin' *I*!'

She only did it to annoy . . . And she hadn't been scalded too badly. Either that, or the hosing had worked.

Sarah had endured all that – bare breasts, bare bottoms, roaring men and screaming women – without batting an eyelid. Yet she'd scarcely said a word. And the smile she'd had on her face when she arrived was still there when she left. She said she'd enjoyed every minute.

'It's a real *family*, isn't it? I've always wanted a real family.'

'You're mad. What bit did you like best?'

'The twins, sitting on heaps of cushions at the table. They looked so sweet, didn't they?'

He couldn't fault her. But somehow he wished he could.

He wished it even more when they arrived back at the cottage and the famous 'Annan' came out to meet him at last. She wasn't a bit as he'd imagined. She was tall and gaunt, with a face so sharply wrought and so strangely immobile that it might have been cast in bronze. She was about fifty. Pewter grey hair had been drawn back from her face and arranged in a simple twist at the nape of her neck. She wore a white blouse, a black cardigan, a plain grey flannel skirt; and Marcus's first impression was of a stern, cold-blooded Puritan, eternally on the lookout for sinners. It was her lucky day . . .

'You must be Marcus.'

Cold voice. Cold eyes. Cold smile. Marcus didn't like

Aunt Hannah, but for courtesy's sake he gave her the benefit of his smile. And although he wasn't close enough to offer his hand, he was quite close enough to see that she didn't like his smile.

'Tea is ready,' she announced frostily. 'You'd better come in,' and she turned on her heel and floated smoothly indoors, leaving Marcus at the gate, almost paralysed with shock.

'I can't stay!' he hissed in Sarah's ear. 'I'm already late for milking!'

She caught his elbow. 'Oh, please! Just ten minutes? She'll be so hurt if you don't!'

For 'hurt' Marcus substituted 'livid'. And so, more for Sarah's sake than for Hannah's, he sighed and went inside.

By the time Marcus returned to the farm, Ben and Little Georgie had almost finished the milking; and Ben, perhaps helped along by the chaos which had reigned at lunch, was in a filthy mood.

So was Marcus. Another potential wife had bitten the dust. Sarah was sweet, but she wasn't worth the trouble that aunt of hers could give him. Christ, she was weird! He'd watched her with appalled fascination as she'd poured the tea (Earl Grey: almost tolerable), and had found not a single line etched into that hard, frozen face; not a single flaw. Dark brown eyes, straight nose, well-shaped mouth. The slightly coarse texture of her skin and her pewter-grey hair had given him the only clues to her age.

But her bitterness was a thousand years old. She'd inherited it from Boadicea (whom she closely resembled; all she needed was a shield instead of a tea-pot): hounded and hunted, raped, flogged, bereaved and disinherited – her bitterness was a thousand years old.

She had spoken almost entirely of the weather, but she'd

made Marcus feel as if he was drowning in poison. He'd never met anyone more repellent. She'd chilled him to the bone. And yet, on the surface of things, there was nothing wrong with the woman. She'd been courteous enough. She'd been sweet to Sarah. So had Marcus been, if only because he'd known it was for the last time. He would not be seeing Sarah again.

'Oh, you're back,' Ben muttered crossly. 'Ten minutes, you said.'

'Yes. I got shanghaied for tea. Knock off if you like, Georgie. I'll finish here.'

Georgie didn't need telling twice. Ben didn't need to be told at all, and Marcus fully expected him to hurry away for a bath, a quiet drink and (twins permitting) a doze behind the Sunday papers. But Ben stayed.

'So you had tea?'

'Yes.'

'With her people?'

'Mm-hm.'

A bright July sun slanted through the cedars on the far side of the yard, and the last group of cows lumbered to their stalls through a downpour of dusty sunbeams.

Ben measured concentrates into the mangers while Marcus stooped to wash the cows and attach the milking clusters. He wasn't in the mood to talk about Sarah. In other circumstances, he'd have walked off and left his father to interrogate thin air; but Ben had done an 'early' this morning, and he'd done most of the evening's milking too.

'Why don't you go in?' Marcus suggested mildly.

'I'm all right.' Ben produced a cautious smile. 'She seems a nice girl. I didn't quite catch her name with all the rumpus we had earlier. Sarah what, was it?'

'Lisle.'

'As in Tate and Lyle?'

'As in island.'

'Ah . . . Been seeing much of her?'

'A bit.'

'And are you a bit – serious? Or just passing the time?'

Marcus ignored him.

'Not that it's any of my business,' Ben said hurriedly.

'True.'

'It's just that if you *are* serious . . . Well, she doesn't seem the right sort for you, somehow. Very quiet girl. Kay was much more your type, I think.'

Marcus kept his peace. When Ben ventured into personal talk it invariably led to a quarrel. A quarrel which – like a well-matched pair of rutting stags – neither of them wanted. So at first they just clunked their antlers together, testing each other's weight, each other's agility, each other's strength. And if, as a result of these tentative calculations, one of them failed to retire . . .

Ten years ago it had been Marcus who'd backed off. Now, far more often, it was Ben. He'd surrendered his superiority where the farm was concerned: a few gentle clunks and he was off. But personal matters were more dangerous, if only because, in personal matters, Marcus was more vulnerable.

'Not,' Ben went on now, 'that I'd have wanted you to marry Kay. Too independent. Very much a city girl, Kay. A bit of a feminist too, wasn't she?'

Marcus kept his peace.

'No good at all on a farm, you see. If the women aren't in tune with the men, you've got trouble on your hands. Once you've committed yourself to a woman, you're committed for a lifetime, and I'd hate you to make a mistake that lasts that long.'

Still Marcus said nothing.

'I think this Sarah Lisle girl is a mistake, Marcus. She's not right for you. Not right for you at all.'

And now – as he'd anticipated – Marcus was angry. He knew he was wrong to be angry – Ben was only confirming his own, barely acknowledged, doubts about Sarah. But he had no right to interfere. Marcus would choose his own wife, and Ben would damn well accept her, whoever she turned out to be!

'Oh,' he said coolly. 'Does this mean you won't be coming to the wedding?'

He had judged this little taunt to be still in the category of antler-bashing; but Ben clearly thought otherwise, for he reared up suddenly, his lips whitening with temper.

'If you've asked her to marry you!'

'*Yes*?' And now Marcus was drawing himself up, squaring his shoulders, gathering his strength for the fray. 'I'll marry the girl I choose, and you'll mind your own bloody business.'

Ben didn't move, but he seemed to retreat a few paces before advancing again for another try.

'Look, all I'm saying – '

'You've said enough!'

During the entire exchange neither man had raised his voice but the air crackled with threat, and the cows shifted uncomfortably in their stalls as if, extra feed nothwithstanding, they would greatly have preferred to be somewhere else.

Ben withdrew, shrugging. 'Damn you then. Go your own way.'

The conflict was over; Marcus had won, and as he walked the herd back to pasture it was almost as if his father had never spoken, as if nothing had happened since he'd dropped Sarah from his life.

But he hadn't actually *told* her she'd been dropped . . . And it wasn't really fair – no, not really – to leave her without a word. She was at least entitled to some warning, poor kid; a cooling-off period; a chance to decide for herself that they'd make a poor match. (He could help her with that!)

Yes, he ought to see her again, once or twice.

She finished work early on Saturdays. Marcus had met her from work before this, arriving two minutes early as a courteous suitor should. Now he was ten minutes late. It was a broiling day. She should have been peeved. (Kay would have given him hell.) But Sarah smiled, just as usual.

'Been waiting long?'

'No. I was a bit late.'

He took her arm and they walked through the market and then along the pretty, glass-roofed arcade which led into Union Street. Sarah adored window-shopping, and Marcus was usually happy to oblige her; but today he didn't.

'Come on, it's too hot to hang around.'

'I promised to pick up some things for Annan at Marks and Spencer. Just stockings. It won't take a minute.'

'That's the other end of town! I've parked in the Circus!'

'Oh.' She smiled again. 'Oh, well, never mind. I'll get them on Monday.'

'Don't be silly.' He caught her elbow and hustled her through the crowds towards the bottom of town. She could barely keep up with him, but she didn't seem to mind.

Marcus tried another tack. 'I didn't care much for your aunt.'

This should have floored her. Had he been in her position, having no one else in the world to care for, or to care for him, Marcus would certainly have taken umbrage. But Sarah just smiled.

'Neither do I, sometimes. It's not easy, knowing I'm all she's got in the world. Without her . . . It's been difficult to live *with* her, but I can't believe I'd have been happier in an orphanage. All I know is that *she'd* have been happier. Without me, she could have married and had children of her own. She could have had some security. Now she's got nothing. Only me.'

Marcus was shocked. He hadn't thought of it that way, had always assumed that Sarah was happy with her life, but how could she be? The poor kid was trapped, for if every man reacted to Hannah as he had reacted, Sarah was never going to get past the starting post. To be stuck in that house, with that woman, with all that appalling bitterness for the rest of her days . . .

And the way Sarah told it, she was the cause of Hannah's bitterness. *Without me, she could have married and had children of her own.* Did Hannah openly blame her for that? The thought made him shudder. And Sarah was such a sweet girl. Nothing seemed to ruffle her or anger her. She was like Helen, in a way. Placid, kind, cooperative . . .

He released her elbow. He tucked her hand into the crook of his arm, and the next time her eyes strayed to a shop window, he stopped and let her look. But the things which attracted her always bewildered him. Cheap costume jewellery, flashy clothes, plastic sandals with mile-high heels. Yet the clothes, shoes and jewellery she actually wore were tasteful and 'good' almost to the point of being boring. She didn't earn much, of course, she had to make every penny work for its living; and perhaps her more ridiculous tastes simply expressed a long-held yearning to be frivolous, poor kid.

The crowds thinned as they passed the entrance to the Abbey Churchyard, giving Marcus a clear view down the length of Stall Street. And there, coming to meet him, were Claudia, Sophy and Alister, hand in hand. Marcus's breath caught in his throat, his heart hammered, and the heat of the day was suddenly unbearable, making his face burn.

They looked wonderful: like one of the perfect happy

families one saw only in television commercials. Alister had completely lost the tired, crumpled look which had marked him out in the past. He was tanned, fit and as neat as a pin in pale blue slacks and a navy summer shirt. Sophy had grown. God, she was lovely! She was wearing new sandals. Marcus guessed they were new, because she was doing a three-year-old's version of the goose-step, lifting her feet as high as they would go to keep them always in view. And Claudia was pregnant . . .

Marcus had often thought that expectant mothers were beautiful, but he'd seen none as beautiful as Claudia. She was glowing. Her fine, ash-blonde hair hung in a thick braid across her shoulder, emphasising the delicate line of her collar bone, the honeyed shaft of her throat. Alister said something, and she turned to him, laughing.

They were happy. They were in love! Claudia was expecting her husband's child. Nothing could part them now . . .

'Marcus?' Sarah's voice was small, desperate – and very, very distant. 'Marcus! You're hurting me!'

'Oh!' He'd been squeezing her hand so hard it was a miracle he hadn't crushed it. 'Oh, I'm sorry.' He kissed it absently. 'I was miles away. Thinking.'

'About what?'

'About . . . termites.'

Yes, in a way, he had. *He* didn't matter. His needs, his loves, his longings: they didn't matter. God didn't answer your prayers. He just made you, and then he left you. And after that, you had to build your nest as best you could – as Claudia had built hers.

'Termites?'

Marcus smiled into Sarah's eyes, but he scarcely saw her. He barely recognised her. Who the hell was she? And who the hell cared?

'I was thinking about you,' he said bleakly. 'Wondering how you'd feel about getting married.'

Chapter Twenty-Four

This was a special day for Claudia, special simply because there was nothing special about it. Thousands of men took their wives out shopping on Saturday afternoons, it was the most ordinary thing in the world. But Alister had never done it before. Not like this: just strolling from shop to shop with Sophy in tow, looking at everything and taking time to choose. It was like an old-fashioned trip to the fair, feeling rich and generous and self-indulgent, buying everything that took your fancy.

They'd come to buy a washing machine, and some sandals for Sophy; but Sophy had come first. They'd had to put her first to keep her from saying, 'Is it time for my new sandals yet? When will it be time for my new sandals? Will I be able to wear them, Daddy? I won't have to have them *wrapped*, will I?'

Afterwards, when they'd arranged for the washing machine to be delivered, Ali had wailed, 'Delivered? Why can't we wear it?'

He was funny and kind and (oddly enough) increasingly good-looking, and Claudia had a comfortable awareness that it was she who had brought about this improvement just by making him content. Making him *happy*.

The business was doing better than ever, and James had transferred joint ownership now, to Claudia and Alister. Ali was thrilled to bits about the baby; and, to make things just perfect, his very first pre-college student, Richard Hiskett (commonly known as Risky), had come back to Murray's, fully qualified, for his first full-time job. He was taking turns to go to market, taking turns to work Sundays – and for the first time since James had been ill, Alister had *time*. Time to go shopping!

There were summer sales everywhere, and in case they missed a bargain they'd been zig-zagging from one side of the road to the other, holding Sophy by the hand. Then suddenly Ali said, 'Oh, hang on!' and released Sophy's hand and dashed across the road to look at Dunn's shop window – just as Claudia looked up the street and saw Marcus Saxon.

A single glance told her everything for he was walking with yet another woman – a stunning Pre-Raphaelite beauty with long, golden hair (Claudia had seen her before, somewhere) – and they looked like a pair of love-sick kids in a hurry to get down Watery Lane. Claudia stared at her feet as they went by (quite literally wrapped up in one another; it would have taken a tyre-lever to prise them apart), but although she was certain Marcus hadn't seen her, she felt as if he had.

It shouldn't have hurt. Why the hell should it hurt? She was happy! She didn't want him! She didn't need him! She had Alister!

Yet the pain was as bad as it had ever been.

And it had all taken no more than a few seconds. A few seconds when Claudia had been blind, deaf, insensate. She hadn't even felt Sophy's hand wresting clear of her own. But she heard her shout, 'Daddy!' And saw her running towards him – into the path of an oncoming car.

'*Sophy!*'

Although in her mind she was flying to the rescue,

Claudia's feet refused to move from the spot. Before she'd managed to take a single step forward, Marcus was there. He must have moved like quicksilver, yet for Claudia it seemed a lifetime. She saw his face first: a wild ferocious mask; and then his arms, flashing out to catch Sophy by the waist, snatching her clear.

There was a moment of total silence. The traffic stopped. The pedestrians stood and stared. And Marcus, his face white with shock, hugged Sophy to his chest as if he'd never let her go. Alister must have moved almost as fast as Marcus had, but he'd had further to travel, and as the traffic stopped and the silence fell, he came to a halt in the middle of the road, gasping with relief.

Sophy, too, had been stunned by the violence of her escape. Her little face was as white as Marcus's, her eyes as wide and staring. But when, from the safety of Marcus's arms, she reached out again, crying, 'Daddy!' Alister didn't move. His face sagging with blank incredulity, he just stood there and stared: first at Sophy, then at Marcus, then at Sophy . . .

He knew.

Until she was five or six, perhaps even seven, Claudia had knelt at her bedside every night, with her eyes closed, her hands pressed together, to recite for her mother the childhood prayer:

Gentle Jesus, meek and mild,
Look upon a little child,
Pity mice in Plicity,
Suffer me to come to thee.

No, she'd probably been as old as eight before those pitiable little mice had begun to seem a touch self-important. Fancy having a prayer all to themselves!

'Mummy, where's Plicity?'

'What, darling?'

'Plicity. You know! Where the mice are!'

Madge had never told her where Plicity was, she'd been laughing too much to speak. But now Claudia knew. It was the place the mice ended up when the cat had finished playing with them; when their hearts had burst with terror and they were no fun any more. Plicity was another name for hell.

Alister hadn't said a word since they'd left Marcus. He hadn't once met Claudia's eyes. Yet when she dared to glance at him as they drove home, his face was as calm as ever. Had he shown the least sign of feeling something – anything at all – she could have coped with it, but this was unbearable! She seemed to be shaking to pieces on the inside. Outside she was like something frozen, not daring to move.

She wondered, knowing that she was verging on hysteria, whether any of this would have happened if only she'd got that prayer right, instead of wasting it on a lot of ungrateful bloody mice! She began to pray, 'Pity my simplicity, pity my simplicity,' as if, in the few minutes she had left, she could make up for a lifetime of error and get God on her side.

Ali knew. He knew! There had been no mistaking that dawning of recognition in his eyes. And when he'd taken the sobbing Sophy from Marcus's arms, there had been no words exchanged, no thanks or expressions of relief. Nothing. And that wasn't like Alister. He'd always been a bit cagey about Marcus; perhaps even a touch scathing about the old family feud; but the two men had talked – not quite like old friends, but certainly like neighbours – that day when the sheep had come in. They'd been courteous, humorous, reasonable. And Marcus had paid for the damage within days of Alister sending him the bill, no questions asked.

But Ali had taken Sophy from Marcus's arms and said nothing. He'd glanced vaguely in Claudia's direction (not into her eyes), and asked, 'You all right?'

He'd walked very slowly back to the car, carrying Sophy, absently patting her back until she'd stopped crying and slipped into one of the staring trances which almost always followed her tears. Now she was asleep on the back seat. When she woke again, what would she find? What would happen next? What would he *do*?

He'd thought her a virgin! She hadn't said she was, but when he'd jumped to that conclusion she hadn't disputed it. Dear God, how many lies had she told to this man who never lied? And how the hell did a man who never lied say what he thought about it? He was just waiting. He was waiting until Sophy was in bed, until James and Cath were safely tucked away with their beloved television. Then he'd take her to pieces!

'*Ali*?' How could two little syllables fragment into a dozen?

He didn't reply.

The next few hours were agony. A stranger would not have known that anything was wrong for Alister behaved just as normal. He didn't crack any of his usual little jokes, he didn't touch Claudia; but after supper he said, as he usually did, 'Thanks, that was good,' and helped her to wash up.

'We have to talk,' she muttered frantically.

He sighed. 'I suppose you realise I'll have to move the sink to get the washing machine in? If they deliver on Thursday . . . Think you'll manage without any water for a few hours on Friday?'

Claudia couldn't speak but the internal shaking was beginning to show on the outside and her knees wouldn't hold her up.

'It wouldn't hurt Sophy to go to bed early tonight,' Ali said. 'I'll see to it. Go and lie down. You're tired.'

'I'm not tired, I'm – !'

'*Hush*. He closed his eyes for a moment, and in that moment his face became a twisted mask of pain. 'Go on. Have a rest. You have your baby to think of, don't you?'

Yesterday he would have said '*We* have *our* baby to think of', and although Claudia noticed the difference, she was half-way upstairs before its import struck her. Did he think that this child, like Sophy, was another man's?

Dear God, she'd never thought of this! If she'd been capable of cheating once, he must think her capable of cheating a thousand times! Even if they stayed together for fifty years, he would never trust her again!

She lay down. She sat up. She got up and stood at the window, wishing she could cry. She wanted to cry, if only to let off some of the steam that was building inside her, building and building until she thought she'd go mad with the strain. But her tears, too, had turned to steam. There was no outlet. No escape.

She must talk to Ali! She must! She had to know the worst. How could she begin to deal with it until she knew what it *was*?

She lay down again and waited for him to bring Sophy up for her bath. But when at last she heard them on the stairs, she almost groaned with horror.

'He *was* the man with the sheep, wasn't he, Daddy?'

'Mm-hm.'

'I *thought* he was! But he looked a bit cross, so I wasn't sure. Why was he cross, Daddy?'

'I can't think,' Alister said. 'Come on, say goodnight to Mummy.'

He carried her in upside down, distracting her – as he usually distracted her – with laughter. She was all ready for bed, wearing her favourite pyjamas which were printed all over with nursery rhyme characters. Her hair was damp at the ends, and she smelled of toothpaste and Attar of Roses.

Claudia caught her in her arms and held her close. 'You've already had your bath!'

'We borried Grannan's bathroom!' Sophy grinned, and her eyes glowed with secret wickedness. '*And* we borried her bath salts! And now I smell like a – ' She turned back to Alister. 'What do I smell like, Daddy?'

'A tart,' Alister said.

'An apple tart!' Sophy chortled happily.

It was the only kind of tart she knew.

For three days after that, Alister said nothing that was not reasonable, gentle, kind. But he spoke only when someone else was nearby. If an opportunity arose when he might talk privately with Claudia, he departed by the nearest exit. She followed him along the cinder tracks and saw him escaping, in the other direction, down another of the tracks. She followed him into the glasshouses only to see him go out at the other end. In bed, he turned his back to her. He said, 'I'm tired. I don't want to talk. Go to sleep,' and left her lying there like a burning log, with no one to put out the flames.

She spent the small hours of the first night pacing the sitting room; the second night pacing the yard. She had never in her life felt lonelier or more afraid. In all the years she'd known him, she had never known Alister to lose his temper or to quarrel with anyone. The nearest he'd come to it had been before the wedding, when he was defending Claudia from her grandmother's wrath; but even then he hadn't raised his voice. He had simply stood firm, been firm – and mildly scathing.

Claudia had thought he'd been just *mildly* scathing; but then, she hadn't been on the wrong end of it – Cath had –

and there was no knowing how 'mild' she had deemed it! If it had been no worse than Sophy's 'apple tart', Cath was still bleeding from her wounds!

But oh, dear God, surely that wasn't enough? The man was in pain; and if he was hurting only half as much as Claudia was, he *must* break. He couldn't keep it bottled up for ever! And then what? Claudia could remember, all too clearly, the wild, 'smash-everything' rages her father had regularly indulged in when Madge was alive. He'd been terrifying enough, God knew, but he'd never really hurt anyone; he'd just been showing off, attracting attention like a toddler in a tantrum. But when Alister let rip it wouldn't be like that. When Alister let rip, he'd kill someone.

Yet by the third night, Claudia was too exhausted to fear anything – violent death included. She might even have welcomed a violent death, just as long as it ended in a long, peaceful sleep.

She went to bed before Ali did, and didn't wake when he joined her. She hadn't had the yellow nightmare since she'd discovered she was expecting Alister's child. Now it came back, worse than it had ever been, and she woke with a yell to find herself drenched with sweat – and quite alone.

Shuddering and gasping, she reached for the bedside light; for even knowing that the light would fix the dream in her mind, she couldn't bear the dark without Alister to hold her, comfort her. The room burst upon her with a dim yellow glow, and she yelled again, for Alister *was* there! He was sitting in an armchair beside the window, watching her, his eyes thoughtfully narrowed.

'It was the dream!' she gasped.

'Yes.'

Claudia sank back against her pillows, drowning in despair.

'Do you hate me?' she whispered.

'I don't know.'

'Oh, I know you won't believe me, but I love you, Ali! I always have! Marcus was – '

'Don't tell me.'

'But if you knew, you'd understand that he – '

'I don't *want* to know. And I'm damned if I want to understand. There's no point. We are where we are. It makes no difference at all how we arrived here.'

'But where *are* we? I don't know where we are, Ali, and it's driving me mad! What are you going to *do*?'

'Do? What can I do? Can I change anything?' He shook his head. 'No. And neither can you. Perhaps you do love me, but whether you do or you don't is of no importance now. I have no way of knowing. I'll never know.'

'But *I* know! And I'm telling you, Ali – '

He laughed shortly. 'Yes. And you can be so convincing, Clo. *So* convincing . . . But only once. Never again. And that's the difficulty, you see. That's where we are. In a place where all the lies are true, the truth is all lies, and the only thing left – '

'*Yes*?'

'I don't know. I've never been here before.'

He looked around the bedroom, into every corner of it, as if *this* was the place he'd never been before. It was a beautiful room: restful, elegant and cool in green and white, with a few touches of pink to enliven the scheme. It was immaculate: but from the pained, bewildered expression on Alister's face, his green velvet chair might have been afloat in a sea of sewage.

It was only then that Claudia knew what she'd done to him. For any man on earth the deception she had perpetrated would have been intolerable, but for Ali it was tantamount to murder. He would never recover from it. To a man who never lied, the truth was life. She might, more kindly, have cut his throat.

She mustn't think of herself any more. She mustn't even

think of Sophy and the baby, let alone James. All she must do now was try to make it easier for Alister. Let him do what he had to do. Let him go.

Or let him stay! It wasn't for him to go out into the wilderness and begin his life again among strangers. It wasn't for him to lose everything he'd worked for! That was for Claudia to do. And she deserved far worse.

'I imagine you'll want to leave,' she began softly. 'But I think – '

Alister's eyes widened. '*Leave?*'

He laughed: a soft, humourless little huffing sound which chilled Claudia to the bone. 'Now why should I do that? I married you for the business, and I've got the business. What more could I possibly want?'

'Oh, Ali!' Claudia wailed softly. 'You didn't marry me for the business!'

'Didn't I?'

'No. Because if you did, you were a liar too!'

Alister smiled. 'Quite.'

'I don't believe you!'

His smile changed to a grin of cruel satisfaction. 'Then why did I marry you? For your sweet temper? For your loving family? For your deathless integrity?'

Tears welled in her eyes. 'For love!' she sobbed. 'You *did* love me! You did!'

Alister shook his head. 'You'll never know.'

Within the space of a week he had returned to normal. He was as warm, as funny and considerate as he had ever been; as if nothing had happened; as if the disaster Claudia had feared for so long had failed to touch him.

Yet it *had* touched him! She'd seen the pain in his face, heard it in his voice!

She watched him now with bewilderment as he stooped in the garden to sweep Sophy into his arms, swing her over his head, tickle her. She laughed, this child who was not his child; and he laughed, this man who was not her father; and their little game ended with a series of smacking kisses which would have warmed any mother's heart. But Claudia's heart was a small, frightened thing, left out in the cold.

She kept remembering how a man looks when his heart is broken. She kept seeing his tears, hearing him scream, 'No! No! No! I *loved* you!'

Ali never said he loved her. Never asked if she loved him. Yet she'd told him ten thousand times. She'd asked him, too; and had for her answer only a sweet, teasing smile. 'Why else would I put up with you?'

Yes, why else? For the business?

She would never know.

When Philip Daniel Chalcroft came into the world Alister wasn't there, but even his absence gave Claudia no indication of his feelings towards her. Her first, thirty-hour labour had imprinted on Claudia's mind the idea that babies, no matter how imminent their arrival seems, like to take their time, put you through hell, make an indelible mark on the world before they even bother to come into it.

So she waited. She kept calm. She said, 'Plenty of time. There's no sense rushing.'

She arrived in the labour ward soon after five in the afternoon, saying, 'It'll be ages yet,' and Ali kissed her and promised to be back just as soon as he'd put Sophy to bed. When he returned at eight-thirty his son was almost two hours old – and the spitting image of his mother.

Claudia would have given her eyes, this time, to have produced a child who was the image of his father; but Alister didn't seem to care. Claudia began to think that she could produce a baby by every man in the village without making more than a small dent in her husband's composure. She almost hated him for that.

'He's yours, Ali.'

'Ours, surely?'

'You know what I mean.'

Ali smiled and measured one of Philip's pink little feet against his thumb. Ali's thumb was almost twice the size. 'Look at that,' he whispered wonderingly. '*Tiny*. I can't imagine him playing rugby, can you?'

It was impossible not to smile. 'Well, he's a bit young for it yet, Ali. Give him a chance.'

And it was impossible not to laugh when Ali, affecting scorn, protested, 'Oh, don't molly-coddle the boy, woman!'

She supposed he'd decided to cut his losses, to pretend nothing had happened, to carry on the same as usual. And either he was the best liar and the best actor in the world, or he hadn't cared much to begin with.

But if pretence was all they had (perhaps all they had ever had) Claudia would go along with it. It was, in many ways, much easier than living as she had lived before, in constant fear of discovery. Yes, easier. But so empty. Ali had been the rock to which she'd clung; a solid anchorage in her sea of troubles. Now the sea was calm but it was endless, featureless. It was unfathomable; and Ali was a part of it.

With Marian almost the only exception, Claudia had never had much time for girls of her own age; and, when these girls had become women, her interest in them had remained much the same. She had no friends except Marian, and Marian had gone away. She was nursing now, in London, as close to Daniel as she could get; and although she still came home from time to time, it wasn't the same.

Mary Foley was as quiet and reserved now as she'd been at the beginning. To all Claudia's attempts at some kind of intimacy, she said only, 'Oh, dear,' or 'Oh, good,' immediately followed by 'I've given the cupboard under the stairs a good clean. Will you look through the rubbish before I throw it out?'

Claudia was lonely. Alister had been her friend for so long . . . He'd advised and comforted her, encouraged, approved – and sometimes disapproved – all her ideas, plans and schemes. She hadn't needed anyone else. He'd been enough.

On the surface, nothing had changed. She felt she *could* go to him, exactly as she'd done in the past, and that he'd respond in exactly the same way. But something always stopped her now. He didn't really care. He treated everyone the same. Cath and James; Mary Foley and her kids; dogs, cats . . . Yes, she'd often seen him crouching in the yard to stroke a cat, to smile and talk as if, barring only a verbal response, the cat was human.

'Had a busy day, have you, puss? Never mind, you lie in the sun while you can. Take a rest. That's the way . . .'

He spoke to Claudia just like that. Stroked her, just like that. And what did it mean? That she meant no more to him than the cat? Or that he had enough love to embrace the whole world: cats, dogs – and tarts – included?

It was odd how deep that shaft had gone. He hadn't even said it to her face – and wouldn't have said it at all if Sophy hadn't prompted him. That had been its power, of course, the fact that it had come from nowhere, and all alone: a tiny dart, dipped in poison. Mildly scathing . . .

She'd known him for so long – and never known him.

It was loneliness which drove Claudia to walk the village with Philip, showing him off to the neighbours as she'd never dared show Sophy. But even now, with Sophy's resemblance to Marcus growing stronger by the day, people still said mawkishly, 'Aw, don't she look like your ma, Claudia? Going to be tall, too, shouldn't wonder.'

She stopped to talk to Diane Bridges, but found no more

to like about her than she'd ever done; and to her sister Carol, who lived in one of Larcombe's only row of council houses. Carol spent most of her time gossiping at her garden gate with bottle-blonde hair forever done up in pink plastic rollers. She screamed at her kids, using language which Claudia hadn't heard since the days of her friendship with Diane. After five minutes in her company, Claudia hurried home again, twitching with rage, with Sophy skipping alongside, asking, 'What does fucking mean, Mummy?'

'I don't know, darling. You'll have to ask your father.'

Sophy did. He laughed like a drain, and to Claudia's indignant protests said only, 'Ah, well. That's life, Clo. They also serve who only stand and swear.'

Claudia laughed. There seemed little else she could do with him.

Eventually, and perhaps inevitably, Claudia ended up where she'd always ended up – drinking tea in Mrs Chislett's kitchen. It was like finding the centre of the world: a place where nothing changed and everything was wholesome, wise and good. Better yet, the cat had had kittens again, which kept Sophy occupied while her mother caught up with the news.

Old Georgie Flicker was on his way out at last: 'Eighty-nine, mind, Claudia, so he've had a good innings, bless him.'

Janice Tapscott was expecting again, Mrs Nod had a kidney stone, Miss Derby was bilious: 'Must have ate something, see, but she says no, she haven't.' And Mrs Burns at the butcher's had developed ulcers with all the worry of the failing business.

'Dang supermarkets,' Mrs Chislett said angrily. 'They'll be the death of the village shops, you mark my words, and it's folks like you's to blame for it, Claudia. Just jump in the car and off to Keynsham. And where's the sense in it? What you saves in the shops you lose on your petrol, see. You don't gain in the end.'

Claudia smiled wanly. No, she didn't gain in the end.

'Yer,' Mrs Chislett said. 'You heard what's been goin' on up over?' Her head jerked towards Saxon's, and Claudia shook her head. It was no use to say she wasn't interested, she was all too interested, but Mrs Chislett was all too observant, and if she hadn't yet noticed Sophy's eyes, they were the only eyes she hadn't noticed. Claudia turned hers to the fire, intending not to look up again until the Saxon bulletin was over. But Mrs Chislett's next words had her jumping in her seat, staring with shock.

'Marcus is married.'

'*What*?'

'Ha! That's exactly what I said! Not a word of it come out till it was over, see, Claudia! Not a blimmin' word.' She bit her lip and added in a pained whisper, '*Register office*.'

'Oh.'

'That's exactly what I said, but Irene said no. That were *all* she said, too! Not that I'm blaming her. Loyalty's a good thing, Claudia. A very good thing – in moderation. But it's the same as all good things – you can have too much of it – and I've had about all I can stand of it just lately.' She laughed. 'Well, how'm I to find out what's goin' on, if nobody won't tell I?'

Claudia's smile was as bright as she could make it, but she felt as if she was dying inside. Register office . . . The girl was pregnant. Marcus had been caught at last . . .

'When?' she croaked.

'A week last Wednesday. Wednesday! For a weddin'! Did you ever hear anything like it?WWent to Paris for the honeymoon. Very nice, too, even if they was only gone five days. A *Saxon* getting wed in a register office, and no word to a living soul! It's never been heard of! Even Ellis done it in church, never mind Gloria was the size of a ruddy barrage balloon!'

'Who's the lucky girl?' Claudia enquired aloofly.

'Ah! Well, that's another thing! I've never heard of her! Comes from over Woodley way, apparently, but – ' Mrs Chislett clenched her fist and thumped it on the table. 'I could kill Vera Harris!'

'Mrs Harris?' Claudia echoed faintly. 'I thought she was dead.'

'She is! That's why I could kill her! Her daughter lives over Woodley, see, so Vera used to keep me up with all the news over there. *Lisle* the name is. Sarah Lisle. But *I* ain't never heard of no Lisles over Woodley!'

'Won't Mrs Saxon tell you?'

'Helen? No, she dang well won't. And that's why I say there's trouble, for there's not a woman alive that's prouder of her sons, and if there was the least thing to boast about, she'd be doin' it! But not a word. She've admitted he'm married, that's all. Then she dives into that car of hers – "must dash!" – you know what she's like, and off she goes. Looks like a ghost, too, she do. Ah, well. It'll all come out, one way or t'other, but if Marcus Saxon's a happy man, Claudia, I'm a blue mushroom with bells on!'

Chapter Twenty-Five

Marcus returned from his honeymoon a frightened man. Sarah returned from hers a virgin.

It had been a difficult beginning to a marriage which, Marcus knew, had been doomed from the start. That box of eggs had been an omen; and although he could be forgiven for overlooking its symbolism, he could not be forgiven for ignoring what had followed. He'd married Sarah in arrogance, pride and defiance; he'd married her, goddammit, for spite!

'You'll marry that girl over my dead body!'

'Fine. I'll marry her.'

'Well, you needn't expect to see your mother at the wedding! She won't be there, and neither will I!'

'Fine. Go to hell.'

Ben had turned purple at that point; and, remembering Tom, Marcus had let out a few inches of rope. 'Okay, so what don't you like about her?'

'I don't know! I can't explain it. It's just a feeling I've got. But I know I'm right!'

'*Right*? The way you were right about Ellis, I take it?'

'He's worth ten of you! Farmer or no farmer, he's worth ten of you! At least he knows how to listen!'

'To do as he's told, you mean? Well, I *won't* do as I'm told!'

That was why he had married her. Because he'd refused to do as he was told, like the stubborn child he had always been when it was Ben doing the telling. And he'd done it because Ellis was worth ten of him. Ellis could sit in a gutter with a begging bowl and, in Ben's eyes, still be worth ten of his brother!

Yet Marcus was in no position to dispute his father's judgement, for with his wife and his children and his pin-striped suit, Ellis had come good at last; and seemed to have managed it all without hurting a living soul. To the best of Marcus's knowledge, all Ellis had ever done to defend himself was to walk off into the blue, searching for someone who could direct his life without breaking his heart. And he'd found her. When Gloria said jump, Ellis jumped. Into a suit, into a job, into a mortgage and some sensible investments. He was happy.

And what did Marcus have for his pride and his strength of mind? Half a farm, half a house, half a daughter. Half a wife.

They had driven back from Paris in almost total silence, and, through it all, Marcus had thought of Luke, of Sibyl Blake – and of Claudia.

There's one thing you don't know about Luke, Marcus. He loved that girl.

Loved her? And raped her? Marcus hadn't believed it. Now he did. The poor bastard hadn't raped her. He'd loved her, and she, the bitch, had led him on until he couldn't help himself. She'd stirred him up to a passion so great that, when the moment came, he couldn't stop.

Nothing like that had happened with Sarah. From first to last he'd been determined that nothing like it would happen again. Sarah must not be hurt. Sarah must not be frightened. And she damn well hadn't been! She'd responded to his every advance with all the breathless passion of a seasoned oak board. Only her lips had moved.

'Don't. I don't like it. I'm tired. Leave me alone.'

'Darling, this is what people *do* on their wedding night. Our marriage won't be consummated until we make love.'

'But I don't want to!'

'Then why did you marry me?'

'I thought it would be nice! But it isn't! I don't like it!'

'Ssh, ssh, you haven't tried it yet, sweetheart . . .'

And she still hadn't. He'd soothed her, wooed her, spoiled and indulged her, he'd wined her and dined her and brought her home drunk. She'd passed out before he could get her shoes off; and that was another night gone.

It was all Hannah's fault – that warped, frigid old bitch! She hadn't been too pleased about the wedding either, and although she hadn't said much, what she'd said had been very much to the point.

'You'll be sorry!'

How right she was . . .

He depended on his parents' good manners to get him through Sarah's first night in her new home. Ben's manners were governed by a strict set of rules: he would never criticise a woman to her face; and he would never criticise a woman to her husband. He could criticise them both behind their backs, of course, but for the moment he would be on his best behaviour; and Helen, bless her, was always on hers.

They did not let him down. They welcomed Sarah kindly, although not with open arms, and Sarah told them her honeymoon had been 'lovely'. She'd never been to Paris before. She told them all about it. Beginning on the ferry. An hour later (they still hadn't arrived in Paris), she was still talking. Ben had excused himself and gone elsewhere, but Helen was beginning to look dazed, and her enthusiastic little exclamations, 'Oh, I adore sea crossings!' had wound down to a dull recitation of 'Good Lord. Oh, really? Good Lord . . .'

Marcus knew how she felt. Sarah was the sort who recounted dialogue as if she were under oath, not daring to leave anything out.

'And then Marcus said, "We'll be there in time for dinner," and I said, "Oh, good! I'm starving!" And I *was*, because I hadn't had anything since breakfast, and then it was only toast and marmalade.'

Marcus swallowed a yawn. He also swallowed a spiteful urge to enquire how many slices of toast, and what kind of marmalade. Thick-cut or thin? Orange or lemon? Instead, he summoned a lover-like smile to his face and suggested an early night. 'We still have to unpack, darling.'

He had only one more shot in his locker, and he used it as soon as the bedroom door had closed behind them.

'You needn't unpack, Sarah. Since you don't like being married, I'll apply for an annulment. You can go home to Hannah tomorrow.'

Sarah tilted her chin and looked sideways at the bed. 'It's just that I don't like being in strange places,' she said. 'Strange beds, you know. I can't relax. And I've only known you a few months. I scarcely know your parents at all.'

'You didn't marry my parents. You married me.'

'But you see what I mean, don't you?'

Yes, he saw what she meant. He'd met her in April, married her in September. He'd seen her at most for ten hours a week, which added up and divided by twenty-four meant . . . They'd known each other a fortnight.

He looked at her then and saw a stranger. He had married a stranger. He didn't know her at all.

He wished he was dead.

*

Ben's herd of Ayrshires was a thing of the past, as were many of his farming methods. There was no more winter grazing. The cows overwintered now in covered yards, and came in to be milked of their own accord on icy winter mornings when sunrise – if the sun rose at all – was still three hours distant.

In spite of the cold and darkness, Marcus enjoyed the first hour's work of the day. Noddy wouldn't arrive until half-past five, and until then it was just Marcus and the cows: a peaceful beginning; a time to think of today and plan tomorrow. Or to ponder yesterday, if he could bear it. He usually couldn't.

Through the still, icy air, he heard Murray's lorry coughing itself awake and felt a part of him reaching out to Alister, the only other man in the village to be out at this time of day. It was a strange feeling: a kind of brotherhood. He often wondered about Alister, asked himself what kind of man he was. A weakling? A fool? Or a wiser, stronger man than Marcus would ever be?

Alister knew about Marcus, yet he was still living with Claudia. Marcus couldn't imagine what kind of marriage they had now. They had looked so happy . . . That was why he'd asked Sarah to marry him, of course. There had been no point in waiting any longer to claim the woman he'd loved and the child he had fathered. He'd walked by, casting them off; and then, as if refusing to be cast off, Sophy had cried, 'Daddy!'

But she hadn't been calling Marcus . . . And now a part of Alister was dead that he'd thought would live for ever: his soul's immortality in Sophy.

How did a man forgive a woman that? How did he live with it? How did it feel? They said it was better to have loved and lost than never to have loved at all, but Marcus had his doubts about that. He had loved once; and since then his life had been a desert. Surely it was better never to have loved?

There was no love now, just sex, for once Sarah had decided to cooperate there'd been no stopping her. But she did it like a whore; exhibiting little desire, no pleasure. She hated kissing; and the preliminary caresses which were so important to Marcus merely irritated her. She just lay there – thinking of England – and, as soon as it was over, turned her back on him and went to sleep. Once, when Marcus had emerged from his near-solitary pleasures, he'd found her calmly unpicking the embroidery from the bedspread.

He'd been furious. Not content with reducing the act of love to something shoddy and incomplete, she'd been doing the same thing with one of the most beautiful things in the house. His grandmother had taken ten years to embroider that quilt and Sarah had destroyed a good six months of it in as many minutes.

When he'd told her what she'd done, she'd been totally bewildered. She hadn't seemed able to comprehend what all the fuss was about. And her ignorance had chilled Marcus to the bone. It was one thing to destroy something beautiful for no reason at all, but to destroy it without even knowing it was beautiful?

He'd caught her destroying other things, too. Mindlessly picking at the arms of the chairs or absently scratching the surface of a table with her fingernails. Once, while she was watching a Hitchcock film on the television, she'd unpicked the sleeve of her sweater right back to the elbow. Marcus had been in his study, writing to Doug Hammond, and when he'd come downstairs to get some coffee, he'd found the whole family watching in awed silence while Sarah gradually unravelled herself.

He'd read all their faces. He knew what they thought. They thought she was mad. Was she?

The church clock struck five. Marcus turned out the cows he had milked. He filled the mangers and let in the next lot, noticing with astonishment that they arrived with human company.

Irene was a treat at any hour of the day but in winceyette pyjamas, duffle coat, curlers and wellies, she was a wonder to behold.

Marcus grinned. 'Hey, where'd you get that outfit? Mary Quant?'

'Oh, gerroff.' She smiled and rubbed sleep from her eyes with fiercely probing knuckles. 'Cor, it's freezing out here!'

'So why are you out here?'

'I wanna talk. And it's private, so . . .'

'Oh?' His eyes widened with astonishment. 'Fire away, then. Your father'll be here soon.'

Irene looked at her feet. 'It's a bit difficult. You won't like it. Promise not to get mad?'

'Mad? Who, me?'

'Promise.'

'No.' He grinned again.

'Ooh, you're a sod, you are.' She sighed and dealt the wall a gentle kick with the toe of her boot. 'Oh, well,' she said. 'It's not a promise you could keep, anyway. I'm thinking of leaving, see.'

Marcus stared at her. Leaving? She couldn't! Well, she could if that was what she wanted, but why should she want it? Where would she go? And how could they manage without her? She and little Tony had fitted so neatly into the family, sometimes it was hard to recall that they *weren't* family. She was like a sister to Marcus, a daughter to Helen. And 'our Tone' had become exactly that: not just Irene's but *ours*.

'Why?' he asked bleakly.

Irene gave him a calculating stare, narrow-eyed and defiant. 'You want the truth?'

'Of course.'

'Well . . . You said when I first come – *came* – here that it wasn't like a job. You said it was share and share alike and everyone doing their bit. I could help your mother with the house and the cooking and you lot'd help me look after our Tone. Right?'

'Right. Hasn't it worked like that? I thought – '

'Of course it's worked! You know it has! Everything was lovely until Sarah come – *came* here! You don't know because you're hardly ever in, but she don't – *doesn't* . . . The thing is, Marcus, she's making everyone miserable, and no one won't – no one *will* – '

Marcus had been correcting her grammar for years. It was just a tease on his part; he enjoyed making her blush. Now he wished he hadn't.

'It doesn't matter how you tell it,' he said gently. 'Just tell it. I promise I won't be angry.'

'Okay, then. She don't lift a bloody finger! She stops in bed as late as she can without missing breakfast, leaves your room in a mess, don't even make the bloody bed! She tells *me* to clear up after her, like I was the bloody maid! And she hates our Tone. She looks at him like he was dirt! He fell off the step in the dining room yesterday, lying there screaming his head off, he was, poor little dab. And she stepped right over him and left him there! Your mother's breaking her heart over it, your dad's going up the wall, and nobody won't bloody well *tell* you!' She stopped, gulped. 'So *I* am,' she added weakly.

Marcus had gone on working while she talked, and he still carried on, his movements quick, efficient, virtually automatic after long years of practice. But he didn't reply. None of what she'd said had come as a surprise, although he hadn't guessed it was as bad as she'd said. But it wasn't Sarah's laziness which angered him most. It was her treatment of Irene and Tony. Why had he never noticed?

Because he hadn't wanted to . . .

'Oh, Marcus!' Irene wailed as his silence lengthened. 'I'm sorry, really I am! I wouldn't have told you – I wouldn't have done nothing to hurt you after you been so good to me and our Tone! It's just . . . Well, yesterday I nearly thumped her one! I don't know how I stopped myself to tell the truth, and – that's why I think I better go. She's your wife, and I got no right to criticise, let alone anything else. Our Mum'll have us back, I expect, and our Carol'll look after our Tone – '

'*Carol*?' In spite of himself, Marcus burst out laughing. 'You're joking!'

'No, I ain't. Our Car's all right. I know her language comes a bit strong when you ain't used to it, but she's ever so kind-hearted underneath. And I'll have to get a job, see, Marcus. I can't manage without, can I?'

'No. And we can't manage without you. This is your home, and Tony's home. The arrangement was that you'd get a job when he starts school, and that, as far as I'm concerned, is the way it's going to be. Never mind about Sarah. I'll speak to her.'

'No! Oh, no, I never meant – !'

Marcus smiled. 'It's all arranged. Now, push off and get warm. I like the outfit, darling, but blue lips don't suit you.'

When Liz and Tom had first married they'd split the house into two. They'd had a sitting room and dining room just to the right of the main hall, and a tiny kitchen, with two bedrooms and a bathroom overhead. They'd even had their own staircase. And, save for the kitchen fitments, no alterations had been necessary. The staircase was already there. Everything was there. The only thing they'd lacked had been their own front door.

The split hadn't lasted long. Helen had been lonely. Liz

had been lonely. It was easier to share. So the little kitchen had been abandoned, and now was used as a store for homemade jam and elderberry wine. It would be simple enough to clear it out.

Marcus presented the idea to Sarah as if nothing more exciting had ever happened to them. Their own little house! Privacy! Independence! 'We'll need a new stove and a fridge, or course. I thought we could go and choose them tomorrow. How does that sound?'

'I can't,' Sarah said. 'I'm going out with Annan.'

'Friday, then.'

'I can't. I'm going to the dentist. Anyway, I can't cook.'

'You'll learn,' Marcus said.

Marcus bought the stove, the fridge and half a dozen cookbooks. Sarah ignored them all. She lived on a diet of milk chocolate, bananas and cheese, leaving the wrappers, the skins and the rinds wherever they happened to fall.

Marcus kept his patience exactly as he might have kept his balance on a tightrope over a pond full of sharks: aware that someone would die if he didn't. He talked, he taught, he coaxed, he offered bribes; and Sarah went along with it all – while he was standing over her. But lambing had begun, the most punishing two months of the farming calendar, and Marcus couldn't spare the time, he hadn't the energy – and his patience was not inexhaustible.

He decided that he could cope with the discomfort for as long as it lasted, but surely Sarah would – *must* – get tired of it and learn how to cope?

She didn't. She came home to sleep. The rest of the time she spent with Hannah; and although Marcus thought of confiscating the Mini he'd bought her, he decided it could do no good. Hannah had a car of her own, and if Sarah couldn't get to Woodley, Hannah would come to Larcombe. Letting Sarah keep the Mini was by far the lesser of two evils.

And it was amazing what a man could do in odd half-hours snatched from the day. Cleaning, cooking, washing and ironing. He often asked himself where he'd gone wrong. And the answer was always: Claudia.

Marcus had never known his parents to quarrel. When they had a difference of opinion they discussed it quietly until it was settled. Sometimes it took one discussion, sometimes ten; but the outcome was almost always the same: Ben won.

This was the expectation Marcus had of his own marriage: that without shouting, swearing or making threats, the differences he had with his wife would be resolved, and he would win.

But Sarah and Helen, although similar in some respects, were very different. Helen, although her tone was always pleasant, always calm, could at least put up an argument before, inevitably, she sighed and admitted defeat. Sarah didn't do it that way. She agreed with everything Marcus said – and then carried on exactly as she pleased. They had the same 'discussions' all through April, all through May, all through June; yet in spite of the frantic work of making silage and hay, Marcus still came home to cook his own meals, make his own bed, iron his own shirts.

It had been a difficult year for haymaking: the weather had been humid and unsettled, and many farmers had watched the mown grass turning black where it lay. But Marcus had been lucky with his timing, and by the first of July the work was over, the bales stacked; and his only worry now was that they'd all go mouldy before he could use them.

He was lying on the sitting-room floor, easing his backache, when Sarah wandered in, peacefully smiling, with her arms full of shopping.

'Look,' she said sweetly. 'I've bought a new dress.'

It was a rag of pink cheesecloth with gilt embroidery

around the hem. She held it against herself and it made her skin yellow, her hair green.

'You have appalling taste,' Marcus said wearily.

'Yes, I know. That's what Annan always says.'

'You waste my money. You're lazy, you're selfish – '

'I know,' Sarah said smugly. 'I'm hopeless. I always was. But Annan told you that before you married me. She said you'd be sorry, didn't she?'

Marcus was astonished. For a moment he was rendered speechless, helpless, incapable of doing anything except stare at her. He stood up, wincing with pain.

'Your honesty does you credit,' he snapped. 'But it doesn't get us anywhere, Sarah! It doesn't change anything. And something has to change. We can't go on like this. *I* can't go on like this. You're making me angry.'

'Yes, Annan said you would be.'

Marcus's eyes blazed. 'Will you shut up about bloody Annan? This is *our* marriage we're talking about! *Our* lives! *Our* future! Do you want a divorce? Is that what you want?'

'No.'

'Well, if you want to stay married, you're going to have to try a little harder. Marriage is a partnership, Sarah. Give and take! You're giving me nothing and taking everything!'

'I know.' She performed a modest little shrug. 'But what can I do? It's how I am.'

Marcus swallowed a scream. 'Shall I tell you how *I* am, Sarah? I'm a man with an uncontrollable temper, and I haven't lost my temper for years!' He sighed, and a wry little voice at the back of his mind whispered, 'Pride ever goeth before a fall, buster.'

True. He was very close to losing his temper; and, having bottled it up for so long, God only knew what would happen when it broke loose at last.

He retreated to his armchair by the hearth. 'What I mean – ' he said steadily ' – is that it doesn't really matter "how you are". You can change yourself. If you really try, you can change.'

'Like giving up smoking, you mean?'

'Yes. If you like.'

'But you have to want to give it up, don't you?'

Again Marcus was struck speechless. He stared at her with his mouth open, his heart thudding with confusion. Was this rational? Was this sane? Suddenly he was frightened.

'Don't you want to change?' he asked faintly.

'No. Why should I? I'm happy as I am.'

'*You're* happy? What about *me*? I'm working myself to death, and you're *happy*? Is that right? Is it fair? Is that what you call a marriage?'

Sarah began to look puzzled and for a moment Marcus knew hope, of a sort. Was she beginning to think at last?

'But there's no need to work yourself to death,' she said pleasantly. 'If we'd stayed in the big house, your mother and Irene would have looked after us. I liked it better in the big house. I get so lonely here. And you're no company.'

Marcus gave up. He closed his eyes. It didn't matter. It didn't matter. There was no point in trying any more. He'd never loved her, and he'd despised her – more or less – since their wedding night. So what was he fighting for?

And the wry little voice in the back of his mind said, 'Your children. What about your children?'

He opened his eyes again. He had no grounds for divorce, and the way Sarah felt about sex, she'd never give him any. But did he want to have children with Sarah? *He wanted children*! But with Sarah? She couldn't look after a cat, let alone a child. Let alone three!

'I think we should have a divorce,' he said gently. 'I'll give you grounds, I'll pay for your solicitor, I'll – '

'I don't want a divorce.'

They were back where they'd started.

'So what the hell *do* you want?'

She smiled; and Marcus realised with shame that he'd never thought to ask that question before.

'Well?' he prompted.

And then Sarah really surprised him. 'I want Annan to come to live with us,' she said.

They used the stone barn now for garaging the farm's vehicles: four tractors, a Land-Rover, a Ford pick-up truck. Marcus was lying under the Ford when he saw his father's feet appear alongside, leaving a trail of wet footprints on the packed dirt floor.

'You under there, Marcus?'

'No. Try the woods.'

'Ah. Right. Perhaps I will.' His feet moved a few paces, towards an upturned oil drum. He sat down. 'Everything all right?'

'The silencer's rusted. Time we had a new one, I think.'

'Silencer?'

'Ford.'

'Ah . . . But you can fix it for the moment, can you?'

'Mm-hm.'

There was a long silence before Ben spoke again. 'How's the back?'

'Better, thanks.' Marcus sighed and stared up thoughtfully into the underbelly of the Ford. They went months without saying anything that was not essential to the efficient running of the farm, and then . . .

'Did you want to talk about something, Dad?'

Ben coughed. 'No. Not really. Just wanted to see you were all right. You've looked a bit peaky the past few days. Not your back, though?'

'No.' Again Marcus sighed. 'Anyone about?'

'No. Nobody. Why?'

'Sarah wants to bring her aunt to live here.'

There was another long silence. 'Have you agreed?'

'Not yet.'

Not ever, he added silently. He hadn't told Sarah he'd rather die. He'd said he'd think about it. And that, if Ben asked, was the answer he'd get, too.

'Marcus?'

'Hmm?'

'Come out of there, will you? I . . . We've got to talk. There's something I should have told you . . . I should have told you a long time ago, and I didn't. I thought . . .'

Ben's feet drew together. He stood up to pace the length of the Ford. There and back. There and back. 'I've buggered up your life,' he muttered passionately. 'I know that, Marcus. Oh, dear God! My own son, and I couldn't even . . .'

Marcus slid out from under the Ford and stared at his father in amazement. The man was almost in tears! He *was* in tears!

'Dad?' he demanded faintly. 'What the hell are you talking about?'

'Pride!' Ben glared ferociously into Marcus's face, his blue eyes bloodshot and glittering. He'd thrust both hands into his pockets. Now he snatched the right hand clear and wagged his finger as if to give his son the telling off of his life.

'Believe me,' he cried hoarsely, 'or don't! As you like!' He stopped speaking and turned away, hiding his hands again. 'I love you,' he went on shakily. 'But we both have too much pride, Marcus. It's always got in the way. Now . . . Now it's ruined you. And it's all *my* bloody stupid fault! *My* bloody stupid pride!'

Marcus was still on the ground, leaning on his elbow. Now he sat up and looked at the back of Ben's head through a mist of tears. He was almost thirty years old.

And his father had said . . . His father had said he loved him. Only words. But after thirty years, surely they meant something?

'No,' he said softly. '*My* bloody stupid fault. *My* bloody stupid pride.'

'No! You don't understand, Marcus! I tried to stop you, but I didn't tell you why! For pride's sake. And your mother's.'

'Mother?'

'This is difficult,' Ben muttered. 'I once had an affair with Hannah Lisle, Marcus. Years ago. Ellis was four. You were two. It didn't last long. She got pregnant and I . . . sent her some money. She was living down Frome way then, and didn't know much about me – I'd told her the usual lies. But she found out where I was. She wrote to me . . . Filthy letters. They terrified me, Marcus. I loved your mother, you see.'

Marcus did not ask the obvious question. Love and sex were different things, and they often slept in different beds.

'Hannah had an abortion,' Ben went on brokenly. 'This was during the war, of course. It couldn't have been pleasant. It seemed to have turned her mind. She wrote such terrible things . . .'

'Blackmail?' Marcus had turned white with shock.

'No, it was more like black magic. Filthy, wicked. She cursed me, Marcus. I deserved it. You . . . don't.'

Marcus wrapped his arms around his stomach to quell a rising swell of nausea. Cursed? Of all the stupid – ! Oh, but Hannah's bitterness . . .

You'll be sorry!

Had it all been some kind of set-up, some kind of revenge?

A knife-thrust of memory twisted in Marcus's mind. He'd thought the same thing about Claudia; and had gone on thinking it in a vague, almost subliminal way. Revenge?

No. One way and another he had brought all his griefs upon himself. There was no one else to blame.

He exhaled, experiencing a strange feeling of satisfaction. He'd thought he'd grown up many times before this, each time as a result of disappointment: hopes crushed, dreams despoiled, confidence shattered. But this was different. This 'growing up' was a gift which somehow marked out all the others as gifts, too. He hadn't accepted the others, until now. He'd rejected them – much as he'd rejected Sarah's tinselled rags – as the evidence of someone *else's* rotten judgement. Yet even that life-long cry of his heart, *My father doesn't love me*! had been a failure of his own perception.

'You must despise me,' Ben said bleakly.

'No . . . It's good to know I'm not the only idiot in the world. But your mistakes are yours, Dad, and mine are mine. I don't hold you responsible.'

'But Hannah?'

Marcus smiled. 'Forget it,' he said. 'Believe it or not, I love you too, Dad.'

Edward Saxon had had bronchitis in April and he'd never quite caught his breath since then.

Olivia offered him little sympathy, but she rarely left his side; and, when she did, it was only to walk outside for a breath of fresh air. Marcus saw her tottering down the garden path with her walking stick, ten paces there, ten paces back, with a deep, spine-stretching sigh to mark the turning point. At eighty-seven she looked very old, very frail now; and it was hard to imagine that she would survive widowhood for long. But her tongue was as caustic as ever.

'What are you looking so sentimental about?'

'Sentimental, Grandma? Me?'

She tilted her head to one side the better to squint up at

him. 'I suppose you think we were happy,' she said. 'I suppose you're envying us our sixty years of wedded bliss. Well, you're wrong. The first forty years were hell. We grew accustomed to it after that. Perhaps you will, too.'

'Just the first forty?' Marcus smiled. 'There's hope then?'

Olivia smiled stiffly. 'There's always hope.'

She turned, and Marcus followed her indoors. 'I'll pop in to see Grandad after I've eaten,' he promised gently. 'Give him my love.'

He turned into his own part of the house. The sitting room was littered with the debris of Sarah's existence; one shoe in the middle of the floor, another in the hearth. A dirty coffee cup on the table, biscuit crumbs on the floor, a cardigan, inside out, over the arm of a chair. Marcus tidied up as he passed through, collecting yet more of Sarah's possessions from the dining room and from the table at the foot of the stairs.

The bedroom was even worse. He made the bed and hurled Sarah's nightdress and blood-stained underwear into the laundry basket. Perhaps it was just his imagination but it seemed to him that she became untidier at certain times of the month, cruelly underlining the fact that she wasn't yet pregnant.

Fuming, he screwed caps on to the many cosmetic jars, tubes and bottles which littered the dressing table, and then swept the lot into the drawer which Sarah (very kindly) had left open to receive them. Save for another coffee cup, the ubiquitous banana skin and Sarah's bank statement – half in, half out of its envelope – the room was tidy again.

He gave most of Sarah's possessions the same respect she herself gave them – none at all – but the bank statement stumped him. He had no idea where she usually kept such things and, deciding that the drawer of her bedside chest was probably the safest place, he put it there.

He'd been working at speed. He had opened the drawer

and shut it again and was on his way out before the significance of what he'd seen struck him. A white paper bag with the corner of a flat, printed carton protruding from it. He'd seen only a part of the brand name: '-ynovlar', but it rang some kind of bell . . .

Marcus had been brought up to believe in the privacy of the individual: a necessity in a family of so many parts. Had Sarah been tidier, he would never have touched her things, never have opened that drawer. And he had no right, now that the bank statement was safely put away, to open that drawer again. He wouldn't open it. He refused to open it. He went downstairs to prepare his supper.

Five minutes later he was upstairs again, white-faced with rage, while the escaped troubles of Pandora's Box seethed about his head like swarming bees.

He didn't eat. He didn't visit his grandfather. He switched on the television and sat glaring at it, barely noticing that, due to the morning's heavy rain, Somerset was set to draw its match with Lancashire at Old Trafford. The only detail which stuck in his mind was that Virgin had been caught out for twenty-four.

Marcus knew another (erstwhile) virgin who'd been caught out. And, in her second innings, which would begin as soon as she arrived home, she'd be bowled out for a duck!

He felt violence had been done to him. When he'd opened that drawer for a second time his rage had boiled in an instant and was frozen in the next. He would crush her. He would destroy the bitch. And he wouldn't so much as lay a finger on her!

He was still lounging in front of the television when she came in. He didn't speak.

Sarah wandered through to the kitchen; and, having

found the half-prepared makings of his meal still on the table, wandered back again. 'Haven't you eaten?'

'No.'

She went back to the kitchen. He heard her filling the kettle. She came back and leaned in the doorway, her hand on her hip.

'Have you thought any more about my idea?' she demanded brightly.

'Did you have an idea, Sarah? When was that? Did they ring the church bells to commemorate the occasion?'

She laughed as if he'd paid her a compliment. 'You know. I asked if Annan could move in with us.'

'Oh? And what did I say?'

'You said you'd think about it. But that was two weeks ago, Marcus. You've had plenty of time to think.'

'Yes,' he said pleasantly. 'I have. And I've decided in your favour, darling. Since you need your precious Annan so much, you can go back to her; and stay with her; and never – if you value your life – come near me, or this house, again.'

Sarah's calm little smile didn't falter. Marcus switched off the television and stood facing her, his hands in his pockets.

'I'll give you a week to pack your things and move out. You may keep the Mini. Anything else – including legal advice – you can find for yourself. I wash my hands of you. As far as I'm concerned you don't exist.'

Still she smiled. 'Why?' she asked sweetly.

He had sometimes wondered if she was crazy. Now he knew. And with the knowledge his rage died. He took the pack of contraceptive pills from his pocket and threw it at her feet.

'Your pills,' he said wearily. 'My children.'

*

Edward Saxon died just after midnight; and the world said goodbye to him with thunder, lightning and rain which beat at the windows in a valedictory drum roll.

Marcus sat at his grandfather's bedside, stroking Olivia's hand, watching her face as if he were watching his own face in a mirror. He knew what she was thinking. Although their memories and experiences of Edward were different, their feelings for him were not. Marcus had known him only as an old man: a man growing gentle with his years; but he knew something of his history, had heard Olivia's assessment of the strong, passionate man he had once been. Forty years of hell? He didn't doubt it. Nor did he doubt the love which had made those years worthwhile.

Olivia stood up at last. She tweaked the bedspread to straighten it, patted Edward's hand. 'Well,' she said softly. 'You always said I'd learn to like you if I lived long enough.' She stroked his cheek and stooped to kiss him. 'And you were right, for once.' She turned, reaching tearfully for Marcus's arm. 'What a lovely way to go,' she whispered.

It rained all the next day. Marcus had had no sleep at all. His mind was operating at dead slow, his body at top speed, his emotions in a nightmarish overdrive with tears and rage very close to the surface. He didn't notice that Sarah failed to go out. But he did notice the steady stream of visitors who trudged up the drive in the pouring rain to 'pay their respects' and offer sympathy to the bereaved.

Marcus was deeply aware of being bereaved, but his bereavement was a confusion he could scarcely bear to confront. In one night he'd lost his wife, his grandfather and what hopes he'd still retained of having a family of his own; and he was guiltily aware that this last 'bereavement' was the worst of them. It shouldn't be. He had loved Edward very dearly and wanted to grieve for him; but there were too many other things in the way.

God only knew how long a divorce would take. He

knew very little about divorce and had an idea that mere hatred of one's spouse would not count as 'grounds'. And Sarah would never divorce him. He would throw her out, but he guessed that that was what she (and Hannah) had been aiming for: that, and the income he'd be compelled to pay her for the rest of his life.

He avoided the visitors. He couldn't listen to their condolences with any hope of keeping a grip on his self-control. But in the middle of the afternoon, when he saw Mrs Chislett arrive, his control deserted him and he went to meet her with tears in his eyes.

Mrs Chislett was eighty-two now and by no means as spry as she used to be. This was her first visit to Saxon's for many months – the drive was too long, too steep for her old bones – yet she had managed it today without aid, without even a walking stick; and in her pink plastic bonnet and her vast plastic mac, with an ancient black brolly bobbing overhead, she looked like some strange, prehistoric reptile lumbering slowly from its swamp.

'Oh heck!' She grabbed Marcus's arm and leaned heavily on it, gasping for breath. 'What a day to die, eh, Marcus? Still, it's a good sign. With the heavens open this wide, he won't have no trouble gettin' in, will he?'

Marcus chuckled in spite of himself. 'You should have phoned,' he chided gently. 'I'd have come to fetch you.'

'Would you, my love? Well, that's nice, but I wanted to come on me own. Make an effort, like. Edward were a good man, and if getting soaked through to me spencers's all I can do to show me respect, it's worth all the trouble, my love. We got the rugs up down there, though. The river'll be out of bed before tea time, I reckon.'

The rain grew heavier. Ben took Mrs Chislett home, and when he returned, soon after five, it was to report that the river was indeed 'out of bed' and the village sandbagged to hold back the flood. Miss Derby, as always, had been the first to suffer. Her beloved garden was already six inches under water.

'Looks like it'll be a bad one,' Marcus said. 'I'll finish milking. You'd better go and help Irene get the hospitality organised.'

As the highest and driest house in the locality, Saxon's had always been a retreat in times of flood. The attic was stacked with piles of blankets and camp beds, a tea-urn and a well-stocked first-aid chest, ready to be brought into use at a moment's notice.

Ben hurried away to prepare for his uninvited guests, and Marcus did not expect to see him again until milking was over. But a short time later he was back, white-faced and trembling. 'I'll take over here! Get in and see to Sarah!'

Marcus asked no questions. It had begun to thunder earlier on, and as he raced into the house the world seemed to fall about his ears in an avalanche of sound: crashings and rumblings so loud and prolonged that Sarah's music was almost drowned by the din. But the thunder ceased. The music did not. It was a Rolling Stones record, being played at full volume. The house was shaking with it. Sarah was dancing to it. And Edward lay dead in his coffin, in Olivia's little sitting room, just down the hall.

Marcus could never recall what happened next. But after it had happened, Sarah lay on the floor, one side of her face stone white, the other scarlet, with a large, purple bruise already developing on her cheekbone. Mick Jagger was silent.

'I *do* exist!' Sarah sobbed. 'I do! I do!'

Marcus sat down suddenly. He felt weak and very frightened and his teeth were chattering with reaction. He had hit her. He had hit a woman, his wife, with the full force of his arm! He could have killed her – killed her, and not known anything about it until it was over!

'Yes,' he said, and was surprised to hear how flat, how

untouched by emotion his voice sounded. 'Yes, Sarah, you do exist. But if you stay in this house any longer, that could easily change. I'm sorry I hit you. I'm very sorry. I'm sorry about everything: our marriage; everything. It was my fault, not yours. But you must go back to Hannah. For your own safety, Sarah. I don't trust myself any longer. I could have killed you just now. You must go. *Go*, please. You can come back for your things tomorrow.'

He didn't dare look at her as she stumbled from the room, and afterwards he didn't dare move in case he was sick. He had hit her. He had hit her! And he hadn't even known he was doing it. He shook his head in shame and disbelief. How much lower could anyone get? Surely this was the bottom of the hole he'd dug for himself? Surely he couldn't fall any lower?

Time passed without his noticing. He might have been there two minutes or two hours before Ben raced in from the yard. 'Marcus! For God's sake, Marcus! Sarah's gone, and she's taken the Mercedes!'

Chapter Twenty-Six

Daniel and Marian's wedding, in June, had been the biggest show of the year. Beribboned Rolls-Royces, glorious hats, a pink and white marquee on the Fairfields' lawn, and champagne enough to sink a frigate.

It had been a curious day for Claudia. She hadn't known how to feel, what to think; and, at the end of it all, when the happy couple had gone away and Sophy had at last been divested of her dark grey bridesmaid's dress (it had begun the day pale pink), Claudia had sat down and cried with confusion.

It wasn't that she wasn't glad for Daniel. It was just . . . Well, she was jealous. Daniel had done everything *right*. He'd arranged his dreams in an orderly line and worked steadily through them, one by one, collecting nothing but honour, admiration and respect on the way. He was a qualified vet, he had a job, he'd bought a house. He'd been married in church to the love of his life. And now . . . Happy ever after?

Marian had said, as she'd kissed Claudia goodbye, that if she and Daniel could be as happy as Claudia and Alister had been, they couldn't go far wrong; but that was as far wrong as she could get. Claudia and Alister were not happy.

They pretended to be happy. They made a good show of it. But it wasn't true. They lived on opposite sides of a deep, narrow chasm; near enough to keep talking across the divide, near enough even to touch had they both reached out a hand. But Alister never reached out. He kept talking, kept smiling – and kept his hands in his pockets.

Most of the time it didn't hurt. Most of the time Claudia could accept things as they were and live her separate existence in a state which almost felt like happiness. For they still shared the business; and the business was going from strength to strength, getting better all the time. They'd built a new office, bought a new lorry and, at long last, a new Land-Rover; and they were better staffed than (in Claudia's lifetime) they had ever been.

The work didn't lessen. With more time at his disposal, Alister had simply improved his standards to compete with the increasing amount of imports from abroad. Their thirty acres had never worked so hard. They'd even reclaimed the old rubbish tip at the bottom of the property, and Madge's abandoned beehives were no more.

Yes, life was very neat, very prosperous and clean. Sophy and Philip were thriving. James and Cath were content and well cared for. Even the yellow nightmare was a thing of the past. Yet Claudia was ever conscious of the chasm which yawned at her feet; the river of lies which ran there. And it was odd: before Alister had known about those lies they had seemed to Claudia a raging torrent which would one day sweep her away. Now they were calm, quiet waters. Ali had robbed them of all threat. But in doing so he'd crossed to the other side and knocked down the bridge behind him.

Daniel and Marian had gone to Greece for their honeymoon. Now, safely installed in their own little house just outside Chepstow, they were receiving visitors. It had been difficult to arrange a day for the visit which would suit them all. Marian was nursing in Newport, Daniel working six days a week (and almost as many nights) in a country veterinary practice, Claudia and Alister as tightly bound as ever to the routine at Murray's. So when the appointed day turned out to be dull, wet and miserable, it didn't seem possible to call it off. Weeks might pass before they could find another day to suit them all.

James and Cath had been invited too, but James wouldn't go and Cath wouldn't leave him, 'just in case'.

'Just in case of what?' Alister smiled. 'Mary's here.'

'Yes, but she'll have to go home to put the children to bed, and if you get held up – '

'We won't. We have children to put to bed, too.'

Cath had discovered a little trick to cope with Alister's unfailing logic. She produced a 'silly old me' smile, nodded a few times as if to admit defeat, and then said, 'Still, I think I'll be happier . . .'

'Don't you want to see Daniel's new home?'

'Yes, of course. Still, I think I'll be happier . . .'

So Cath and James stayed at home. And even in Ali's huge Volvo estate car (also new), it was easier without them. Philip couldn't go anywhere without his pushchair, his nappies, his food supplies, his toys and three changes of clothes. Sophy needed her books, her doll and her puzzles. And they all needed mackintoshes and gum boots just in case it stopped raining and a walk became possible.

They set off soon after lunch. Claudia had spent the morning in the office, and all her time since then organising the children for their outing. She hadn't seen what effect the rain had had on the river, and as they drove out through the gates was shocked to see it so high. Yesterday the bridge had had deep arches, solid stone legs reaching down into the river bed. Today, just thin crescent moons of daylight showed under the hump-backed road, and the stone supports were entirely underwater.

'That's the beans drowned again,' she said. 'If this keeps up they'll be washed right out.'

'Or they won't be,' Alister said cheerfully. 'They're usually all the better for a good soaking.'

Claudia had long ago forgotten her childhood fear of the bridge, but now, as they drove across it, she shuddered with revulsion. The stones of the parapet looked even more reptilian than usual: greened over by lichens; cold, slimy and glistening with rain.

'It'll clear up,' Alister said. 'You watch. As soon as we get to the Severn Bridge – '

'The *new* bridge, Daddy?' Sophy piped up excitedly. 'Are we going over the *new* bridge?'

'Yes, and the weather's always different on the other side,' Alister said firmly. 'When it's sunny here, it's raining there; and when it's raining here . . .'

'You were saying?' Claudia enquired cynically when they crossed the Severn an hour later.

'Perhaps we ought to go home,' Alister grinned. 'It's probably sunny there. It's *always* different on the other side of the bridge.'

The best part of another hour had passed before they found Daniel's home: a quaint, redbrick keeper's cottage which, although standing within spitting distance of the roadside, was so well shielded by trees that they'd driven past it three times before they glimpsed it through the rain.

On a fine day it would, Claudia knew, have been a beautiful spot; set high on a hillside with huge pine forests shielding it from the north. But now it looked dank, dark and unwelcoming, its garden a wilderness, with only the steady drip-drip of rain from the trees to break the silence.

'Does Uncle Daniel live here?' Sophy asked anxiously. 'It doesn't look very nice, does it, Mummy?'

'It looks lovely!' Claudia lied brightly. 'And I'm sure it's very cosy inside. Come on, let's go and see, shall we?'

Luckily for her own state of mind, the front door flew open at that moment and Marian, Daniel and a small Labrador puppy came hurtling out to welcome them. 'We'd given you up!'

'We got lost! We passed it three times!' They hugged, kissed, fussed, laughed, fell over each other. Marian cooed over Philip, Sophy cooed over the puppy, Daniel cooed over the Volvo and Alister looked towards heaven, his hands held palms up and a beatific grin on his face. 'See, I told you!' he said. 'The rain's stopped!'

It started again a short while later, but no one noticed. The little house was indeed very cosy inside, although Claudia never worked out why this should be, for it was virtually empty of furniture and in dire need of fresh paint and wallpaper. But there was a bright log fire in the hearth, a kettle boiling in the kitchen, and a wonderful old-fashioned tea of dainty sandwiches, strawberries, pastries and Dundee cake.

They talked as if they hadn't seen each other for years. The newlyweds spilled out their plans for the house, tales of their honeymoon, reports of new jobs, new friends and colleagues; while Claudia and Alister reported news of the family and passed on the latest village gossip. It was a wonderful visit: warm and relaxed; and Claudia had realised, long before it was over, that this was the first time in a year (yes, they'd had that washing machine a whole year . . .) that she hadn't been lonely.

It was over too soon but, swiftly as it had passed, they left more than an hour later than they'd intended. It was still raining. They hadn't noticed it inside the house for the surrounding trees and the deep mulch of leaf-mould which covered the ground had lessened its force, muted the sound of its fall. Claudia stood in the doorway while Alister and

Daniel packed up the car under the shelter of an enormous black brolly.

The brolly reminded Claudia of Mrs Chislett. And the river. If it had gone on raining in Larcombe all day, the river would be out of bed by now, slithering across the road into Mrs Chislett's front parlour; and poor Miss Derby would already be up to her knees in muddy water.

'I think I'd better ring home,' she said. 'Dad'll be worried if we're late.'

'No,' Marian said. 'You get on your way. I'll ring.'

The children were asleep before they made their return journey over the Severn; which was just as well, for there was something frightening about the rain now. Claudia had never seen anything like it. Neither, to judge by the grim expression on his face, had Alister. It wasn't like driving through rain; it was like driving under a vast waterfall. When Claudia leaned forward to look up into the downpour, she saw not the usual diagonal lines of rain arrowing out of the sky, but a near-solid torrent of water. The windscreen wipers were rendered useless. Work as fast and as furious as they might, the rain worked faster; and the noise, as it pounded against the roof of the car, was a continual roar.

'We've lost the beans,' Claudia said flatly.

'Nonsense. This won't be general. It's just a squall.' Alister didn't speak again until they left the motorway at Bristol East, where the exit roundabout sat in a hollow between high embankments. The road was under a foot of water. 'Oh, dear,' he murmured, and there was something in his tone which scared Claudia rigid.

After that, they covered the rest of the journey at dead slow. The torrent eased slightly, separating into rain drops which, when they hit the windscreen, made circles the size of dinnerplates; and even on the highest and 'driest' parts of their route they were ploughing through water three inches deep. In the dips and hollows, smaller cars than Alister's plunged into floods which covered their wheels; and one car, a Hillman Imp which plunged in too fast, had its engine drowned before it could climb out again.

As they left the suburbs of Bristol to join the country roads, the sky was rent by lightning, and a moment later a terrifying crash of thunder was added to the continuous roar of the rain.

Claudia was very frightened now. 'The village'll be six feet under,' she gasped. At that moment Sophy woke up, crying with fright as another deafening clap of thunder sounded overhead. Claudia turned in her seat, her eyes wide and bright with manufactured excitement. 'Isn't this fun, Sophy! Look! The fields are all under water! I wonder if we could catch some fish for Grandad's supper!'

Sophy was not impressed. 'We'd get very wet,' she said disapprovingly. 'Are we nearly home?'

'Yes. Not far now.'

'I don't like it,' Sophy said tearfully. 'I wish I had Uncle Daniel's puppy. I could look after him, couldn't I? He needn't be frightened if he was with *me*.'

'Philip's teddy looks a bit nervous, too. Perhaps you should give him a cuddle. Tell him we're nearly home.'

'You just told him,' Sophy said.

'Oh, he doesn't believe *Mummy*,' Alister said grimly. 'That's the trouble with the teddy bears of this world: they don't believe a word Mummy says! Tell him again, Sophy. Tell him we're nearly home.'

This jibe, added to the other agonies of the journey, was too much for Claudia. 'We *are* nearly home,' she snapped bitterly.

'Yes, as the crow flies. But crows don't fly in this sort of weather and we've got that almighty dip at the bottom of Kilner's Hill to get through yet. If it's flooded, I think I'll have to walk ahead to find the shallow bits – if there are any.'

The 'almighty dip' was flooded but a few cars on the other side of the road were managing to creep through and Alister waited until they'd gone before crossing the road to follow the route they had taken.

When they were safely through, Claudia's nerves were screaming with tension. They were now two hours later than they had planned. Mary Foley would have gone home and James and Cath would be alone in the house, watching the waters inexorably rising. It was no good to pretend they'd be feeling sanguine about it. The beans must surely have been ripped from the ground by now. That entire six acres alongside the road would be drowned, the topsoil washed away, and the packing shed would be a foot deep in water. Even for Ali it would count as a major disappointment but for James and Cath, with the rain still falling as hard as ever, it was nothing less than a horror story: perhaps even a total wash-out, the dread of their lives.

Claudia shuddered at the thought. A year's work, a year's profits, gone in a single day! And it wasn't just one year they'd have to worry about. It could take five years to recover from this sort of disaster for while you worked to rebuild, you lost markets, lost capital, lived on your fat – and after all the investments they'd made during the past year they hadn't much fat left to live on. If they had a total wash-out, they'd be ruined!

Now Claudia began to pray. Let it stop, let it stop, please God, let it stop. But, as with most of her prayers, this one had the opposite effect to the one she'd intended. The rain came down harder than ever.

As they climbed slowly towards the high crest of the Bristol road, a new and far worse horror seeped into Claudia's mind. It was still daylight. Until now it had been that dim, grey, cheerless light to which darkness is often preferable but now Claudia noticed that the sky was not grey at all. It was a strange shade of yellow, as thick as pea soup and yet eerily luminous, as if the sun, even in the midst of the deluge, was struggling to break through. Just as they reached the brow of the hill, the clouds were again lit by lightning, a terrible forking flash which seemed to hang in the air for an eternity. Before it had faded, the thunder came and it was as if the world had broken apart: an ear-splitting crack, a terrible rumbling; and then more lightning, more thunder. They seemed to have come to the very centre of the storm.

But it wasn't the thunder which terrified Claudia. And it wasn't the lightning. It was that dreadful yellow sky; the yellow light. She seemed to be drowning in it.

No, she told herself firmly. It isn't the dream. You're awake. And you mustn't be scared. Not with the children here. You mustn't be scared.

'Mummy!' Sophy whimpered. 'I don't like it.'

Claudia couldn't speak. If she spoke, she knew she would scream.

They rounded the brow of the hill and where Larcombe church tower should have been was nothing but thick yellow mists.

Claudia's eyes closed. And flew open again as, for the first time since she'd known him, Alister swore. '*Holy shit!*'

Larcombe was under water.

'*Down by the station, early in the morning* . . . Come on darling, sing! It'll make the thunder go away. *See the little –*'

'P-p-puffa billies,' Sophy whispered.

'*All in a row! See the little driver – ?*'

'I can't! What if Daddy gets d-drownded? Mummy!'

'Hush, darling, hush.' Alister had parked the car in the lay-by outside the church gate, where the hearse always waited when there was a funeral. Claudia had climbed into the back seat to comfort Sophy, while Alister walked downhill to see if, by a miracle, a way still existed to the far side of the bridge, home and safety. Home and safety! The Murray house had never been flooded, not even in a total wash-out, and Claudia knew that if only they could get there . . . Oh, if only they could get there, she'd never complain of anything, ever again!

Poor Sophy was terrified, and it wasn't just the thunder which had frightened her. It was Claudia's own fear: not of the floods so much as of the terrible yellow sky. It was so like her dream! Not the same, but so like it! She couldn't stop trembling. She couldn't control her voice. And Sophy could feel that fear, hear it, smell it!

'He won't drown, Sophy! How can he drown? No! Look, darling! He's coming back!'

As Ali trudged back to them through the downpour he looked like a photograph slowly developing in a vast, glass-sided tank; getting more substantial with every step. He'd been soaked through to the skin before he'd closed the car door on his way down. Now, although he couldn't have been any wetter, he seemed very much happier.

'It's not as bad as it looks on this side!' He fell into the car and slammed the door behind him, panting with exertion.

'We can get through?'

'Yes. The top of the bridge is still clear. It's deeper on the other side, but the top of Miss Derby's garden wall's just level with the water. If we go now, we can get through. Wake Philip. I'll carry Sophy.'

'Carry? You mean we're *walking*?'

Ali laughed; and then, noticing the state she was in, he knelt backwards in his seat and reached for her hand.

'We have to,' he said gently. 'The water's half-way up my thighs on this side. It would drown the engine. I'll leave the car here.'

'But if it's up to your thighs . . .'

'It'll be up to your waist, I know. But I'll help you, Clo. We'll do it in stages. Both of us to the middle of the bridge. Then you wait with Philip while I take Sophy home. I'll come back for Philip, and then I'll come back for you.'

'H-how long will it take?'

'About half an hour, I should think. Don't bother putting macs on, they're worse than useless. Just get the belt out of yours and tie Philip around your waist. That'll leave your hands free to hang on to me.'

As she had known he would, Philip began to cry as soon as he was wakened; and he refused to cooperate when, with trembling hands, she attempted to tie him to her. Even with Ali's help, it was ten minutes before they set off, and the minute Philip found himself exposed to the rain, he screamed blue murder and bucked in her arms like a frightened calf.

From the church gate, with the rain reducing visibility to a few yards, her view of the village had been no more than an impression: an endless sheet of muddy yellow water, with only the roof of Miss Derby's cottage rising out of the gloom. But when they reached the bus-stop at the foot of the hill and the damage became more evident, Claudia almost fainted with shock.

She had prepared herself to see the village turned into a lake. What she hadn't expected was that the village had been turned into a river. The water was forcing itself through the narrow gap between two hills – on one side the hill behind Mrs Chislett's cottage; on the other the hill behind the high street; and then raging down the valley in an almighty torrent. Most of the low-lying cottages were already drowned to a depth of four or five feet. Miss

Derby's ground-floor windows had smashed and the river was surging in one side, out the other. The road, on both sides of the river, had disappeared entirely.

'Ali! I can't walk through this! It'll knock me off my feet!'

'No, it won't. I've already been through. It's not as strong as it looks. Hold on to me. Get your hands through my belt and don't let go.' He turned and smiled. 'Not even to repair your lipstick.'

He'd had to yell to make himself heard over the din of the rain, the river, Sophy's sobs, Philip's screams and the almost continuous rumble of thunder. Claudia was amazed that he could crack jokes at such a time. Amazed and grateful for if he could crack jokes, they *could* get home. If he could crack jokes they were safe. It wasn't as bad as it looked . . .

But, oh God, it looked awful! And it felt worse, for as soon as Claudia stepped into the flood, the force of it rocked her sideways, and pebbles, gravel and twigs, stirred up by the rushing water, clawed at her ankles like cold, grasping hands.

'Ali!'

'It's okay! Stand still for a minute! Get used to it! Then walk against the current! One step at a time!'

It seemed to take forever; and at the deepest part, just as they reached the bridge, Claudia was lifted off her feet for a moment. But Ali seemed to have anticipated this and lunged forward suddenly, dragging her to safety between the parapets.

Only a six-foot stretch, the highest part of the roadway, was not underwater; but having reached it at last, Ali turned to gather Claudia and Philip in a hard, reassuring hug. 'Brave girl!' he yelled. 'See? I told you you could do it!'

He pushed her into the spurious shelter of the passing

place and set Sophy down for a moment, crouching to cuddle and reassure her, giving instructions for the next part of their walk. Poor little Sophy. She had stopped crying but was in an agony of fear, her face white, her teeth chattering, her dark hair plastered against her skull like waterweed. Claudia was certain she couldn't understand what Ali was telling her. Like her mother, she was simply trusting him to get her through, to take her home, to make her safe again.

But should they be trusting him? He was human; he could make mistakes . . .

'Ali!' Claudia cried suddenly. 'Let's go back! Please! I'd rather spend the night in the car than . . .'

But Ali either didn't hear or wouldn't listen. He lifted Sophy on to his back: 'Hang on tight, Sophy!' and turned again to Claudia. 'You too. I'll be back before you know it! Don't follow me, whatever you do. Just wait.'

He took one step away from her and then turned again. He spoke, but Claudia heard nothing above the roar of the flood.

She bowed her head, sobbing just once before noticing that her legs were torn to ribbons by the detritus of the flood. Oh, God, she'd had enough! She knew she couldn't take any more without going crazy! If only the rain would stop! If only the noise would cease! She couldn't catch her breath! She was suffocating!

When she looked up again, Ali was just climbing to the top of Miss Derby's garden wall. The wall was still above water, he'd said, but that had been ages ago and now it was several inches below! Even if he managed to get Sophy to safety, he surely couldn't come back for Philip!

Then, as if called to the scene by heavenly intervention, the headlights of a vehicle shone through the trees at the foot of Saxon's drive. A moment later Claudia saw the nose of a Land-Rover creeping down to the edge of the flood and Marcus jumped out with a coil of rope over his arm.

'Oh, thank God!' Claudia whispered. The water had reached the very edge of the woods, but there seemed to be little current there to impede Marcus's progress. He yelled something to Alister and then, clambering along the bank until he came level with Miss Derby's wall, he tied one end of the rope around a stout tree trunk.

But now Claudia became conscious of another sound: a terrible sound, an intense, deafening roar which turned her heart to ice. She whirled around, her eyes wide and staring with horror.

But all she saw was a vast wall of yellow water, bulging and swelling between the hillsides, carrying everything before it as it thundered towards her. And in the instant before she ducked, shielding Philip's body with her own, the bridge reared up under her feet – as she'd always known it would – and swallowed her alive.

Chapter Twenty-Seven

The telephone line hissed and crackled. Thunder roared overhead. But the duty policeman who had answered Marcus's call seemed to be falling asleep on his nose. 'Ah,' he said. 'Oh, dear,' he said. 'Not insured to drive it, is she? Ah, well, that *is* nasty, sir. The whole of that valley's under water so far as we know, and there's nothing much we can do at the moment. Our radio links were cut more than – '

At that moment the line went dead and Marcus hurled the telephone down, hissing a curse.

'Ring Hannah!' Ben urged frantically. 'You haven't seen the state of that road, Marcus! She'll kill herself!'

'The bloody line's gone dead!'

'Try again, for God's sake!'

Marcus dialled again, and, to his surprise, Hannah's number rang. Marcus didn't trouble to introduce himself. 'Sarah's taken the Mercedes,' he snapped angrily. 'Has she arrived? The road's flooded. She could kill herself!'

'When did she leave?' Hannah's voice was as soft as milk, but even Marcus could hear the chill note of dread in it.

'About fifteen minutes ago.'

'Then she should be here. I'll go – ' There was a clatter as Hannah dropped the receiver back in its cradle.

Marcus hid his face in his hands. 'She hasn't arrived, Dad. I'll have to go down. Perhaps the Land-Rover'll get through.'

'From what Miss Derby says, a bulldozer wouldn't get through! She only just made it out of her cottage!'

'I'll try,' Marcus said wearily. 'My God. What a day . . .'

He had climbed out of his waterproofs an hour before and now didn't bother to put them on again. If he found Sarah in difficulties he'd need his wits about him, need his freedom, and it was amazing how the stiff folds of a waterproof suit could hamper a man's progress.

But he had doubts about the wisdom of his decision when, within seconds of his stepping outside, the rain had penetrated every stitch he had on. He'd never seen anything like it. 'Bucketing down' had never before seemed so appropriate a phrase. Even to feel it lashing his face gave him a sensation of drowning; and that sensation wasn't noticeably lessened as he crept off down the drive in the Land-Rover. The windscreen wipers were helpless against such an onslaught; it was like having wipers on a submarine, trying to sweep the sea away.

He had never expected to be frightened by anything the weather could do but this was truly frightening. There was barely a moment between one flash of lightning and the next, and the thunder never ceased. But the strangest thing was the quality of the light, the colour of the sky: a queer, luminous yellow which transformed everything to the faded sepia tints of an old photograph.

Grandma and Grandad standing beside a laden haycart with pitchforks at the ready. Luke and Sibyl Blake, with poor Jim Murray, laughing by the river bank . . .

The old family tales of triumph and tragedy had often seemed to Marcus to be figments of someone's imagination: the truth stretched and embroidered, like one of Olivia's tapestry hassocks, to make an hour by the fireside more interesting and pleasant.

'And then poor Jim Murray took a scythe off the wall and chopped our Luke's arm off.'

'He *didn't*, Grandad!'

It no longer seemed so incredible to Marcus. A few hours of love, a moment of black rage . . . Isolated from all the years of a man's life, such hours and moments seemed of little significance; yet they could not be isolated, they were each a part of the whole. A few hours of love, a moment of rage, and suddenly the whole world was tumbling; not just for the perpetrator, but for everyone his deeds had touched. Marcus had loved Claudia; and from that moment on the repercussions had never ceased. Today, Marcus had struck his wife (dear God, he could have killed her!); and he'd struck her because, five years ago, he had loved Claudia.

You raped me!

Why had Claudia said it? Marcus might never know, but he'd always suspected that it was because, fifty years ago, Luke had loved Sibyl Blake. They were like dominoes standing in a line. Knock one down in the second decade of the century and they were still falling in the sixth. And how could you stop it? By taking a few dominoes out? By taking Marcus's children out of the line?

The thought wrenched at his heart but as he reached the foot of the drive and stared, horrified, at the scene of devastation which met him there, even this thought was driven from his mind.

He'd seen the village flooded before, but never like this! The road was two feet underwater! Sarah would never get through! She might be drowned! And Ben was probably right: even the Land-Rover might not get through. But he had to try. Hitting Sarah had been more than his conscience could stand. Leaving her to drown? Never!

He eased the vehicle forward and then stopped again as

another horror came into view. Alister? What the hell was he doing? He'd never get across that wall in one piece!

Marcus had jumped out of the Rover and made a grab for a coil of rope before he'd even noticed that Alister was carrying Sophy. When he did, his heart leaped with terror, and then stilled. This was his child. This was his future. The only shred of the future he still possessed.

'Stay there!' he yelled. 'Sit down! Don't move! I'm coming to get you!'

It was amazing that Alister heard him over the deafening roar of the flood, but he did. And he obeyed, lowering himself down to straddle the wall with Sophy clinging to his back like a limpet. Marcus clambered along the edge of the woods until he came level with Alister, selected a strong young beech tree and tied one end of the rope around it.

He was still knotting the other end around his waist when a new and infinitely more terrifying sound filled his ears. Filled his ears, possessed his mind, seemed almost to run in his veins and become a part of him. It took no more than a second, yet in that second his expectation changed from saving Sophy's life to losing his own. Whatever that noise was, no one could survive it. His eyes staring with terror, he looked up. He saw Claudia and her baby in the centre of the bridge, and behind them a vast wall of water, rearing up, crashing down . . .

He screamed. His legs were knocked from under him and he was carried away, carried under, with no breath left in his lungs to sustain him. He knew he was dying; and yet even with that knowledge in his mind, and the flood squeezing his lungs to bursting, he thought of Sophy, and held out his arms to catch her. Something hard crashed against his legs, something with spikes and talons clawed at his face, something strong caught at his waist and snatched him backwards, hauling him clear of the torrent. He'd forgotten the rope!

There was a moment of light, a choking gasp of air before he went under again, his arms flailing with panic; and into his arms there came something soft, something yielding. Sophy! He pushed her up with all his might, and at the same moment felt solid ground under his feet. He caught at the rope, took a single, desperate step forward and breathed at last.

'Marcus! Here! Marcus!'

He couldn't see. He floundered on, his lungs roaring for air; knowing only that he had Sophy in his arms and must save her.

Strong hands grasped him. They snatched his burden from him and hauled him, still roaring, into the shelter of the woods.

He opened his eyes and let out a howl of anguish. Claudia and her baby lay dead at his side. But Sophy wasn't there.

He seemed to sit in his darkness for hours before Titch Flicker shook his arm. 'You all right, Marcus? Anything broken? Move around a bit, will you? See if you'm all there.' He stroked his hand over Marcus's face. 'You'm bleedin' like a pig. Can't see where it's comin' from, though.'

Marcus touched his head and winced. 'Just a cut,' he murmured. His legs moved. His spine was still in the right place. 'I'm all right, Titch. Leave me.'

'I can't. We got to get Claudia and the babby up to Doc Fairfield's. They'm alive, Marcus, but I don't know for how long if they don't get help pretty damn quick.'

'They're *alive*?' Marcus was on his feet, howling with pain as one of his many unnoticed injuries made itself felt.

Titch was right. They were both alive, if only just, and the child, by a miracle, seemed to have been unmarked by his ordeal. Claudia, on the other hand . . .

'Quick,' he said. 'Get that tarpaulin from the back of the Land-Rover! No! No, we daren't move her. Stay here, Titch. Hold the baby face down, rub his back, keep him warm. I'll go and get Dennis Fairfield.' He burst into tears. 'Please God, oh, please God, let him be there!'

Marcus was still crying when he arrived back at Saxon's an hour later. He stood in the hard grip of his father's arms and sobbed like a child. He fell to his knees, beat the ground with his fists and wept until he was exhausted.

His mother washed his face. His father stripped off his sodden clothes and eased his bruised arms into the warm folds of a dressing gown. Marcus began to weep again. 'I had a daughter,' he whispered. 'She was so beautiful, Dad, and she's dead!'

Ben seemed unsurprised, but Marcus was beyond caring what effect his words might have on anyone.

'We don't know that yet, Marcus,' Ben said gently. 'We don't know anything yet.'

'You didn't see it, Dad! No one could survive that! If I hadn't tied that rope . . .'

'But you did. And because you did you pulled Claudia and the baby out. They're alive, Marcus! And Titch was there to help you. Someone might help the others as well. You mustn't give up hope. Not yet. And there are others needing help. Mrs Foley says James and old Mrs Murray are still down there. We've got to get them out, Marcus. For Claudia's sake, hmm? Think of Claudia. If you're right, if Alister and the child . . . We've got to get James out of there.'

'Yes.'

'And Mrs Chislett, if she's still alive.'

'Dear God. Isn't she here?'

'No. I thought she must have gone up to Fairfields', but Titch says there's no one there except the Burns family and – er . . .'

He seemed to have deemed it more tactful not to mention Claudia again but Marcus couldn't get her out of his mind. Poor little thing – she'd looked like a slab of raw meat, beaten and bruised, gashed, grazed and swollen almost beyond recognition. Yet Den Fairfield could find only one broken bone in her body: her right arm. She might still die of shock or pneumonia, and Philip too might die if they couldn't get him to hospital in time, but if they lived . . . If Alister and Sophy were dead . . . If Claudia had to face that . . .

'Give me five minutes,' he said. 'We'll get down there as soon as I've dressed.'

'And eaten!' Irene snapped angrily. 'You ain't going out there again without something hot in your belly!'

She was already brandishing the soup ladle, and, to his amazement, Marcus found himself searching his jumbled thoughts for a joke to comfort her. But he didn't find one. He found Sarah instead. How strange! He'd been going down the drive to look for her . . . And, since then, she hadn't even crossed his mind.

'Did Hannah ring back?' he murmured faintly. 'Dad?'

'No. But the lines are out. She still might have got through, Marcus.' Ben reached out to grasp his son's arm. 'Don't think about it. Think of what you *can* do, not – '

'Yes,' Marcus said.

It was still raining and very dark by the time Titch and Ben, using the tractors, had cleared a path through to the Murray house. But the headlights and an odd flash of lightning had shown them what they could expect when they finally reached the house. The gates had been ripped from their posts, the packing shed was a ruin. But at least the flood had receded enough to allow the Land-Rover through.

'You and Titch had better go in,' Ben said quietly. 'If they're still alive, the sight of me will finish them off.'

'Is the sight of me likely to be any better?' Marcus asked wanly.

'Don't worry about that, Marcus. Even I don't recognise you at the moment.'

Marcus had felt his left eye closing some time before. Now he raised a hand to his cheek, and found it swollen beyond hope of anyone's recognition. He wondered what it was that had hit him. One of the huge boulders which had been ripped from the bridge? Or the roots of the enormous elm tree they'd just trundled out of the road? How the devil had Claudia survived it? And how *could* Sophy survive?

With Titch sitting beside him, Marcus nosed the Land-Rover into Murray's yard, its headlights blazing.

'Aw, poor devils,' Titch groaned. 'They've had it, Marcus.'

It seemed as if they had, for although the old house was still standing, the ground-floor extension had been reduced to matchwood and rubble by the weight of yet another tree – a beech this time – which the flood had hurled at it and left behind. Now the roots of the beech hung in mid-air, decorated like a Christmas tree with the limp, dripping debris of the storm.

They slithered out of the vehicle into deep mud, carrying flashlights and ropes and – Helen's idea – a thermos of hot coffee and brandy 'just in case'. Marcus didn't suppose it would be needed. It was common knowledge that James and old Mrs Murray slept downstairs. Even if they'd had warning of that almighty surge, they couldn't have moved fast enough to escape it.

'I – I ain't got much stomach for dead bodies,' Titch said tremulously.

'Okay,' Marcus muttered through swollen lips. 'I left my stomach behind hours ago. Just yell out to them, will you? And pray for an answer.'

But before Titch could do his bit, they heard a wild, quavering cry from inside the house and both men heaved great sighs of relief.

James and Cath were sitting on the stairs, just inches above the flood-line. The water had receded now, leaving deep, slimy mud in its wake, and neither of the terrified victims was in a fit state to wade through it.

Marcus knelt on the step below them, murmuring the few words he could think of to calm them. 'It's all right now. We'll soon have you out of here.'

'Claudia!' Mrs Murray wailed. 'Has anyone heard of our Claudia?'

'Claudia's fine,' Marcus lied stoutly. 'She's up at the Fairfields'. Take a sip of this coffee, Mr Murray.'

'C-can't. C-can't.'

'He can't hold the cup!' Mrs Murray sobbed.

James was almost rigid with shock, and Marcus had to force back his head and hold him like a child before he could drink. But that strong, physical contact was enough to give him the solution to at least one of his problems. James was as thin and as frail as a rabbit. He could be carried out easily.

Mrs Murray was another matter. She wasn't stout, but she had the broad-based solidity typical of a strong woman past her prime and Marcus had an idea she would not take kindly to the indignities of a fireman's lift. Another difficulty was to shut her up so that he could think.

'It smashed in through the front door!' she gasped. 'Like a whirlwind! We'd just been through to the kitchen – oh, if we hadn't, I daren't think! Just there! We were standing just there!'

She pointed down to the foot of the stairs. 'And in it

came! Crash! I don't know how we got up here, for neither of us can walk, but we did it, we did it. We damn well did it!'

Marcus managed a painful, one-sided smile. 'Just goes to show what you can do when you have to, Mrs Murray. And you have to get out of here now, I'm afraid. If we help you, d'you think you can walk down?'

'Oh!' She chuckled hysterically, 'I can do anything, now, young man! You just name it!'

Marcus named it; and a few minutes later, with Titch supporting her in front and Marcus behind, Mrs Murray walked out of the house on her own two feet. She shuddered and moaned as her slippers disappeared into the deep slime at the foot of the stairs, but she said not another word until she was safely stowed in the Land-Rover. Then, her teeth chattering, simply, 'Thank you. Whoever you are, young man, you're a gentleman.'

'Take her home, Titch,' Marcus said quietly. 'I'll fetch Mr Murray out as soon as you get back.'

He went back inside and found James weeping, like a child left alone in the dark. Marcus put an arm around his shoulders. 'It's all right, sir,' he said kindly. 'You're safe now. A hot bath and a warm bed, and you'll feel fine again.'

'I did it all wrong,' James said bleakly.

'We all did, Mr Murray. Every one of us.'

'All my life I've lived in fear of this, you see. Yet now it's happened, it doesn't seem to matter.' He shivered and huddled closer to Marcus's side. 'You're the Saxon boy, aren't you?'

'Yes. I'm Marcus.'

'I heard you took a doctorate. In chemistry, was it? I envy you that. A good education . . . Mind you, I used to read a lot when I was younger. Not fiction. I never saw much point in studying other people's pretences. Exploration, that was what I liked. Brave men – climbing mountains, hacking through jungles: the sort of thing I could never do. But I can't hold a book now. My hands shake. Just a few lines and I'm lost. But I can read a few lines, and I found this little book a few weeks ago. One of my wife's. It made me wish I'd read more fiction while I still could. It made me realise that it's not so much a pretence as a way of thinking things through. That's something I've never done, you see. I've never thought things through. I was too afraid.'

Marcus held him more tightly, closing his eyes on despair. 'You aren't the only one,' he croaked hoarsely.

'This little book,' James went on. 'I don't really understand it, to tell the truth. It's a sort of poem, and I think – I might be wrong, of course, not knowing much about poetry – I think the chap might have sacrificed his sense to make his rhyme. But the start of it made me think of you. Of your father, I mean. Your family. "I fled him down the nights and down the days; I fled him down the arches of the years; I fled him down the labyrinthine ways of my own mind; and in the mist of tears I hid from him."

'And here he is, saving my life, Marcus. Here he is, holding my hand.' He chuckled softly. 'Good phrase that: "The labyrinthine ways of my own mind." I got myself well and truly lost in there, didn't I?'

Marcus couldn't reply. To have brought James to wisdom at this point in his life was surely the most cruel trick Fate had ever played on him. For tomorrow . . . Oh, God, what mist of tears would cover him tomorrow?

'Come on, Mr Murray,' he said gently. 'Let's get you out of here, shall we?'

He stayed at the house only long enough to ensure that the Murrays were comfortable. Then, prompted by an awed whisper from Titch Flicker, he went back down to the village, and Mrs Chislett's cottage. He'd noticed the tractor standing there as he'd driven away from Murray's, and wondered why Ben had turned the headlights off. Now Titch told him. It had been to save James Murray from a heart attack.

The headlights were on now, blazing into the muddy remains of Mrs Chislett's bedroom. The entire front wall of her cottage had been ripped away.

Ben was in tears, but there was nothing anyone could do. The rickety old staircase had been reduced to a heap of wet kindling, half buried in silt. A dead calf lay straddled across it, its back legs tangled in the legs of Mrs Chislett's upturned sideboard.

'It must have been that tree,' Titch said. 'Got stuck in one of they winders, I expect, and took the whole wall with it. Poor old dear . . . She'd have been sluiced out o' there like a spider out of a bucket.'

And as they stared, appalled, into the wreckage, the rain stopped. It stopped very suddenly, as if the floodgates of heaven had slammed shut. And it was only as this analogy came to his mind that Marcus remembered his grandfather. He began to laugh; and, still laughing, he shook his fist at the sky. 'Took you long enough to get in, Grandad!' he roared. 'Did you have to take so many with you?'

He laughed and laughed. He fell against the tractor and laughed, and it wasn't until his father and Titch pulled him away that he realised he was screaming.

He didn't know much after that. He never knew who had done the milking the next morning, for he didn't wake until after seven, and might have slept until noon had not the police come to find him.

He had slept in his old room: the rest of the house had been taken over by guests; and Helen brought him coffee and gently warned him of what was to come.

'They've found the Mercedes, darling. I'll show them up

here, if you don't mind. It's the only private spot left in the house.'

Mutely, Marcus stared up at her with his one good eye. She was as white as a ghost, with huge purple shadows around her eyes; and in the bright sunlight of a glorious July morning the wrinkles on her face looked twice as deep and twice as many as he remembered them. She had grown old, it seemed, overnight.

'Did you sleep at all, Mother?'

'I had an hour, I think.' She smiled and squeezed his hand. 'Irene's been marvellous, though. I couldn't have managed if she and Liz hadn't been here.'

'Liz? Oh, of course. She came for Grandad . . .'

He scowled with bewilderment. His grandfather's body still lay downstairs but how were they to bury him? The bridge had gone. They couldn't even get to the churchyard . . .

He crept painfully out of bed, eased his bruised and aching body into a dressing gown and sat in the study to receive his visitors.

They were very kind. The Mercedes, with Sarah's body still in it, had fetched up two miles downriver, in the middle of someone's garden shed.

'I'm afraid we'll have to ask you, or perhaps one of the family, to identify her body, sir. They've taken her to Bath. Can't get through to Bristol at the moment. All the bridges are out.'

Marcus swallowed. 'Have you found any other . . . bodies?'

'Just the one, sir.'

'A child?'

'A man.'

'Alister.' Marcus shook his head. 'No child? A little girl?'

'It's a terrible mess out there, sir.'

Marcus gazed blankly through the open window at a

clear, azure sky full of swooping housemartins and swallows. It was hard to imagine the 'terrible mess' which lay at the bottom of the hill; hard to picture Sophy lying in a coffin of cold mud. He closed his eyes, bowed his head. Poor little girl . . .

A loud clattering noise suddenly tore through the dreadful peace of that moment and Marcus's head flew up. 'What the hell – ?'

'One of our helicopters, sir. The old lady in the cottage near the bridge? She's up in the loft. They're going to winch her out through the roof.'

'*Mrs Chislett*?'

The policeman smiled. 'In a terrible paddy, she is, too, sir. Been giving us hell ever since we found her. Nearly killed one of the firemen she did. Threw one of the roof slates down to call attention to herself. It only missed him by an inch.'

The next few days passed like a nightmare: one of the strange, disjointed nightmares which sound more funny than frightening when you tell the family about it at breakfast.

When they brought Mrs Chislett out through her roof, Veronica, tied up in Mrs Chislett's cardigan, leapt from the old woman's arms with ten feet still to go between mid-air and dry land, and disappeared into the woods, cardigan and all. The cat showed up again two days later. The cardigan never did.

Edward Saxon travelled to his grave by a thirty-mile detour. Ben bought drinks and pork pies at the pub for the mourners on the church side. The others travelled thirty miles home again and had whisky and ham sandwiches in the drawing room at Saxon's. Olivia was her usual scathing self. 'Trust Edward to make a show of it,' she said crisply. 'He was always one to draw attention to himself.'

The Army moved into the old stone barn and set up camp there while they demolished what was left of the old bridge and built a Bailey bridge in its place. The three officers dined each night at the Saxons' table: charming, kind, humorous men who made everyone forget – for a few minutes at a time – that they were living through a nightmare.

But a nightmare it was. Seven people, caught by that vast surge of water on its devastating race down the valley, had died in the floods that night. And two of the bodies still were not found. Hannah Lisle's. And Sophy's.

Hannah's disappearance was a mystery no one could fathom. Her cottage had been flooded but it was clear that she hadn't been inside it at the time. Her car was missing which seemed to indicate that, after Marcus's call, she'd driven off to look for Sarah. But no one had seen her go. And her car was nowhere to be found. It was easy to imagine that a child's body could be dragged to the river bottom and buried by silt and debris, but a car? As the waters slowly receded and the river went back to its bed, surely they should find something?

They found many other things. Drowned sheep, cattle and horses; bicycles; other people's cars. The horsehair and leather-cloth sofa, last seen in Mrs Chislett's front parlour, turned up in the playground of a primary school, three miles downriver. This would not have been remarkable save for two small details: the first that the playground was surrounded by walls ten feet high; the second, a linen and lace antimacassar, still neatly arranged across the sofa back.

John Murray and his wife had come to take James and Cath to their home in Bath, and what a strange meeting that had been. Marcus and John had never – since they'd first learned to swear – exchanged a civil word; but now, in spite of the sadness which attended their meeting, it was as if they'd been friends all their lives.

Even so, it was hard for Marcus to enquire after Claudia, who, with her baby, had been taken to hospital in the same helicopter which had rescued Mrs Chislett.

'They're alive,' John croaked fervently. 'Thanks to you, Marcus.'

'That was a stroke of fate. No credit to me. Has she been – told?'

'No. Daniel's coming tomorrow, to be with her when . . .'

'And the baby?' Marcus asked hurriedly.

'He's okay. A bit of a chest infection, but they'll soon have that cleared up. Thank God she'd tied him to her. Otherwise she'd have lost everything. Husband, children, home . . . The business. Oh, God, Marcus, what had she ever done to deserve this?'

Marcus couldn't reply.

Chapter Twenty-Eight

Claudia was going home tomorrow. 'Home' was the place you were in when you weren't in hospital. It was the place the nurses spoke about when there was still an hour to go until the next dose of tranquillisers, and there was nothing left to hold on to, and all Claudia wanted to do was to scream.

'Never mind, Mrs Chalcroft. You'll be going home on Friday.'

They knew, and Claudia knew, that home wasn't there any more; yet they still said it. They held her hand and said it. Said it in soft, cloying voices which, she gathered, were meant to be comforting.

And now Marian was saying it, holding her hand. 'Never mind, Clo, we'll take you home tomorrow.'

But the thought of Daniel and Marian's gloomy little house, with its trees and its leaf-mould and the soft, drip-dripping of rain, filled Claudia with dread. She and Ali had been happy there; happy for a few hours: their last hours together. She couldn't remember very much after that. Just little images, little phrases which jumped into her mind like fanged beasts, tearing her apart.

Every four hours they put those little beasts to sleep:

knocked them out with tranquillisers; and every three hours they woke up and yawned, making Claudia's stomach swoop with despair. Then they stretched, digging their claws into her heart.

Ali was dead. They'd buried him two days ago and heaped up his grave with flowers. Claudia had not been there. She'd been lying on her bed, having forty-three stitches removed from various parts of her anatomy: her head, the backs of her legs and her shoulders. Save for a few bruises and a broken arm, she'd taken all the damage from behind. They'd said she must have curled herself into a ball to protect Philip. Done it instinctively, they'd said. But she could remember nothing, and now bore her protective instincts nothing but resentment. For in saving Philip's life, it seemed she had saved her own; and she didn't want to be alive. She wished with all her heart that she was dead.

If they had only found Sophy, perhaps she could have borne everything else, but almost two weeks had passed since the flood and they said there was no hope . . .

In the cotton-wool existence which endured for three hours out of every four, Claudia could tell herself there was no hope. She could tell herself Sophy was dead, and believe it. Yes, believe it and be thankful, for death was a thing she had never feared. Ever since her mother's death she'd lived in envy of the dead. They had won through to the far shore of the sea of troubles and need never suffer again.

But as the effects of the tranquillisers began to wear off, all Claudia could think of was Sophy: a tiny baby nestling between the curve of her arm and the curve of her breast, and the passion and the power of that moment. *Nothing will harm you while your mother's alive*.

But Claudia *was* alive! And Sophy was lost, lost, wandering in the darkness and the rain all by herself!

Mummy! I don't like it! Mummy!

She was only four!

'Still,' Marian said now, 'you must be feeling more comfortable now they've taken the stitches out. They get so itchy, don't they?'

'What?'

'And when that plaster cast comes off your arm you'll begin to feel more like your old self, Clo. We'll help you. You mustn't worry about anything. John's going to see to the house – '

'She isn't listening, darling,' Daniel murmured gently.

No, Claudia wasn't listening, but she could hear very well. She had heard every word, looked it over carefully and set it into line with its fellows. 'You mustn't worry about anything.'

It was good, plain English. It made perfect sense. But it didn't mean anything. It was like the phoney painted food they put inside refrigerators at the Electricity Board Showrooms. Roast chicken and tomatoes; celery and trifle. It made perfect sense. But it wasn't real!

'John's going to see to the house.'

House? House? *House*? What did it mean? What was Marian talking about? *House*? What about Sophy? Why wasn't anyone seeing to Sophy?

'We'll help you.'

So why didn't they find Sophy? It was all the help Claudia needed – and no one, no one would do it for her! Oh, yes, the police had searched. Five miles downriver, under every fallen bridge, every tangled weir. But what if she was *six* miles downriver? Who had looked there? And what if she wasn't in the river at all?

'Mrs Chislett's couch,' she said abruptly.

She realised she'd said the same thing before, many times, but no one had listened. No one seemed to care.

Now, sighing, Daniel murmured, 'Here we go again,' and came to put his arms around her. 'That's different, Clo.'

'No. No, it isn't different! If Mrs Chislett's couch could be thrown over a ten-foot wall . . .'

'But then what, Clo? Someone *found* Mrs Chislett's couch. If Sophy had been thrown clear, someone would have *found* her.'

'Not if she had wandered away. She could have – ' Panic caught at her throat and squeezed her lungs until she was gasping. 'She could have – wandered off – Daniel! She'd have been so – scared!'

'Clo, you were only in the water a few seconds but *you* didn't wander off when they pulled you out. You were unconscious. And even if you hadn't been, you couldn't have walked!'

Claudia eyed him narrowly, noticing that he looked mildly exasperated, as he'd sometimes done when he was trying to help her with her physics homework. He'd been good at physics. He'd known all the answers. He just hadn't been able to explain the questions, and he still couldn't. He didn't even know what the question *was*! It wasn't – as he seemed to think – 'Is Sophy dead?' but 'Where *is* she?'

Claudia shook her head. 'You don't understand.'

'I do, Clo.'

'*No*!' Rage leapt into her eyes. Rage and hatred for this brother of hers who had never lost a child he had loved, never sacrificed a single thing he had wanted. 'No, you *don't* understand! She's not dead, she's not dead!'

'Clo, she must be. You've got to try and accept – '

The door opened, a nurse came in and Claudia reared back in her chair, her eyes darting wildly in search of the drugs trolley, hoping for another few hours of the strange, leaden peace which only drugs could bring her. But the nurse had come empty-handed.

'Oh, dear,' she said briskly. 'Not getting upset again, are we?'

'No,' Claudia snarled. 'What have *we* to get upset about?'

'You've another visitor, dear. But he won't come in without your *express* permission. So what'll I tell him?'

'Try telling me who he is,' Claudia snapped. 'If he's selling insurance, I don't want any!'

'Now, now . . .' The nurse apparently decided that Claudia was too 'upset' to handle and turned to Daniel instead, whispering, 'A Mr Saxon?'

'Oh . . . yes. He said he might come. It's Marcus, Clo. Will you see him?'

'Marcus?' Claudia felt her colour draining away, but whether with hope or with horror she couldn't tell.

'No,' she said faintly. 'No . . .'

'Oh, Clo . . . Clo, please. He saved your life.'

'He didn't have to! I didn't want him to! I wish he hadn't!'

Now Marian took her hand again and patted it firmly. 'Clo, listen. You say, very rightly I think, that we don't understand how you feel. We do try, love, but how *can* we without . . . ? We loved Ali and Sophy, Clo, but not as you loved them. How *can* we understand? But Marcus has lost his wife, Clo. He's bleeding inside just as you are. See him, love. Will you?'

Claudia turned her head and stared into the corner of the room, a very interesting spot where two pale green walls came together in a cold, straight line. She had stared into that corner for two weeks now, trying to work things out. But this was the first time it had given her a single iota of help.

He's bleeding inside just as you are.

Yes . . . Oh, yes. He *would* understand! He was Sophy's father!

'Yes,' she breathed. 'I'll see him.'

*

Marcus had not crossed the threshold of a hospital since a year before Callie's death, but the smell of a hospital was something one never forgot and could never wholly analyse. Now, waiting for the nurse to emerge from Claudia's side-ward, Marcus decided that it was the smell of the struggle between bad drains and disinfectant. The drains were winning.

He shrugged and looked at his watch. He inspected his cuff-links, brushed a hair from his sleeve.

He'd bought this suit for his wedding: a steel grey worsted which, the tailor had remarked obsequiously, brought out the steel in his eyes. It had done that, all right. Either brought it out or hammered it in, he wasn't sure which. He'd worn the suit quite a lot, just lately. To the mortuary. To the police station. To three Godawful funerals.

He'd had a charcoal grey suit which had been more suitable for funerals but . . . He clenched his teeth, sickened at the memory. Sarah had gone to his wardrobe after he'd hit her, and slashed all his clothes with a razor. She'd have slashed this suit too, had he not hung it under his sheepskin coat. She'd carved the coat to shreds . . .

No, he mustn't think of Sarah. Think of Claudia. But even Claudia scarcely bore thinking about. He didn't really want to see her. He wasn't certain why he had come. He was actually frightened, had been afraid since it had first crossed his mind that this was something he should do. No, not *should*. Duty most certainly wasn't a part of it, although this was the only certainty he had. Nothing seemed to mean anything to him any more. He felt . . . steely. Stony. Cold. He didn't even want to know why he was here, waiting for Claudia. It didn't matter. Nothing mattered any more.

The nurse emerged from the ward on tip-toe. She had a very large bosom, inadequately supported. 'Express permission granted,' she said. Then, drawing the door closed for a moment: 'Try not to stay too long, sir. She's still a little bit upset.'

'Just a little bit?' Marcus echoed sarcastically. 'Thank you. I'll bear that in mind.'

It was odd. He'd seen Claudia bleeding from virtually every pore just ten days ago yet in the meantime, when he'd thought of her, he hadn't remembered her like that. He'd remembered her tanned, pregnant and beautiful with her hair caressing her shoulder in a soft, flaxen braid. It was this Claudia he expected to see now, and the shock of seeing her as she really was . . .

Never had he been more grateful for the habit of self-control. He didn't gasp, hesitate, close his eyes. The smile he'd produced outside the door was still on his face when he reached for her hand, but something else was happening to him on the inside. Steely? Stony? Cold? Another of life's little illusions . . .

She looked like a dead thing: tiny, pale, almost skeletal. Her face was still bruised, her legs and hands a tapestry of half-healed cuts and grazes. Her eyes were enormous, glittering and burning, with deep, purple crescents scooped out beneath. And they'd cut her hair! He could see why. An ugly, six-inch gash ran from her temple to her crown with the inflamed marks of the sutures still evident. God, she looked awful!

'Are they looking after you?' he asked gently.

She didn't reply. She was trembling and it seemed she couldn't look at him for as soon as he'd touched her hand she looked beyond him, into the corner; and now seemed quite fascinated by what she saw there.

'How's Philip?'

'He's fine, thank you. Much better. They take him to the children's ward during the day. He doesn't know, you see. He still wants to – play.'

'That's good.'

'Yes. I thought he would miss Sophy . . .'

'Too young, perhaps.'

Her gaze stayed fixed upon the corner of the room but her grief travelled in another direction, towards Marcus. It made his skin prickle, his arms ache to hold her. But, save for her hand, he didn't dare touch her. Just the plaster cast on her arm made him wince with borrowed pain.

Suddenly she laughed – a hard, brittle little sound. 'Well,' she said, 'who'd have thought it? My father was here yesterday, singing your praises, and even John can't stop saying how much we owe you.' She threw back her head and laughed again. 'So it's all over! Fifty years of hatred – gone!'

Now, for the first time, she turned to look at him, her eyes narrowed to slits of burning rage. 'Isn't – that – *wonderful*?' she sneered bitterly. 'They've turned you into a bloody saint! You saved our lives! An old woman of eighty, a helpless invalid, and *me*! You bastard! You should have let us die!'

Marcus bowed his head, covering his eyes, shaking his head. He felt Claudia's hand snatching clear of his own and was about to stand up, clear out, when that same little hand touched his cheek, stroking it gently. 'Oh, I'm sorry, Marcus. You almost killed yourself to save us, and I know . . . I know I should be grateful, for Philip's life if not my own, but – '

'No,' he whispered brokenly. 'You're more right than you know. I didn't even realise I'd fished you out, Claudia. I thought you were Sophy. But I . . . missed her, and now she's . . .'

'Don't! Don't say she's dead, because – !'

'I know.'

Somewhere behind him he heard Daniel utter a groan of despair, and Marcus knew what he meant. He understood.

But he understood Claudia, too. Sophy wasn't dead. Not until they saw her dead. Until then, she was just a lost little child: wandering, crying, turning her face up to the rain. This thought, among many others, was something he had not faced until now; had refused to face. That Sophy was dead, must be dead, was a *fact*. It was a fact he had accepted, and had accepted almost with gratitude, for with the life taken from her, she could suffer nothing, feel nothing. She couldn't be afraid. But facts and feelings . . . They didn't necessarily walk hand in hand; and until they found Sophy's body, she would live for ever: a tormented, terrified little girl, all alone.

'Find her,' Claudia whispered. 'For the love of God, Marcus, find her!'

'I've tried. We've all tried, Claudia. The police – '

'Police!' Claudia spat the word. 'What the hell do they know? What do they care?' She raised her hand, balling it into a fist which she brought down on his knee like a hammer. 'Find her!' she shrieked. 'Find her! She's *your* daughter! Don't you know? Don't you care?'

Claudia curled up in her chair, sobbing with rage. Now, white-faced, Marcus turned to look at Daniel and Marian, who seemed to have been glued to their chairs with shock.

'I'm sorry,' he said wearily. 'I shouldn't have come.'

'Please!' Claudia wailed. 'Marcus! Help me!'

But he couldn't look at her again. He closed his eyes, reached for her hand and felt it come to his palm like a homing bird. 'Yes,' he said. 'Don't cry any more, Claudia. I'll find her.'

But he was lying. Every able-bodied man and woman in the county had searched for Sophy. Policemen, firemen and frogmen; farmers, poachers, hunters; people out walking their dogs. There was nothing more to be done.

*

'Tuff-tuff, tuff-tuff.' Philip scooted up and down the sunny lawn on the expensive little steam engine Daniel had bought him. 'Tuff-tuff, Mummy!'

'Chuff-chuff,' Claudia echoed dreamily; and then, realising she should make a little more effort: 'Blow the whistle, darling. Whee!'

'*Not* wee! Tuff-tuff!'

'Oh.' She nodded. 'Right.'

It was hard to play with him. It was hard to do anything. Even doing nothing was hard. She was still taking the tranquillisers; and although they turned her mind into something resembling a tepid bowl of porridge, they did nothing to relieve the physical restlessness, the physical weakness which made her wish, every moment, that she was dead.

Daniel had been home for lunch. She'd promised Marian she would cook lunch for him, but hadn't quite pulled it off. The potatoes and peas had turned out beautifully, but she'd completely forgotten to turn the oven on and steak casserole wasn't so good raw. They'd opened a tin of mince instead. Since then, she'd washed the dishes, and this task (relatively simple even with one arm in plaster) had taken more than an hour to complete. She couldn't concentrate. She couldn't settle to anything.

Marian had taken her to Newport to buy some new clothes but after a mere ten minutes she'd been half dead with exhaustion. Ten minutes after coming home, she'd been half dead with boredom, prowling about the house like a caged tiger and wishing, since she was prowling anyway, that she'd prowled around the shops instead. She couldn't read. Her intellectual challenge of the day was reading *The Gambols* cartoon on the back page of the *Daily Express*. With her broken arm she couldn't knit or sew. She couldn't even watch television; for every word and every image reminded her of something she wanted to forget.

And that about summed it up. She wanted to forget everything: past, present and future. She couldn't cope with any of it, especially the future. In her more lucid moments, when the porridge of her mind thinned to watery gruel, she looked into the future exactly as she might have fallen off a cliff: wanting to scream, yet somehow knowing she'd hit the rocks before a sound could emerge. What was the future without Ali? What was the future without Sophy?

'Tuff,' Philip said. 'Tuff-tuff-tuff.'

Claudia smiled wearily. 'True,' she said. 'And then there's you, sweetheart. What are you going to do without your daddy?'

'Daddy,' Philip said thoughtfully. 'Gone.'

But he didn't mean Ali. He seemed to have forgotten Ali. Three weeks dead, and his son had forgotten him. 'Daddy' was Daniel, and the postman and the milkman. Daddy was anyone in trousers.

It was a hot, rather sultry afternoon and when Philip tired of his train Claudia fetched him a bucket of water and a plastic beaker and stripped him down to his nappy. He'd play for hours with water; and as long as Claudia sat and watched him, he would ask nothing more of her.

'Dawter! Plash!'

Claudia gritted her teeth and squeezed her eyes shut. Christ, who needed television? A little child who couldn't yet talk and he'd reminded her of everything, *everything* she wanted to forget!

She sat in a deckchair and closed her eyes. It was too soon. Everyone said it was too soon, yet already it felt like a million years, and the future wouldn't go away. One day she'd have to deal with it; not just for Philip's sake but for Daniel's and Marian's. They'd only been married two months. They were both new in their jobs and hoping to do well. But, first with hospital visiting and now with Claudia on their hands for God only knew how long . . .

They didn't dare leave her for more than an hour. With her broken arm, her drugs and her death-wish, she could hardly be counted as a responsible guardian for her own son. Yesterday she'd had the curate to keep her company, the day before it had been the community midwife on her day off.

Today, some anonymous neighbour would be calling in and the very thought of it turned Claudia's stomach. They all knew, they'd all had to be told, and none of them knew how to cope with it. None of them knew what to say. Poor devils. They arrived feeling sorry for her, and, long before they left, Claudia hated their guts for making *her* feel sorry for *them*!

She heard a car purring to rest in the drive but didn't open her eyes until she heard Philip say, 'Daddy!'

Drat! It was the curate again. Oh, well. Ten out of ten for courage . . .

'Philip? Stay on the grass, darling.'

'No. Daddy.' Still carrying his plastic beaker, he waddled past the corner of the house, out of Claudia's sight. With difficulty, she hauled herself upright to go after him. But before she could go further her knees turned to jelly and she sat down again, ramming her knuckles between her teeth. *Marcus* . . .

'Hi there, buster,' he said warmly. 'What've you got there? *Hey*! Oh, well, I did ask, I suppose.'

He emerged with Philip in his arms and a dark, watery stain down one side of his shirt. Philip, having done what damage he could with the water, was now happily bashing Marcus with the empty beaker.

'Help! Oh, ow! I give in!'

He set his persecutor down on the lawn, crouching with him to examine the depleted contents of the bucket. 'Ah, this is where you keep your ammunition, is it?'

'Dawter,' Philip explained smugly. Then, looking for

something else to show off, he pointed to his engine. 'Tuff-tuff!'

'Tuff-tuff?'

'He means chuff-chuff,' Claudia whispered.

'Ah.' It was the only communication they shared for the next half hour. Marcus ignored her. He got down on his knees and played trains. He took Philip's hand and strolled about the garden. He put Philip on his shoulders and played horses. And when Philip at last tired of all this and became fretful, Marcus threw Claudia a wink and asked smoothly, 'Time for a nap?'

'Er – yes.'

'Which way?'

Philip had done something nasty in his nappy but even this didn't bother Marcus, and his nappy-changing technique was immaculate. Philip screamed throughout – he hated having his nappy changed – but Marcus didn't seem to notice. He got on with the job, picked Philip up, cuddled him, thrust him at Claudia's face for a kiss, and then slotted him neatly into his cot with his teddy bear.

Claudia could only gaze and blink. The curate had had a hell of a time with the nappy, and hadn't entirely recovered before Marian had come home, two hours later. But Marcus hadn't even worked up a sweat, let alone a full-scale panic.

'Coffee for the grown-ups now,' he said.

'Are you – ? Have you done this sort of thing before?'

'Once or twice. Tony Bridges. Ellis's lot. I've observed more than I've participated, but it's not difficult to get the hang of. Babies are like lambs: a good deal tougher than they look.'

'They didn't tell me you were coming.'

'No.'

'Why?'

'Would you have been pleased?' He'd put the kettle on and found cups, saucers and spoons.

'No.'

He smiled. 'Well, then.'

'I didn't say . . . I forgot to say that I . . . I'm sorry about your wife.'

'Thank you. So am I, although not for the obvious reasons. We weren't happy. We'd quarrelled. I'd told her to leave. I hadn't realised . . . Up on the hill there, you get no real idea of . . . I didn't know the road was flooded although I realise now that common sense should have informed me. I'd never seen rain like that in my life, and God knows I've seen floods enough. So I feel . . . I *know* I killed her. It isn't something one can forgive oneself. Sugar?'

'No. Thank you.'

Claudia felt sick and dizzy. She groped her way to a chair and sat down, gulping for air. Marcus followed with the coffee, but he set it down on the table and came to crouch at her feet, holding her hand. 'Tell me,' he said. 'Tell me. If you don't it'll drive you mad, and you mustn't go mad, Claudia. Philip needs you, and he'll need you for a long time yet.'

'It seemed . . .' she whispered. 'I didn't . . . When we . . .'

'Yes?'

'He couldn't forgive me. He loved me. And I . . . I loved him, Marcus. But he couldn't . . . After that day . . . in Bath, he didn't believe me any more. We didn't quarrel. We never quarrelled. But sometimes he said things, just little things, to remind me that I'd spoiled everything. I killed him twice, Marcus. The day I married him, and the day . . . The night . . . That night.'

She sank further back in her chair, sagging with weariness. 'I knew . . . When we reached the middle of the bridge I wanted to go back, go back to the car. I knew something terrible was going to happen! I'd *always* known it!'

'Known it?'

'Yes, yes!' She was crying now. 'Ever since my mother

died, I'd dreamed of it without knowing what it was! That terrible . . . yellow. But that was all it was, just – yellow, and – and drowning. And I'd always been scared of that bridge! All my life! I knew, Marcus! I *knew*! But I only said it once, you see. I said it once: *Let's go back to the car* . . . And then I let him go! I should have fought him, Marcus! I should have done anything to stop him! Stop him – taking – Sophy! But I didn't, I didn't! I let him go!'

She was screaming with pain, and barely noticed Marcus's arms coming around her, scarcely noticed when he lifted her from her chair. But she noticed his hands rubbing her back, noticed that he was rocking her, rocking her. She noticed his tears, scalding her face.

'Oh, Claudia!' he howled. 'What did we *do*? I *loved* you!'

This was where the pain had begun. And this was where it had brought them.

There was no way out.

Chapter Twenty-Nine

Marcus had finished his business at Frome market and now strolled up through the town, trying to remember his mother's shopping list. Three large melons – '*Not* water melons!' (how did one tell the difference?) – two skeins of white embroidery silk and a pack of cheap ballpoint pens from Woolworth's.

Marcus had felt ill since his afternoon with Claudia the previous day. They'd cried like a pair of babies, and now he had a crashing headache, not helped by the scorching heat of a bright, August morning. On the other hand, he felt better where it really mattered. Since the night of the flood he'd been like a zombie, able to identify only the most simple of his feelings: a cold, unforgiving self-hatred. He still hated himself; he still knew he would never forgive himself for sending Sarah to her death; but somehow, just to know that Claudia's sufferings were so much worse than his own had helped him to put things into perspective a little.

She was a brave kid. She'd pull through. He had no doubt of it. And, if she could do it, so could he. One day, life would begin to mean something again. One day, he'd look up at the sun and laugh – instead of wincing and reaching for his sunglasses.

He hated wearing sunglasses except for driving. They made him feel like a tourist. But everyone looked like tourists today. Hot weather seemed to bring out the crazy side of the British character; and while this might look okay in Carnaby Street, it looked very weird in the narrow hillside streets of this little Somerset market town.

Girls in groin-high shorts and high-heeled shoes, men in open sandals, with bare, hairy toes sticking out. The hairy toes made Marcus shudder. The groin-high shorts did not; although he wasn't as interested in them as he felt he should have been. They made him feel cynical and world-weary. He observed them critically, decided that they all looked like paired sets of coloured balloons, and vaguely considered arming himself with a pin.

As he disappeared into Woolworth's, however, he noticed one woman who was not dressed for the weather. She was standing at the bus-stop, wearing a long, belted Burberry and heavy, old-fashioned shoes. He ploughed through to the stationery counter for his mother's pens, thinking how odd it was that after five minutes' exposure to bare toes and tightly clad bottoms, the good old English Burberry had somehow seemed so alien. But no, it wasn't the Burberry. It was the sunglasses she'd worn with it. God, people were strange!

Pens. What else? Christ, he'd forgotten . . . Melons. Embroidery silk. Something else. What the hell was it? He stood hovering for a moment on the pavement before turning back up the hill. Embroidery silk. Melons. The woman was still there. Her hair had been cut too short before being permed, and a revolting foam of frizzy grey curls adhered to her skull, looking more like an old man's beard than a hair style. Two young girls joined her in the bus queue, laughing and shrieking, pushing one another.

The woman took a step forward and turned to face the road, her chin lifting with puritanical disdain.

Marcus's heart slid into his boots and bounced back again, quivering with shock. Dear Christ, for a moment there, he'd thought . . . He stared at her. No, of course not. She was dead. Yet he still found himself stepping sideways into the doorway of a hardware shop; he still stood there, staring at her. It was! No, it wasn't, it couldn't be! She was dead!

He turned away and, at the same moment, two things happened which, although resolving none of his doubts, made him act as if they had been resolved. He began to tremble violently and, at the same time, saw two shirt-sleeved policemen strolling across the street at the foot of the hill, heading towards the cattle market.

Marcus leapt out of his hiding place and raced downhill, zig-zagging across the road between a slow-moving cattle truck and a murderously fast Austin Healey. Both drivers yelled curses at him.

'Hey!' He caught one of the policemen by the elbow and collapsed against the wall, fighting for breath.

He could barely speak. 'Floods!' he gasped. 'Last month! My wife's aunt disappeared, presumed drowned. Police – m-messages on the radio. Remember? Hannah Lisle!'

'Yes, sir?' The chap smirked as if he was having his leg pulled. Marcus wanted to hit him.

'I – I think – I'm almost certain – that the woman . . .' He flapped his arm towards the main street. 'Woman – wearing Burberry – at the bus-stop – is her. I know I could be wrong. But – '

The policemen both looked at their feet.

'*Quick*!' Marcus hit a note he hadn't managed since his voice had broken, many years before. 'If the bus comes, we've lost her!'

'You sure about this, are you, sir?'

'No. If it is, she's changed her hair style. And the sunglasses . . . But I'm – pretty sure.'

'Right you are, sir. Stop there a moment. If I remember rightly, it was a Miss, wasn't it? Miss Isles?'

'Lisle!' Marcus groaned.

Only one of the policemen approached the woman. The other waited on the corner with Marcus. He said, 'Don't build up your hopes, sir. These things happen when people disappear. You keep looking for – '

He stopped speaking just as a shriek of wild laughter echoed down the hill. 'Er – just a moment, sir.' And he strode off up the road to join his partner.

Shuddering, Marcus crept from the shadows and stared up the hill. It *was* Hannah. She had taken a two-handed grip on the bus-stop post and was laughing fit to bust: horrible, crazy laughter.

He crossed the road again, his legs shaking, and staggered weakly towards her. The policemen weren't touching her; but one of them was smiling and quietly talking, encouraging her, it seemed, to do her worst.

She was surrounded now by a circle of staring onlookers. Although still clinging to the post, she was sitting on the ground, grinning up at the crowds as if, like a tube-station busker, she was performing for money. It was extraordinary how pleasant she looked with a smile on her face. Marcus had never seen her smiling, or even frowning; just that straight-faced immobility which had made her look like a statue, cast in bronze.

She caught sight of Marcus and burst out laughing again. 'Oh! Here he comes! Saxon pig! Just like his father!' She turned her head to look at the crowd of onlookers, her face falling, her mouth drooping at the corners like a theatrical tragedy mask.

'Killed my baby,' she said pitifully, almost singing it: a soft, wailing lament. 'His father did. He killed my baby.

And *he* killed my little girl.' Now she began laughing again. 'But I've got *his*! And she'll die, too, before he finds her! Oh, yes! She'll die too!'

'Who's she talking about?' one of the policemen snapped urgently.

Marcus's face was wet with cold perspiration. He was freezing with dread. 'I – I think . . .'

The policeman caught his arm, steadying him. 'Come on, sir. Come on. Don't pass out on us, now!'

'I think – I think she's got – my daughter,' Marcus whispered.

He sat in the police station for almost three hours. They plied him with sweet tea, asked questions, took statements. He didn't know where they'd taken Hannah. He knew only that they'd brought in a doctor – a shrink, he supposed – to wring some kind of sense out of her. He felt as if he was dying. His heart was palpitating, his lungs seemed to have shrivelled to nothing. He couldn't breathe, couldn't stop trembling, couldn't think.

If she had Sophy – ? The hope almost crucified him! But if, as she'd said, Sophy was dying – ?

'For God's sake,' he groaned. 'Hurry!'

He envisaged himself cracking Hannah's skull open, rummaging inside it for an address. But he felt as if his own skull had been cracked and rummaged into. He'd spilled out every detail of his private life, trying to explain who Sophy was, who Hannah was; Sarah, Claudia, Alister. He'd almost told them about Ben's affair with Hannah – anything to be helpful, anything to find Sophy! But he'd stopped himself at the last minute. His mother didn't know, must never know . . .

'Right, sir. How are you feeling, now?' The station sergeant stood over him, smiling kindly.

'Bloody awful.'

'Hm. Well, sir. This little girl, Sophy. I know she's your daughter, but in the circumstances . . . What I mean is, does she know you? Would she recognise you?'

'You've got an address!'

It was miles out in the country. A tiny, galvanised bungalow with a lean-to garage at the side. Hannah's Morris Traveller languished inside it with a flat tyre, its wheels still caked with the thick, yellow mud which had buried the river valley.

The police had contacted John Murray and now he and Marcus sat side by side in the police car, mute with terror, while three police officers, one of them a woman, went inside to search for Sophy.

When at last he and John were called inside, the first thing Marcus noticed was the smell of the place: dank and musty with an undernote of creeping fungus and dry rot. Then he heard the voice.

'Eh? *Eh*? What d'you say? You'll have to speak up! I'm deaf in the one ear, and can't hear in t'other! *Eh*?'

'Hannah Lisle!' the policeman bellowed. 'Do you know her?'

'Eh? *An animal*? Where?'

Marcus followed the sound of the voices, down a narrow, plaster-board passageway where ancient strips of beige wallpaper hung in ribbons, brushing his face.

A skinny, buckled old man sat in a broken armchair beside a banked coal fire, craning his neck to hear what was being said to him. The policewoman was crouching in a corner, beside a similarly broken couch. She was holding Sophy's hand.

Marcus pushed John back into the passageway in his hurry to get outside again and be sick, not so much with horror at the state Sophy was in, but with rage; a rage which had no outlet save through his stomach. For Hannah was mad and whoever the old man was, he was old – too old to be held responsible for the child who lay so small, still and bewildered in that horrible little room. No one would be punished. No one would pay. Only Sophy, only Claudia. Oh, God, it wasn't fair!

Another three hours passed before Marcus saw Sophy again, but he saw Claudia first: a little wraith who, with Daniel at her side, fled through the hospital waiting room as if all the goblins of hell ran at her heels. Twenty minutes after that, Daniel came to fetch him.

'Sophy wants to see you.'

'Sophy?'

'Hannah's told her . . . Told her. She wants to see – her father.'

'Oh,' Marcus said.

Sophy looked a little better now, but thinner and paler than any child had any business to be, her eyes huge saucers in a tiny, haunted-looking face. She had bronchitis, and a deep gash in her leg, untreated since the night of the flood, was so badly infected that if they hadn't found her . . . Hannah had been right about that. She would have died.

Claudia had been crying. Now, her face irradiated with joy, she just stared into Sophy's face, almost eating her with her eyes. She didn't look at Marcus. Sophy did.

'Well? Do you know him?' Daniel asked gently.

'Yes.' She took a shallow, rattling breath.

Marcus felt very shy and deeply ashamed, for the eyes of this child, his daughter, were old, wise, and full of pain. She was four years old. Just four! Oh, they should have saved her from this! They should never have let this happen to her!

'Are you my daddy?' she asked bleakly.

Marcus didn't answer at once. He wanted to, but didn't

dare without first thinking it through. To a four-year-old child, however old and wise she had become, 'Daddy' wasn't so much a name as a whole world: a world he had never been a part of.

'No, Sophy,' he said at last. 'Your daddy . . . died. I am your father. That's something very different, you know.'

Sophy produced a faint little smile. She folded her arms and sank back against her pillows. 'Huh,' she said smugly. 'I knew she was wrong!'

Everyone laughed. And everyone cried.

Claudia reached out her hand to Marcus, smiling through her tears. 'You said you'd find her,' she whispered. 'I didn't believe you!'

'You weren't the only one,' he said.

James and Cath Murray moved to the little house in Chepstow. Claudia and Philip moved to Bath, to stay with John and his wife while Sophy was still in hospital.

Claudia was still taking tranquillisers, and, strangely enough, she felt she needed them even more now that Sophy was safe. The future loomed even larger now. It seemed even more empty, more terrifying, for if such things could happen to a woman and her children while Alister was alive, what worse things could happen now that he was dead?

Everyone seemed to think she'd go back to Larcombe as soon as her arm was mended, as soon as the builders moved out. But they were wrong. She couldn't go back there! She couldn't face it. Not all alone. She'd rather be shunted between John and Daniel for the rest of her life than go back there!

But John's wife had other ideas. Three weeks of living with James and Cath had already tired Laura of her husband's family. She was patient and very kind but Claudia began to suspect that beneath that cheerful smile of hers, she was hiding a core of steel.

'The first thing we've got to do with *you*, Claudia, is to wean you off those bloody pills. You've got a lot of thinking to do during the next few months, and you can't do it with your head all fogged up, now can you?'

Claudia smiled dreamily and left the room, murmuring something about seeing to Philip. A lot of thinking to do, eh? she thought grimly as she went upstairs. Try it yourself, ducky!

Yet she knew in her heart that Laura was right. The cliff she had to jump off – one of these days – was not just her own future, but Sophy's and Philip's. She couldn't just drift. She couldn't expect Daniel and John to look after her for the rest of her life. Other women lived alone. Other women supported their children. Well, of course they did! Just look at Mary Foley! But Mary Foley was so alone, so sad . . .

No, no. Claudia couldn't do it. She'd do it one day, perhaps, but not yet. Not – just – yet.

She spent six hours of every day at the hospital with Sophy, trying to answer all her sad little questions; trying to figure out how her mind was working. But it was difficult to reassure her. She had fallen off the world; and when she'd come back to it, everything had changed.

'*Your* mummy died, didn't she, Mummy?'

'Yes, darling.'

'Mummies always die, don't they?'

'No, some of us stay alive until we're very, very old, Sophy. Think of Grannan. She's Grandad's mummy, and she's still alive, isn't she?'

'I don't know. Hannah said – '

'Darling, Hannah told you a lot of wicked fibs. She told you I was dead, and I'm not. And Philip's not. Grannan's not. Grandad's not.'

'But Daddy is. That wasn't a fib, was it?'

'No, sweetheart . . .'

The doctors said that nothing would reassure Sophy until she'd seen all the things that were familiar to her and settled back into her normal routines. But Ali had been an essential part of the normal routines. Ali had been everything: work, play, mealtimes, bedtimes. How could life even go on without him, let alone get back to normal?

Marcus came to the house to enquire after Sophy a week after he'd found her. He was pale, tired, and thinner than Claudia had ever seen him. But, as on the first occasion he'd met Philip, he picked him up and talked to him, played with him for a short while, and then sat down, still holding him on his knee, to ask how Sophy was.

'Better. She'll be . . . home in a few days.'

'Is she still scared?'

'Yes. Sometimes I think she always will be.'

He said nothing; but he looked at her narrowly over the top of Philip's head, almost as if he thought she could do more than she was doing to help Sophy.

'I'm scared too,' she said defensively.

He smiled. 'You'd be mad not to be. And speaking of madness . . . I've been down to Wells today.'

'Wells?'

'The hospital. Hannah wouldn't see me, but I had a long talk with the psychiatrist.' His mouth hardened. 'It seems they know her well. Had I realised that before I married Sarah, I'd have run a mile. But it's no good to think of that now. All we can do is to fit the pieces together . . . And go on as best we can.'

Marcus put Philip down, watching as he toddled across the room to play with his bricks. 'He's great, isn't he?' he grinned.

'You seem very at ease with children.'

'Well, I was one once, you know. I remember it very

clearly, and I was exactly the same then as I am now – only smaller. I remember that when I was three – or perhaps even younger – I thought I should be respected; and was always shocked rigid to find that no one gave a damn how I felt or what I thought.'

He seemed very angry; contained, but very angry.

'I do respect my children!' Claudia wailed. 'But what can I do, Marcus? I've lost everything! How can I help them now?'

But she saw at once that Marcus hadn't been accusing her. His mouth fell open with astonishment. He clapped a hand to his forehead and sighed wearily. 'Oh, Claudia, I didn't mean that!'

'But you are angry?'

Again he sighed. 'Yes. Aren't you? We made mistakes, Claudia. We both did. We all did. And, taken in relation to the history of the world, they were small, trivial mistakes. It seems unfair and unspeakably cruel that so much tragedy has come out of them. That's why I'm angry.'

'Yes.' Claudia closed her eyes. '"The sins of the fathers will be visited upon the sons unto the third and the fourth generation." Is that how it goes? I always thought how unfair that was. It seemed . . . vengeful and threatening. But now . . .'

Marcus leaned forward. 'Yes?'

'It wasn't. It was just an explanation of how the world works. My father always hated field poppies. He used to tear their heads off. "Kill one poppy and you kill ten billion," he used to say. I think mistakes are like that. Let one flourish, and you've got ten billion. That's why I'm so scared, Marcus. I've made so many mistakes. How can I hope not to make more?'

'You can't,' Marcus said gently. 'But you can try. So can I.'

John and Laura came in with a tray of coffee and Claudia

realised with a new start of guilt how out of touch she was becoming when John asked urgently, 'You've been to Wells? Any news?'

'Yes. I didn't see Hannah, but she's talked to the shrink. Apparently she did take the car to look for Sarah. She realised the road was impassable just before the surge came through. I'm not certain what happened next, where she went, but afterwards she came back, hoping to find Sarah – and found Sophy instead. She'd been carried through on a tree – it seems she didn't go under as Claudia and Philip did – and when Hannah realised she was alive . . . I don't know. I suppose she also realised that Sarah must be dead, and took Sophy as a – replacement. She knew Sophy was mine. Sarah had recognised her . . . She'd recognised her one day in Bath, when we met Claudia and Alister. That was before we were married. I still can't believe she married me, hating me . . . I suppose it was Hannah's doing, like everything else.'

'But who was the old man?'

'Hannah's father. She hadn't seen him for twenty-odd years. He threw her out when . . . When she was young. She didn't even know if he was still alive.'

'Is he crazy too?'

'No. Just old. And very deaf. He didn't understand what was going on, poor devil. And Hannah . . .' He shrugged angrily. 'Sane or crazy, kidnap is a serious crime. She'll be staying where she is for a long while yet.'

Lured by Marcus's description of the New England fall, Ben and Helen took a holiday in America that year. Marcus, viewing the depleted gathering at the Sunday lunch table – just Olivia and Irene and little Tony – let out a deep sigh and stared glumly at the wall.

A moment later, he was hit in the face by a roast potato,

and Tony, who had accidentally perpetrated this misdeed, stared at him for a moment with wobbling lip and then, torn between giggles and tears, explained tremulously, 'My knife slipped.'

'Hmm.' With difficulty, Marcus smiled. 'That's what they all say. I should have ducked, shouldn't I?'

But his shirt and his face were spattered with grease and gravy and he excused himself and went off to clean up. Afterwards he found that he wasn't hungry and sat for a while on the edge of the bath, thinking about Claudia and her 'mistakes snowball'. She was right, of course. That 'sins of the fathers' line had not been as he, too, had always thought, a sadistic threat, so much as an explanation of the knock-on effects of Nature. Kill one poppy and you kill ten billion. Cut down one oak, abort one child, rape one woman, smack one little boy for throwing roast potatoes about . . .

Yes, he had been in the mood to smack, or at least to snarl at Tony, and Tony had been well aware of the fact. He was a sensitive little kid. By no means bright, but – like his mother – affectionate and eager to please. He adored Marcus. And had Marcus indulged his mood at that moment, Tony would have adored him no less. That was the awful part. He'd have blamed himself for a silly accident and been nervous of his table manners for days to come.

That was how it worked. Marcus remembered his own childhood too well to imagine otherwise. One smack made you nervous, the next made you angry, the next – marked you for life. And if a few little smacks could do so much harm to a child, what harm had been done to Sophy?

Again Marcus took himself back to his own childhood, analysing his feelings then, asking himself how the tide could have been turned back. Discipline, of course, was necessary; but Marcus was certain that Ben could have disciplined him adequately if he'd just explained things, put

Marcus in the picture, recognised his *intelligence*. Sophy was intelligent. She could read. She could think.

But thinking was all she did now; and her thinking was not informed, not logical. She believed that if she let Claudia out of her sight for one moment, Claudia would disappear again. Not only disappear, but leave her at the mercy of lunatics. And in terror of those lunatics she trusted no one but Claudia, would speak to no one but Claudia, let no one but Claudia touch her.

Marcus had not attempted to touch her. He had politely ignored her, concentrating his attention on Philip in the hope that, if only out of jealousy, Sophy would eventually butt in. But she hadn't yet, and her relentless reserve frightened and hurt Marcus more than anything ever had. Somehow, somehow, they must turn the tide. Somehow they must heal her. But how? Claudia herself wasn't healed. Neither was Marcus.

They said it could take three years for a normal adult to pull through a sudden bereavement, and Claudia's bereavement had been more than sudden. It had been cataclysmic. Say four years, then? But four years, three years, two years or one – it was too long for Sophy. They had to help her *now*.

Ben and Helen came home from their holiday tanned, happy and full of praise for America, American hospitality (they'd stayed with Marcus's friends), American luxuries and American food.

'Thinking of emigrating, Dad?'

'No.' Ben smiled and gazed from the window into a fine, grey, November drizzle. 'I love old England. I just can't, for the moment, think why.'

'You missed Mrs Chislett, I imagine.'

Ben laughed. 'Yes, I think that's probably it. I see her cottage has been patched up. What about Murray's?'

Marcus sighed. 'The house is fine. Rebuilt, redecorated,

refurnished. Mary Foley's been marvellous. But Claudia won't come back.'

'Are you – still in love with her, Marcus?'

'I don't know,' he said bleakly. 'I care about her. I care about the kids. I want to help them, Dad. But I don't know how; and I'm scared.'

'Scared?'

'Of making another mistake.'

It was another week before Marcus visited Claudia again. He arrived in the middle of the afternoon, wanting to see Sophy; but Claudia had taken both children to the park, and Marcus was not inclined to follow them.

Laura gave him tea. She knew he didn't like the stuff, but she always seemed to forget; and, even while regretting his bad manners, Marcus sulked.

The silence lengthened. 'Feeling crabby, Marcus?'

'Yes.'

'Hmm. That makes two of us.'

'Oh? What's your excuse?'

'Guess,' Laura snapped bitterly. She crossed one leg over the other and pursed her mouth. 'Anyone would think I didn't have my own life to live. Anyone would think I didn't have a husband. It's Claudia this, Claudia that, and we must think of the bloody children. I *am* thinking of the bloody children! What kind of life is this for them? Their mother's a zombie, they've got nothing to call their own, nowhere to play, no friends! If she doesn't pull herself together soon, I'll be going up the bloody wall!'

'I see,' Marcus said frigidly.

'Like hell you do.'

Now they were both sulking. Marcus glowered at her over the narrow expanse of the coffee table. John Murray had married a complete package when he'd married Laura. She was as tough as old rope: bright, cheerful, pretty, humorous and totally indomitable. Marcus had guessed as much the first time he'd laid eyes on her, for there were very few women who weren't shy of him at the first meeting, and Laura had been one of the few. He'd liked her for that. He'd liked her for a great many things, and perhaps it was unfair of him – plain crabby, in fact – to dislike her now for merely saying what she thought. She was right about the children. And Claudia was, virtually, a zombie . . .

'I'm sorry,' he said brusquely. 'It's just . . . I know how Claudia feels.'

'No, you don't,' Laura said. 'You know how she *might* feel if she weren't always stuffed up to the eyes with tranquillisers, but take my word for it, Marcus, she doesn't feel a thing! She doesn't think, she doesn't act, she doesn't – '

'Hey! Just think back to what you said at the outset. "Anyone would think you didn't have your own life to live; anyone would think you didn't have a husband." It may have been put on to the back burner for a while, but you still have your life, Laura. You still have your husband. Claudia's lost everything, and – unlike you – she can't get it back again!'

'*Rubbish*! She's still got her children, her home! She's still got friends and family! She's not hard up! Alister was insured up to the hilt and so was the house, the business! And if she'd just stop taking those bloody pills . . .'

'How can she? How can she face it yet? Christ almighty, Laura, it's hardly been five months!'

'Five months, five years! It makes no difference, Marcus. One day she's got to face it, and the sooner she faces it, the better'll it be for everyone!'

'For *you*, you mean!'

'Yes! For me, for John, for Claudia and the children! And let's not forget Daniel and Marian. Has it crossed your mind what they're going through? They'd barely got back from their honeymoon before this lot hit them! What kind of start are *they* getting? No privacy, no time. They daren't even kiss each other in that poky little house for fear of embarrassing the old folk!'

'Huh! Perhaps you didn't notice that Claudia and Alister had that problem, too! Or that they took the full responsibility for James and his mother while you lot were all swanning around doing what you liked! Where would Daniel have been if Claudia hadn't taken the business on?'

They'd been openly yelling at one another, but now Laura smiled and lowered her voice to a venomous hiss. 'And where would Claudia have been? I'll tell you, Mr Sanctimonious Saxon. She'd have been out in the street, with your brat in her belly!'

Marcus turned white with rage but before he could say another word, Laura returned to the attack. 'Claudia wasn't doing anyone any favours! Claudia was just doing what she had to do, to save her own neck! And where were you then, my noble Sir Galahad? *Hmm*?'

'I'd better go,' Marcus muttered. He stood up, and had almost reached the door when Laura spoke again.

'Coward! You're as bad as she is. Well, all right. Run away and take a pill. It'll wait. And, while it's waiting, it's destroying two good marriages, two beautiful children, and a woman who refuses to stand on her own two feet.'

Marcus smashed his fist into the wall. 'That's not *fair*!'

'Isn't it?'

Marcus looked at his hand. He'd skinned the knuckles and they hurt like hell, but he wasn't angry any more. He just felt sick. Laura was right.

'Could we stop quarrelling?' he asked flatly.

'Yes. As long as you stop defending her.'

'How can I help it? She's so small, Laura. She's so young. And she's been through hell.'

'Yes, but there's one thing you're overlooking. She's been through hell before. She's good at it, Marcus. She's strong inside, she's tough, and she's a damn good mother. But the pills are hiding all that. I'll tell you something else, too. If she could get back to that house and take a look at the wreckage of the business, she'd have it – and herself – back to normal before you could say sucks!'

'On her own? Don't be ridiculous!'

'She doesn't have to do it on her own. Risky Hiskett'd come back like a shot if she asked him. And Mary Foley. Between them they could do it, Marcus. Believe me.'

'I *don't* believe you.' Marcus went back to his chair, rubbing his knuckles. 'Alister was the guts of that business. All right, Claudia helped him, and perhaps he couldn't have done it without her, but on her own? No. She can't even drive the lorry, let alone – '

Whenever Claudia had returned from her walk, they'd been yelling too much to hear her. Now the door swung back on its hinges and she came in, her fists clenched, her dark eyes smouldering with rage. She glared at Laura and, if Marcus had been laying bets, he'd have put his money on Claudia taking Laura's eyes out before another word could be said. But, to his complete astonishment, Claudia turned on him!

'Who says I can't drive the lorry? Who says I can't do it on my own? You – you – stuck-up, patronising, no-good bloody *Saxon*! I'll show *you*!'

She was trembling with fury, scrabbling in her bag with shaking fingers to fetch out – what? A revolver?

But it was her bottle of tranquillisers. She clutched it in her fist and stared at it: desperately, almost lovingly, her knuckles whitening, her arm vibrating with an unholy passion.

Then: 'Here!' she screamed as she hurled it into Laura's lap. 'Suck that! And I hope it damn well chokes you!'

Chapter Thirty

Claudia arrived home on the first of December, almost five months since she'd left it, and she was almost as scared now as she'd been then: her heart hammering, her teeth chattering, her fingers quivering with terror.

She'd anticipated every gulp, gasp and palpitation, and had elected to sit in the front seat of John's car, leaving Laura to cope with the children in the back. But Sophy had sensed her mother's fear and begun to cry; and now, instead of falling apart as she'd expected, Claudia was forced to be bright, brave and cheerful, even – or so it felt – in the grip of a major heart attack.

'Oh, look, Sophy! See the frost shining on those branches! Doesn't it look lovely? Just like diamonds! See, darling? See?'

'Yes,' Sophy whispered.

'Oh, goodness! We've got a new bridge! Oh, that's much nicer than the old one. And look at Mrs Chislett's cottage, Sophy! She's had it painted pink!'

'Bink!' Philip yelled. 'Bink! Bink! Bink!'

It always happened this way. Sophy stayed locked up in her misery, whatever anyone said or did. But Philip was easy. Tell him a bowl of cold noodles was thrilling and he'd go mad with excitement.

But as they turned left, just beyond the foot of Saxon's drive, Claudia swallowed a wail of dismay and grabbed John's arm. They'd knocked down Miss Derby's cottage! It wasn't there any more! The wall where Alister . . . The garden, the cottage . . . It was as if they'd never existed!

'Miss Derby!'

'She's okay, Clo. The foundations had gone anyway, but even if they hadn't it would have had to go. They're building a new bridge – '

'We've already got a new bridge!'

'That's just a Bailey bridge. The Army'll want it back, eventually. No, they're going to build a real one: concrete, with two lanes. And they're putting in new flood defences, Clo. All the way along the river. It'll never happen again.'

Claudia didn't want to think about that. 'But where's Miss Derby?'

'In Old Georgie Flicker's cottage. She loves it, too. Bigger garden. Higher up.'

Claudia had swivelled her head to see again the patch of naked ground where Miss Derby's cottage had been. Now, straightening up, she looked towards Murray's where an enormous banner had been hung across the gateway, with 'WELCOME HOME' painted out in red, white and blue.

'Oh! *Oh*! Oh, hell, where's the packing shed?'

'Damn the packing shed. Look at the house!'

Someone had laid a red carpet on the front steps and there was bunting all over the porch, balloons floating at the windows.

'Oh . . .' Claudia breathed. 'Oh . . . Who did this?'

She'd been told that the house had been wrecked, but it looked as good as new, and almost the same; except that the new extension had a pitched roof rather than the flat one James had given it.

But inside . . . It felt very different inside. It smelled different, looked different. Fresh paint, new carpets, new windows, new doors. *Central heating*! Panic assailed Claudia: a terrible swooping feeling which could only result in tears. It all looked so beautiful – but it was empty. Alister wasn't here!

'John . . .' she whispered.

'Mummy!' Sophy wailed.

Laura shoved them down the hallway, using Philip's feet as a battering ram. 'Come on, you lot,' she said briskly. 'Hurry up, put the kettle on! We haven't got all day!'

Claudia could have thumped her. How insensitive could you get? Laura had made it plain enough that she couldn't wait to get rid of her unwanted guests, and now she couldn't wait to clear off and leave them!

'Are you sure we've *got* a kettle?' Claudia snapped bitterly.

Laura wrinkled her nose in a catty little sneer. 'There's one good way to find out, isn't there?'

Claudia stormed through to the kitchen and then stopped, her mouth dropping open to see the place full of people: Daniel, Marian, James, Cath, Mary Foley and her children.

'Welcome home, Clo! Welcome home, Sophy!'

Claudia burst into tears. She hugged them all, thanked them, turned to hug John – and then Laura. 'Ratbag!' she hissed tearfully. 'I'll get you for this!'

'Oh, yeah? And you so small? So young?' She prodded Claudia in the stomach. 'Ha! She can't even drive the lorry!' She laughed and kissed Claudia's cheek. 'Aren't men daft?'

But now a very humbling thought crossed Claudia's mind. 'Not all that daft,' she said. 'I've just remembered something. We haven't got a lorry.'

*

No lorry, no tractor, no glasshouses, no packing shed. No Alister. Nothing. Just the most appalling mess Claudia had ever seen. She walked the frozen ground in a daze of depression, shuddering at everything she saw. Hedges ripped from the ground, tree boughs, stones from the river bed, broken glass, twisted house-frames; the old tractor and the lorry still embedded in frozen mud. It would take her a thousand years to clear all this. Another thousand to rebuild and start again. No. She'd sell the land to Saxons and let them have the worry of it. They deserved it.

As Christmas approached and the days became darker, her depression deepened. It seemed such a long time between getting up and going to bed each day. James and Cath had settled back into the house as if they'd never left it, but for Claudia it remained very strange, empty and cold.

Sophy had rallied a little when she'd seen that her precious grandad and grannan were still in the land of the living; she'd even managed to say a few words to little Andrew Foley; but now she was as sad as ever, clinging to Claudia's hand, sometimes crying, never laughing, scarcely saying a word.

Claudia dragged Sophy up the hill to visit the Fairfields, and, with surprising ease, across the Bailey bridge to see Miss Derby in her new home. She felt no fear at all on the bridge although with its loose, rumbling boards and metal railings, it seemed a good deal less substantial than the old bridge had ever done. How strange . . . Had she really had a life-long presentiment of that night? If she had, it was gone now. Gone. Like everything else.

She didn't want to see Mrs Chislett. Mrs Chislett was tactless, sometimes to the point of brutality, and Claudia couldn't face that sort of thing. Not just yet. Even a 'sympathetic' remark about her appearance would probably slay her. She still remembered the one, years ago – when? – oh, yes, the day of Marian's party – when Mrs Chislett had said she'd seen better legs on a pigeon. Bloody nerve! But it was truer than ever now. She couldn't eat much. Food just seemed to stick in her throat, and even when she managed to swallow it, it made her feel sick. She was as thin as a lath. She looked pathetic. She felt pathetic. And she had a nasty feeling Mrs Chislett would tell her to pull herself together . . .

But she met Mrs Chislett by accident one day, and was shocked to see how very old and frail she looked. The floods seemed to have taken all the strength out of her.

Claudia took her arm to help her down her front steps, and then could hardly refuse to go in and have tea.

'Now mind where you put your feet, my love. Our Veronica's had kittens – '

'What, again?'

'Ah, well, she run a bit wild while I was staying down our Ernie's, Claudia. The neighbours was all very good. They put down food for her regular, but – and for the life of me I can't think why – they never gave a thought to her morals. Ha! Gone right off the rails she has. Put the kettle on, Clo. I can't . . .'

She sat down in a new, high-backed armchair, gasping for breath. 'Ooh – ah. I think I'm gettin' old, Clo. It ain't never fair, is it? Just as I was beginnin' to enjoy meself, too.' She sent one of her most tender smiles towards Sophy, who was hovering shyly at the kitchen door. 'See if you can find them kitties, my love, will you? They gets all over the place. Did you hear about me goin' up in a helicopter, Claudia? Me and Veronica. Though *she* never took to it much.'

Claudia laughed, and then almost choked on a sudden rush of tears. She'd laughed! Trust Mrs Chislett to pull that one off! But oh, it had felt so good, so good!

'Did *you* take to it?' she asked huskily.

'Take to it? I never had no blimmin' time to take to it! They hoiked me out of that roof so fast! Blimey. I ain't caught me breath ever since! But . . . Call me daft if you like, I feels quite proud of it, Clo. Goin' up in a helicopter at my time of life. I was terrified, mind. I'll admit that. But I'm sorry it didn't last longer. I kept wondering about it, wishing I'd took more notice. But I had me eyes shut from start to finish, and me stomach's still up in the loft!'

Claudia laughed again. She put her arms around Mrs Chislett and hugged her gently, her eyes brimming with tears. 'I do love you,' she whispered.

Mrs Chislett's eyes were overflowing too, but she wiped them hurriedly. 'Not in front of the little one, Clo. Come round another day, and we'll have a good bawl together, eh? Did you hear how I got up in the loft? Now that *was* a miracle! One of my psychic warnings, I reckon. See, I'd wore meself out a bit, goin' up Saxon's in the afternoon – '

'Mummy?' Sophy had found the kittens and was now trying to cram them all into their basket – without much success. 'Mummy, Veronica's the kittens' mother, isn't she?'

'Yes.'

'But where's their father?'

'Er . . . Well – '

'Oh, he lives somewhere else,' Mrs Chislett explained hurriedly. 'Up Saxon's farm, I reckon.'

Sophy sighed deeply. 'So does mine,' she said.

Claudia froze, but her face turned crimson.

Mrs Chislett laughed. 'Think I didn't know?' she asked softly. 'She's the picture of him, Claudia. Has been since the day she were born. Did Alister know?'

'Yes.'

Mrs Chislett nodded. 'And loved her just the same,' she said. 'Yes. That was Alister. Good all through, my love. Good to the bone. And that's why the Almighty took him, you know. We only stays alive while we still got summat to learn.' She laughed. 'So anyway,' she said briskly, 'when you'm arranging my hundred and tenth birthday party – '

She was eighty-three, and although Claudia laughed, her heart felt like lead. Mrs Chislett hadn't much more to learn.

Marcus came to visit James in the second week of December. It was the first time Claudia had seen him since that awful row at John's house, and she'd had a feeling then that she would never see him again. She couldn't remember what she'd said to him: something very rude, certainly; and even at the time she'd known how unfair she was being. She'd overheard most of the shindig with Laura and the one thing that had come over most clearly was that Marcus was very firmly on Claudia's side.

But he'd cut her to the heart with that remark about Ali being the 'guts' of the business. He'd made it sound as if Claudia had been no more than Ali's little helper, on virtually the same level as poor Timmy Marsh! (Poor Timmy. He and his mother were living on National Assistance now . . .)

Why she'd been so furious she had no idea now. Probably because it was true. She would never have been able to manage without Ali; she'd just deceived herself that she could. But she couldn't. She couldn't. The business was as dead as he was.

'Hi.' Marcus smiled as she opened the front door and then jumped backwards down the steps and came in on all fours, growling like a lion. Philip, who'd been clutching her leg on one side, retreated down the hall, screaming with laughter. Marcus caught him, picked him up, and proceeded to 'eat' him. 'Hiya, buster!'

'Hiya, buzzer!'

Marcus laughed and, tucking Philip into the crook of his arm, he now noticed Sophy, who was still clutching Claudia's other leg. 'Hello, Sophy,' he said, and without waiting for a reply, 'Is your father in, Claudia?'

'He never goes out. In the sitting room.'

Marcus tipped his head to one side, his smile mocking her. 'I'd know where that is, of course?'

'Oh. Sorry.'

How strange! He'd been so much a part of the family just lately, it was hard to realise he'd never set foot inside this house except when half of it was missing and the other half under water!

'Second door on the right. I mean . . . third.' She blushed, stalked past him to open the door, and before she quite knew what she was about, snapped, 'Would you care to be announced?'

His face stilled, his eyes lost their mischievous sparkle and became like pools of ice. 'I think I'll manage,' he said softly.

He took Philip with him. Claudia closed the door and stood for a moment with her hands over her eyes, feeling like death. Why had she been so snappy with him? He'd been so good to her, to them all! There wasn't a single life in this house they didn't owe to Marcus! *He'd found Sophy*! Yet all the old animosity was still there. He scared her, and because she was scared, she couldn't seem to help biting his head off. But why was she scared?

The answer passed through her mind like an arrow – in one side, out the other – leaving a trail of pain in its wake.

'Come on, Sophy,' she said wearily. 'Let's put the kettle on. I suppose he'll want coffee.'

She was still setting the tray when Sophy said, 'Is Marcus Philip's father, too?'

Claudia hesitated. 'No, darling,' she said at last.

'He plays with Philip, though. He doesn't play with me.'

'No . . . but – '

'Why isn't he Philip's father?'

'Er – well. Well, that's hard to explain, Sophy. Some people have two fathers and some people don't.' She smiled and took up the loaded tray. 'Will you open the door for me, darling? My hands are full.'

She hadn't even asked herself why Marcus had wanted to see James. Now she stood amazed to hear Marcus saying, 'But it isn't just a question of philosophy, is it?' He pointed to the book James had laid open on the arm of his chair. 'That's one of the finest poems in the English language, yet it makes very little obvious sense. It just stirs things inside you, deep, fundamental things you'd barely realised were there.'

James laughed. 'You've lost me. But I'll read it. Thank you. It's quite interesting this, you know. Finding something new, at my time of life.'

'Coffee, Marcus?' Claudia smiled, trying to apologise for her earlier bad manners; but Marcus's eyes skidded past her, to the ever-present Sophy.

'"*A damsel with a dulcimer*",' he quoted softly, '"*In a vision once I saw. It was an Abyssinian maid, and on her dulcimer she played –* "'

'What's a dulcimer?'

Claudia almost dropped the tray. Sophy had spoken to him! She'd spoken quite angrily – indeed, very angrily – with her bottom lip sticking out, her pale eyes blazing.

Marcus didn't reply directly. He said, 'What's a dulcimer, Claudia?'

Claudia blinked. 'It's a – isn't it something like a zither?'

'Or a xylophone?'

'I've got a xylophone,' Sophy announced sharply. 'No, I *did*. But the floods took it away. *And* my scooter. *And* my daddy.'

Marcus reached out his hand to her, but he spoke to James. 'Now that's an interesting point. If a dulcimer's like a xylophone, the sense should be the same if you said, "A damsel with a xylophone". Same number of syllables, you see. But it – '

'What's a *damson*?' Sophy left Claudia's side and stood a few feet from Marcus, clenching her fists under her chin.

'Damsel,' Marcus corrected gently. 'It's a girl. A pretty little girl, just like you. A damsel with a dulcimer.' He grinned. 'Shall I buy you one for Christmas?'

She took a few more steps forward and rested her hands on the arm of his chair. 'What will you buy for Philip?'

'Philip? Oh, he doesn't want anything.'

Sophy smiled. 'He does!'

'Does he? What does he want?'

Sophy thought about it. 'A tricycle,' she said at last. 'Quite a big one, just in case I want to borrow it sometimes.'

'Yes, I see. Fine. I'll buy Philip a tricycle.'

'But you're not *his* father, are you?'

'No.'

She crept cautiously around the front of the chair. She laid her hand on Marcus's knee. 'Do you think it would have a bell?'

'Philip's tricycle? Oh, yes, I'm sure it would.'

She stepped between his knees. He picked her up, held her close; and over her head he met Claudia's eyes with a grin of pure triumph.

Claudia didn't know what to say, what to do, how to feel. He'd won Sophy over with patience and gentleness and – damn him – with an all too clever perception of the female psyche. He'd made Sophy jealous!

And now his long, strong fingers were stroking Sophy's hair; and all the fear, all the doubts and the tension were draining out of her; for in the hard, protective circle of that man's arms . . .

Claudia's eyes widened with horror at the path her thoughts were taking. No, oh, no! Ali was dead! He was dead, and she couldn't – !

'Something wrong, Claudia?'

'What? No! No, I was just – '

Just what? Just surrendering to his all too clever perception of the female psyche!

'Just wondering if you could loan me a tractor,' she finished lamely. 'I can't clear the ground without one.'

It rained through most of January. Froze through February. Snowed in March.

When the sun came out at last, Marcus shed his woollens and waterproofs and strolled through the lambing pasture to the gap in the hedge from which – if he stood on his toes – he could see into almost every corner of Murray's land.

And she was at it again. Up to the waist in mud and broken glass, breaking her back for a task that was well-nigh impossible. Why? Why did she have to do it? It certainly wasn't for the money. Now that all her insurances had been paid up she was loaded. At least until she started to invest again. New glasshouses, new vehicles, new buildings, wages and salaries. And then she'd lose the whole damn lot!

His eyes burning with frustration, Marcus turned to walk back to the house, noticing, as he passed, a ewe straining to eject her halfborn lamb. Marcus waited for the next contraction, caught the lamb on its way out, wiped the yellow mucus from its muzzle and then laid it under its mother's nose.

He'd often despised sheep their stupidity; but, just lately, he'd wished people could be as simple. The complexity of human emotions, his own included, was beginning to seem like a maze, with all its exits closed.

Claudia loved him. She wanted him. *She wouldn't bloody well touch him*! And he understood. He understood. Grief, guilt, all that. But he loved and wanted her more than all his grief, all his guilt. Grief? Well, guilt, anyway.

But after all Claudia had been through, one would think (if only for the children's sake) she'd be glad to let it all go and accept the things she'd been made for: his love, his protection, his strength. But his love most of all. He had so much to offer. He'd waited so long . . .

And nothing stood in her way! Mary Foley actually *wanted* to move in with the old folk! The kids loved Marcus; Marcus loved them! But there she was. Up to the neck in mud. Refusing even to talk about it.

Well, two could play at that game. She could buy her own bloody tractor. Perhaps, when she saw the whacking dent it made in her capital, she'd begin to see sense at last.

He washed his hands at the stone sink in the gunroom, lathering his arms, scrubbing his nails. Through the open kitchen door he could hear Irene and his mother chatting, but didn't begin to listen until he sat down to ease off his boots.

'No,' Irene said. 'It's not the money, honest. It's just . . . Well, I've been so dependent on you for so long now, it's beginning to scare me.'

'Scare you? How?'

'I don't know. It's hard to explain. It's just . . . Well, think of the floods. Think how they changed people's lives. We none of us had any idea, did we? We got up in the morning, thinking it was just another rainy day. And at the end of it . . . It's Claudia, see, Helen. She's woke me – woken me up.'

'Oh, I see! You mean you're afraid you and she – ? When Marcus and she – ?'

'No! I like Claudia. Always have. She used to be my watchyacallit when I was little. Model, sorta thing. I always wanted to be like her. That's why I worked so hard to pass for the Grammar, because I wanted to be like Claudia. Funny, really. Didn't stand a cat's chance with my looks, did I?'

'Oh, *Irene!*'

'Well, it's true. No, what I meant about Claudia was . . . Well, look at her. She was like me in a way, Helen. Got herself into trouble and found herself someone to lean on. She had Alister. I had you. And then – phht! No Alister. No bloody nothing. Overnight. It's no good saying it can't happen to me, Helen. It can. It can happen to any of us. And if when it happens we've never learned to stand on our own two feet . . . See what I mean?'

Marcus closed his eyes. He smiled. Yes, he saw what she meant. Claudia had to stand on her own two feet, just once, just to prove that she could. It might take a few years; she'd be in mourning for a few years too; but Murray's *would* help to heal her. And after that? He'd have her!

He stood at the entrance to Murray's yard, smiling at his beloved. Barely an inch of her was not either plastered or streaked with mud, but she looked terrific. Furious, too. An impossible task? No, not for Claudia. She was, and always had been, like Marcus – a worker. If she hadn't broken her arm, if she could have come back to this six months ago, she'd never have needed those Godawful pills. She'd have taken it out on the land and cured herself in no time at all.

'Farver!'

Marcus laughed and ran to meet Philip, who was racing down the garden path towards him. He was the image of Claudia. Perhaps a little more sturdy, but just as beautiful.

'Hiya, buster.' He picked Philip up, kissed him, put him down again and looked around for Sophy. She had begun to call him 'Father' at Christmas, and although when he thought of it objectively it made him feel very old, he rarely thought of it objectively. It was the sweetest name in the world. Those soft little arms about his neck, those warm little lips at his ear . . . *Father*.

Sophy sidled around the corner of the porch, her eyes bright with mischief. 'Guess what I been doing!'

'I can't. Nothing naughty, I hope?'

She giggled. 'No. I been making cakes! For you!' She glanced importantly at the Mickey Mouse watch on her wrist, which was set permanently at ten past four. 'Five minutes. Then you have to come in and try one. *Okay*?'

'Okay. Five minutes. I'll just have a word with your mother.'

Claudia had seen him. She waded out of the mud, flapping her hands to shed her glass-proof gauntlets, shaking her feet in vain hope of shedding some mud.

'How's it going?'

'Okay. I think I've got all the glass out, anyway.'

'Good. I'll bring you a tractor tomorrow. Will a week be long enough?'

'A *week*?' She stared at him, appalled.

'Well, what do you need to do? Clear all those trees and boulders off the top, plough, spread some muck? You should manage that in a week. Do you want the muck or will you get it from Dando's, as usual?'

Claudia's eyes had been getting wider, her face paler under its streaks of mud. Now she turned pink and burst into tears.

'I can't do it!' she wailed. 'Oh, Marcus, Marcus, I can't! Not on my own!'

He squeezed his eyes shut and clenched every muscle in his body to stop himself grabbing her into his arms, telling her she needn't; that he'd do it all, do everything for her.

This was something he mustn't do. If he did, she'd live in fear for the rest of her days. He couldn't do that to her, any more than he could do it to Irene. They had to find their strength, know it, have faith in it. Stand on their own two feet.

Marcus took a few steps away from her. He set his chin at its most aloof, disdainful angle.

'Well, well,' he sneered softly. 'Isn't that typical of a Murray?'

There was a short silence. A brief moment of utter peace. Then Claudia let rip. 'You bastard! You lousy . . . You lousy, stinking, bloody *Saxon*!'

She bent down, filled her hands with mud and slung it at him. Marcus dodged. He laughed.

'My grandfather did it!' she shrieked. 'He had a wash-out and he did it! My great-grandfather did it, too!'

'Yes.' Marcus shrugged. 'But they were bigger than you.'

She threw herself at him, flailing her fists, and Marcus caught her, held her.

'Hey,' he grinned. 'This is just like old times, isn't it?' And he saw her rage begin to melt, her tears change to reluctant laughter.

'Ooh, I hate you!'

'No, you don't.' He straightened and looked down his nose at her, making certain she knew he was being serious. 'No more lies,' he said softly. 'Do you hate me?'

She stilled. She closed her eyes and Marcus bit his lip, watching breathlessly as the gaunt angles of her face softened and warmed, making her beautiful again.

'No,' she whispered.

He laid his hands on her shoulders and bent his knees to look into her eyes. 'Good,' he said. 'Because I want to ask you something.'

'Oh? What?'

He'd had it all worked out but now didn't know how to say it. He felt shy and afraid, silly and excited, like a young boy asking his first girl for a date.

'Let's do something normal,' he said at last. 'Let's do some of the things we should have done years ago, if we'd only had half the sense we were born with. Let's start living again, shall we?'

Claudia blushed and bowed her head. 'What do you mean, exactly? I can't – '

'Can't jump in a bath? Put a decent dress on? Come out to dinner with me? That's all I ask, Claudia. Something ordinary and civilised. Something friendly. We are friends now, aren't we? At last?'

The reply was slow in coming. Claudia was still blushing, and – judging from the way her mouth was working – struggling to come to terms with what he'd asked. Alister, of course . . .

'Depends,' she said thoughtfully at last.

'Hmm? On what?'

She tipped back her head and grinned. 'Loan me the tractor for *two* weeks – and you're on!'